Other Books by
Jess E. Owen

SONG OF THE SUMMER KING

BOOK II OF THE SUMMER KING CHRONICLES

JESS E. OWEN

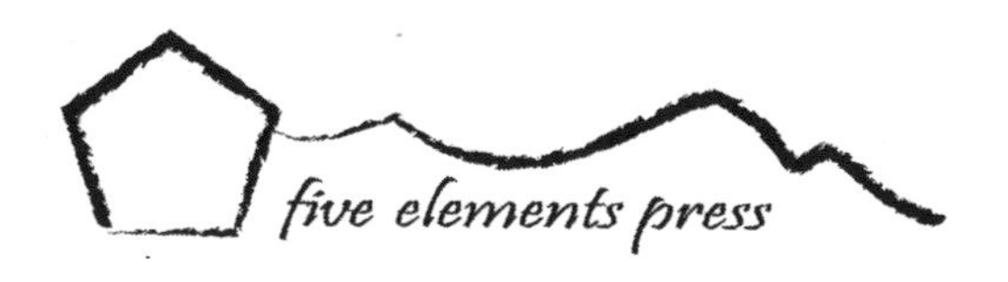

Five Elements Press
Suite 305
500 Depot Street
Whitefish, MT 59937
www.fiveelementspress.com

PUBLISHER'S NOTE

Cover art by Jennifer Miller © 2013
Cover typography and interior formatting by TERyvisions
Author photo by Jessica Lowry
Edited by Joshua Essoe

ISBN-13: 978-0985805876
ISBN-10: 0985805870

FIRST PAPERBACK EDITION

My second book is dedicated to everyone who read the first.

Table of Contents

Skyfire

He is borne aloft by the Silver Wind
He alone flies the highest peak,
And when they hear his song at battle's end
The Nameless shall know themselves
And the Voiceless will once again speak.

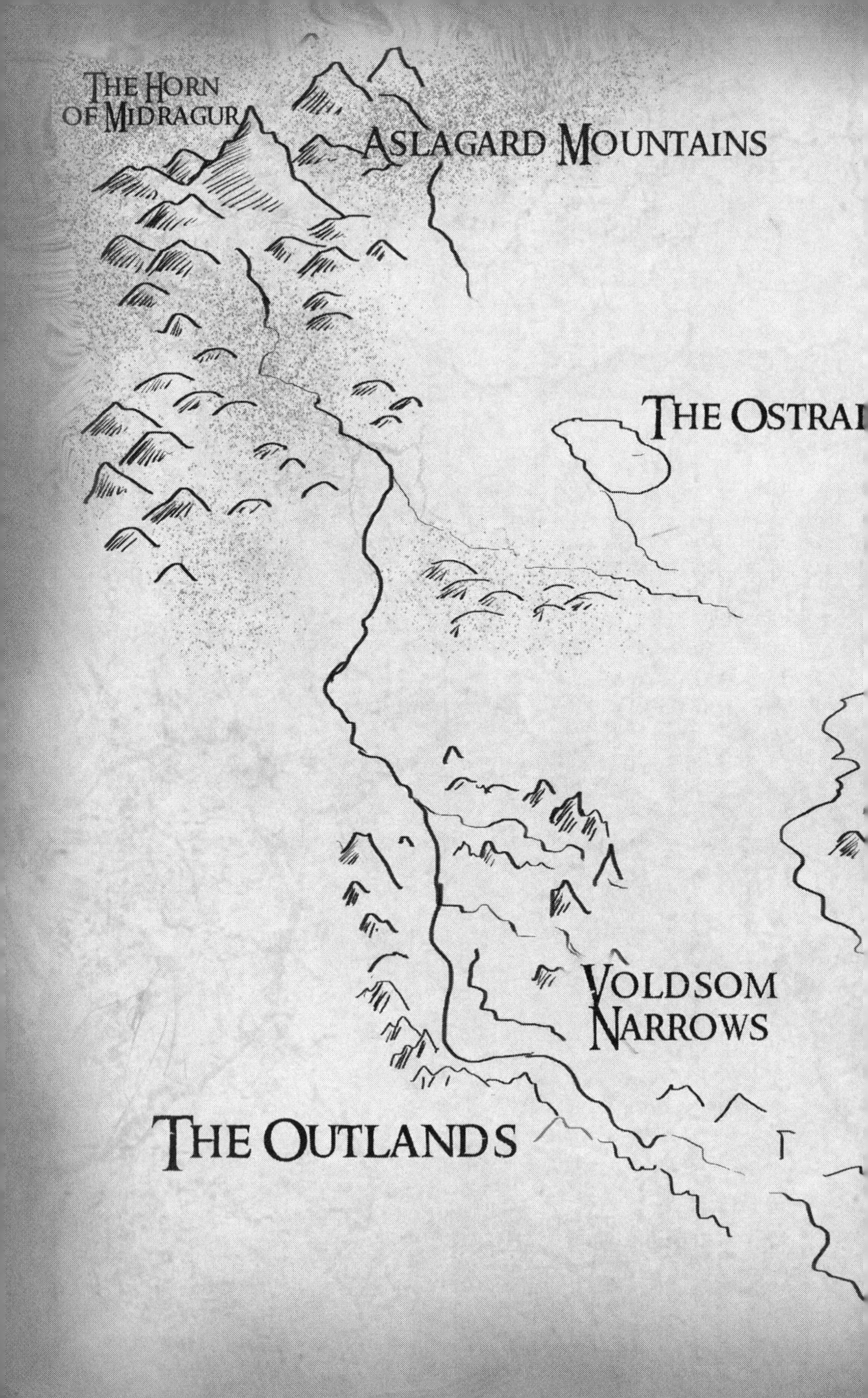

THE HORN
OF MIDRAGUR
ASLAGARD MOUNTAINS
THE OSTRA
VOLDSOM
NARROWS
THE OUTLANDS

Starward
Nightward
Dawnward
Windward
HORES
THE WINDEROST
DAWN SPIRE
THE DAWN REACH
THE VANHEIM
SHORE

1
The Highest Peak

ICY WIND LASHED ALONG VERTICAL slabs of black mountain rock near the highest peak of the Sun Isle. Few creatures ever ventured there.

Shard clung to the mountainside, talons caught in tiny crags, hind paws purchased on a feather-thin groove in the rock below. The wind soared past and Shard tightened his wings to his sides, swinging his long feathered tail out for balance. Snow swirled, stinging his eyes, and the wind howled like a wolf close to the kill.

The mountain was angry.

One wing stroke, then another. Unbidden, his uncle Stigr's voice came to him. *One foot in front of the other.* Even though he wasn't on the mountainside with Shard, his mentor's advice stuck, and the words made him groan. He perked his ears and peered down to check his height.

Surely the peak is close. This is mad, mad, mad. He sought a vision on the mountain, at what felt like the top of the world. The past summer had changed everything he knew. Now it was his responsibility to solve the injustices he'd discovered—but he had no path.

His idea to seek his vision on the mountain top seemed less and less like a good idea, for at that moment, he saw nothing.

A whorl of white and gray met his eagle stare. Not even his gaze could pierce the wall of wind and snow. No longer able to see the floor of the canyon between the jagged peaks, Shard turned his face upward and shoved his muscles back into a sluggish, lurching climb.

The wind shifted again, dry as wood and cold from the top of the world. Shard ground his beak and shoved his talons up higher. *One. Foot.*

"In front of the other," he gasped. Snow soaked even his wings, oiled and resistant to water from his diet of fish. The climb, hours in the wind and snow, had broken down all of his defenses. If Shard tried to open his wings he would meet his end smashed into the cliff face. The wind changed direction and angle every three breaths, made it impossible to fly. The snow made it impossible to see more than two leaps ahead. Everything felt impossible. He dragged himself another notch higher, muscles beginning to lock and quiver.

He hadn't eaten in five days.

The memory of another's voice drifted into his head, a she-wolf from another, much warmer place, *"Only when we are empty as pelt do we know what truly lies under fur or feather and bone."*

Her words, the wolf song sending him on his way, and his uncle's advice flickered in and out of his mind like falling feathers. He knew he was still climbing, but it seemed to happen without him. A ledge loomed above. If he could drag over the top of that ledge, he was sure he would be close to the pinnacle, or at least high enough for his challenge.

One will rise higher.

Another voice. His father. His dead father. That spirit had spoken to him so clearly once, appeared before him as if in flesh, advised him, and then gone. Shard hadn't heard another word since then. He'd had no visions, no guidance, no ideas, and there were things he needed to know before winter came. The last time he'd made wrong decisions, too many lives were lost. He couldn't take that chance again.

We wolves go on a quest for our life vision, his friend had told him, a wolf seer named Catori. Her fur had burned bright and ruddy in the red autumn woods. In the lowland, it was the quarter of the year the wolves called the time of red rowan, not for the leaves, but for the berries that grew in red bursts. Cold stole the nights and the leaves of red and gold only served as a bright warning of winter.

The brisk chill of the lowlands was nothing compared to the White Mountain.

We wear down all that is flesh so the spirit may rise and show us the path.

Catori had told him her own vision that she'd dreamed as a pup before her eyes even opened. A gryfon nest and a whelping mother, but out of the mother's belly came wolf pups, and Catori knew by that vision that the future of wolves and gryfons was linked. They must befriend each other again, and she was to be a link between them.

It was autumn when it became clear to Shard that he didn't know what to do, and didn't like the choices he had, so Catori had encouraged him to go on a vision quest as the wolves did, and seek his answers that way.

He is borne aloft on the Silver Wind
He alone flies the highest peak...

Words from a song overlapped the memory of Catori and Shard shook his head, squinting up and around. Fast-flying snow stung his eyes and he ruffled his feathers, shaking it off again. The ledge loomed dark overhead.

There. That is as high as I can go. The place had to challenge him, to strip him to his essence. Then, as Catori said, a vision should come to him. The wolves didn't seek their visions on the White Mountain, but Shard had chosen the highest point on the largest island in all the Silver Isles. It felt right that a gryfon seek his vision there. He remembered choosing the point on a warm autumn evening, gazing at the distant peak, surrounded by friends and a warm sunset.

Shard would have laughed at his stupid choice if he'd had extra breath. A nice glide along the seashore, seeking his vision by sunset light, sounded better every moment.

One foot in front of the other.

He slapped talons against a solid-looking outcropping. The ice that had looked like rock cracked and crumbled under his weight. Shard swung down, clawing for purchase, shrieking. His voice fell dead in the wind, dry from thirst. His claws scraped as he slid down on rolling rocks and ice. Wild for balance, he flared one wing.

The wind swooped in, knocked his wing wide and threw him spiraling off the rock face into the air.

Shard kicked his hind paws out straight and lashed his tail into a fan to rudder himself, stretching the other wing to try soaring. Sick of climbing, blinded from snow, Shard ducked and curved with the wind. The long canyon between the two white peaks sent winds circling and lunging like caribou, knocking him toward one face, then the other.

Panicked, aching and blind, Shard forced his thoughts to leave him. He was nothing but wings and air. He knew only that he wanted the pinnacle of the mountain.

I won't be defeated by wind!

He twisted and flapped, testing the air, straining all his skill. At last he found what he needed–a sliver of wind slipped under his wing like a guiding friend. Latching onto it, he curved his wings to follow only that current. It was warmer than the others. The single, tiny, warmer current lifted him higher.

After wild moments that felt like hours, Shard saw where the mountain slopes met. The canyon between them ended in a solid wall of white snow and black rock. Ice crumbled down its face, chunks falling into the hazy gloom below. Shard, heart slamming, had barely enough strength to react.

Pull up pull up PULL UP! Even his wings screamed until Shard realized he was shrieking also, wordless, mindless as he flapped his wings against cold air, unable to fight the wind that he rode straight toward a solid face of rock.

Shard screamed an eagle cry into the wind and shut his eyes—

—and a warm draft shoved him straight up and over the canyon rim, and higher. Free of the circling winds, Shard angled his wings to catch the draft, soaring, soaring high until he saw a flat, round expanse jutting out from the highest peak. No wider than a gryfon at full stretch, it was large enough to land on.

The thin air made him gasp. Snow dragged his wings like stones. Happy to be freed from climbing like a wingless beast, Shard shoved through the gray air until he reached the ledge below the peak and landed, tumbling in the snow. Awkward and exhausted as a fledge after its first, miserable flight, Shard lay panting, barely comprehending the blanket of snow under him, and that now the wind was whispering and soft.

Snow fell gently around him.

He had landed in the shadow of the great, pointed peak of the mountain, sheltered from the wind. It felt like a calm winter day.

In the corner of his vision, something moved, like a little hump of snow.

Shard tried to stand, but his legs quivered and collapsed under him. He lay on his belly, beak resting on the snow, and perked his ears as the hump of snow became an owl.

"Son-of-Baldr," sang the owl, and her deep voice perked his ears again. "Son of the Nightwing. Rashard, son-of-Ragna the White."

The sounds and words became his name and Shard blinked slowly and raised his head. He had, for a moment, forgotten his name. Forgotten that he had one. With his name, everything else snapped back. Why he had come, his need for guidance, the wolves singing him away with blessings on his vision quest.

"I know you," he whispered. "You guided me once before, in the forest. What are you doing here? You can't live up here."

He failed to keep the disappointment from his voice. In that moment he realized keenly that he'd craved to see his father again, and nothing else. Instead, his deadly, awkward flight had attracted the attention of this creature, an old friend. Or at least an acquaintance. He wondered if this flesh and blood owl could answer his questions any better than a sparrow could. She had helped Shard before, when he was lost. Perhaps she meant to again, but he would've preferred a vision of his father.

Still, it was good not to be alone.

"My prince. I came here for you. " The white owl stretched her rounded wings in a bow, and blinked large fierce eyes, yellow as the summer moon. "What brings you to the brow of the Sun Isle?"

"I need help," Shard whispered. His tongue stuck to his beak. Warmth rushed his head. Then the owl lost focus in front of him, the mountain slanted, ready to tip him back down to the bottom of the world, and he fell from blinding white into blackness.

2
A Divided Pride

ON THE LOWLAND, WINDWARD COAST of the Sun Isle, gryfons gathered for a hunt. Autumn reigned on the slopes and in the scattered woods that sprawled around the Nightrun River and cold nights glazed the dying grass and birch in gold. Rowan berries gleamed like clumps of ember in those little forests, and all the animals of the Sun Isle rushed to fatten up for winter.

All the animals but us, thought Kjorn. Prince of the gryfon pride, a head taller than most and gold from the tips of his ears to his feathered tail, he paced as his father spoke to the gathered hunters.

"They will be vulnerable now, focused on their autumn hunting." Sverin, the Red King, now called the War King by some, paced level with his warriors.

Kjorn stood at the back, watching their faces as Sverin spoke on about their enemy, the wolves, and the importance of the wolf hunts. They must drive the enemy out. They must seek revenge for the wolves' horrific attack on their nesting cliffs that summer past. Most of the warriors' eyes were narrowed. They nodded and their wings rustled in agitated agreement.

Gryfon fledglings and elders and even initiated warriors had died in the wolf attack. Though some believed Sverin's aggression triggered it, it would not be easily forgiven.

Kjorn watched his father speak and knew in a sense he was right, but he grew wary of winter closing in on them.

This isn't the time for war.

The pride was growing lean. The females who were newly mated should have been getting plump and soft over autumn, but all still stood sleek with wiry summer muscle, their eyes gleaming with a weary, dangerous edge. They were still early enough in carrying their kits that they could hunt.

But not for long, Kjorn thought. Over the long, dark winter, it would be up to the males to provide.

Bright blue flashed above, a gryfon circling. Kjorn watched as the older warrior stooped to land. Caj was the only gryfon in the pride who might talk sense to Kjorn's father, but so far he'd done nothing. Kjorn wondered if Caj agreed with Sverin and wished only for revenge on the wolves. They had, after all, also turned Shard against the pride.

Against Caj, Kjorn simmered. *His own nest-father. And against me.*

Caj landed and trotted to Kjorn, one ear flicked toward the king's words. The king's wingbrother stood tall and broadly muscled, his flanks scarred from countless battles.

"What news?" Kjorn muttered, unconcerned about missing his father's speech. Sverin spoke often those days, whether to reassure the pride or himself, Kjorn wasn't sure.

"A good herd of red deer on the nightward coast of Star Isle," Caj said under his breath. A chill breeze swooped between them, ruffling feathers. "Fat and happy from nuts and berries. Even some late summer fawns."

"What news of the *wolves,*" Kjorn amended.

Sverin paused his speech, ear twitching, and Kjorn lifted his head to make it look as if he'd been paying attention. But he didn't need to pay attention. The words were always the same.

Honor. Vengeance.

Glory.

War.

I wonder if he tastes the words anymore, Kjorn thought. *If he wants revenge on the wolves, or on Shard, who is already dead.*

Caj shook his head, ears slicking back as he turned his narrowed gaze to the king. "No sign of wolves, my prince. There's never any sign. The den lies cold. Trails are days old. Tracks lead to cliffs that drop into the sea. They've disappeared."

Kjorn clicked his beak against angry words. It wouldn't do to lose Caj's confidence and support. "They haven't disappeared. You heard what Shard said this summer. There are caves under the islands. That's where they're hiding." Kjorn looked to the sky, as if bright Tyr might hold an answer. The sun stood at middlemark, but in autumn, middlemark was so low in the sky it was almost evening.

Caj stretched, scarred flanks twitching. "The shadows grow long. Winter stalks us, my prince. I wouldn't go into those caves for all the fawns on Star Island. We must be allowed to hunt food."

"You can feed on wolf flesh."

"Only if we can find wolves."

"Can't you tell him to stop this?" Kjorn whispered fiercely, turning so his father wouldn't notice them arguing. "We can have our revenge in spring. Can't you tell him to focus on hunting food? "

"Can't you?" Caj asked.

Kjorn shifted. "He's your wingbrother."

"He's your father."

Kjorn had thought Sverin's gaze was intimidating, growing up, but staring now into Caj's even, pale eyes gave him a true taste of what Shard had faced, raised by Caj.

"You should be the one to speak," Caj continued, so quietly Kjorn might've dreamed the words. "But speak carefully. Winter is not the time to rebel, not the time to split the pride."

"Tell that to my father," Kjorn muttered. "He would have us go to war."

"Your father's concern is real," Caj said. "The wolves could very well attack again. Tread softly. Learn to handle situations like this now, if you plan to be a decent king."

That he would presume to advise Kjorn on kingship was the last insult he could stand. Kjorn flared his wings out and snapped his beak. Caj backed down and hunched into a respectful mantle, his wings curved up over his back, bowing his head. The gathered hunters parted to see the commotion and the aisle between them led straight to Sverin's hard gaze. Kjorn backed away, tucking his wings as he stared down the length of peat and grass into his father's eyes. Kjorn had his mother's eyes, pale summer blue, but Sverin's were merciless gold.

"Did you have something to add, my son?"

A soft snort drew Kjorn's ear. In the corner of his eye he saw a smug look on green Halvden's face. He was an arrogant warrior, younger than Kjorn, who preened for favor every chance he could.

Kjorn raised his head. Caj's warning rang bitterly true. *He's my father. If I can't stand up to him, I'll be a poor leader.*

Sverin looked huge in the late light, crimson around his face fading to scarlet down his back and wings like flame. He wore golden chains, bands and gleaming jewels his grandfather had stolen from the dragons in a war long ago. The Red King. The War King. He wore the whispered title proudly, though Kjorn wasn't sure if it was a compliment.

Kjorn settled his feathers and met his father's eyes as calmly as he could. He'd done nothing wrong, after all. "Caj has sighted a herd of deer on the Star Isle. Fat and happy with autumn. I think—"

"Perfect," said Sverin. Kjorn perked his ears, hopeful as Sverin paced away. "Go to them." The others lifted their ears, looking refreshed at the thought of easy meat. "But leave them be," Sverin said, crushing the expressions on every gryfon's face. "Their presence will draw the wolves out of their cowardly hiding and you may catch them with their guard down."

"Father—"

"Go. Now. The day grows late." He looked to the fading light. The sons and daughters of Tyr could not see well in the dark like owls, and so it was forbidden to fly at night. Sverin had exiled gryfons from the pride for that crime. Now with winter stalking near, exile meant certain death.

But Shard flew at night.

And well it did for him, Kjorn thought back at himself. Words and arguments gathered and stuck in his throat. The others watched Sverin, then Kjorn, waiting for his lead. He felt their tension, felt Caj's attention and disapproval at his back. He ignored them all and bounded into the air. The others, muttering, followed.

Caj had been no help at all. He'd practically said that Sverin was right, and not to cause trouble by splitting loyalties. And Kjorn decided he wouldn't. He would speak to Sverin alone, wouldn't challenge him in front of the pride. But he would make sure they had something to eat that night.

When they reached a good height, Kjorn drifted close to a younger gryfon of copper-brown coloring.

"Einarr," he said over the wind.

"My prince." The young gryfon had a mate to feed and a family so shamed by a number of exiles that he would never speak up against the king. He also wouldn't betray his prince.

"Take two hunters with you back to Sun Isle."

"My lord?" Einarr's wide eyes tried to catch Kjorn's, and his wings tensed. Kjorn glared forward.

"We need meat. The caribou will be low, feeding in the foothills of the White Mountains. Hunt along the Nightrun and take your kills back to the nesting cliffs."

"But your father—"

"You're only obeying me." Kjorn looked firmly at him. "My father's hunger for vengeance can't overshadow even his need for meat."

Relief tainted by fear filled Einarr's face. "Yes, my lord."

He keened two names into the wind, his own mate and another huntress. They angled in an arrow starward—the direction so named for a star that shone at a fixed point in that quarter of the sky. A bank of low-lying clouds covered the mountain range on the starward edge of the Sun Isle.

Caj glided in on Kjorn's side. "That was well done, my lord."

"Let's hope so," Kjorn muttered.

"You must still talk to your father."

"I know." He glanced away, staring over the length of the Sun Isle to the mountains that crowned its starward edge. The brief, bleak thought of his wingbrother Shard crowded his mind. Former wingbrother.

Shard was dead. He had fallen into the sea.

After betraying me.

Kjorn keened a warrior cry into the wind and led his hunters to the great, wooded Star Island.

3
Autumn Omens

*T*HE VISION HAD A FAMILIAR *scent to it now, hot wind and strange, tangy plants. Pillars of red rock crowned a sunlit plain. He strained to follow a dark gryfon who soared in a cloudless blue, a bolt of skyfire in his claws.*

"Father!"

But the gryfon wasn't his father, and didn't answer. Beyond the range of the vision he felt disappointment. This had been his father's vision. It was not his own. It was nothing new.

Wind like waves surged and pulled him back to stare ahead at what the vision offered him.

In the distance, a jagged range of mountains beckoned. One peak soared high above the rest, covered in snow, jutting like a fang against the sky.

Then, to Shard's amazement, something happened that hadn't, before.

A sound.

A song floated from the snow-covered mountain, in a voice unlike any other creature he'd heard–at the same time like a lark, and a hawk, fierce and beautiful and far away.

"Which rises first, the night wind, or the stars?

Not even the owl could say,
whether first comes the song or the dark…"

"Who are you?" Shard cried. The song silenced. The question echoed back to him from the rocks, as if the singer wondered the same about him. "Who are you?" Shard called again. "Where? Did you know my father? Am I supposed to find you?"

"Which fades last, the birdsong, or the day—"

A shadow blinded him. A huge, leathery, veined wing knocked him from the sky, and everything fell dark. A deep, instinctive fear grasped Shard's heart and he twisted violently away from the beast that attacked him.

Wind woke him, howling against the mountain peak. Shard rolled to all fours and stared around, beak open in a pant. His muscles cramped and locked and he sank back to his belly in the snow.

The owl, watching, tilted her head around. As if it were a spring day and he'd only taken a nap, she fluffed her spotted feathers. "Did you find what you sought, young prince?"

Shard switched his tail back and forth. Exhausted, hungry and cold despite his warm autumn down, he grew gloomy at her question. "I don't know. I sought a vision the way the wolves do."

"Yet you are not a wolf."

"No, but I thought…I thought it would help."

"And did it?"

"I don't know," he admitted, and she tilted her head around in the opposite direction. "I saw my father's vision again." He felt foolish telling her, but she was the only one there, the only one who seemed interested in what *he* wanted to do. Stigr had his own plans. Catori and her family seemed convinced the gods would show him the way and he had only to wait. He knew he had waited too long.

"Twice now, then," the owl chirped. "Once in the summer, and now. Does that not make it your own vision?"

Shard hadn't considered that. Wind shivered past, though most of it was blocked by the last bit of mountain rising above them. "Does it? He told me that he died because he'd tried to fulfill his second vision, his vision of peace in the Silver Isles, without following the first."

The owl just watched him, yellow eyes deep and waiting, until he answered his own question.

"Then I must fulfill his vision before I do anything else."

"If you think it right," answered the owl.

Shard flattened his ears and glared. "That doesn't help! The last time I did what I thought was right, I was wrong both times and wolves and gryfons died for it. Is the vision sent by Tyr and Tor?"

"You are a living Vanir," she said. "Your own ties to the living earth and the sky and the things happening now should tell you what to do. Not a vision of a dead gryfon, great Baldr or no, or any god, or anyone but yourself."

"That's—ridiculous!" Shard's head reeled and he regretted his long days of fasting. Surely he would think better with some fish in his belly. "Where do the visions come from, if not Tyr and Tor? Ravens? The wind? I want to do the right thing! I want to do as they intend the Summer King to do, but you tell me only do what I think is right?"

Again she blinked as if surprised, and ashamed heat flushed his face. *I'm taking out my anger on her, and she only came to help.* He lowered his head, mumbling an apology.

"Prince of the Vanir. Chosen of Tor. Summer King." She intoned all the names and with each one Shard first felt smaller, then more determined. "If Tor stood before you now, what do you think she would tell you to do?"

His talons clenched. *Tor herself? How could I know?*

But some part of him did know. A whisper in his own heart suggested, and he answered the owl out loud.

"To..." he sighed. "To do as I think is right."

Her eyes squinted in a kind expression and she fluffed her feathers. "I think so, too. And perhaps visions do not come from the gods. Perhaps they come, indeed, from ravens who hear all to tell great Tyr at world's end. Perhaps from the wind, and the sky and the sea and the rocks beneath your claws. Heed and weigh and make your choices."

"What if it's the wrong choice?"

She hooted and opened her wings. "Oh, gray prince, I see that you aren't afraid, perhaps, to do the right thing, but that you want more information, before you make a decision?"

Relief made him fold his wings again. "Yes. More information. Not a vision. Not a riddle. If I tell Stigr of my father's vision again he'll only argue that the fight is here. If I have more to add to it—"

"Then follow." She hopped up and hovered, wings round and silent over his head. "You try to serve many masters. Your father's spirit, your uncle, your own heart. I know one who may help, for he hears the word of the wind, and he longs for the peace between gryfons and other great beasts of the land that endured while the Vanir hunted from the sea."

That was new to Shard. The only other great beast of the land he knew had been the boar king Lapu of the Star Isle, slain in Shard and Kjorn's initiation hunt.

"A storm comes, my prince. Let us go seek my old friend, who should be a friend to you."

Shard dragged to his feet, flinching when aches lanced every muscle, bounded twice and jumped roughly into the air. Recalling his last disastrous flight around the mountain, he held his wings tense, alert for rogue gusts and more snow.

The white owl led him in a low, spiraling flight along the swirling gusts, skirting the canyon between the peaks to sail down the steep, icy face of rock and snow toward the foothills.

Shard took a breath, feeling easier away from the unpredictable winds of the peak. He tucked his talons into his chest feathers and let his wings relax.

Slender pines thrust up like splinters below and boulders and barren fields laced the lower slopes. The forests grew thicker the lower they flew. The movement of small animals caught Shard's eye and his belly clawed, but he followed the ways of the old Vanir. He took his food from the sea, and didn't hunt on land, unless with the wolves. And he didn't want to lose the owl, curious where she meant to lead him. He scoffed at himself.

A fine prince of the Vanir I am, hoping an owl can show me what to do.

Then again, perhaps she was impressed by his coming there. Perhaps she wouldn't have come at all if he'd remained, indecisive, in the safe forest of the Star Isle. Twice now the owl had helped him—he wondered what he might owe her in the end.

The storm she spoke of roiled on top of the mountain. The weather moved so swiftly there. Shard was used to seeing weather for leagues out and having time to take cover.

Movement in the trees caught his attention again. A herd of caribou stood alert as Shard's shadow flickered over them, then as one, broke into a run toward the wooded hills. Shard watched them run and his belly snarled again—but even if he hadn't vowed against hunting on land, taking a fully grown caribou alone would be too dangerous.

Snow disappeared as they reached the foothills. Mud and dying grass and golden birch sprinkled among the evergreen pines and their scent rose into the wind. The scent of autumn.

The owl banked to begin a graceful descent and Shard followed. He admired her flight and tried to think how old she must be. She'd once said she was a friend of his father. He didn't know how long owls lived.

Shard snapped to attention as they flew lower, careful not to crash into the looming pines. The scent of the Nightrun River wafted to him and he breathed deeply, smelling rich autumn, fermenting leaves, damp earth and frost in the air. Normally the weather wouldn't trouble him, for he was fit from easy fishing and had the fine, soft winter down of the Vanir growing in for winter. After his quest on the mountain top though, the snow had soaked his feathers and he shivered against the chill.

The owl dipped down into the trees. Shard looked for a wider opening between the pines and dropped down to land on the cushion of needles and yellowing ferns. He turned to see the owl perched in a tree. She gave a warbling, whistle-call into the forest. First like a bird sound, and then like a word. *A-oh...*

"Aodh!"

A shiver glided down Shard's spine to his feathered tail.

It wasn't a word. It was a name. He was sure of it. Mist drifted through the woods from the river.

"Behold!" called the owl. Shard turned, lifting his ears.

A caribou strode forward through the mist, velvet ears angled toward Shard. Instinctively, Shard backed three steps away, intimidated by his sheer size.

At the shoulder he stood twice as tall as a gryfon and his antlers branched up and swept back in a massive crown like a rowan tree. The long winter coat held no trace of soft brown, only silver and gray.

Shard didn't question the owl, only bowed low, mantling his gray wings in a gesture of respect.

"Prince of the Sun Isle," greeted the caribou. Shard was accustomed only to the voices of wolves and gryfons and birds. This creature's voice lilted, light and oddly musical, like the long whistles of young bucks in earlier autumn. At Shard's look of surprise that the caribou knew him he added, "You have your father's look about you. It has been many years since a gryfon sought our company." Eyes as deep and dark as a winter night met Shard's, and he knew the caribou wasn't afraid.

"I've waited for you."

4
THE PRINCE HUNTS

KJORN FOCUSED ON REMAINING STILL, though every nerve vibrated at crouching so close to the herd of fresh, warm, oblivious red deer. His mate crouched in perfect stillness beside him, irritation flooding from her in waves so strong Kjorn could smell it.

"My mate," Kjorn chanced, barely above the volume of breath, intending to ask her what was wrong. His belly snarled and he winced when a doe lifted her head, soft ears swinging to and fro. Thyra twitched. Thyra, daughter-of-Caj, Kjorn's chosen mate and future queen, had a presence that usually made Kjorn feel strong and secure—except when she was angry with him.

That time, her anger was not at him.

"Fools," she breathed after another moment, glaring across the field and through the herd of deer toward where Halvden and other males crouched. Sunlight glanced off their gauntlets, chains and other dragon-made trinkets. Favors from the king. "I told them not to wear those."

"They're only showing off."

"And every wolf within a league will smell gold or ruby, or see a flash of light that is not from sun on a stream." Thyra's feathers, pale lavender and subtle, blended decently with the forest shadows. It was only in bright sunlight that they showed the faintest iridescent blue. "Do they think the wolves are fools?"

Kjorn tightened his own bright wings, wishing they'd left hunting to the females, or at least that they'd left Halvden on the Sun Isle.

Suddenly the herd broke. Whether it was their own whispers, something the males across the field did or another, unknown sense, the deer scattered, bounding toward the tree line.

Thyra swore. "*Mudding*—Kenna, Birgit, fly, to me—!"

She shot forward before Kjorn could move, and two huntresses met her in the field, all targeting the same old stag. In awe, Kjorn watched the other females leap out in well-orchestrated clumps, felling deer as neatly as if it had all been planned. He ran out from his hiding spot, shouting, to at least frighten deer back into the field when they scattered toward the woods.

His father wouldn't be pleased, but the trap was ruined anyway. No wolves would come, the deer would flee, and so they might as well have a meal.

Four deer fell before the rest of the herd escaped. Caj barreled up to Kjorn from a far corner of the field like a thunderhead.

"What happened?"

"The honored prince was talking," drawled Halvden as he trotted up to join them. "I could hear him across the field."

"Silence," Kjorn ordered, lifting his wings and giving Halvden a single hiss of warning. "More likely it was your armor that spooked them. Never wear it on a hunt again."

Halvden's eyes narrowed. "My lord, the king has given me—"

"You argue with your prince?" Caj demanded, tail slashing through the high grass. "Be still. Know your place. If you can't hunt properly, I'll make sure Sverin has you flying patrols over Pebble's Throw."

"Go," Kjorn said to Halvden, relieved for Caj's support. "Help butcher the kills."

Halvden's gaze darted between them, then, without a word or a bow, he spun and shouted orders for dividing the meat. The females gave him cursory looks, all of them more experienced than he.

"He needs to learn how anyway," Caj muttered, watching the green gryfon darkly. "If he expects to feed his mate this winter."

"And he should," Kjorn said. "If Kenna gets hungry, I think it's him she'll take a bite out of."

Caj chuckled and then ruffled his feathers, looking grim. "Your father won't be pleased."

A breeze smelling of sweet, dying grass and the sea brushed Kjorn's face. He thought he caught another, musty smell, but if it was a wolf, it was far away or old. "I'll speak to him."

Caj appraised him. "Good. I know you think it's my duty, Kjorn, but it's not." The old warrior watched him frankly. "It's yours. He's your father. It will be your pride. If there's a wrong, it's yours to right."

Kjorn inclined his head, not irritated that time. It was true enough, and Caj stood beside him against Halvden.

But I wonder, whose duty was it to set Shard right, before he got himself killed? Caj, his nest-father? Or mine? Or all of us?

The smallest and easiest part of him to dismiss wondered, in the end, if Shard had actually been wrong.

"What about Halvden?" Kjorn asked quietly.

"He's just showing off. A braggart." Caj fluffed his feathers again. "Shamed by his mother leaving and his father's death. Winter will cool him. I should make sure he's doing properly over there."

He bowed to Kjorn, and turned away to check that Halvden was being fair in the division of meat. Kjorn remained where he was, watching them, standing guard at the tree line. There were more predators than wolves in the forests of Star Isle, though he doubted any would interfere with a gryfon hunt.

The musky scent came again, then the whisk of movement in the brush.

Kjorn whirled, his breath catching.

The bright autumn woods didn't help him, despite his sharp vision. The forest lay still but alive, tricking him with light and shadow. Leaves became birds and tree trunks became wolves and shadows became ravens, all laughing, silently, as he strained and stared through the trees.

"Your Highness!" Caj called. Kjorn leaned toward the trees, then Thyra called his name, and he turned away.

If there had been a wolf it was gone again, or had never really been there at all.

5
Autumn Song

THE CARIBOU WAITED FOR SHARD to answer. Shard glanced back at the owl, who opened her wings encouragingly and tilted her head.

"I am Shard, son-of-Baldr. I'm honored to meet you..."

"Aodh. Leader of the Low Hill Clan." His voice lilted in a strong brogue, rolling and rising like a river. His long velvet ears swung back and forth, listening. "I speak for all the hoofed creatures from the foot of the White Mountains to the seaward end of the Nightrun, and I have the ear of the hoofed clans of the Star Isle and the horses of distant Crow Wing, if I should have news for them."

Shard bowed low again. He barely had the ear of his uncle, two ravens and two exiled gryfons who had left the isles.

"What brings you here?" asked Aodh again, looking hopeful, Shard thought, for news to send to the other hoofed creatures of the islands. Shard wished he had better to tell.

"I sought a vision, as the wolves do, of how I can bring peace to the Silver Isles. And..." Somehow he couldn't finish. The next part still didn't ring true in his mind.

"And how you may reclaim your birthright as king?" A breeze stirred the caribou's silvering coat and he shook his antlers. "I hear much, for in listening, is survival. The winds have told me much, and the wee birds. How deeply the Red King hates you, and hates the wolves, and indeed, the Silver Isles and perhaps even himself. How you love his son as your brother and will not fight again. Is this your dilemma, young prince?"

The musty, warm meat scent of the rest of the herd filtered through the trees. Shard ground his beak and didn't answer. Claiming his birthright would mean overthrowing Sverin, the king. Worse, it would mean betraying his own wingbrother, Kjorn. Again. He had already sabotaged the king's war on the wolves and challenged the king himself to battle. That had ended with no clear victor. The king fled to his nest, and Shard dove into the sea, letting them think he was dead. He couldn't declare full on war against Sverin and Kjorn. So he'd waited.

He was done waiting.

When Shard didn't answer, Aodh strode forward and lowered his head until his dark, soft nose almost touched Shard's feathered brow. Shard held very still. The caribou's breath stirred the small feathers between Shard's ears and Shard breathed slowly, wary of antlers and cloven hooves.

Aodh's eyes slid half shut, and he might've been dozing if he hadn't started to speak.

"The Silver Wind stirs about you." His voice drifted, for Shard's ears alone. "I have heard a new song in the autumn air, and birds whisper it now. I have waited for you to come, to tell it to you. And indeed I knew if it was for you, that you would come."

Shard shivered as Aodh's voice dropped deeper, quieter, echoing his secret from the wind.

"The Song has been sung, the first battle won
And summoned a prince of summer.
The Silver Wind speaks
And the king it seeks
will be son, and brother, and father."

For a moment, Shard, Aodh, the white owl and the forest stood in impossible silence.

Then Aodh flung his massive head up and shook his antlers as if waking out of a dream. Shard startled back, frustrated.

"What does that mean? The king it seeks will be son, and brother, and father? Is it the Summer King? Is it for me? I'm not a father."

Aodh stamped and Shard flinched. "It is only mine to listen. It is yours to see and know. I cannot know your fate. I can only tell you what I hear."

He must have sensed Shard's restlessness, for he lowered his head, speaking patiently again. "The time of red rowan is on us, young prince. The time of storing up strength, of waiting, of change. The gryfon pride in the low land waits. But you, son of the Nightwing, must find the summer in yourself and you must act. Your strength must be greater than all others. The song has been sung. You have answered. You are the Summer King."

Shard stared up into Aodh's endlessly black eyes. Though the new riddle maddened him, he couldn't take it out on this wise beast. Huddled away in Sverin's pride, there was so much he'd been blind to. *When we hunted from the sea, did my father speak to caribou? To all Named souls?*

"How do you hear these things?"

Aodh tossed his massive head, amused. "It is for gryfons to see. To hunt, to chase, to catch. It is for us, the hoofed, to listen, to stand, to hearken to the wind and earth. I listen. I hear the Silver Wind itself in my dreams. You must see, and fly."

"What must I see?" Shard asked. "I don't understand, how do I see?"

"You look," Aodh said simply, and his large ears twitched, hearing the breeze. "I must tend to my family now. Danger draws close."

Shard stifled a growl, not heeding the warning of danger. Aodh was worse than Catori. It did little more than warn Shard *something* was to be done, but what or where he had no idea. The owl had promised him more information, and he'd gotten more riddles instead.

Still, he couldn't beg the creature to stay and tell him everything, like a kit pestering its mother. Surely if Aodh knew something clearer, he would have said it.

"Thank you, honorable Aodh."

Aodh tilted his head, long ears swinging back and forth once. "The time is long passed when my herd treated with gryfons. The red kings turned from the bounty of the sea to hunt us, but I see the old Vanir in you, and know that none will hunt my family under your reign. When you rise, son of Baldr, I will be there to honor you."

The caribou lowered his crowned head and turned to stride again into the pines. Mist prowled in behind him.

Shard blinked and began to turn also, when a new scent flickered to him. He tensed. Movement drew his gaze. Shard dropped to a crouch, peering through the brush.

A flick of movement. A feathered tail.

Shard's heart tightened and his wings clenched.

There, hidden in the ferns and trees, blind to Shard's presence, a gryfon stalked Aodh.

6
Einarr's Secret

SHARD SHRIEKED A WARNING JUST as the other gryfon leaped—a streak of copper feathers, then heard Aodh's whistle of surprise. Shard sprang forward, talons splayed, to crash into the other gryfon. His coloring was familiar. His scent. Then his shocked face.

"Einarr!"

They hit the needled forest floor and rolled. Aodh pivoted to charge, bellowing a challenge.

Shard twisted and shoved to throw the younger gryfon to the ground, shouting at Aodh. "No!"

At his word Aodh reared up, flashed his hooves and belled again. Einarr dropped low and rolled away. Shard stood his ground between them, words flowing from his chest that were the caribou's language, the words of the earth. "Honorable Aodh, spare my friend!"

Aodh snorted, stamped fore-hooves to the earth, and cantered back to his herd, whistling warning through the trees. The pounding of hooves vibrated the ground under them, and Shard faced Einarr.

They had gone on the same initiation hunt. Einarr had been a friend.

What would Stigr tell me to do? Now Einarr is only another member of Sverin's pride. I can't think of him as a friend.

"How dare you hunt a Named creature on the Sun Isle! How…" Shard stopped, his gaze flicking over Einarr again as the younger gryfon stared at him, beak open in a panicked pant. His feathers and coat looked too dull. His ribs showed against his pelt at a time when he should've worn a sheath of fat for winter. Shard had seen great herds of lazy deer wandering the Star Isle. So he couldn't figure out why Einarr was so lean, or what would drive him so far up the Sun Isle, seeking such dangerous prey.

"Sh–Shard?"

Cold crept down Shard's veins. No gryfon of Sverin's pride could know he lived. Now Sverin would hunt him, or take his anger out on Shard's family, who still lived with the pride.

Unless he never found out.

"The pride is starving," Einarr said when Shard just stared at him. "We had to hunt here."

"I didn't know how desperate you were," Shard said slowly.

Einarr pushed to his feet, ruffling pine needles from his wings, and ignored the question. "I can't believe you're alive! We saw you. We saw you fall into the sea!"

"I didn't fall," Shard said, distracted by other sounds. Einarr wasn't alone. There would be others hunting with him, but he hadn't raised an alarm. Maybe there was a chance that Shard could keep Einarr's silence, if he said the right things.

"But…"

"I dove," he clarified when Einarr didn't catch on to why he wasn't dead. "I dove on purpose. Vanir don't fear the sea."

Einarr's beak fell open. "You—"

"Don't tell Sverin you've seen me," Shard said firmly.

He expected Einarr to argue, but something hardened in the younger gryfon's lean, hungry face. "He already leads us on a mad hunt for the wolves. The pride is hungry. I shouldn't give him a reason to hunt something else."

Shard let his breath out.

"But. . . ." Einarr's eyes lit. The wind brought scent of other gryfons, calling for Einarr through the trees. He ignored them, staring at Shard with narrowed eyes. "If I brought news of *you*, it would mean honor for my nest. My mate. Maybe even more food."

"Einarr—" Shard checked himself as a growl built in his throat. Violence was not his way. And surely that, selling Shard to the king, was not Einarr's way. He was only desperate.

Shard straightened, standing tall among the ferns, letting the scent of the river and the feel of the White Mountains at his back give him strength. He thought of a hundred different things to say—to remind Einarr he was the true prince of the Vanir, that he planned to reclaim the islands, that it was his right. Promises and threats swirled into his head, and he tried to think what Stigr would recommend, or what his own father might have done.

But, gazing at Einarr's desperate, frightened face, all Shard could utter was, "Einarr, your brother and your father live."

Einarr's ears turned forward, and his expression softened.

"I've met with them," Shard continued. "They're well." He took a deep breath. "And they follow me. . .as I welcome any to follow me. Even now Dagr has flown to find your father and the other Vanir, to return to the Silver Isles. I mean to find a peaceful, just end to all of this. Do what you have to, and fair winds, Einarr."

Shard turned and dodged into the trees before Einarr could respond. He remained on the ground to make sure the other gryfons didn't see him. Einarr didn't call after him or give any kind of attack cry or, as far as Shard could tell, any indication at all that they had spoken.

But there was no telling how long that would last.

Shard sprinted through the forests of the low slopes as fast as a wolf, faster than any gryfon on foot for he ran more often than any gryfon. A small black shadow swooped on his left.

"Hugin," he panted, glancing over at the raven, who gave a clattering call. "My friend. Watch him for me."

The raven tilted his head in acknowledgement and veered back the way he'd come. Shard ran, and when he reached the foot of the mountain again, leaped into the sky and turned toward the Star Isle.

"The herd scented us, my prince." Einarr stood with his head bowed, wings splayed down from his back in a respectful mantle. "I didn't plan well. We failed. We brought hare, quail, and other small game from the forests…"

Kjorn stood tall over the copper gryfon, feeling cold. He could hardly be angry with Einarr, after his own hunting band had failed to find wolves and given in to hunger instead. They divided the meat as he spoke to Einarr, based on family rank, age, and who had helped the most in the field.

Sverin watched from the top of his rocks with a surprisingly patient expression.

Good, thought Kjorn. His father could hardly argue with feeding the pride, and Kjorn suspected he was hungry too. Still, when Kjorn had landed with a deer haunch in his talons and no word of wolves, the Red King turned from him, climbed his rocks, and didn't speak again.

The light faded toward evening and long golden shadows stretched across the Sun Isle. Each day grew shorter than the last. Kjorn focused back on Einarr.

"You tried." He forced his voice to sound calm and forgiving. "It was a chance thing, hunting them. They're too wily. Too large."

Einarr nodded once but didn't lift his face. "My lord—" his voice cracked. Kjorn perked his ears. The evening wind had fallen still and the scent of gathering frost pricked the chilly air.

"Yes, what else?"

Distantly, in the woods by the Nightrun, a raven called. Einarr lifted his head and fear gleamed in his eyes.

Am I that frightening? Kjorn thought in dismay. *As frightening as my father?*

Surely he wasn't. Surely Einarr knew Kjorn wouldn't punish him for a failed hunt.

"Nothing," Einarr whispered after a moment of thought, staring at him with huge eyes. "Everything is fine. I saw nothing else in the mountains."

Kjorn flicked his tail. "Go see that your mate gets a meal from our hunt."

"Thank you, my lord." He bowed again and trotted away.

Kjorn narrowed his eyes. He walked through the golden grass until he found Caj, who watched the division of meat with a sharp eye. A raven called again and that time Kjorn saw it, winging toward the deer meat to try stealing a meal.

"Caj," Kjorn said.

Caj turned an ear his way and left the group to walk to Kjorn's side. Clouds drifted across the lowering sun and the golden shadows deepened to violet.

Kjorn recited wisdom Caj had once given Shard and him when they were kits. "When does a gryfon answer a question that wasn't asked?"

Caj eyed Kjorn for a moment and rumbled, "When he's lying."

7
HALFNIGHT

NIGHT PRICKED THE SKY WITH stars and the wind blew frosty, signaling that the true, final days of summer had faded to autumn. Shard dropped lower in the sky, scanning the forest for any indication of gryfons before he landed.

From overhead, the former wolf den looked like an enormous rowan grove. Only by flying lower, landing in the forest and walking up to the den itself had Shard learned that the branches all sprung from a single, ancient, massive tree. As the leaves died off, red berries glittered like tiny flames.

Shard landed many leaps off from the guardian rowan tree and trotted through the ferns and pines, scenting cautiously in case there were gryfons near. Sverin hunted the wolves, and he knew the den's location, but mostly he had given up hunting there. It was too obvious. Though cautious, Shard doubted Sverin would leave scouts at night, even out of desperation.

Above all things, Sverin feared the night.

Shard perked his ears as he stepped out into the clearing. A short cliff jutted up from the forest floor, a crumbling mass of stone clenched together by the curling roots of the giant tree, the crags and holes once forming wolf dens.

Now the wolves lived under the Silver Isles, in a network of caves formed by water, wind and earthfire in the First Age. But every night they came out to hunt.

The cold wind combed Shard's feathers the wrong way and he lifted his beak with a shiver, uttering a low, raspy imitation of a wolf howl. Delighted yips and yowls answered him and before he could twitch his tail the wolves flooded from the den to surround him.

"Windbrother!" called a male wolf from the top of the cliff. The largest of the pack, his reddish fur darkened to black along his back and into autumn gold along the slabs of muscle on his shoulders.

"Ahanu." Shard bowed before the young wolf king. Before he could continue, summer pups swarmed him, still soft and lanky, and a red she-wolf trotted up, her ears and head high. As the light faded he just caught the bright amber of her eyes. Night was for the wolves. Shard could barely see in the dark, but his other senses helped, if he paid attention.

He dipped his head to the she-wolf. "Catori."

"My friend." Her eyes shone. "I see some success in you. What did you see?"

"There's a lot to tell—"

"Shard!" cried one of the summer pups. Wolves whelped in spring, as gryfons did, but they grew faster and these pups had become taller and lanky over the summer. Shard reeled. When these pups, now his small friends and admirers, had been born, Shard had still considered wolves a vile enemy.

"Play songs! Play riddles!"

Catori nipped at them fondly. "Away with you. To your mothers!"

Shard laughed and opened his wings as the cubs yawned and rolled under him.

"I want to fly!" whined the littlest.

"You're getting too big," Shard laughed. Once or twice he had gripped a young wolf in his talons and took them soaring over the woods and sea. Now they grew large, their bones sturdy and heavy and their bodies plump for winter.

Shard wondered what Kjorn might have said, to see him giving wolf pups joy flights over the water.

Ahanu loped down to them while the rest of the pack milled and warbled, excited and waiting for news of Shard's vision quest.

"Brother," Ahanu greeted, lifting his nose. Shard touched his beak to the young wolf king's nose and they shared a breath. Ahanu smelled warmly familiar, his wolf scent tangy and comforting to Shard now. They'd had a successful hunt, for he also smelled blood and shreds of meat. "Were you successful?"

A gray feather, woven into the fur of Ahanu's neck by clever raven claws, swiveled in the breeze. Like his sister who wore two of Stigr's black feathers in her fur, he wore one of Shard's fallen feathers to show he was a friend to gryfons.

"I think so," Shard said, distracted by the noise and commotion of the wolf pack after so many days alone.

"Good!" Ahanu declared. "I would like to hear, but first, you'll feast. Your uncle fishes along the shore to gather special meats for the Halfnight. We will honor bright Tor as she comes into her season. Then tell us what you saw on the mountain."

Shard dipped his head, then blinked. "Halfnight? What's that?"

Catori gave a soft *wuff* of surprise. "Sverin and the Aesir don't recognize it? Your uncle didn't teach you?" She turned in a circle, tail swishing happily. "The night when summer gives way to autumn. When Tor begins her reign. The nights grow longer. The days shorter. But this day and night, she and Tyr share equal time in the sky." She trotted forward to sniff him, then stepped back. "Your ordeal was long. Your nights of fasting and the mountain climb changed your sense of day. All told, you've been gone a fortnight. Bright Tor is almost full."

"A good omen," Ahanu declared. "Good that you returned this night. It is a rare Halfnight that we see her at her brightest."

A howl rose off in the woods. A shudder seemed to run through the pack, as if they shared a skin. The moon was calling. Shard perked his ears and suddenly Ahanu dodged away laughing, then whirled and braced his forepaws on the ground like a pup at play.

"But come now. We have food to eat and songs to sing!"

"Sing with us!" Catori bumped Shard's shoulder. "Feast! You need meat. Stigr waits for us by the shore."

Ahanu spun around and loped into the forest. Wolves streamed past Shard to follow. Catori turned and followed her brother into the forest. The howls rose. Shard, slower than the wolves for his poor night vision, followed them on a well-worn trail through shadow-dappled forest toward the saltwater scent of the sea.

The new song from Shard's vision rolled through his mind in time with his quick footsteps.

Which fades last, the birdsong, or the day…

Several times, absorbed in his thoughts, Shard ran face-first into a sturdy fern or a bramble, and finally he focused on the night around him. Wolf laughter and panting filled his ears, the swish of fur in the undergrowth. He kept close to Catori until they burst out of the woods and trotted in a long line down to a beach on the dawnward coast.

Waves crawled in and out. The moon perched imperiously above, huge and round as a pregnant gryfess, washing all in silky light. Wolf pups zigzagged around the adults as they reached the pebbly sand, bellies full, laughing and howling.

A dozen wolves already occupied the shore, enjoying a meal, playing races and sparring. Shard scanned those gathered and saw the distinct silhouette of a gryfon among the wolf pack. He was stretched out on the sand, holding court to a group of yearling pups and telling tales of the Conquering and the days before, when he and Baldr the Nightwing had wild adventures from one end of the Silver Isles to the other.

"Stigr!"

"Hail, nephew!"

Shard picked up to a trot then stopped, feeling suddenly dizzy.

"Have a meal!" Stigr called, seeing that Shard wouldn't be much good until he'd eaten. He remained where he was, with wolf pups climbing on him, begging to learn how to fish.

Catori and Ahanu led Shard to the carcass of a deer that still held good chunks of meat. "We wanted to eat here," Catori explained, "to bask in Tor's full light."

"And we thought you and Stigr would enjoy it," Ahanu said, his tail waving as he saw that Shard was, indeed happy with the arrangement.

"Thank you," he said.

Catori sniffed his ears, then stepped away. "We'll leave you to eat and rest awhile, then hear your tale."

Shard inclined his head to them again, tore a haunch from the carcass and settled on a pile of mussel-crusted rocks where he could see all the activity.

Their thoughtfulness for him struck a bright note in his chest, and in a strange way, made him feel more like a king. He knew they had done it because they were friends, not because they considered him the Summer King and heir to the Sun Isle, but it still made him feel undoubtedly regal. He would have to think of a way to show them the same regard.

And remember to enjoy it, he thought, gnawing on the deer haunch. He stripped the meat slowly, wary of his tight stomach, and of eating too much rich meat too fast. Like Stigr, he only ate prey from the land when the wolves gifted it, or allowed him to hunt with them. He'd only learned a few moons ago that prey should always be honored and thanked before killing, that they had Names and a soul just as Shard had.

The moon climbed in the sky, and Shard watched, hearing bits of tales that floated his way, letting his muscles relax and his stomach ease, and savor the feeling of returning home. The moon neared middlemark before he'd finish eating. He gazed at it, thinking of his mother, Ragna, wondering how she fared under Sverin's reign. He'd had no chances to speak with her since he'd learned she was his true mother, and had lied to spare his life.

One of the pups howled to Shard to stop staring at the moon and play, and Shard tossed him the thigh bone of the deer, promising, "Later!"

Then he fell under the attack of two wolves who ambushed him from behind.

Catori and Ahanu had leaped silently, but burst into laughter when they crashed into Shard. Squashed against the rock under their playful nips and growls, Shard cried traitors and summoned Stigr for aid. He managed to shove his wings open, and the wolves tumbled away, laughing.

A rough wind buffeted them and Shard rolled to his feet, shook vigorously, and looked up to see that the wind gusted from Stigr's wings, beating the air as he landed in front of them.

The old warrior was taller than Shard, feathers as black as Ragna's were white, hard and lean and bearing the long, shaped wings of a pureblooded Vanir. Scars laced his flanks but the worst mark came from the Conquering, from Shard's own nest-father Caj. Where Stigr's left eye should've been was only a nest of scar, and when he spoke he always swiveled his head to see whomever he was speaking to.

"We're allowed to disturb the prince now?" His single eye gleamed in the moonlight. He rumbled the jest kindly, Shard chuckled.

"Yes. you are. I think I've got my head on mostly straight again now that I've eaten."

"I don't know about that," Stigr tapped his beak together, in a fine mood. "But you look better anyway."

Shard folded his wings neatly, lifting his head. He hadn't realized how he'd missed his uncle, and his friends, until he was among them again. "Is this the respect you show your prince?"

Stigr chuckled and made a show of bowing, mantling his black wings handsomely. "Perhaps if you'd show some respect to your elders…"

"I'll try harder," Shard said. It was Stigr who had taught Shard better flying and fighting techniques. Stigr who'd waited alone in exile for Shard to come of age, sought him out and taught him everything he knew about the night, about Tor, about being a Vanir. Stigr, Shard thought, to whom he owed nearly everything—the good, and the bad. His birthright, and his exile.

Ahanu padded up to bump Stigr affectionately, sniffed his wings, then turned to Shard, eyes bright under the moon. "Tell us of your vision quest."

"I'd like to hear it," Stigr said, and sat.

Shard glanced to Catori. He'd hoped to tell her alone, to get her opinion before he talked to Stigr. Ironically he recalled a time when he hadn't wanted her opinion or even her friendship. Stigr, she feared, had a tendency to speak from bitterness toward all of the Aesir gryfons in the world.

But Stigr will not be king of the Vanir, Shard thought, feeling edgy. *I will.*

As the wolves below settled in for their own stories and songs and the wolf pups collapsed into sleeping, fuzzy heaps on the sand, undone by the excitement, Shard told Ahanu, Catori and Stigr his tale.

He told them everything about the mountain, the owl, Aodh and even Einarr.

Afterward they sat quietly, each considering, and heard only the voices of the wolf singers below, telling the autumn tales.

Shard broke the quiet. "The song from my vision. Is it something you've ever heard? Any of you?"

"The Song of Last Light," Ahanu said.

"Song for the dying," Stigr clarified.

"Whoever sang it in my vision," Shard said quietly, "felt as if they were trying to call me. What is the rest of the song?"

Catori lifted her head, reciting toward the moon.

> *"Which rises first, the night wind, or the stars?*
> *Not even the owl could say,*
> *whether first comes the song or the dark.*
> *Which fades last, the birdsong or the day?*
> *Not even the sky could tell,*
> *Whether last stills the sun or the jay."*

Ahanu joined her, singing the last line, and indeed it was just like the Song of First Light that Shard had learned that summer.

> *"Only the long day brings rest*
> *Only the dark of night, dawn.*
> *When the First knew themselves, the wise will say,*
> *They took their Names to the Sunlit Land*
> *But their Voice in the wind sings on."*

"What does it mean?" Shard whispered, shivering once.

Catori lowered her face from the moonlight and shadow darkened her eyes. "Someone is dying."

Stigr huffed, tilting his head to watch Shard. "What does this have to do with anything?"

Shard's wings twitched in a shrug. "I don't know. It's the song that was coming from the mountain. But I know it was calling someone. It was calling me."

"It was calling nothing." Stigr cocked his head, first at Shard, then at the wolves who stayed out of the argument. "It was a rhyme. A kit's nest rhyme."

"A last song," Catori argued.

Shard met Stigr's gaze. "I think…" He drew some courage from the moon and the endless sea. "I believe I'm supposed to find that mountain."

"You can't leave the Silver Isles," Stigr said flatly. "I know you don't wish to fight your wingbrother. I know you fear the Red King, and you want the best for all. But sometimes you have to fight."

A strange coolness glided through Shard. "I don't fear Sverin. I bested him once—unless you've forgotten."

Stigr's tail lashed as he grew angrier and Shard fought the urge to shrink back, for he couldn't be Stigr's student forever. He let his uncle speak, meeting his gaze in silence.

"Shard, son of my wingbrother. The fight is here. Your pride is here. Dagr and Maja will return in spring with whatever Vanir they can gather home. You must be *here*." Stigr stood and paced, black wings opening halfway in agitation. His eye narrowed, his voice was low and firm. "Baldr didn't fight until the end. If he could be here now, I truly think he'd council you not to wait any longer. Not to avoid the fight as he did."

The coolness in Shard's blood revealed itself as confidence.

"Uncle," he said, making sure his voice carried the respect he felt. Stigr was his mentor, his uncle by blood, his friend, his father's wing-brother and his own most steadfast ally. But Shard would be his king. "Thank you for your counsel. I need to think everything over."

The air seemed to thicken. The hackle feathers along Stigr's neck stood up as if he faced a challenger. He realized, Shard knew, that Shard wouldn't always do exactly as he said anymore.

He wanted me to be his prince, Shard thought grimly, feeling a little regret at the betrayed expression in Stigr's face. *His king. Surely Baldr followed his own heart in the end.*

Though in the end, Baldr was killed.

"My counsel," Stigr growled at last, "is always yours. My prince." He gave Shard a cool nod, glanced to Ahanu and Catori, then shoved from the rocks to glide back along the seashore. Shard leaped forward and opened his wings, biting back a shout. Catori whined and Shard whirled instead to face her.

"He has no right to be angry. He wants me to be a prince and make decisions, but only when it suits him!"

"That isn't true," she said. "He only fears for you."

"For the Silver Isles," Ahanu added.

Shard sighed and folded his wings again. He inclined his head to Ahanu. "Brother, I'd like to speak to Catori alone."

Ahanu yipped a laugh. "Of course. I must let the seers have their counsel."

"Thank you again for the feast," Shard said quickly, swishing his tail in the way of a pleased wolf. Ahanu bowed, stretching long legs out toward Shard.

"Of course. For the next feast you can bring me fat salmon from the sea."

"I will," Shard promised.

The wolf king left them, loping down to the shore to settle a dispute over the last of the deer carcass. His stern, rolling growls prickled the skin on the back of Shard's neck. There had a been a time when they were not friends, and he remembered those growls.

Catori stood next to him on top of the rocks, ears perked toward her pack as well. Shard noticed that some of the wolves were pairing off and trotting up the beach, or away up the footpath and into the woods again. Catori looked over her shoulder at Shard as he sat, and her eyes caught the light of the moon.

"You're wondering about the things Aodh said."

Shard shifted, surprised. "How did you know?"

"It's natural."

"A son, a brother, a father? I'm not even mated. Does it mean I'm to find a mate?"

"You will be king," she said, dipping her head to sniff idly at the mussels bunched on the rock. "You'll need an heir."

Dismayed, Shard stood. "But there's no one in the Silver Isles who I'd want or who would want me, no one—and it makes it sound as if I have to be a father before I can fulfill the promise of the Summer King."

Her ears twitched to and fro. "It may not be exactly that. Perhaps it means you'll be a father to the Vanir. A king. Perhaps your mate will be among the returning Vanir."

Shard hadn't thought of that. Hesitant excitement warmed his chest. He was not the last pureblooded Vanir in the world. Two gryfons of his pride, Maja and Dagr, had flown to gather any lost Vanir they could find from other corners of the world. Maybe among them would be a young huntress who might…

He shook his head.

"That won't be until spring."

Catori shook herself, sat, her forepaws tucked together, and looked at him a moment, as if trying to see through him. "I think it will be revealed to you, Shard. You're already a son and a brother, without trying. There is obviously some other task for you that has been whispered in the wind. A task for the Summer King."

Restlessness crawled up his skin. Instead of clarity, he had more riddles. "Stigr thinks my task is here."

"You answered the call of the Summer King. I think if you are called again, you will answer again." She displayed the points of her teeth in a playful expression. "I do know that the snow owls speak to very few. We wolves know they are the closest creatures to Tor, that they see her when she is dark and the sky is only stars. They know of death, and of the future."

Shard considered his conversation with the owl. Below their rocks, a young male wolf told a raucous joke that left all the males howling, and the females scattered them with indignant nips and growls.

"She seemed very practical to me. She only said to do what I thought was right."

"Sound advice," Catori said, lifting her nose to the wind. The scent of autumn came to them, a distinct, frosted edge to the air.

Catori stared into the wind. "One day," she whispered, her face and amber eyes traced by the moon, "I see a fine, gray king, as humble and strong as the washing wave, as steady as the mountain, with a hunting queen and strong fledging warriors under his wing. We are not yet who we will be, Shard."

She looked at him and a chill soared up Shard's back. For a heartbeat he was back in the rowan grove where he'd met her. He saw behind her eyes that she listened, like Aodh, and heard things no other heard, saw things in the moonlight and the dark that others didn't.

"It will be the paths you run," she paused in amusement, nose crinkling to reveal the points of her teeth , "or *fly*, that temper you. The battles you fight. The foes you conquer."

"Or don't," Shard muttered, thinking of how he'd rabbited when fighting Sverin. He could have kept his grip and dragged the fanatic king into the sea and drowned him. He could have ended it then. "I should have ended it. Sverin should have died in the sea as my father died in the sea."

"Or not," Catori mused, and Shard's throat felt dry. "We all have a voice in the song. Sverin may yet have an unfinished destiny."

"And what's that?" Shard scoffed. "To kill *all* the Vanir of the world before he dies in glorious battle somewhere?"

Just as he realized he sounded more like his uncle than himself, Catori hopped to her feet and nipped his ear. "If anyone should hate Sverin, it's me. I think you speak out of regret and fear. But Shard, you aren't weak because your aren't a conqueror or a killer. Because you consider the ripples of the stones you drop doesn't make you a coward."

Shard lifted his wings, and had no answer. He looked down to the beach, perking his ears at the wolves. Two more pairs circled each other as if in a dance, laughing, and disappeared up the shore into the woods.

"Are they hunting again?"

Catori threw her head back and laughed. "Oh, no. It is on the Halfnight that we choose our mates, as gryfons choose theirs in summer."

"Oh." Shard shifted uncomfortably. *A son. A brother. A father.*

"When there is peace," Catori said, looking politely away from him, "I know you will find a fine huntress to help lead your pride. Don't worry." She stretched. "Myself, I think I'm not ready either." She tilted her head, watching the wolves cavorting, and pups stumbling through all their legs. "It has been my duty to watch and dream for my pack."

Shard sensed her changing the topic from his visions and he was grateful for the respite. They both knew what he was going to do in the end, but it wasn't *her* opinion on it that he feared.

He stuck with the change of subject. "I wasn't ready either, this summer."

"Catori!" called a male wolf. She lifted her head and Shard swiveled his ears. In the dark it was hard to recognize coat color, but the voice was familiar.

"Catori, run with me!" He loped up and hoisted to his hind legs to slap his paws on the rock near Catori's feet, panting and delirious with the moon. A gray feather of Shard's flickered against his neck fur, a sign of their friendship.

Catori tilted her head in to lick his face while Shard watched, bemused. "Not this night."

His ears flattened in disappointment, then he darted his face in to wash her cheek vigorously. "Then I'll wait another night, and another, until it's the next Halfnight." He tilted his head the other way and stopped panting, serious for a moment. "And the next, until you run with me."

"You'll be old and gray, Tocho," Catori mused. "Find an eager young female to run at your side."

"I'll never find her." Tocho's eyes shone under the moon. "For I can see none but you."

With that he shoved from the rock and bounded away, laughing, to dive into a wrestling game with the pups. Shard looked inquiringly to Catori.

"Perhaps." She turned her ears toward Tocho. "Perhaps when there is peace in the Silver Isles again."

Shard chuckled. He didn't know Tocho well, but knew he was good. Once, Shard had saved his life from another gryfon, and for that Tocho hadn't attacked the gryfon's nesting cliffs that summer past. For that, they would always be friends.

None of that helped Shard think of a proper mate for himself, though. What Catori said was true. He would need a mate.

A queen.

A son, a brother, a father.

He shook his head, feathers ruffling up as if against a cold breeze. It was too much to think about, and there was no gryfess in the Silver Isles now that Shard could picture mating with, much less making queen. Perhaps the Vanir who were yet to return, as Catori had said. Perhaps there was a young Vanir huntress among them, who wouldn't have known of Shard's past as a runt among Aesir, an outcast. A female his age, demure and quiet, who would know him only as the prince who returned peace to the Silver Isles.

The thought was strangely cheering and he'd just begun to form an image of this phantom gryfess in his mind, with keen eyes and feathers like twilight...

A shout went up among the wolves.

Shard and Catori exchanged a look and jumped down from the rock to find Ahanu. Pups and young and old wolves alike clamored around them.

"What is it?" Shard asked. "What's happening?"

All looked to the sky, questioning and staring, different wolves circled asked, "Gryfons? Is it the War King?"

"No, it's sunrise!"

"Too early," grumbled an old wolf.

Shard looked up, scanning the sky, and he shivered in awe. A soft, bluish light crept forward from the starward quarter of the sky. It glowed like moonrise, but from the wrong quarter and much too early.

Suddenly Stigr was at Shard's side among the knot of excited wolves, ready to protect him against attack. He tilted his head at the sky. "What's all this?"

"I don't know," Shard breathed, excitement beating through him. Some new magic was revealing itself under Tor's blessed light, on the Halfnight. Maybe it was a final sign for him. He had to see.

He crouched and shoved into the air, his wing beats scattering wolves as he soared up high, ignoring Stigr's shouts to come down.

8
STARFIRE

CAJ SPRAWLED ON HIS NEST, watching edgily as his mate stood near the mouth of their den.

"No wolves sighted at all, you said?" Sigrun stood with her dove-brown wings half open to catch the moonlight that peeked in from the dawnward sky. She was Caj's mate, healer to the pride, and that night she looked like something from an old, eerie Vanir legend. Wolf howls drifted clearly to them from across the sea channel between the islands.

Mocking.

"Not during the day," Caj confirmed, tracing the line of moonlight down her wingtip with his gaze. He rarely remained alert so late into the night, but Sigrun's restlessness and the large rising moon had kept them both awake.

His ears twitched at the last of the howls before they fell quiet. "They hide in their caves, laughing, and come out at night."

Sigrun turned, her face soft, eyes fierce. "Perhaps the king will finally consider hunting at night."

"Doubtful." Caj shifted and then thought better of standing. He didn't want her to feel threatened. Instead he extended his wing to invite her back to the nest. "Come away from there."

She perked her ears. A draft stirred up the strong scent of herbs and Caj sneezed, making Sigrun laugh. "Are you afraid I'll fly away into the night?"

"No." There was something about the moonlight through her wings and Caj hadn't figured out if it was beautiful, or terrifying. She had survived the Conquering and accepted Caj as her mate, but that didn't change who she was. A pure Vanir. For half a breath, he saw in her everything his wingbrother feared. Darkness. The cold moon. Magic.

Nonsense.

The only skill he had ever seen her practice was mending flesh and bone and spirit. That, she did with splints, herbs of the earth and her calm voice and heart. Not magic. And she had never lied to him, even about Shard. Once they were mated and she felt safe, she had told him that Shard was really the son of her wingsister, the son of the slain Vanir king. With her, Caj had kept the secret, had raised him under Sverin's gaze, had tried to make him a loyal member of the Red King's pride. Had failed.

He shifted again, closing his wing when she didn't move to come to him. "Does Shard live?"

Sigrun turned, wings folding, and didn't seem surprised that he'd asked, though it had been half a season since Shard's battle with Sverin. "I don't know."

Caj pushed himself up to walk to her, to the edge of the cave, to show he wasn't afraid of the night. That answer was her way of not lying to him. He knew it. "Or should I ask, did he survive his fall into the sea?"

"He didn't fall," she said, almost curtly. "He dove."

Caj shuddered, feathers prickling up. "So he did survive."

She looked down, ears laying back. "He would never harm Kjorn."

"Kjorn isn't my wingbrother."

"He released Sverin before hitting the water, and he didn't have to. You know him, Caj. You helped raise him."

Caj stifled a growl. "I hardly helped." Shard hadn't let him, too aware that Caj wasn't his true father, though Caj had tried many times to be a father to him.

Sigrun's wing brushed his and she seemed to ignore his answer. "What will you do, now that you know?"

"What I've always done." He hesitated before he touched his beak to the soft feathers behind her ear. "Protect you."

She loosed a breath of relief and Caj began to turn, but she nipped his feathers. "Stay. Stand with me, watch the rise of the Halfnight."

"I don't observe the Halfnight," he muttered, eyeing the moonlight that grew brighter on the sea beyond the nesting cliffs. It cast a pale, glimmering path along the water straight toward them as if the moon invited them down a strange new trail. *A cursed trail. Is there a land of Endless Night, where Tyr's light never touches? A land where the cowards and oath breakers go to suffer when they die?*

"It's a cursed time," Caj went on when she didn't speak. "The beginning of cursed winter."

"I observe it," Sigrun answered quietly, looking out again. Caj hesitated. She had never shamed him, never flown at night, never spoken openly of the old beliefs where others could hear. Only to him. Because she felt safe.

After another moment, Caj sat slowly next to his mate. They sat there in silence for a little time. He became aware of Sigrun humming, a low, timid song in her throat. She never grew louder, and didn't add words, but the song seemed to match the moon.

It was late, middlemark, and Caj's weariness ate at him, but he'd decided to let Sigrun determine when they would sleep.

Just as he'd begun to think the moon had a little of its own kind of beauty to it, a strange, growing unease warmed his stomach. The many deep scars lacing his skin began to ache the way they did before a storm, his nerves as tense as if an enemy approached.

Glancing furtively to Sigrun, he saw her eyes widening, and her ears laid flat against her skull. They both sensed something, like a storm, something growing thick but invisible in the air, as if the night were coming alive.

He looked back out into the dark, and they saw it at the same time.

Ice chilled Caj's heart.

"What is that?" Sigrun breathed. She crouched, staring at a strange, growing light in the starward quarter of the sky.

"I don't know," Caj answered, as calmly as he could, though his feathers had begun to stand on end. "But it's been seen before."

Shard flew so high the thin, frosty air spun his thoughts in giddy circles. Below, Stigr's swearing barely made it through the cold wind.

The Isles spread out below Shard in the moonlight, the tides pulled away by mighty Tor to reveal land between each island, to reveal that the Silver Isles were really one. Each isle thrust up from the sand and glittering back sea, bunched in the shape of a gryfon's hind paw.

Shard gulped cold air, his wing beats slowing, but strong enough to keep him aloft at the dizzying height. His mind alight with mystery, he swung about to stare starward. That quarter of the sky was so named for the Daystar that shone high above in the night and day and could be relied on for direction from any quarter. Now all the stars were washed out by the strange pale light.

"Impulsive—foolish—" Stigr's gasping reprimand cut short as the older gryfon decided to save his breath. He flapped hard to hold steady next to Shard as they stared. From that height they could see the slight curve of the world, like the edge of an egg with light behind it, and the starward sea beyond the Silver Isles glowed blue.

White Tor stood high at middlemark. The Halfnight. Shard could just picture Tyr, standing perfectly on the other end of the world, waiting for his time.

The moon laid heavy light on them, turning Stigr's black feathers to molten silver.

A slow coil tightened Shard's belly as he waited, staring starward. At first he saw only the fixed, guiding Daystar.

The cold, growing light crawled over the mountains and trees and tops of all the Isles. At last the source of the glow came over the earth of the horizon.

"Great Tor's wings," Stigr breathed, and Shard could only agree.

A stream of fire glided across the sky.

Shard had seen stars fall, bright motes dropping like sparks and dying. This wasn't the same. As if a star had grown wings, a ball of pale, bluish fire trailing a long, bright tail soared slow and blazing across the night.

Something flashed before him, a dream image in front of his open eyes.

A white serpent in the sky. Swan wings shaping the wind. A gleaming pearl in a black cave under a sky swathed in stars.

"Only the long day brings rest..."

"Only the dark of night, dawn!" Shard sang back desperately, hoping for an answer. "Who are you?"

"Tyr's beak." Stigr's second remark broke Shard from the vision. "It's headed this way, Shard."

Instead of a serpent, Shard saw the starfire again. He blinked hard, eyes streaming against the dry, cold air as he reoriented himself.

His heart ignited with glee. It was a final sign. It had to be, fire from Tyr but colored like the moon and sea, a sign from both Tyr and Tor to show him his path. Aodh was right. He'd only had to look. The line of fire split the sky in half, drawing a clear arc toward the windward quarter of the sky.

Windward. Toward the home of the Aesir. The home of the conqueror, Per the Red.

Baldr's vision, now Shard's vision, was of the homeland of the Aesir.

I'm suppose to go, Shard knew with utter surety. *Whether or not Stigr likes it.*

Maybe he could find allies there. Maybe some of his own Vanir pride had fled there, waiting for him to find them, or for news that he had risen so they could return. Maybe he could learn a way to make the

Aesir in the Silver Isles leave peacefully if he knew more clearly why they had come. He would find the white mountain from the vision, and the singer who called to him, and fulfill whatever the vision meant to show him.

Any solution he wanted that involved not confronting Kjorn as a rival prince or challenging Sverin would be found in the Aesir homeland.

And I knew it, Shard thought grimly. *I knew, and it shouldn't have taken Tyr's talons raking the sky to see it.*

"Fly down with me," Stigr growled, for though the starfire showed no sign of awareness or life, it flew nearly straight toward them.

Shard didn't want to chance an encounter with the fire, and followed Stigr down. The older gryfon was more experienced and heavier than Shard, but Shard spent his time practicing flight. He'd learned the way that falcons dove at eye-defying speeds to catch their prey. He sleeked his feathers tight and twisted his body, contorting until the wind slipped like river water around him. He outpaced Stigr in a heartbeat and hurtled toward the beach, flaring only a few leaps' height above the water, slowing just enough to land hard and sprint to Catori and Ahanu.

"What is it?" Shard asked, breathless, feeling hot and tense and ready to follow the fire across the ocean. Stigr thumped beside them, nearly knocking two cubs over. "What does it mean?"

"It shows a path," Catori murmured. "Our family has seen it once before."

Shard blinked, and Stigr made a rough sound. "Tell us what it meant to you, then."

"I will tell the tale," said Ahanu, and even the pups trotted close to listen, and learn the name of the fiery creature in the sky.

"Kajar's Sign," Kjorn breathed.

He shouldn't have been awake. Aesir were children of the day. But he couldn't sleep with the moon shining in and the wolf howls in the night. He'd almost decided to break the laws of his father and Tyr and fly to the Star Isle to hunt the wolves down, if only to get his last couple hours of sleep before dawn.

Then the sky had brightened. Too bright for night, and too early for dawn, so Kjorn had risen from his nest and paced to the mouth of his den.

Fire streamed across the sky. Kjorn's heart lit and pounded.

"My mate," said Thyra, slipping up beside him. She was calm, as if they only observed a new breed of deer walking past. A cool huntress to the core. The moon and strange starfire lit her lavender feathers with an other-worldly pale blue glow. "What did you call it?"

She didn't look afraid. Kjorn had never seen her afraid of anything and recalled again why he loved her, had chosen her. He hesitated to tell her, but the old stories drifted to him, and he had promised himself he would never keep anything from her.

"There's a story. A true story. My mother told it to me once as a kit, but my father wouldn't tell it after she died. He doesn't like omens or talking about the past. Aesir look toward the future."

"Tell me," Thyra urged. "Your past is my past now, too. I should know it."

Kjorn watched the majestic progress of the starfire as he spoke. "My mother said that the starfire comes every few generations, and has flown since Tyr and Tor created the world. She said it first led the gryfons from the realm of Tyr and Tor down into the world, and when it's seen, it's a sign of things coming, or where to go."

Thyra huffed, looking concerned and practical, traits from both her parents showing as she studied the starfire. "Do you know what it means now?"

"No." Kjorn lifted his wings, staring at the starfire. *Is it a sign for me? It can't be.* Kjorn, like his father, didn't truly believe in omens, but only in real things that he could do and control.

Surely it was only a strange occurrence of the night, like the moon and stars.

"I don't," he said firmly, looking at Thyra. "But it's been seen by my family once before. Great-grandfather Kajar saw a starfire trail like this, and believed it would lead him to his destiny. He followed it all the way across his own territory and the sea beyond, into the arctic land of the dragons, and started his war to conquer their land and seize their gems. He took gems and by all accounts won his battles, but…"

He trailed off. "That's all Mother and Father ever told me of it. When Kajar died, our families and allies were strong enough that my grandfather Per led us all to conquer the Silver Isles."

Thyra seemed to hold her breath a moment. Her scent drifted to Kjorn, always a comfort, and now with a new edge. The scent of their unborn kit in her belly. His kit. The thought of it tightened Kjorn's muscles with pride and sudden fear. He wondered if it would be male or female. He pictured a male kit with his strength and Thyra's sharp wit. He could take him hunting along the Nightrun as a fledge.

What if it's a little huntress? he thought in dismay. He wouldn't know what to do with her besides protect her from pushy males. But she would have the best mother to teach her all she needed. *Either way. A little warrior or a huntress. It will be Thyra's and mine.*

And he would do whatever he had to do to make the world right before his offspring came into it.

Is this how my father felt about me?

Thyra nuzzled him out of his thoughts. "What will you tell your father? He'll be sleeping fast. He won't have seen it. What will you tell him?"

Kjorn stared at the fire in the sky, blood racing as if he were about to plunge into battle. He thought of his father's relentless hunt for the wolves, his distrust of the native Vanir gryfons, his fear of the night. He thought of his own new suspicion that Einarr was hiding something. He couldn't imagine what Sverin would do if he learned of the starfire.

They already struggled to prepare for winter.

Unrest already grew.

Thyra watched him quietly, waiting. Kjorn set his ears back, turned from the night and said, "Nothing."

9
SHARD'S CHOICE

WIND DRIFTED ALONG THE SHORE, wind that carried the scent of dying autumn leaves, ripe berries and the promise of cold.

Ahanu's voice was deep and mild, as the end of the starfire grew dim in the windward sky, over the far horizon.

"Our mother's mother saw it, two generations ago." He sat slowly, nose crinkled in amusement as Shard tried to count the years. "We wolves grow faster but live longer than gryfons, I think."

"My dam'a," Catori said, affirming Ahanu's words. "She was almost as old as a raven when she died."

"And she saw the starfire," Stigr prompted, tail sliding in irritation across the sand.

Ahanu looked toward the stars, as if his mother was there. "Yes. She was a snow wolf from beyond the mountain range of the this isle, from the cold starward edge of the Star Isle where the snow barely melts in summer. She saw the starfire many, many years ago, and dreamed one of her pups chased it down to the sea."

Catori finished the tale. "And when our mother heard our father's song, she went down from the mountains just as in the dream."

For a moment, Stigr and Shard stared at them. Shard realized he'd never met Catori's mother, actually, hadn't even known the she-wolf lived. Stigr lifted his wings and stretched out his talons, digging long trenches in the gravelly wet sand.

"That's all very well for wolves—"

"Summer King," said Ahanu to Shard, just as Catori said, "Star King, Prince of the Sun Isle. What does it mean to you? Surely this is your sign."

Shard could have told her right then what it meant. Something in Stigr's expression stopped him and his gaze darted to the dark sea. "I have to think about it."

The wolves took his hint, and Stigr narrowed his eye. "Enough songs for this night, I think. Tomorrow we need to make a plan before winter lands on our tails, Shard."

"Yes, Uncle," Shard said quietly.

For another mark of the moon the wolves milled on the shore, wishing Shard well and offering help with whatever path he chose. They took Ahanu's word that the starfire was a good sign for them, not a warning, that it was Tor's harbinger of strong things to come. Shard avoided the topic of it any further and pressed Stigr and Catori for lessons on the Halfnight itself.

He learned that this night was when one should stop singing the songs of summer and sing those of winter. He learned that bright Tor ruled high in winter, when the world turned its face from Tyr's light and the days grew short and cold.

When at last the wolves couldn't keep from yawning and the pups sprawled exhausted in the sand, Stigr and Shard bid their farewells.

Shard touched his beak to Ahanu's nose. "Good hunting."

"I will see you farther down the path, brother," Ahanu said quietly. Shard closed his eyes a moment, then they stepped back and he went to Catori.

She dipped her head. "Be safe, my friend."

"I'll miss you," Shard said.

She shook herself, almost laughing. "Mind your dreams. I might not be so far away. Fair winds, my prince."

Shard displayed his wings in respect. "Good hunting to you. Catori…if you see Kjorn, somehow, tell him—tell him I want his forgiveness. And that he has mine." She dipped her head. Then, as Ahanu had said, "I'll see you farther down the path."

"I think it will be so," Catori said. With that, they parted.

He and Stigr chose to stay that night on the Star Isle, flying up to the abandoned dens of the short-lived gryfon colony of Windwater.

"Fair dreams," Stigr rumbled from the ledge outside his chosen den. Shard nodded, memorizing his uncle's face in that moment, happy, with a belly full of fish and a heart full of songs.

"Rest well, Uncle," Shard said, feeling suddenly strained. "Thank you for all you've done for me. It means everything."

Stigr huffed, giving him an odd look, but seemed to take it as an apology for their argument earlier. Shard had hoped he would. "See you in the morning," Stigr said, and disappeared into the den.

Shard remained on the ledge outside his own temporary den and didn't answer. He settled down and rested for a quarter mark, waiting until Stigr's growling snores reverberated from the cave.

The moon sat large and full in the nightward quarter, and stars ruled the sky.

Shard stood up and faced the sea. For a moment he lifted his face, taking in the scent of pine, of wolf, the faint, familiar scent of his uncle, of earth and leaves. The scent of home.

A slow thrill climbed his muscles.

"I'll return," he whispered to the night, to the Isles themselves, to anyone who might've needed to hear his promise in the wind.

Then he leaped silently as an owl from the cliff face and soared out over the black and silver waves.

10
The King's Guard

"This honored guard," Sverin declared to the gryfons in front of him, "shall consist only of initiated males, whether mated or bachelor. Your sole task is the protection of the pride, from threats both without and within."

Kjorn listened from the front of the group. Morning light washed the Copper Cliff in warmth, though the chill of autumn stalked at the edges in every little breeze. Inspired by Kjorn knew not what, Sverin had summoned all initiated males to him at sunrise, but more than males gathered to listen. Curious fledges looked disappointed that they couldn't participate, and the huntresses exchanged worried glances. Sverin listed further duties of the King's Guard as Caj stood beside him, watching and weighing each gryfon's expression.

Kjorn wondered if Sverin had seen the starfire, but nothing suggested it.

No. He hates the night. He would've been sleeping fast.

"Most of you will be given the honored task of hunting wolves and seeking out any exiles still in hiding in the Isles." Sverin's gaze probed each intent face before him. "We will post a new watch, night and day, over the nesting cliffs. We will not suffer another ambush from the enemy."

An irritated female called, "And what of the hunting, my honored lord? Sire? Will the females be expected to hunt in winter, carrying kits in our bellies?"

"No." Sverin sought out the speaker, and so did Kjorn. Kenna stepped forward—Halvden's mate, a proven huntress and leader, vivid violet against the yellow grass. Sverin addressed her with calm respect. "Of course not. Some will be assigned to continue training as hunters for winter—those who have proven themselves as able hunters, those of your choosing."

"We want Einarr!" called one huntress.

Kjorn chuckled to himself as other names were called. He noticed with pleasure that Halvden's was not among them.

"And the prince!" cried another.

Sverin laughed, lifting his wings to still the voices. He cast a surprised, proud look at Kjorn. "Indeed? Lady Thyra, and Kenna, discuss the best male hunters among yourselves and then tell me your choices. The rest will serve as honored members of the Guard, with Caj as your captain, the First Sentinel."

Kjorn felt as if the earth swept from under him. Perhaps the huntresses wanted him for hunting, but *he* should be captain of the Guard.

What is my father playing at?

"Take a few moments," Sverin said as talk erupted among the new male Guard, and the leading huntresses. "And see me after with your decisions. Kjorn, my son, come here."

Eyes narrowed, feeling brash, Kjorn trotted forward, ready for an argument. The expression on Sverin's face shook him. It was not haughtiness, not arrogance, but concern. Caj took the moment to slip away from them and listen in on the debate between the huntresses and the new Guard.

"My son," Sverin said. "Know that I would've made you the captain, but your place is closer to home. The pride must see you, safe and healthy, and providing for your mate."

Kjorn's feathers prickled a little at the word 'safe,' but he stopped himself from speaking too quickly. *Is it the pride that needs to see me safe and healthy, or my father?*

Winter would fall too quickly. With winter, darkness and cold and the memory of losing his mate would haunt Sverin deeper. Kjorn knew it. He saw it each year. Perhaps that summer and losing so many members of their pride had sharpened the Red King's caution.

And Kjorn could hardly argue that serving with the huntresses wasn't a place of honor.

That, he knew, would get him banished from his own nest for a fortnight.

At last he bowed his head. "Yes, Father. I know you're right."

Sverin lifted his wings. "Besides, how could I deny the huntresses one of their chosen?"

"Indeed," Kjorn muttered, casting a sidelong look at the group. "I don't want to know what Thyra would say if I told her I argued to be in the Guard instead."

"I wouldn't advise it," Sverin said, with the faintest edge of humor, and they shared an amused look. For a moment, Kjorn felt closer to his father than he had since Shard's death.

Then Halvden's voice broke over the discussion, he already taking the opportunity to boss others around.

"He takes too much liberty," Kjorn said, wary, for he knew that Sverin admired Halvden and had admired his father.

Sverin's eyes cooled and Kjorn felt the moment of connection evaporate.

"He's ambitious. Give him time. He has his father to avenge and the shame of his mother to overcome."

His mother. Maja. One of the old Vanir, who had left the insult of a fish outside Sverin's den before putting herself in exile. Kjorn supposed she got whatever she deserved, alone, with winter coming.

Something caught Kjorn's gaze at the edge of the field, a movement of white.

Ragna the Widow Queen watched the proceedings in silence. *Shard's true mother,* Kjorn thought bitterly, and now that he knew, the resemblance was obvious. The slight, graceful build, the slender wings and pale green eyes. That morning, she looked oddly smug. As Kjorn watched her, she turned and caught his gaze. Trapped for a moment, Kjorn stared back at her. A strange, electric knowing shot through him.

She had seen the starfire. Somehow he knew it.

What does it mean to her? What does it mean to any of us?

"Leave that one alone," Sverin warned.

"Why do you let her stay?" Kjorn turned his back to the widow and faced his father full on. "She lied and subverted you and she makes the Vanir restless."

Sverin's gaze darted away and for a moment he was silent. Kjorn wondered what else he didn't know about the Conquering, what other great lies like Shard's parentage, and secrets, those who'd lived and died, what battles were fought and what lives spared or taken. But he never asked, and Sverin volunteered no more information.

Aesir didn't live in the past.

The king answered abruptly, "Exiling her would cause unrest."

Sverin's gaze strayed as he spoke, and he and Ragna watched each other across the expanse of grass. Kjorn couldn't judge her expression, except that it certainly wasn't fear.

"Her son and heir is dead," Sverin held her gaze as he spoke quietly to Kjorn. "She knows they are truly, finally beaten. We will breed them out and the Vanir will be gone. I'll allow her to die here among the dregs of her kind. She does nothing now but wait for death."

Kjorn agreed that she seemed as if she were waiting for something, but he didn't know if it was death. "She did nothing before, and look what happened."

Sverin looked at him with a strange, haunted look, then he loosed a slight hiss. "Question me again, my son? We are establishing a new order. I need you by my side. Trust that I know best, for all that you didn't trust me before."

Kjorn blinked and hunched down a little in acquiescence. Before, Sverin had advised against trusting the Vanir. Now, for all purposes, he appeared to be instructing Kjorn to leave them alone. Or at least the Widow Queen.

"You remember," Sverin added very softly, "what happened the last time you doubted me."

Kjorn hunched lower and dipped his head. "Yes, Father."

"Well this feels a bit more like home." Caj, perhaps sensing the brewing argument, trotted up boldly between Kjorn and the king. He pressed his wing to Sverin's as if to steady him. "Already the males clamor for rank and recognition like the tier-climbing fools of our old nests."

Sverin chuckled, immediately soothed by his wingbrother's presence, Kjorn saw. "A smaller pride. They will all be recognized."

"I think the division is good," Caj said. "Hunters and sentinels. Everyone chose well. They'll ask your approval of course."

"Good."

Caj glanced at Kjorn, as if waiting for him to add something. When Kjorn said nothing, Caj went on. "A wise move too, my brother, to divide us into hunters and guard. The pride needs meat before winter. They should know to trust your decisions, Sire."

Shame coiled in Kjorn's belly. Those were the words he should have said, and the sentiment he should've felt. Sverin had invented his own compromise before Kjorn had to intervene at all, and the tensions in the pride already lessened.

"I agree," Kjorn said belatedly, and Sverin inclined his head to both of them.

Thyra, Kenna and Halvden approached and mantled, ready to give their decisions.

"My lord," Caj said to Sverin. "May I borrow the prince while you speak to these three?"

"Of course." Sverin waved them away with a wingtip and Kjorn, puzzled, followed Caj away across the grass. They walked, not minding the whispers and gossip that already circulated about the Guard, what it would mean for hunting and for the Vanir left in the pride.

They stopped a good distance from the King's Rocks, where gulls and the crash of water below would drown their conversation from prying ears.

Caj spoke, looking out toward the sea. "Last night was what the Vanir call the Halfnight."

"Yes." Kjorn glanced around uncertainly. "What of it? It marks the turn to autumn."

Caj studied him closely, as if he had actually asked a question and now awaited the answer.

A gull cried, shooting over their heads. The sound jarred Kjorn and he looked around, restless, remembering his father's warning, thinking of the night, of the starfire.

It struck him like a stone and he looked back at Caj.

He saw it. He saw it too. Kjorn's beak slipped open and he lifted his talons to take a step, then found he didn't want to move. *What does it mean to him?*

Caj's expression twitched just slightly in acknowledgement. He'd wanted to know if Kjorn saw it. If Kjorn, like his grandfather Kajar, had watched the starfire split the sky.

"I think it best," Caj said in his low, rumbling burr, "that we follow Sverin's rule as it benefits the pride. If you question him, then challenge him outright and take over the pride. Otherwise, show respect. Trust him. Follow him."

"Winter is a difficult time for him," Kjorn agreed cautiously, listening through the spoken words. *Don't speak of it,* Caj had said without speaking. *Don't speak of it to anyone, and certainly don't follow it as your great-grandfather did.* "I won't disrupt the pride," Kjorn added.

Before they could speak further or Kjorn's head spin any more, Halvden glided in to demand Caj's time, something about an argument between the hunters and the Guard already, and Kjorn followed them back to the group.

So, he would remain in silence about the starfire. Thyra would not mention it if he didn't. He cast a long, hunting look across the pride as they walked.

His gaze ended on the hill where Ragna had stood, but she was gone, and Kjorn could only ponder the distant White Mountains and plan his moves. He would need to watch Einarr and, if his father showed any new signs of poor judgment, to act swiftly to correct it—or, as Caj suggested so bluntly, to take over the pride.

You remember what happened, the last time you doubted me.

Kjorn closed his eyes against the bright autumn day, for all he could see was Shard, plunging to his death in the storm-tossed sea.

11
The Windward Sea

Dawn lit the sky at Shard's back. He'd followed the trail of the starfire as well as he could remember it. Still it burned in his mind, an invisible line in the sky, Tyr's unquestionable direction. As the light grew, Shard's heady excitement from the night faded.

Endless washing sea stretched away in every direction. The scent of brine and fish wafted to him on the morning wind. No scent of earth, trees, forest creatures or rowan berries touched the air. Shard peered behind him and saw nothing of the Silver Isles. A slow, creeping panic edged into his muscles.

The exhilaration of seeing the starfire shriveled.

What was I thinking?

A madness had overtaken him, to suddenly leave the islands and fly blind over the sea.

Of course he'd been thinking it all along. Ever since Stigr had hinted that summer that he thought Sverin, his father Per and the rest of their Aesir clan had fled something, not come to the Silver Isles as conquerors. Ever since he'd shared his father's vision.

Shard had known he would fly to the windward land. He hadn't planned to leap headlong after a racing starfire trail, without thought or plan or any kind of goodbye.

He tightened his talons and locked his wings into an easy glide that picked all the little currents up from the waves. His wings, Vanir wings, stretched longer and with more curve than the broad, blunt wings of the Aesir. Like a gull, or a fishing eagle. If the Aesir had made the flight, so could he.

Water rolled under him. Endless, fathomless blue water. Panic prowled just at the edge of his steady flight.

"Per the Red made this flight," he whispered. "And Sverin, who fears the sea."

Dawnward, the sunrise bloomed like a wild rose. Nightward, Tor's pale rim still peeked just above the sea. If he kept sun and moon on his flanks, Shard knew he would remain pointed windward, and eventually find land.

Eventually.

Sverin had rarely spoken of his windward home, what Shard's family had always called the greatland, or the windland, mentioned only how vast it was. Larger than the Silver Isles. One solid mass of land so big that even the gryfon clans hadn't fully explored it. Mountains, plains and coastland, forested realms and great stretches of red desert. Suddenly every rare tale Sverin and Caj had ever told of their home came rushing back to Shard, and he rolled the information over in his mind as he flew.

The ocean remained still and blue and far below. The panic he'd first felt edged away with the simple focus of flight, and the salt wind kept his mind clear. Soon, fear slunk away in the face of boredom, and Shard almost laughed. For now, his wings felt strong and tireless.

If the Aesir could do this, so can I. Son of Baldr, the Nightwing. Prince of the Vanir. For all that means. A prince in exile.

He should've bid farewell to his mother, somehow. At least he had told Catori, so she could explain to them, to Stigr.

How he wished he could've told Kjorn that he was flying to Kjorn's homeland! To the realm of his fathers. If only Kjorn was still his friend, and flying at Shard's side. It was a journey they had spoken of taking together, though Sverin halted such talk any time he heard it.

Shard realized that for as much as Sverin hated and feared about the Silver Isles, he seemed equally reluctant to return home.

What drove Sverin and his father Per away?

He got no answer from the sky, the wind or the waves.

The day stretched into a long, hot blue. Blue above, blue below, and salt scent everywhere. Like his blindness in the snowstorm of the White Mountain, Shard's eyes played tricks with him, seeing ripples in the sky that weren't there, and shimmering shapes on the horizon that became whole flocks of gulls or gryfons or islands and then faded.

Just after middlemark, Shard's belly snarled. He hadn't eaten since midnight. He sank lower in the wind to see about catching fish. The water seemed to heave and dazzle and invite him in out of the heat. Shard cast his gaze back and forth across the surface of blue.

Nothing.

There was nothing out that deep. Stigr told him tales of deep fishing, brave gryfons who hunted in deep water for the mighty silver-back fish and sailfish. Apparently Ragna had gone on one of those wild hunts in her younger days, but Shard just couldn't picture it.

Even if he saw a sailfish, it would be foolish to hunt it alone. It took at least four skilled Vanir to bring one down.

Or up, Shard thought giddily. He shook his head and stared hard over the water again. *Didn't Per and his family eat anything on the journey? Or if they were fleeing something, maybe they just went hungry.*

Stigr had told Shard that the native Vanir offered the Aesir gryfons help and shelter and food, and been answered with attack.

What must they have looked like, when they arrived? How hungry, exhausted and desperate they might have been, he would never know. Shard, a nestling, had only been aware of scents and sounds at the time. Sigrun, standing over him in the nest and begging Per the Red to spare his life. Fainter, he remembered the scent of Ragna standing near.

Something silver flickered at the corner of his vision. Shard peered through the bright air. He couldn't tell if it was another illusion.

Another flicker caught his eye, like a white bird leaping from the ocean, then fell back into the water. Shard blinked twice to clear his eyes.

Then, without warning, small, bright fish surrounded him in the air. Flying. They glided along the surface for the length of two leaps before plunking back into the sea. Leaping, splashing, bumping into his hind paws when they didn't seem to realize he would be there. For a moment he thought he'd gone completely mad, then his hunger took over and he snatched one from the air. A very real, wiggling fish with fins like wings was his prize.

Laughing, he gulped it down and dipped lower to catch more, eating his fill. *Who knows if Tyr will bring this bounty to surface again?*

He wondered if Stigr had ever seen flying fish, and guilt gnawed him for leaving his uncle behind.

The waves grew choppy as a heady wind rose, and Shard navigated the blustery currents carefully, tucking his talons up against his chest. Almost mindlessly, he relaxed his wings and soared, dipping and rising along the wind, dodging waves that grew larger with each passing sunmark.

Day passed into night, and Shard kept the Daystar directly at his back, which would keep him oriented properly windward. The night air refreshed him, and he kept a close eye out for land. *Did the Aesir ever rest? Or were they desperate or just strong enough to make the long flight without tiring?*

Shard determined he wouldn't tire—or if he did, the last thing he would do was fall out of the sky. He flew on the through the night, and into the next dawn without resting.

The Song of Last Light threaded through his mind, whether remembered or sung by the creature from his vision on the mountain, he wasn't sure.

> *...they took their Names to that Sunlit Land*
> *But their voice in the wind sings on.*

To pass time on the second day, Shard decided to imagine his perfect mate.

He had never spent much time thinking about it as a younger gryfon, for the king only allowed a few select males to take mates. The day yawned long and blue like the last, with wispy threads of cloud creating spiraling wing-shapes above him. Over land, those kinds of clouds usually signaled a drastic change in weather. Over the sea, Shard had no idea if it meant the same.

He imagined his future queen's feathers like twilight. Not dull and gray like his, but soft with an edge of dusky blue. He could picture how it would feel to have a warm mate to curl up to each night, to hunt with, share secrets.

The wind grew cooler and Shard half noticed a new, sweet scent that wasn't salty. Rain. He checked the sky above and around. High and cool, only feathering clouds. Another illusion of the long flight. The waves grew choppier below, and he rode the currents with ease, though his wings were tiring.

He tried to figure out if having a mate would be like having a female wingbrother. In his mind, his perfect mate would be a little like Thyra—maybe a different personality, but a friend, and so much more.

Shard rolled along the wind, drawing in his mind an elegantly curving beak and intelligent eyes. She would know of the Vanir ways too. They could explore the night together and find places that belonged only to them. She would admire Shard's flying abilities, not just that he was a prince, and she could teach him secret hunting techniques.

He thought of the Daynight pledge, of clasping talons and falling together under the bright gaze of Tyr. Then, that night—

A surging wave knocked him into the sea.

Stunned, he held his breath as the water sucked him under, the rolling wave flipping him over and around. Shard released a gasp of bubbles and forced his wings to move, dragging through the water to pull himself up. He kicked hard and his face broke the surface. Gasping, a moment of sheer panic seized his muscles.

Then the unbidden thought of Stigr laughing burst in his mind, and he loosed a chuckle at himself.

Stigr often said females were a worse distraction than fleas, though Shard was certain it was only because Stigr had ended up a bachelor. Shard almost glanced around to make sure no one had seen. But there was no one there to see him. Far off he thought he saw a white bird, an albatross perhaps on its long, lonely migration, but that was all.

"Behold the mighty Summer King," he said to the empty waves.

He splayed his wings and floated along the swells for a moment, savoring the rest. If nothing else, he'd discovered that he could rest in the water, though it took a little effort to float, it was less than flying. The ocean grew restless, higher waves and a heady wind. He would have to pay more attention to his flight.

"No more thinking of you, my queen," he chuckled to the air. "You're not even real and you're already causing me trouble." He chuckled again, slightly delirious. All alone in the middle of the ocean, with no one to hear, the word didn't sound as absurd or frightening to him as it had on the Star Isle.

Queen. A mate for him. *A mate for the king of the Silver Isles.*

Shard closed his eyes, breathing deeply of the sea. "I am Rashard the Stormwing," he whispered to the water, and it lapped up to splash his beak. "The son of Baldr and Ragna. Prince of the Silver Isles." All alone, with no one to hear but himself, it felt real and powerful. "*King* of the Silver Isles," he declared to the vast and empty sea.

A wave rocked under him and he flexed his wings and kicked his hind paws to remain on top of it, and rode it down again. The water grew choppier. He had to fly out before it grew too difficult. The brief rest had felt good on his wings and the cold water reinvigorated him.

He worked forward into a hard swim, kicking and stroking, and when the next wave shoved him up he lurched out, flapping hard. Water rolled from his wings like a gull's and he climbed back into the sky.

Wary of the growing waves and tiring of the wind currents, he flew higher to gain more leagues, faster.

Did the Aesir rest? Is there any land between here and the next coast? The only reason Shard could land in and escape from the water again was his diet of fish and sea creatures, which gave his feathers an oily sheen. The Aesir had no such protection.

Weariness crept back in by the time the sun hung toward his second evening at sea.

Sverin never spoke of how long the journey had been. Shard clung to that thought. If the Red Kings could fly over the sea, then so could he, a true Vanir, make the journey with ease.

Then, Sverin never said it had been easy.

By the last rays of evening sunlight, Shard saw storm clouds piling in the dawnward quarter of the sky.

12
Raven's Daughter

The scent of damp soil and fermenting pine needles infused the woods of Star Island. Sigrun slipped through the forest with her two apprentices following, just old enough now to have made the flight. Three grown warrior males stalked with them, two along their flanks and one ahead, though Sigrun knew she would be safe.

Am I not a huntress as well? And what beast have they even seen on the Star Isle to frighten them? The guard had been Caj's doing, and she wouldn't fight him on it. The new sentinels of the King's Guard needed something to do, after all.

And how would it look, to say I'm more afraid of their arrogant warrior males than of the wolves?

After all, she was one of the Vanir who had hidden Shard. It made her a traitor, but most had understood her plight. She, a healer, couldn't let a kit die, not a little nestling.

"There!" cried one of her eager apprentices, and bounded forward to a sprawling nettle. Already the plants on the Sun Isle gave in to the nightly cold, and so they had to range abroad for the proper medicines to ease the discomfort of the pregnant females.

"Well done," Sigrun said. They trotted forward to the nettle brush and Sigrun trilled to let their escort know they were stopping. Standing alert, Sigrun watched as her apprentices selected what living leaves remained on the bush, careful not to sting themselves on the ready thorns.

"I can't believe they must put *plants* in their water," scoffed the oldest. "I am never having kits. Ever."

"Me neither," piped the younger. She'd barely made the flight over, just having molted into her winter feathers that made her strong enough to fly.

Sigrun cocked her head and chuckled. "Plants aren't so bad." *If only we could fish. Then they'd have all the extra nutrition they need.*

That time of year used to be the richest of all, when the salmon ran, and the mackerel and sardines fled in schools away from the seals of Crow Wing. Memories of the days of fat, happy, pregnant females ran through Sigrun's mind. She remembered watching Ragna waddle through tide pools, laughing and failing to catch the slowest fish. Back then, being pregnant was almost a joy. A break from hunting, from worry and work, and watching the males fly in proudly with the game they'd hunted for themselves.

Before the Aesir.

Sigrun had carried Thyra under the wary eye of Per the Red. And that first winter, that harsh, awful winter, Sverin's mate got herself killed, trying to swim in the sea.

That had been the end of fishing for the Vanir.

Together with her father who had trained her in healing, Sigrun dug deeper and deeper in herb lore to learn what could replace the rich gifts of the sea. Now her father was gone, free in the Sunlit Land with Tyr and Tor. Sigrun would not see females lose kits under her watch as healer. Not only would the tragedy of it break her heart, but Sverin would no doubt suspect her of purposeful negligence.

Tor, watch our females in this time, she prayed silently, breathing deeply of the woods and the heavy cedar. *Wrap them in your wings and keep them strong.*

"That's good," she said to her apprentices once they'd picked the nettle clean. "We'll see what else we can find before sunset. Each of you range with one of the males."

The young gryfess healers exchanged an excited look. "By ourselves?"

"With one of the males," Sigrun repeated. "But yes. You know what to look for. At the first evening sunmark, we'll meet at the forest edge where we entered."

They whooped and trilled and bounded off three-legged, nettle leaves gripped in the talons of one foreleg. Two of the males followed at a trot, having heard Sigrun's instructions.

Sigrun rustled her wing feathers in amusement and turned to walk deeper into the woods. It had been some time since she'd been to Star Isle. *Not since summer,* she realized sharply. It had been the last time she'd seen Shard. And Stigr.

The scents of the forest summoned heavy memories of young days as fledges, daring each other to go deeper and deeper into the woods with the hope of seeing wolves.

The hope, she thought ruefully. The hope, not the worry. Of course, the wolves never bothered them, because they didn't go to the woods to hunt. They only flew to the Star Isle to explore, to gather herbs or fish the streams. Sigrun fell into fond memories. Ragna, Sigrun, Baldr and Stigr, the inseparable quartet.

We thought we could conquer anything. She narrowed her eyes and ruffled out of the past.

"Healer, wait!"

Sigrun's guardian bounded up to her. He was younger than Thyra. A full-blooded Aesir from a pair who'd flown already-mated to the Silver Isles, but only succeeded in bearing a kit a few years into their lives there.

"Vald," Sigrun said. She'd helped to bring him into the world. It was almost an affront that he felt she needed nest-sitting. "I appreciate your concern. I'm perfectly capable—"

"Caj commanded I guard you. All respect, but I follow his command, not yours." He stood nearly as tall as Kjorn, with feathers of rich orange. Sigrun couldn't fathom their plumage. Nothing any gryfon ate could turn their feathers that color, and she couldn't imagine that even the windward land of Per the Conqueror held plants so bright that an Aesir would blend in with feathers like that.

Not that it mattered. They had arrived, and brightly colored, and she treated them as any other gryfon. She wouldn't win an argument with him, and any argument would make it back to Caj.

But she didn't need a barnacle on her tail during her herb gathering.

She flattened her ears as if in worry and widened her eyes, swiveling her head to stare into the woods. "Did you hear that? Off over there." She spread a wing out, pointing vaguely, and when he glanced that way she added, "Something large."

He slanted one ear, uncertain, and peered at her doubtfully. Then to his great surprise, and Sigrun's, a crashing racket in the brush beyond them sent birds spiraling up out of the trees.

"Stay here," he barked.

"Mm-hm." Sigrun watched him go. *Maybe it's a deer. Maybe we'll have meat.* Sigrun had no illusions that it would be a wolf, and even if it was, she wasn't particularly worried.

Maybe I'm being too flippant. I have eaten meat of the Star Isle, after all, and they might consider me an enemy and a thief now too.

With the brave young warrior busy with a mission, Sigrun trotted forward under the cedars. Far ahead she saw the blaze of rowan berries through the trees, and larch pine turning as yellow as the birch trees. Sun filtered through the trees, a little warmth reaching the day. For a moment she felt free, and only then realized how trapped she felt on the Sun Isle between Ragna, Sverin, Caj.

I am a healer with each sunrise, she reminded herself. *And healers take no sides.*

"Daughter-of-Hrafn!"

The clattering title drew a squawk of surprise from Sigrun. She whirled, then looked up to the trees. "Who speaks my father's name?"

"Daughter of Hrafn, the healer, the Raven, ha! Daughter of the Raven, they say!"

A raven shuffled about in a high cedar branch. Sigrun realized then what had saved her from the young male gryfon's protective company. A raven, playing tricks.

He hopped from the tree and let himself fall three leaps before flinging his wings out to land, bouncing twice, in front of Sigrun. He mantled, mockingly, as a gryfon would to a king.

Or a queen, she reflected.

"Fair winds," she said, gaze flicking to the side to make sure no other gryfon from her little band was in sight or earshot. It wouldn't do to be rude to the raven, in any case. She had learned that early on.

"Does no one speak great Hrafn's name on the Sun Isle anymore? He was a friend to ravens."

"He was named for them," Sigrun confirmed. Her father had been a healer so talented and powerful many whispered that Tor had granted him healing magic. Or ravens had. Sigrun wasn't sure about that. She had never seen that ravens had special powers other than speaking and being particularly clever and bothersome and perhaps intruding on dreams.

"Raven's daughter!" The black bird called into the forest, and Sigrun winced at his volume even though the others would probably only hear a raven's chatter. They didn't listen properly.

"What is your name?" she asked, straining for courtesy. As easily as the raven had drawn the male gryfon away, he could draw him back to Sigrun, and would, if she offended him.

"My name is the way I am called," he answered, strutted three steps away, then four toward her so that his large black beak nearly speared Sigrun's leg. "My task is to know the songs, to know all names, to weave the tales and weave the tellers too, and at the end of days I will fly to bright Tyr's shoulder—"

"Munin," Sigrun said wearily. "How good it is to see you again."

He stopped, not used to being interrupted. Far off, Sigrun heard another raven call, drawing Vald deeper into the woods. It seemed both ravens conspired to get her alone, and there had to be reason for that.

"You needn't be so twitchy, daughter-of-Hrafn. My brother has your escort well in wing."

Despite his strutting and his riddles, Sigrun trusted that much, and relaxed. "Very well. What can I do for you?"

He fluffed and laughed, surprised, hopping away with his wings spread. "For me! How kind! How utterly thoughtful. A healer to the core. The Raven's daughter from tail to toes."

Sigrun waited. It was good that Munin was supposed to be the storyteller, as much as he liked hearing himself speak. As a younger gryfess Sigrun had riddled with him, unafraid and without irritation. She wondered how long ravens lived, or if they died at all, if these two Named creatures really would be alive all the days of the world. Or maybe they had already died and simply taught their hatchlings to be exactly the same as they had always been.

"But is there nothing I can do for *you?* My sister, the Raven's daughter?"

"No," she said quietly. "You know the state of the islands. I'm not like my father, thank you."

"Ah, but you are. Great healer. Great trickster. Daughter-of-Hrafn."

Sigrun stood rigid. "I'm not a trickster."

He stopped hopping around and peered at her, his black eyes gleaming. "Are you not? Mother of Thyra, now a princess. Nest-mother of a prince, not a prince, mate to the Aesir, yet servant of white Ragna? Who could say what name the daughter of ravens will take today?" A beat of silence, then he guffawed at his own cleverness.

Sigrun slapped her talons on the ground. "Stop this now! What do you need of me?"

He stopped. Again he spread his wings as if he were a humble servant. "I need nothing. I have the wind, carrion to feast, and enough to watch and keep me amuse—"

"Tell me what you came to say."

The woods were silent. Sigrun wondered why it couldn't have been the other, saner, quieter raven to come and speak to her with whatever news or need they had. Then she realized Hugin had probably chosen the task of distracting the escort because Munin would've thought it funny to bring Vald back in the middle of conversation.

She shuddered and wondered what Sverin would think of that—and Caj. She couldn't humiliate Caj that way.

"Winter stalks you," he intoned, and Sigrun kept quiet, hoping he would give his news and go. "You must be prepared. There will not be enough meat."

"What do you know," she argued in spite of herself. "Sverin has come to his senses. He sends the males to hunt. They will hunt this winter."

"They will hunt shadows and catch snow," Munin whispered. "They will hunt the king's nightmares. They will hunt, but you will feed on fear and songs."

At last, Sigrun crouched down to hear him, for his voice had changed to his dream tone, to prophesy and promise that held no trace of mockery. Munin blinked up at her, then pecked the ground hard, three times. "A prince has followed a flying star. But he will arrive Nameless, and not a prince, in the red, windward land."

"Shard," she breathed. "He followed the starfire? He left us?"

The raven seemed to blink back to himself and laughed. "Left the Isles. Never you. Always, he's with you. Be alert, daughter-of-Hrafn. No one trusts a raven. Be alert."

He cackled and flapped away, his wings slapping Sigrun's face. She shuffled back and opened her wings, expecting attack at that moment, never knowing if Munin's warnings were for the immediate present or something yet to come.

In his wake he only revealed Vald returning, bounding forward through the dim woods.

"Mudding birds!" he swore, then saw Sigrun and dipped his head. "Forgive me, healer."

Sigrun fluffed her wings, trying to look normal, and remembering that she'd pretended to be worried about noise in the brush. "No wolves then?"

"No wolves."

"A relief," she muttered. Munin sang a bawdy song somewhere off in the woods, and she twitched, looking the opposite direction. "This way, then."

She and Vald explored the woods without further incident, his only duty to assist her with carrying. Sigrun found willow to dull aches, dying but plentiful chamomile to assist with sleep, and other herbs to ease the anxieties of her pregnant charges.

At the appointed time, she met her apprentices back at the edge of the woods.

They were buoyant with success. They'd found watercress and a rabbit. Their harried escorts trotted after them, covered in burrs and pine needles.

"Well done," Sigrun managed to say as her apprentices showed off their bounty. In the woods behind, a raven called.

No one trusts a raven. But I'm not a raven. Or am I? Not taking sides, or seeming to change sides, only trying to protect those I love? Does Ragna even trust me? Does Caj trust me? She thought of the escort he'd sent and wondered if they were to protect Sigrun, or to protect her from herself. Threats without and within.

"That's enough for today," Sigrun said, her stomach tightening as she recalled Munin's warning.

"Then back to the Sun Isle," barked Vald, looking nervously out beyond the islands. Sigrun saw the source of his anxiety. Far away on the dawnward horizon, a dark storm brewed. Sigrun shuddered, thinking of Munin, knowing it was only a harbinger of the storms to come.

13
WINDWALKER

THE GALE STRUCK JUST AFTER midnight. Shard curved his wings like a falcon and tried to outpace the wind and clouds, and for a time he succeeded. Racing over the broad, black sea, under the light of the moon, he had laughed at the storm. But the storm had faster wings than his.

Lancing skyfire illuminated the lunging waves. Three times the height of the highest trees on the Star Isle, the waves rose like cliffs around Shard and threatened to knock him from the sky. If he fell, it would be no easy trick to get back into the air as he'd done before. Clouds flocked overhead, their roiling edges lit silver, then muddy gray as they covered the moon.

Caught between surging clouds and a surging sea, Shard dodged along the coils of wind, breathless with weariness that ignited into fear. He tried to pretend he was back on the White Mountain, dodging cliffs.

The rain began. He heard it like a rush of a thousand caribou. It wasn't like the cold, slushy rain of the Silver Isles. Hard sleet pelted down with the force of a waterfall. Shard's feathers shed the water as if he were swimming but it beat his wings—his head—his face. Shrieking into the black storm, he challenged an enemy that he couldn't fight.

His muscles screamed protest at battling the wind and lashing rain. A wave swelled and Shard banked hard, tail skimming the water. Another wave launched toward his face. Just like in a mountain canyon, Shard soared in a tight, angling flight between the massive walls of water. Once, the wind almost slapped him down, but he beat his wings against the water and fought to remain aloft.

A sound distracted him from his choice. A sound, either hallucinated from his panic, or an impossibly far distance away, made him fling around in the storm to seek its source. For a moment it stole his world. He knew the words.

Like a bird song, they sought an answer.

"Which fades last—"

Skyfire crackled in claws above and the pounding thunder that followed drowned out the song.

It didn't come again.

Gasping, drenched and hardly able to breath through the rain, Shard angled upward. He had to fly above the storm.

Icy black cloud closed around him. Within the raining, blinding fog, flashes of light spooked him in different directions, first one side, then the other, down, and up again. His feathers stood high at each stroke of skyfire. If he was struck it would be the end of him.

Shard shrieked again.

"I am Rashard the Stormwing!" So his uncle had nicknamed him, when he survived a storm flight against Sverin and a dive into the sea.

"I don't fear you!"

Voice raw, wings leaden and aching, Shard found he had lost all sense of *up*. Or down. He wheeled and flared, peering around.

Bright Tor help me. Father…

Then he remembered. His father's spirit no longer dwelled in the sea. Once locked there, Shard had helped to redeem him, and so his father's spirit flew on to the Sunlit Land.

Will I join him now?

He had to find up and down. Sucking a breath, Shard shut his eyes, closed his wings, and fell. Wind shoved him, but he felt the drop. With *below* established, Shard flared, stroking upward again.

Every muscle screamed.

Shard pumped his wings harder, desperate to escape the tempest before a freak wind shoved him into the sea, or a massive wave dragged him under.

The rain slacked, then was gone.

Gentle, misty cloud swirled and broke before him, and Shard burst from the top of the thunderheads into the high, clear night beyond.

His chest tightened against the thin air. Cold clamped his soaked feathers and the sodden fur of his hindquarters. Shard fanned his tail and glided, soaring higher under the still, white light of the moon.

A distant flash of white caught his eye.

It can't be skyfire.

It remained, floating, like a star.

A bird. Shard's mind reeled. *It can't be the owl, not here*. Another trick of the eye. Shard flew toward it anyway, wondering if the strange song in the storm had come from the bird.

Long, shaped white wings shone against the dark sky, like a gull, but too large.

Shard stretched his wings against the cold and aches, shouting in the language of birds. "Wait! Please!"

The white bird turned in a long, lazy sweep to fly back toward Shard, and he recognized it. An albatross. It flew in close to Shard and turned so that they glided side by side through the night.

"You speak to me?" inquired a light, windy, male voice. A little scratched, as if he didn't often speak.

Shard knew then that the bird hadn't been the source of the strange, high music in the storm. That was something else, some madness of his own, some remnant of his last vision.

"A gryfon," prompted the albatross, "lord of sea and land?"

"I'm no lord. I wanted to…to greet you." Shard found the current on which the albatross rode, and glided along. He tried not to sound disappointed, but he still puzzled over the song in the storm. *If not this bird, then who? Or what?*

The bird's long, long wings stretched almost the same length as Shard's though he was a fifth Shard's size.

"To greet me?" The seabird made a low, soft noise. "I saw you challenge the storm. You fly over the sea, and in the night, a gryfon. Yet you come to greet me?"

"Yes." Shard tried not to feel guilty that he might not have cared about greeting the albatross had it not been for the mysterious song.

"Then, greetings." The albatross caught a draft and bumped higher. He seemed to float, effortless, not a feather twitching. Shard stared, and followed as the bird spoke again. "Where do you fly?"

"Windward," Shard answered. "To the home of the Aesir, to find a white mountain peak, and maybe meet with the Aesir clans there."

"Windward. Aesir." The albatross let out a long, singing breath, and drew another. "I would not go there. I fly there no longer, not after the darkness fell."

Shard's heart leaped, but not in joy, at getting some form of news. A chilly wind shivered his feathers and he glanced at the moon for courage. "What darkness?"

"Speak of darkness, and darkness comes. I will speak no longer."

Befuddled, curious and so close to information, Shard winged in closer. "Please. I must know what's happening in the windward land. Visions have called me there."

The albatross flew in silence. Shard blinked at him. His eyes looked distant, bright, full of only sea and sky. He looked witless. Nameless. Shard had seen wolves and gryfons lose themselves briefly in hunt or battle and this looked the same, but he needed information, not a silent, witless companion.

"Friend," Shard said firmly. "Bright flier, sea brother, windwalker—speak!"

One wing twitched and the albatross peered over at him. "Have you named me, prince of the sky?"

"What? Surely you already have a name."

"We of the winds have no names. Eagles of the windland do, perhaps, in their arrogance. But have you met a gull, a jay, an owl with a name?"

"Yes! I—" Shard paused. He couldn't remember if the white owl had ever told him a name. The only birds he had ever known to have names were two ravens back in the Silver Isles. "Only ravens."

"Ravens were tasked by Tyr at the dawn of the First Age," the albatross said. "Tasked to watch and remember, so that at the end of days they may fly to him again, and tell him all the tales of the world."

"But you speak."

"Having a Voice is not the same as having a name. Many speak and remain a nameless part of the earth and sky. Just as the wind may speak. The earth may speak. But you have named me, lord, and I will keep it." He gave a low, laughing call to the white moonlight and the storm that now roiled far below.

"Windwalker," Shard said quietly. "Will you tell me, now, of the darkness over the greatland?"

"No."

Before Shard could argue, Windwalker added, "But I will lead you there."

He silently lowered one wing and turned. Shard realized he had been following blindly, with no care to which direction. He could have followed the bird all the way back to the Silver Isles.

"Why do you help me?"

For a moment Windwalker flew in silence. Then, soft as a breeze, he sang.

> *"One will rise higher*
> *One will see farther*
> *His wing beats will part the storm.*
> *They will call him the Summer King—"*

"And this will be his song," Shard finished for him. "How do you know that song?"

"It has been sung, and everything in the winds of the world finds a way to me. If you are that one whose wing beats can part the storm, then I will take you where you wish to go. I will teach you to ride the wave winds, as I do, to fly like a sea bird wherever you wish to go."

Shard could only say, "Thank you."

"Since you'll be flying far, and over the open sea, I have advice for you. Old advice, from my father and his, and his mother and hers, since the beginning of our kind."

Shard held his breath, talons clenched together. "Yes?"

Windwalker tilted his head, peering with one bright yellow eye. "Never fly out farther than you can swim back."

Shard relaxed his talons and laughed. "I'll remember that."

"Now this." Windwalker looked forward again, and Shard watched him. "This long flight, my lord, comes at a price. You cannot think. You cannot think, 'Oh, how tired I am.'"

Windwalker stretched his wings, then settled them into a glide again, and Shard imitated him. Stars rippled above and the moon bathed them and the top of the storm clouds in silver.

"You cannot think, 'Oh, how far I have to go.' You cannot think at all. For this long flight, you must give up yourself. To journey across the windward sea, you must let go of your name, and become part of the sky."

"My name?"

"But it will come back to you. In time. Son of Tyr and Tor. You cannot truly forget, you who parted the storm, and named me. I don't think you can forget."

"You don't think? But are you sure?" Shard had forgotten himself once, briefly, after almost drowning in the sea. Witless, he had climbed to safety on pure instinct, and woken to remember himself just before meeting Stigr for the first time.

"Trust you will remember. Too many thoughts will weaken you. You must be a bit of wind and sky, like me." Windwalker stared ahead, unconcerned. Shard watched him, breathless fear crawling forward. "Remember only to follow me, brother of the sky. Remember only that."

"If I'm Nameless, witless, I might attack you."

"If you do, I will flee. But I think you will remember, Stormwing."

"My name is Shard. Rashard, son-of-Baldr." He still savored saying his father's name, for he'd spent so much of his life not knowing it.

"Rashard. Now forget."

The stars blazed. Shard took a breath. Then another. He didn't know if he could forget himself on purpose, or if he wanted to. But if that was the price of long sea flight, he had to pay it. He wondered if Sverin and the other Aesir had forgotten themselves in their journey over the sea, and remembered only when other gryfons called out to them from the Silver Isles.

Was that why they had made war? Nameless, witless and wild, maybe they had attacked the Vanir of the Silver Isles as animals, no better than witless hawks battling over territory, and remembered themselves only later.

"You will never make the flight if you cling to your thoughts," whispered the albatross.

Shard shook his thoughts.

"You are wind," Windwalker intoned. "You are feather and bone, and hunger, and thirst. And wind."

Shard focused on his feathers, loosing a breath. *I am wind. I am feather and bone.*

I am wind. Feather and bone.

Wind. Feather. Bone.

Flight and blood and bone. Anything else is death.

Hunger, thirst and hunt.

Flight, feather and wind was life.

Blood. Feather.

And wind.

14
Einarr's Choice

The fat ptarmigan Einarr had stalked for the last quarter mark burst from the brush in a rage of cackling squawks when two large male gryfons blundered through the woods. The banks of the Nightrun River on the Sun Isle were proving rich in smaller game and Einarr took his free afternoons to refine his skills there when the huntresses didn't need him.

Usually, it also gave him time to be alone. Apparently that was not Tyr's intention for him that day.

The two approaching gryfons hooted and laughed after the small bird. The autumn sun flashed off of the gaudy bands that weighted their forelegs and necks. Einarr had no such favors from the king. He wasn't sure he wanted any. The king seemed to bestow favors on the loudest braggarts of the pride, and if that was the company, Einarr didn't want it. He had wondered, since his failed hunt for caribou in the White Mountains, if a different kind of king would reward different kinds of behavior.

He wondered if it mattered.

"Windblown *slugs,*" he muttered, jumping up from his cover in the brush to watch his mate's supper fly away.

"Language, young hunter!" called a familiar, mocking voice. "You wouldn't have gotten within a wing's reach anyway."

"I was in a wing's reach!" Flushed under his feathers, Einarr glared as Halvden and his second, Vald, trotted through the underbrush. The fat brush bird would've been a nice delicacy for his pregnant mate, and he could have proven his skill at more refined hunting. "Are you patrolling for rabbit and fowl now? I know they're frightening, but really not so bad, once you—"

"Big words from a little gryfon," Vald said. He was Einarr's age, but larger, a full-blooded Aesir.

Shard didn't need to be large to be strong, Einarr thought, lifting his head defiantly. The thought of the wiry gray gryfon who had been a friend, who was still alive, who had challenged even mighty Sverin, lit an ember in Einarr's chest.

"Not that it's your business, hunter." Halvden strolled past him, bumping him hard to one side. "But if you must know, survivors from the ambush last summer said the wolves arrived and left from the direction of the Nightrun. So the entrance to their secret tunnels is somewhere in the area. If the tunnels even exist. I think it's some kind of witchery, myself. Anyway, the Guard are searching along the banks today."

"I wish you luck then," Einarr said, his hackles prickling. "It's a long river." He didn't like being alone near Halvden, who was known for bullying, nor Vald, who seemed to be taking his new position as Third Sentinel for all it was worth.

Third Sentinel. Whatever that means. The new ranks and titles only gave them more reason to strut and preen, as far as Einarr had observed. It didn't make them more responsible, or more useful. If anything, it made them worse. He stepped aside before Vald could push him too.

"There's a series of rock cliffs a league down," Einarr told Halvden. "It seems a likely spot for a cave. I would check there."

Halvden looked downstream, apparently bored by the idea. "I didn't ask for your advice."

A glint of blue caught Einarr's gaze from the direction Halvden and Einarr had come. He glanced furtively in that direction, but saw only a pine jay dart up from the bush. Nothing else moved, no more gryfons joined them.

"We might as well look," Vald said, trying too hard, Einarr thought, to also appear as unconcerned as Halvden.

"Perhaps." Halvden cast a look around, as if he knew a great deal more than anyone else there. "Oh, Vald, I learned something new today."

"Oh?"

"Yes, how do you tell the difference between a hunter and a crow?"

"I don't know," Vald said, eyeing Einarr slyly.

"One eats vermin," Halvden said, "the other is a bird."

Vald laughed, slapping talons against the fallen leaves. "Oh, Halvden, what do you call a young gryfon who wishes he was in the King's Guard?"

"Why, I don't know," said Halvden. "What?"

"A *hunter*."

They exploded in laughter and headed off, Halvden hitting Einarr in the face with his tail as they left. Einarr stood, shaking with anger, but locked to the ground.

A scuffle overhead made Einarr look up, and he saw a raven peering down at him. It bobbed its head at Einarr and he blinked, looking quickly away. Some said Shard had spoken to ravens.

Maybe they carried news for him.

The thought of that gave Einarr an odd sense of hope, and strength. He hadn't told Sverin that he'd seen Shard, hadn't told anyone. He clung happily to the news that his own father and brother lived, and remained silent.

He watched as Vald and Halvden strutted through the brush, down toward the clear area nearer the riverbank, exchanging jokes and thinking up new insults for male hunters. He didn't understand why, for as far as he knew, hunting was as hard as patrolling, and it had always been done this way—the males hunted in winter when the females couldn't.

Einarr thought of his mate, sweet Astri, working so hard to feed the pride, of Thyra, of Halvden's mate Kenna. He was sure Halvden only meant to mock male hunters, but it insulted all of them. Einarr knew he'd been lucky to get away from the encounter without a fight. He should just take his chance to leave.

The memory struck him of Shard, lock-talon with Sverin as they fell toward the sea.

"I have one," he called.

Both gryfons stopped, looking over their shoulders at him.

Halvden narrowed his eyes. "You have what?"

"A joke," Einarr said. "I have one. What do you call a sentinel whose mate hears of his jokes about hunters?" He waited, anxious, but anger spread through him like heat.

"What?" Vald demanded.

"Hungry," Einarr said.

Before he could flee, Halvden crashed back through the woods. He slammed Einarr to the ground and locked talons around his neck. Einarr coughed against the grip, one wing bent and pressed against a rock.

"But Kenna won't hear of it," Halvden warned. "Will she."

Einarr gurgled an answer and Halvden loosed a lion's growl in his chest.

"I didn't catch that."

Einarr's first instinct was to give in, to let Halvden have his moment of pride and then get on with his day.

The raven above cackled and hopped to another branch, calling raucously through the golden birch. Something in Einarr turned. *What if Shard could see me?* If the raven was spying for Shard, Einarr wanted him to give a good report.

Drawing a tight, shallow breath against Halvden's grip, he twisted his own hind quarters sharply and jabbed a paw into Halvden's stomach.

Halvden coughed and his grip loosened enough for Einarr to squirm and roll to his belly.

Vald bounded in to help Halvden. Einarr flung a wing out to strike the orange gryfon's face. He caught Vald straight in the eye and shot forward, but Halvden lunged after him.

"You muddy little—son of an exile! Brother to a coward and the son of a traitor!"

Starlings and whatever small animals were left fled the woods in a scuffle of wings and calls. Einarr stopped hard, dug his hind claws into the earth and kicked dirt into Halvden's face. The big gryfon fell back, swearing and shaking his head.

"Who's muddy now?" Einarr taunted. Too late he saw that Vald, recovered, had circled around. The orange gryfon crashed into him from the side and they rolled, clawing and kicking. They bumped into a boulder, Einarr pinned on his side, crushed under Vald's weight. Halvden, eyes red from dirt, shoved through the underbrush. He cuffed Einarr's head so hard that lights exploded before his eyes and he heard a bright ringing. Vald jammed a foot into his belly for good measure and Einarr gasped, shaking his head.

"Hold him," Halvden rasped. "I think I'd like some copper feathers to line my nest. And we'll see how well you hunt birds with a broken wing."

"Halvden," Vald said uncertainly, though he held Einarr pinned. "We should get on with our work. It was just a joke—"

"I said hold him!"

Einarr squirmed with an animal shriek as Halvden's talons closed on the muscle near his wing joint.

"I think that will do, Halvden."

The voice, not Vald, stopped Halvden, though the talons pierced Einarr's skin.

Einarr blinked dizzily, still reeling from Halvden's blow, and saw a patch of blue striding forward through the trees. The flash of color he'd seen before. It was a gryfon.

It was Caj.

"Let him up," he barked at Vald, who couldn't obey fast enough. "What's all this? I thought we were patrolling for wolves, not each other."

Einarr fell over onto his belly and forced himself to stand. Halvden mantled before Caj, all humility.

"We…were…this runt—"

"A spar," Einarr cut in, his voice rough. He shook leaves and dirt from his wings and looked Caj in the eye. "We met in the woods and I challenged them to a spar."

Caj watched him incredulously. Sometimes Einarr found him more terrifying than Sverin himself.

Anyway, I did challenge them. I just lost.

"Well I'd say you quite won," Caj growled at Halvden. "Let me never hear a threat about wing breaking again from *any* of you. Back to your work. Our group has found a place downstream worth investigating. Find them. And you." He studied Einarr up and down. "Focus on hunting. There are more important things to fight this winter than each other."

"Yes," Einarr agreed, glancing to Halvden and Vald as they left, muttering. "I agree."

For a moment he caught Caj's gaze, and Caj hesitated, waiting to hear what he had to say. Einarr wanted to ask if Caj had actually waited, hiding in the brush, and watched the entire fight unfold. He wanted to ask if Caj knew that Shard, his nest-son, was alive.

But he met the hard gaze and said nothing.

Finally he dipped his head to Caj to indicate he had nothing to add. The blue gryfon huffed and trotted after Halvden and Vald.

Einarr stood still for a moment, regaining his breath and letting the dizziness fade. The raven was still in the trees above. It had followed the fight. It had followed him, Einarr was sure of it.

"Tell…*him*," Einarr said, wary of any other unseen Aesir listening in, "I can't leave my mate in winter. I can't leave the pride. But tell him I…I was glad to hear of my father and brother."

The raven gabbled back at him and flapped out of the trees as Einarr watched, feeling foolish. Once airborne it loose a laughing call, and Einarr could have sworn there were words within its clattering voice.

"*Long live the gray kings. Long live the Vanir!*"

"Long live the Vanir," Einarr whispered, set his wings back, and bent to the task of recovering his lost ptarmigan.

If he were going to tell anyone about Shard, he would've told Caj. The blue gryfon had always seemed fair and just to Einarr, if harsh in his ways, but he was also the king's wingbrother. So Einarr decided he wouldn't tell anyone. Not Caj. Not his own mate. Certainly not the Red King.

Einarr decided in that moment he would tell no one that he had seen Shard, and that the prince of the Vanir was alive and well.

That *his* prince was alive and well.

15

A NEW LAND

A GREATLAND PEEKED THROUGH BREAKING CLOUDS below. The cragged, broken shoreline crawled out as far as a gryfon eye could see.

He stared down, ears swiveling, eyes searching. He wasn't sure how long he'd been flying, but a steady ache in his wings and a sharp claw in his empty belly told him it was time to come to earth and find a meal. The land swept off and away in broken hills and plains and became low mountains far, far away. In the other direction down the coast, the earth continued in a long, seemingly endless grass plain, swelling now and then into golden hills.

He had never seen so much land that he could recall, but then, he couldn't now recall much more than the sea. Cloud drifted under him and he banked to angle along the coastline. A herd of deer grazed among the hills and he focused on them.

White movement caught his eye and he glanced over, staring at an albatross who watched him steadily in return. An albatross would make a stringy but filling meal.

Ra-shard! cried the bird, a strange sound.

He chuckled to himself and banked hard, swooping toward the albatross and swiping his talons to try and catch a white wing. The albatross shut his wings and dropped fast, repeating the same odd sound as before. Then, curving his wings like a tern, sped back out over the sea.

The gray gryfon blinked at the empty sky. Before he could regret losing his meal, a commotion below drew his ears and eyes. The grazing deer had broken into a run across the hills. The wind sent the grass rippling in a golden wave, and from the air, he saw what caused the pronghorns to flee.

Two gryfess hunters and a pack of eight strange, painted wolves clashed in the shorter grass where the pronghorns had grazed just moments before. Nothing about the scene was familiar, but familiar faces flashed through his mind.

A lavender gryfess, beautiful and fierce as the sun, stalking through a dim woods.

A she-wolf, red as autumn, laughing under the moon.

He shook his head at the dream-things and dove toward the fight. If he helped the gryfons, they might reward him with food. Strange warnings and a sense of foreboding he couldn't explain tightened his muscles. A strange urge seized him to pause, to examine, to even fight on the side of the painted wolves. He shook it off. In a clash between gryfons and other beasts, he would side with his own. Shoving doubt aside, he quickly scanned the fight and saw where he was needed.

A young, tawny huntress the color of the sand coast fell under the attack of three painted wolves. He shot down like a falcon and slammed against a big male wolf, shrieking a battle cry.

More dream things flashed before his waking eyes, blinding him briefly from the fight.

Twin wolves sprang at him in attack, angry eyes, heavy fur, snarling with fangs and claws bared.

He and the big wolf rolled down a hill, tearing the earth and flattening the grass as they struggled to snag the other's ears, eyes or throat.

The others who had ganged up on the smaller gryfess followed them, snarling.

He tore free of the big male and fanned his wings open wide in a threat display, hackle feathers lifted, beak open in a low, dangerous hiss. It curled into a lion growl in his chest, reverberating in the earth under them.

The big male wolf padded off to reconsider him, head low. Large, rounded ears lifted as the other two wolves joined, circling. A female with a keen gaze muttered commands in a low, growling warble.

They weren't like wolves he knew he'd encountered before. He had never seen anything like them. They stood shorter than Silver Isles wolves, their sleek coats patterned in broad, rangy spots and swirls of pale brown and white. Slather hung off their dark muzzles. Their blunt jaws lay open in exhausted pants. They lifted large, rounded ears toward him, then laid them back in threat, eyes glittering darkly.

Silver Isles, he thought wildly, distracted by his own odd memory. *What am I remembering?* Large, lanky wolves, with heavy coats for long winters, pointed ears, long muzzles, feathers of friendship tangled into their fur. The wolves of home.

Home.

"Wait!" he shouted as the big painted wolf lunged in to attack. "Earth brother—" he fell and rolled out of the way, muscles leaping into practiced action. He had fought wolves before. The other two skittered forward, heads low and jaws snapping for his open wings.

He fought, dizzy with the sudden awareness that he was missing something, that he was lost, that he had a Name he could not remember, that this was not his home.

The female wolf ran in barking, and latched jaws onto his heel. Hot pain seared up his hind leg and he writhed around, swiping talons toward her face. She leaped back but followed her males in again to attack. The three converged on him, fangs clamping on his tail feathers, heavy paws with sharp claws raking across his shoulders and chest. A younger male lunged for his throat.

Something ripped the wolf off of him.

A new gryfess joined the fight, catching the wolf's shoulders in her talons and dragging him off with heavy beats of her wings. The wolf yelped as he broke free, tearing his own fur to escape, and the gryfess landed hard, flinging open her wings in warning.

The wolves retreated and he, straining to remember himself, stood back to back with his new gryfess ally.

The wolves lunged in again, though they seemed more hesitant now that he was not alone. His body fell into practiced fighting movements—defend, attack, flare a wing to block a wolf from leaping at the gryfess beside him. Her haunch pressed to his, their tails lashed together—it was as if they'd fought side-by-side their whole lives and he was grateful for the help.

The rest of the pack streamed down the hill and they couldn't break out of the fighting to fly. Moving liquidly together in defense and attack, they shrieked warnings and held each other's backs.

Words came to him, rich, guttural words that echoed the growling of the wolves.

"*Hunt brothers,*" he snarled as a young wolf darted in at his side. His gryfess partner hissed and slashed her talons to warn him away. "Earth sisters, stop this!"

The keen-eyed she-wolf fell back, jaws closing to a growl as she lifted her dark, round ears toward him. Through the dust and what strands of grass remained standing, he saw comprehension in her eyes.

Before she could answer, if she would have, a harsh, gleeful singsong voice called from high in the air. "Filthy painted poachers, muddy dogs, attack my kin? I'll line my nest with your pelt!"

The she-wolf's gaze shot upward. Most of the wolves scattered as two more large gryfesses thudded to earth only a leap's length away. Now facing four enraged gryfesses and himself, the wolves barked and howled to each other and scrambled to retreat.

The she-wolf caught his eye briefly, bared her fangs, and whirled to run through the grass, growling for the others to follow. The newly arrived gryfons chased them a moment, taunting.

Then it was quiet.

Wind carried off the dust and brought the scent of the sea. More memories clamored at him, but he had no time to sort their meaning. The gryfess who had fought beside him so perfectly circled around now to face him.

Three things struck him. She was as sturdily built as a full-blooded Aesir, but shorter than the average he'd seen, stocky and strong. Her ruddy feathers were the plain, wholesome color of a red hawk, faintly iridescent under the sun, but not outlandish like Sverin or the others. The final detail held him captive—her oddly familiar pale gold eyes, shining brightly above a splash of vermillion flecks along the paler feathers of her face.

Sverin's eyes. Sverin. The Red King. The Silver Isles.

The Aesir.

Words and names and memories swamped him and he strained to remember who he was in the middle of it all. His muscles twitched and shuddered with exhaustion and he fought to remain on his feet. His wings hung down at his side and his hind leg bled freely.

Not a good first impression, he thought grimly.

The gryfess spoke and the words slowly began to mean something to him.

"I am Brynja, daughter-of-Mar." Her voice lay clear as an icicle in the air. A name. It was her name. He tried to find his voice but it was buried in his long silence, flitting in the winds over the sea. When he didn't answer, Brynja strode two steps forward, lifting her broad wings in assertiveness. "Of the sixth tier of Dawn Spire, fourth huntress to his majesty Orn, son-of-Throsver. You fought well, stranger. What's your name, and from where do you hail?"

The older female who'd saved them trotted back from chasing off the wolves, with a gray companion beside her.

The older female's coloring was similar to Brynja, though she was leaner, taller. "From the Vanheim Shore?" she asked airily. "He looks it. Well? Speak up. You trespass here."

When he couldn't answer, she scoffed. "Outlander then, and witless. Nameless, useless. Off with you, shoo!" She fanned her wings and fluffed, waving her wings as if he were a crow. The dusty gray huntress who'd arrived with her twittered in amusement. Still his voice escaped him.

Far off on the shore, a gull cried. It sounded like the albatross, before. What sound had it made?

Rashard.

It brought him the memory of a red she-wolf. A black, sharp, laughing gryfon male. A golden prince with a bright stare of summer blue. That golden gryfon's mate, a sleek huntress the color of lavender dawn. *Catori, Stigr, Kjorn, Thyra.*

The memories rushed in and became him. Love and memory swelled in his heart, and knowing them, he knew himself again.

"Shard," he whispered to himself, relieved. Windwalker had left him. Gave his name back, and left him. Shard wondered if he would ever have a chance to thank the bird, realizing with shame that they'd parted because he, not knowing himself, had attacked.

"What?" asked the gryfess named Brynja. She watched him expectantly with eager eyes, curious, winded from the fight. Knowing himself, Shard was suddenly overwhelmed by his own name, past, and purpose, and more aware of the details around him. He shook himself, fluffed his feathers—and paused, studying Brynja and the others closely.

The gryfess band before him stood now in a neat wedge, Brynja and the older gryfess at the front, the younger two behind. Shard had expected to see Aesir gryfons like Sverin's pride. These four carried themselves like Aesir. They sounded like Aesir. Their builds were as strong and sturdy.

But their feathers were as natural and plain as Shard's own.

Thrown off, he tried to gathered words. Were these some other, foreign, strange breed of gryfon?

They can't be Vanir. They're nothing like me. Yet...

Brynja's eyes, beautiful yet severe, were chillingly similar to Sverin's.

A distant cousin? Shard thought, bewildered. Nothing was going as he'd planned or hoped.

"Witless," said the tall, oldest huntress again, stepping forward and raising her wings. "A witless, Nameless, trespassing, poaching Outlander."

"He isn't a poacher," Brynja said, watching Shard intently. "He flew down to help Lisbet." She nodded toward the tawny huntress, who dipped her head in thanks to Shard. Brynja nodded approval and returned her attention to Shard. "Tell us your name."

Slowly, Shard found the voice buried in his chest. He knew he could speak. *But what should I say? Should I lie until I know more? Until I know them, and where their allegiance falls?*

He had spent all summer lying. Lying to his uncle, to himself, to his friends and family and his former king.

Windwalker's call echoed in his mind.

"My name is Rashard," he said, his voice scratchy from disuse, but firm. "Son of Baldr. Prince of the Silver Isles in a far corner of the starward sea."

He extended his wing starward, to indicate the direction he'd come, in case anything in his introduction confused them. Brynja didn't look confused. Her gaze lit and she searched his face, then whirled to face the older gryfess at her side.

"Valdis, did you hear? Silver Isles. That's what the other one said too."

"Then maybe he was telling the truth," Valdis murmured, studying Shard.

Brynja looked beside herself. "Do you think—"

"Be still, daughter of my brother. This bears some thinking."

"What other?" Shard asked, looking from one to the other. "Who else spoke of the Silver—"

"Quiet, Outlander," Valdis cut him off. "Maybe you are what you say. Though I've never seen a prince quite so…" she eyed Shard up and down and didn't bother to finish. By her expression, Shard was glad she didn't. She cast a look behind her to the two younger huntresses. "Sigga, Lisbet. Fly a circle out to make sure the dogs have truly left our grounds. We'll meet you at the outpost. Find the pronghorns and take one for our supper. We'll deal with…Prince Rashard."

Shard narrowed his eyes at her tone. She didn't look at him again, but Brynja did, and he caught her gaze. The bright, eager look in her face soothed him a little.

Sigga and Lisbet dipped their heads and loped off, taking wing without question. Shard ached to sit down, but he stood strong, refusing to show these females weakness.

"The starfire," Brynja burst out once the others were gone from ear shot. "It came from the Starland Sea. And now, these two gryfons. I told you it was a sign."

Starfire. Before Shard could respond, she spoke again, aflame with excitement. "If you truly come from across the Starland Sea, then you must bring tidings." She stepped forward and he caught the warm, sweet scent of her on the rising wind. "Please. What news of our lost kin?"

"News?" Shard asked.

Valdis stepped forward between them. "That's right," she said slowly, as if she'd decided Shard was dull-witted, not merely confused. "News. What news of a pride of Aesir who left these lands ten summers ago?" Her look was one of deadly focus. "What news of Per the Red?"

16
REUNION

"PER IS DEAD," SHARD MANAGED after a moment of surprise. It was all he could think to say. "He died years ago and I'm sure he flies with Tyr in the Sunlit Land."

Valdis made a low, dangerous noise at his flippant tone. "What else?"

Shard resisted the urge to growl. "I'm not an envoy for Per and his kin." If Valdis was somehow allied with Per, he had to tread carefully. He *didn't* have to let her press him underfoot like a nestling. "I have questions for you, too," he added evenly. "I'm sure we'll all be able to answer each other's questions in time."

I just rescued one of her huntresses. All his life he'd been overlooked as a runt and an outcast and the last born Vanir, valued only because of friendship with Kjorn. No longer. And certainly not in a new land, where all they would know of him was what he presented. Valdis cocked her head, amused.

Brynja trotted up so Valdis no longer blocked their view of each other. "Of course. Valdis please, let him be an honored guest at our outpost. Lisbet would've been killed if not for him."

"She never should have come in the first place. Just because her father sits Second Tier. She's no replacement for Dagny in any way."

"Should we speak at the outpost?" Shard prompted, wary of hearing many more names before he figured out who he was talking to in the first place. There were enough questions to go around. Namely, what other gryfon they'd met who spoke of the Silver Isles. *Friend or enemy?* And how they knew Per the Red.

"Yes," Valdis said, her tone forcibly civil. "The outpost. Let's fly."

"My wing is sprained," Brynja said. "I can't fly, so if we want to make it before nightfall…"

Shard had never thought embarrassment could look so charming, and caught himself staring at the details of Brynja's face. When she looked at him, he lifted his wings in a shrug. "I can walk."

Valdis muttered but they set off, and Shard immediately regretted it. The painted wolf's jaws hadn't broken bone in his hind leg, but they had gouged and torn. Blood oozed down his paw and the bite sent a lancing stab up his leg with each step. For awhile he kept up, head high, his pace steady.

They trekked nightward through the rolling grass hills. After the first few moments of silence, Shard caught up to Brynja. "What is this place called?"

She laughed, ears flickering uncertainly. "You really aren't from this land at all, are you?"

"Or he's playing you for a fool," Valdis warned. Her gaze swept the hills and the plain beyond. Shard wondered, with a chill, what she searched for so alertly other than wolves. Brynja tossed her head, dismissing the idea, and lowered her voice so only Shard could hear.

"For what it's worth, I believe you. But watch yourself around my aunt, and watch your words when we reach the Dawn Spire. Loyalties become complicated and I would rather see you become the hero who saved a young gryfess than a meddling Outlander."

"The Dawn Spire? Is that the outpost?"

Brynja stared, then laughed again in disbelief, as if Shard was the best thing the world had presented her with all day. He didn't particularly enjoy being laughed at, but he sensed no malice from her, and the sound was rich and hearty. "It's our aerie. It's where the united clans of the Winderost make their home and where the king rules."

"King Orn," Shard said, recalling her earlier introduction. "And this place, the Winderost, how far does it go? How far does your pride rule? Is it one pride, or many? You said clans."

She gave him a keen look. "You ask good questions, Prince Rashard." Skyfire lanced from his tail tip to his chest to hear her say his title and name. "The Winderost stretches from this quarter—the Dawn Reach—to the Vanheim Shore, past the Dawn Spire, nightward to the Voldsom Narrows, starward to the Ostral Lake shores."

Shard nodded slowly, but his look must have been blank, for she chuckled again. "When my wing relaxes again in the morning, we'll fly high and I'll show you our boundaries. It's important to know. Particularly where the Outlands begin. Where the enemy lives."

"The enemy?" Shard wondered, for her tone changed and her voice fell low. "The wolves?"

"No." Her expression closed, and she seemed confused that he didn't know. "The great enemy, the other…you really don't know?"

"I don't," Shard said, wondering how many times she was going to ask. "Who is the enemy?"

"It's better you don't know," she said, gaze darting away. "We don't speak of it. But I can tell you anything else."

"As well teach him the names of all the ruling families, our ties, and any other secrets you might know," Valdis growled. "That's quite enough of all this."

"Our boundaries aren't secret," Brynja replied. "If you'll look at him and listen for more than a moment you can plainly see he isn't from here. And he certainly isn't from the Outlands."

"If you'd look and listen," Valdis said smoothly, "You'd see he's certainly no prince either."

"As for the other gryfon," Shard began, not wanting to argue her, "who you said mentioned the Silver Isles—"

"Best to travel silently," Valdis cut in, raising her voice over the wind and acting as if she hadn't heard him. "If the wolves try to ambush us, or the grass cats are trespassing again. Best to be alert. And silent."

The last she said over her shoulder to Brynja, who ruffled her feathers in silent reply. She gave Shard a wide-eyed look, and he ground his beak against a laugh.

They walked inland, and a part of Shard despaired when he could no longer hear the crash of the sea. In the Silver Isles he was never more than a quarter mark's flight away from the water.

The late afternoon crawled toward evening, and without the conversation to distract him, every needling ache became sharper, and Shard bit down hard to keep from groaning with each step. His hind leg shuddered and cramped and he could no longer walk steady and straight, but let himself limp to relieve the pain.

The hills stretched longer and broken, the grass stubbly and dry from wind. The sun crouched on the horizon, washing orange light across the hills. Brynja and Valdis grew more tense, and picked up to a trot as darkness crept from the nightward sky.

"Brynja," Shard began. "Is there something dangerous about the night?"

"Be silent," she reminded him, though not coldly. Shard noted how wide her eyes were, her tight stance as she walked. So, she was as fearful of the dark as any Aesir of the Silver Isles, and of traveling on the ground.

But it is half our birthright.

He couldn't argue philosophy at that moment though. Any time she looked his way, he only made a point of looking unconcerned.

The falling night brought chill. It dropped from a crisp, sunny dusk to a cold worthy of the Silver Isles, and Shard fluffed against it. Already tired from his flight, the fight with the wolves, and the long walking, he struggled with his limp and resisted asking how much farther.

As the sun slipped below the horizon, they reached their destination. The hill they climbed rose steadily in a long, high slope before dropping sharply into a dusty rock cliff. Valdis led them single file up a long narrow trail that wound from the slope around to the front of the cliff. A single long cave gashed the rock face like a fish's mouth, agape.

"We're here," Brynja confirmed for Shard, over her shoulder. "You'll be able to rest and eat."

Raw with exhaustion, Shard only grunted acknowledgement. The breeze brought the scent of meat and he knew Lisbet and Sigga had succeeded in their hunt for pronghorn. His belly roiled with hunger but he feared his long fast would make him nauseous and vowed to eat slowly.

"Inside," Valdis ordered. "Quickly now, it's almost dark."

Shard limped after Brynja, trembling. The cave at last cut the endless wind and it was gloomy as night inside. All Shard heard was the scuff of paws and talons on rock. Lisbet and Sigga sat near the entrance with a fresh doe carcass, and exclaimed cheerfully at seeing Valdis and Brynja.

Relief quivered under Shard's feathers and it took all his strength not to curl up and fall into oblivion. There were still questions he needed to ask, and Brynja had offered food.

"*Shard?*" demanded a familiar voice from blackest corner of the cave.

Shard whipped about to peer into the darkness. Valdis folded her wings as she looked between Shard and the speaker he couldn't see. "Ah, so you do know each other? The Silver Isles must be a small place."

"Very small," Stigr rumbled, stalking out of the shadows.

17
Forbidden Songs, Forbidden Sea

Cold hovered over the Silver Isles like a falcon stooped on its prey. Sigrun paced among the young gryfess hunters. A beautiful, clear, cold day for hunting. Chill wind wove between their legs and cold nights had hardened the peat under their talons.

Six females preened and fluffed against the wind, waiting Sigrun's inspection, their bellies growing plump with kits. They stood at the top of the nesting cliffs above Sigrun's den, several long leaps away from the King's Rocks where Caj and Halvden gathered a band of the King's Guard for a wolf hunt.

"The herds will be going inland now," Sigrun said to her daughter.

"I know." Thyra fluffed, looking hard at the horizon. Everyone tried not to stare over at the male hunters, praying to bright Tyr they succeeded. Even though Sverin had been pleased with his newly formed Guard, their continued failure to bring back a single wolf hair seemed to gnaw at the last of his good will.

"Beware of the boar this time of year," Sigrun added. "They guard their feeding grounds ferociously."

Thyra tossed her head. "Mother, I *know*."

Sigrun straightened. The damp scent of frost mocked every breeze, and the sky blazed icy blue. "I can pull you from the hunt if I feel you're unfit."

Thyra dipped her head, ears still flat. "Thank you for the advice."

Sigrun slanted an ear toward the end of the line. Ragna was murmuring something to the young huntress there, a pale, snowy gryfess with shy eyes.

Astri, thought Sigrun. *Einarr should've chosen a stronger mate, to make up for his meekness.* Sigrun turned her ears to hear what Ragna was saying. Other hunters perked their ears, and Ragna's warm, low voice came to Sigrun in a singsong.

> "*...when all was Nameless, the wise will tell*
> *It was only by knowing the other*
> *That they came to know themselves.*"

Terror swept Sigrun and she flung open her wings.

"You're all fit to fly! If you feel overheated or dizzy, you must stop and rest immediately, for the life of your kit. Don't be proud in this." The females dipped their heads at her instruction and Sigrun drew a deep breath. "I smell frost in the air, maybe even snow. Go now and do us well, before the weather changes. Thyra, wait a moment."

The young females warbled and flapped happily, and Ragna swiveled to stare at Sigrun, tail swinging slowly. Sigrun met her stare across the peat, narrowing her eyes.

"Mother? You needed something?"

Sigrun looked at Thyra. "Yes. Bring me half the meat from your kills. Down to the shore at even light."

Thyra tilted her head uncertainly. "Why?"

"You know why."

Her daughter's soft brown eyes widened, and she glanced furtively toward the king's rocks, where Halvden, Caj, and a band of others took wing. "And what shall I tell the king when we have little meat to show?"

"That the hunting was poor. That the lesser beasts have gone to ground."

"Lie to the king? My mate's father?"

Sigrun paused, wings tensed, and stared at Thyra flatly. It had been Sigrun's lying to the king, Caj's lying, Ragna's, that had saved Shard's life many years ago during the Conquering.

I risked my life for the life of my prince, for my wingsister's son. For everything. And now Shard is in exile and has left the islands, for what? The fight is here.

None of that mattered now. All that mattered was surviving the winter, and if that meant further deceit, so be it. She had to take Munin's warning seriously and prepare.

Thyra shifted, talons pressing the frozen ground. Then, under Sigrun's silent stare, bowed her head. "Yes, Mother. Hunters, to me!" she called into the still, bright air, and the plump hunting band pushed into the sky.

Sigrun waited, but Ragna didn't walk to her. She had once been the queen, after all, and expected others to come to her. After a moment, Sigrun did.

"Ragna. Why would you sing that song?"

"Sometimes all we have are songs." She looked to Sigrun, and the semblance of her green eyes to Shard's lanced a talon through Sigrun's heart. *He was my own. My own son….nest-son. That was all. Adopted. Raised. At the end of the day he is Ragna's blood. Prince of the Silver Isles.*

Where he was, no one could say. Munin said he had followed a flying star, if that had even been the truth.

Sigrun shook herself of warnings and ravens and fear, and spoke to Ragna. "You'll get her in trouble, maybe even exiled in winter. You don't fear Sverin as you should." Ragna lifted one wing in dismissal and Sigrun ruffed. "Hear me, sister! You can't fly this wind alone. You can't skulk at the edge of the pride, ready to flee, unafraid of the king while you put others in danger. Because your mate is dead, your son in exile, doesn't mean the rest of us wish to die. Obey the king. See us through winter, stop spreading old songs and seeding unrest until Tyr is strong and may guide us again."

"In winter, I listen not for Tyr, but wise Tor." Ragna turned, pale as a spirit. "I don't wish to die. But I don't fear it. I don't fear songs, or the past, or the night. Do you? Tell me, sister, when did you become an Aesir?"

The words locked Sigrun's chest.

"Everything I do," she whispered, "I do as healer to this pride."

"Now is not the time for healing," Ragna murmured. "We are at war. Sverin knows it, though he, like I, will not split the pride in winter. Not before they have seen Shard again, have seen the prince, the king they could have. But we are at war. There will be wounds. There will be pain. I sow the seeds for Shard's return and not all will welcome him with heads bowed." She turned her head to survey the distant gryfons and the edge of the nesting cliffs. "I am still queen of the Vanir, and I will see my son stand on the top of the Copper Cliff, as king of this pride."

Sigrun stared at her. To others, Ragna seemed quiet, wise, the distant, gentle widow of the conquered Vanir king. Sigrun knew the gryfess behind the quiet. She knew that the quiet masked plans, not meekness. Sigrun knew the gryfess who had won Baldr's shy heart, who had, in her youth, slain a sailfish in the middle of the sea. A queen who relished prosperity and peace and exploration, who now burned under every feather to have to stomach the rule of greedy, arrogant Sverin.

Before she was a queen, she was my wingsister. The sister who Sigrun had pledged to fly by until her last breath died in the wind.

I will see my son as king of this pride, she'd vowed.

Sigrun bowed her head. "So will I."

Ragna made a soft sound of acceptance, and Sigrun lifted her head to meet Ragna's eyes again. "But you're also my wingsister. Help me see this pride through the winter."

"So I will," Ragna whispered.

Dark clouds rolled against the horizon and Sigrun shuddered. "I must go to the seashore. Distract the king?"

"The king is already distracted," Ragna said, and it was true. He spoke now to Kjorn, purposefully keeping him behind, Sigrun thought, safe from hunting meat or wolves, safe from anything. "Go, sister."

Sigrun hesitated, then stretched out her wing. Ragna fluffed, surprised, and, with a glance toward the king, opened her wing to cover Sigrun's.

"Wind under me when the air is still."

Sigrun spoke the next line. "Wind over me when I fly too high."

"Sister by choice."

"Sister by vow," Sigrun spoke the words to herself as much as to Ragna, and the last line they said together under a rising wind. "By my wings, you will never fly alone."

They broke, before any could see, and Sigrun loped to the edge of the cliff. Carefully she climbed down toward the craggy rocks, toward the pools and crevices of salt-crusted stone.

The smell of seawater, fish and salt gathered so thickly that Sigrun knew no gryfon would track her scent there. There, where tide pools looked haphazard to anyone who didn't know what else to see, Sigrun knew there was a stash of salt. The Vanir built the gathering ponds in the Second Age when they arrived in the Isles, and used them to preserve meat if omens portended a long winter, or bad fishing. It became a matter of raking talons through the crusty stones and gathering the salt into her wings, dropped down and cupped inward, the same way she carried herbs and flowers from the woods. It would be long and tedious work to gather the salt, and then to preserve the meat, all in secret.

Sverin would not approve. In her deepest heart, Sigrun knew he would not approve of using salt from the sea. The sea that he didn't understand, and feared. The sea that had drowned his beloved.

Still it had to be done.

In the corner of her eye she spotted a raven, watching her.

"Do you follow Shard's dreams?" Sigrun asked. The raven didn't answer. It had to be Munin. "If you do, guide him to us. Let him see how the War King rules, tell him of the harsh winter to come, that his pride might starve. If you really do hear all things in the wind, then I hope you can tell us soon of his return."

The raven gabbled darkly and took wing into the chill blue sky.

18
Strange Nestfellows

"Why didn't you tell me you were leaving?" Stigr demanded.

Shard stretched on his belly a few steps outside the cave, digging the last of the marrow from a leg bone—all that was left of the meal they'd given him. The meat sat heavy in his belly but he relished it slowly. Stigr had let him eat before swooping in with questions, and Shard's head cleared enough to hold conversation. They had moved outside of the cave, as far as Brynja and Valdis would let them go, to speak in private.

"It was time," Shard said without meeting his uncle's gaze. "And I knew you would try to stop me."

Stigr huffed. He look a little battered and Shard imagined that his uncle hadn't been as courteous to the huntress band as Shard had tried to be. The last glow from the sun faded and stars pierced the darker air. Shard glanced toward the cave, but the gryfesses spoke among themselves, perhaps about what to do with their captives. Or guests, as Brynja said.

"*Time?*" Stigr drew his attention back. "Time to fling yourself headlong over the sea without so much as a word? I had to ask a gull if it knew your direction. A *gull,* Shard, do you know how maddening they are, when they're bright enough to speak at all? Worse than ravens, the lot of them, because they think they're clever and they're not."

For the first time, irritation fluffed Shard's feathers. *He calls me his prince but treats me like a kit. I don't owe him an explanation.* So Shard didn't offer him one.

"How did you get here before me?"

Stigr glanced toward the cave. "It was only a matter of hours, nephew. I flew high. Covered more distance. I saw a storm and took a more windward route. After that I just…flew." His eye narrowed. Shard studied his uncle's severe face, wondering if Stigr had lost himself the way Shard had.

Shard also wondered, idly, if Windwalker had known Stigr was following, and led Shard to avoid him. Surely Stigr wouldn't have tried to take him back to the Silver Isles, not after the decision was made.

Brynja walked out of the cave. "You should come in now that it's dark."

"Hm," said Stigr, but deferred to Shard, who agreed. Whatever put the fear of the dark into the Aesir, he didn't want to face it. Yet.

As they walked back in, Brynja's face, amused and curious, was the opposite of Valdis, who only looked suspicious and irritated. Brynja settled near her aunt against one wall and Shard and Stigr sat opposite them. Lisbet and Sigga had retired to the back of the cave, though Shard suspected they still eavesdropped.

"Now," said Brynja, "why have you come?"

Shard found himself briefly locked in her gaze, glinting through the gloom. Stigr's presence beside him suddenly filled him with relief, instead of irritation.

At Brynja's question, Stigr gave him a warning look. These females were harsh, but reasonable, though Shard had no way of knowing how much power they had in their pride, or how the rest of the Aesir would receive him. Better to have Stigr at his side, even if he could be too narrow-minded.

With that thought Shard realized Stigr wasn't angry that Shard had left, but angry that Shard had left him behind. He addressed Brynja's question.

"First, you must believe we're not just Outlanders."

"Whatever you mean by that," Stigr grumbled, eyeing Valdis.

"It means you're not of our aerie," she said coolly. "If that's simpler for your simple mind."

"Listen, female, I've had enough of your mudding—"

"Uncle!" Shard stood, touching his wing to Stigr's. They couldn't afford to insult these Aesir. Deeper in the cave, Sigga twittered and laughed at Stigr's swearing.

Stigr only flattened his ears. "Nephew. You haven't been nest-sat by these nattering fish hawks all afternoon. You don't understand."

"I understand," Shard said quietly, and managed to catch Stigr's eye. *I understand you're humiliated to have been captured and held. I understand you hate the Aesir. But I need you now.*

It was good to have a friendly face near, but Stigr's intolerance could very well cost Shard his purpose. Reading Shard's expression, Stigr looked away.

"Forgive my uncle," Shard said, looking first to Valdis, who loosed a derisive chirrup, as if Stigr's opinion couldn't matter one way or another, then to Brynja, who only watched with steady curiosity. Shard found himself wishing they could have met differently.

"As I said," Brynja began after a moment of waiting for Shard to speak, "you're here now. What are we to do with you? Why did you come? You spoke of silver islands, and flying over the sea."

"You're going to have him repeat what I've already told you, I see." Stigr's one-eyed glare bore down on Brynja. Soon it would be too dark too see his face at all, but Shard could still see the venom there.

He moved to step between them, but paused and watched as Brynja turned to face Stigr. After the two stared at each other for a moment, Brynja lowered her head and mantled.

"You're obviously a seasoned and accomplished warrior, Stigr, from across the sea, who doesn't stand for nonsense, and your sense of pride is strong. For that I hold you in high regard." She stood tall again, neatly folding her wings, and held Stigr in her gaze, calmly bewitching. "I hope that as we come to know each other, you'll also hold me in high regard. And yes. I would like to hear the story as Rashard tells it, if you'll advise him to do so."

Shard kept still, delight springing up in him to see his uncle speechless. When Shard met his gaze, Stigr gave the slightest nod.

Satisfied, Brynja turned back to Shard. "So."

They want to see if our stories match, he thought, and fluffed his feathers calmly, as if he were among friends. He had a feeling Stigr had told them as little as possible. He probably wouldn't want to mention the Conquering, or that Shard was a prince.

Too late for that.

Shard drew a breath.

"Years ago our islands were overrun by Aesir conquerors. Per killed my father. The king." At that statement, Valdis and Brynja exchanged a quick look, and Shard continued, watching their expressions while Stigr loosed an irritated breath. Shard didn't look at him. He'd spent his entire summer hiding the truth and lost all those dear to him for it. He wouldn't start out that way in this land.

"Many of the native gryfons, we of the Vanir, were exiled, killed, or forced under the rule of the conquerors." He watched as Brynja's expression searched him. "You said Per was your kin and I don't know if you're a friend or enemy now. The Aesir are turning tyrant, banning Vanir ways, repressing any talk of the past, and threatening exile or death to any who don't follow their laws. I don't know if this is the normal way of your kings, but we won't have it any more."

When none of the gryfesses responded to that, Shard strained to see Brynja's expression through the dark. *Will she laugh, become my enemy? Is that just the way of the Aesir kings?* He couldn't read her, and she was silent.

"Nephew," Stigr warned, but Shard gave him a look that suggested silence. *He has to let me do it my way.*

He took a step toward Brynja, ignoring Stigr's seething expression. "I was raised among them and don't consider them my true enemy. Though I know it's the way of the Aesir to conquer new lands, we don't think they came at first as conquerors." He drew a deep breath. "I want to make peace, but I need to know why they came. They arrived with all their possessions, as if they were fleeing something. They came with young kits, and dragon-made treasures."

"Dragon treasures," Brynja breathed.

Shard's heart pounded. Perhaps they were close. "Yes," he said intently, as if he spoke only to Brynja. "Do you know why—"

Brynja whirled and flicked out her wings in excitement, nearly smacking Shard's face as she blurted to Valdis. "Only one family and followers would bear those! It has to be the truth!"

Valdis's face was unreadable. "I advise silence, Brynja."

"But it was a sign! Kajar's Sign, it was for us after all, to watch starward, to tell us of the return—"

"Be still!" Valdis crouched back in the face of Brynja's excitement.

"Kajar's Sign?" Shard asked, heart thudding. "I followed a starfire windward. Is that what you speak of?"

In answer, Brynja only whipped her head back to stare at Valdis, and her excitement felt like an updraft in the cave. Shard's wings twitched. He took a slow breath.

"This *is* the truth. Per is dead. His son Sverin rules. His son Kjorn was my wingbrother, before I learned the truth and tried to right the wrongs in the pride. Neither of them knows I'm alive."

"Sverin," Valdis murmured, as if tasting the name. Shard noticed Stigr watching her closely, waiting for reaction, but she had mastered a neutral expression. "And Sverin's mate? How does she fare in these Silver Isles?"

"Dead," Stigr said, as if he'd been waiting for the chance to deliver bad news.

Valdis's expression shifted to disdain. "You seem pleased by that."

"Your kind killed my king," Stigr growled. Shard tensed as his uncle gathered into a crouch. "Per killed my wingbrother and threw his body into the sea. Your kind overrun our home and kill and pillage the forests as they please, making enemies of all the other creatures in the Isles. Your precious Sverin would have killed my nephew, my prince, if Shard hadn't been a better warrior."

Valdis scoffed. "A better warrior than the son of Per? This dull, strapling—"

Stigr lunged at her. Brynja and Shard jumped between them at the same time and collided. Stigr smacked into Shard, knocking him down as Brynja tore away to one side to stop Valdis, who shrieked a battle cry.

Lisbet and Sigga scrambled forward from the back of the cave, then hesitated in joining the fight when they saw that Shard was handling Stigr. He managed to hook his talons around Stigr's wing joints and drag him back. Pain shot up his hind leg when he put weight on it and he yelped.

"Enough, Uncle! We need them."

"We *don't*," Stigr roared, having borne the last insult he could stand. He crouched again. Shard shoved him to the rock wall, pinning the best he could, and heard Brynja.

"Valdis," she pleaded, shouldering her aunt toward the far wall. "Stop this. Don't you see what their arrival could mean?"

"Call your best!" Stigr shouted at Valdis, though mostly in Shard's face. "Take us to this Dawn Spire and call the best warrior in your whole mudding pride, and see Shard throw him down."

Distraught at the fighting, but distractedly pleased with Stigr's faith in his ability, Shard kept a tight grip on his uncle's shoulders, squeezing in warning. Stigr's breath was ragged, at last his wings sagged in defeat.

"Stop this," Shard whispered. "Please, Uncle. I need you." At last Stigr met his gaze. Shard heard Brynja murmuring a similar request of her aunt. To his surprise, Stigr relaxed his ears and lowered his head.

"Forgive me, my prince. I won't hear anyone speak ill of you while I have breath."

"Thank you," Shard murmured, and meant it. "But let's not make enemies our first day."

Stigr ground his beak so hard that Shard winced, and he knew the argument Stigr was biting back. *They're all our enemy. All of the Aesir, everywhere.*

Except, they weren't. Not to Shard.

"You can let me go now," Stigr said. "I'll be good. Unless the *lady* feels the need to insult you again."

"She doesn't," Brynja said. She glanced also to Lisbet and Sigga, who'd fallen back once they saw that Stigr was contained. "None of us do. We're all weary, and it's been a very strange day. Please, stay with us here and rest. Peace between us?"

She looked around to each them through the dark, enough starlight reaching in that Shard saw the outline of her face.

"For now," Stigr muttered. Shard kicked his foot. "Peace," he said.

"Peace between us," Shard said, echoed by Valdis, Lisbet and Sigga.

A breeze filtered into the cave, refreshing the air. Shard let go of Stigr. "We'll talk again tomorrow. After everyone's rested."

Stigr muttered and settled where he stood. To clear his head, Shard limped to the front of the cave to study the stars, to see the familiar beasts that Stigr had taught him to see. The Wolf Pack, a cluster of eight bright stars, the Daystar that would guide him starward and home when he was ready, and the Dragon, a sprawling serpent named Midragur that spanned the length of the sky.

"Come in please," Brynja said, walking only to the mouth of the cave.

Shard looked at her, surprised. "I was looking at the stars"

"It isn't safe. Please." She peered past him, as if she expected attack. "Rashard…or, is it Shard?"

"Shard, if you like." He turned and left the night, walking back in the cave to sit beside her.

Brynja relaxed once he was inside. "Please forgive my aunt. And, forgive me, but, you against Sverin. It is a little hard to believe, if he's everything my aunt has told me he is. As far as a warrior, and…"

"Size," Shard finished for her, and she ducked her head, apologetic. "I know." He almost told her more, about how he'd used the sea to his advantage, and that it wasn't strength but his skill in flying that won out. Instead he remained quiet, and enjoyed the soft huff she made as she tried to imagine him winning a fight against the Red King. Then he wanted to ask how she knew him, how close kin they were, why Sverin's pride had fled and she and Valdis remained, and why their feathers weren't the color of gemstones.

"Forgive my uncle, too," he said instead, his mind fuzzy with weariness. "But everything he said is true. He's lived in exile these last years because of them, and stayed in the Isles only so he could help me."

For a moment she just looked at him. "Valdis and I didn't invade your home or kill anyone close to you."

"I know that."

"Tell Stigr that, please."

"I'll remind him."

The scent of sweet grass and a musty, lion-like smell came to them on the wind. Brynja noticed him sniffing.

"The grass lions. They live in prides like gryfons. They're insufferable poachers and we're forever chasing them back to their own lands."

Shard thought of the wolves of his home, and how clear the boundaries were there. He resisted asking Brynja if the grass lions or the gryfons had lived in the Winderost longer.

"Have you ever tried making a pact with them?"

She chuckled, cocking her head. "Don't be ridiculous. They don't listen, and they don't speak."

"Ah." Shard squinted into the dark, and knew better to argue further. "I have so many questions."

Brynja was watching him, and he felt an odd flush under the feathers of his face. "Me too, Shard."

"Enough, gaggling like geese over there!" Valdis called. Brynja and Shard flattened their ears, chagrined. "Time for sleep. Questions in the morning."

"Here, here," muttered Stigr.

"At least they agree on something," Brynja whispered to Shard.

"It's a start," he agreed, and they parted. Shard curled up at Stigr's side, grateful for his familiar bulk and scent, and stared at the long line of Dragon stars outside in the night. He'd flown to the Aesir homeland, the Winderost, to follow his father's vision. He knew he must still seek the white mountain and figure out who or what had called to him in the strange song, and determine the meaning of Aodh's rhyme. But something drew him to Brynja and Valdis in their pride.

If they can answer my questions about the history of Per and his kin and those who conquered the Silver Isles, they might be able to help us.

Though why they would want to, Shard didn't know. Valdis had seemed interested in the mention of Per.

Friend or rival? Shard wondered.

Movement outside in the dark made him lift his ears, but he didn't move, not wanting to wake Stigr, who already snored beside him. Starlight glinted off a pair of eyes, though whether a wolf or a lion he couldn't tell. He met the gaze, and they stared at each other until Shard's own eyes slipped shut. Black wings seemed to close around him and lift him away.

19
Raven Dreams

Pale half light shone down on the Silver Isles. Shard stood at the foot of the King's Rocks on the Copper Cliff and stared around, noting small glimmers, as if he looked at the rocks and peat and distant river through a thin curtain of water.

A flurry of black feathers made him spin around, and he heard a raven's laughter.

"Munin! What have you done? I can't be home already."

He strained to remember what had just happened, couldn't figure out why everything looked so pale, as if the moon shone, but there was no moon in the sky.

Munin landed in front of him, oddly huge and small at the same time, as if Shard were looking at a constellation of stars that formed a raven, but also a small raven within.

"But it is the Halfnight!"

"No it isn't." Shard strained to find the moon. "That was days and days ago…I think."

"You flew over the sea. Forgot your Name. Forgot yourself."

Shard stepped forward, raising his wings. They felt large and light, as if he could fly up to join the stars. "I didn't. I am Rashard, prince of the Silver Isles."

Munin laughed and spread his wings in a bow. "Welcome to the dream place. Your father knew it well. From here you return to your life, or fly on to the Sunlit Land." He speared his beak dawnward, where Shard noticed an enticing, steady glow. Enticing, yet terrifying. "Would you like to go with me, beyond the Dawnward Sea?"

"No one flies back from that sea," he murmured. "Where is this place? I'm dreaming. This is a place of dreams? Can I see things that are happening here, at home?" Suddenly alert, he looked around eagerly, but no one he knew showed themselves. The nesting cliffs stood eerily silent in the unending twilight.

"Things that are happening, or have, or will. It's hard sometimes to tell."

"Are you to guide me? Where is Hugin?"

"HA!" Munin's voice boomed and rolled like thunder through the dream realm, and Shard winced. "My brother deals in a different realm."

"Is this real or not?" Shard asked wearily.

"Are you really dreaming? Yes." Munin hopped around twice, then flapped up into the sky without a word. Crying out, Shard followed. Before he could blink they were landing in the woods of Star Isle.

"Catori!" he called.

In the flash of her name she sprang from the brush and bumped into Shard. They laughed, circled and raced to an ever-receding tree line, then flopped down in the grass. Her amber eyes looked more real than anything else in the dream. "So you reached the windward land."

"The Winderost," he said, and told her everything. Munin wandered around their feet, mumbling. "Catori, is this real? Can I see the Isles?"

"If you try," she said quietly. "But beware of Munin. He doesn't always tell what has already happened, or what is only a possibility, or only a fear. I don't trust my own dreams of you, because your path is linked to many others, and their changes change you. But perhaps if we dream together, we'll know the truth."

She told him all that had passed in the Silver Isles that she knew to be true.

"Enough!" Munin cackled. "My wings grow weary of carrying you, dear prince."

Shard's chest tightened and he became aware that Munin's slender claws wrapped round him, that the raven beat the dark night furiously, and he was huge and made of stars.

"Thank you!" Shard managed, knowing it was best not to insult the strange raven. Catori's howl followed him across the sea, where Munin dropped him back in the Winderost, back in the cave next to Stigr in the dry, foreign land.

Before the raven could say anything, an animal scream ripped the night.

The dream shattered like smashed ice around him.

Shard shot awake, stumbling over Stigr toward the cave entrance. Soft, quiet dawn spread over the broken hills. A couple of sparrows startled from Shard, and the rich scent of earth and dew lay heavy in the air. It was silent. No animal had screamed. Behind him, the gryfesses yawned awake, watching him curiously.

"Shard," Stigr said, walking up beside him. His feathers looked sleek black against the morning, and he seemed rested. "What did you see?"

"I…I don't know." He murmured the dream to Stigr while it was fresh in his mind, and Stigr pressed a comforting wing against him. When Shard mentioned the scream, Stigr shook his head, swiveling to look across the hills.

"I didn't hear it. You have Baldr's gift of sight. Maybe stronger. Beware of raven dreams, though."

"Catori felt real," he murmured.

"I'm sure she was. Just remember. Trust your own heart."

"I will."

"Since you're quite awake," Valdis said, "we must make a plan." Shard and Stigr turned to face her, and Brynja.

"I'd like to see your aerie," Shard said. "And meet your king."

The two gryfesses exchanged a look. Brynja answered, "Of course. Let us guide you, and introduce you. Whatever you came here to do, it's better that the king know of you, so the Guard doesn't mistake you for trespassers, Outlanders or spies."

"Listen well," Valdis said firmly. "Listen all of you, Brynja, Lisbet, Sigga, and you…" She hesitated, sizing up Stigr and Shard again, and seemed to come up with an agreeable description. "…starlanders. The king is not to be trifled with. His support spans far and wide in the

Dawn Spire and he will not take well to any news of Per and his kin, if what you say is true."

"You seemed eager to listen last night," Stigr said. "Had the whole night to decide we're liars or spies, did you?"

"Be still, please, Uncle." Shard lifted his ears to Valdis. "I understand. We'll make ourselves known and then continue on our way."

Brynja looked uncertain. "It might not be so simple. You'd do better to stay with us awhile."

"Oh yes?" Stigr asked. "Is that a rabbity way of saying we've gone from guests to captives?"

Valdis growled low, but Brynja lifted her wings in a gentle shrug. "I believe you when you say we're not your enemy, when you say you're here to learn truth, and not cause unrest. But we can't let you wander. There are outlying enemy clans, our own Guard who might attack you, other creatures who threaten our borders. Let us help you."

"Then take us to the king," Stigr growled. In the dawn light, his left, missing eye made him look more dangerous. "I've had enough bandying about with hunting parties who play sentinels."

Valdis flared her wings. "Give us orders? Who do you think you are?"

"Valdis," Brynja said calmly, "let's take them. It isn't ours to decide what should be done, and it'll take another day to fly home. I don't want to be caught in the dark again."

Valdis was silent, weighing everything.

I fly there no longer, not after the darkness fell. Shard wished that Windwalker had told him what creatures roamed the night that even the gryfons feared.

He couldn't help but wonder, with a strange thrill, if it could be dragons.

Kjorn's great grandfather had started a war with dragons, stolen their gems, and Per the Red took them to the Silver Isles. To Shard's home. Stigr thought that the Aesir had started a war they couldn't win, fled, and taken over the Silver Isles, exiles from their own lost war.

But why only Per and his kin and friends? Why not Brynja's family? Valdis? The king they speak of?

He had to know. If the starfire had led him there, if he was to be the foretold Summer King, then surely all these things were happening for a reason.

He thought, stealing a look at Brynja's lovely face, that surely he was meant to be exactly where he was.

"You need the help of the king," Valdis said at last. "Brynja and I are not in a position to make decisions for the pride on what to do with…guests. It is Orn's to decide what you should know and where you should be allowed to go. If he mistrusts you, he'll banish you to the Outlands without blinking."

Stigr stretched his wings and chuckled. "I'd see him try."

Valdis hissed, beak wide. "I'll see you laugh when he calls down fifty of the King's Guard on you."

"Fifty," Shard breathed. "Fifty gryfons?"

"And that's only part of the Guard," Brynja added, watching Shard's face. "Is your home pride much smaller?"

Shard couldn't even answer. Fifty gryfons was half his own pride. And they claimed that was only the size of the guard. He swallowed dryly and shifted his talons against the grass. "A bit," he mumbled.

"This is what we will do," Valdis said, and Shard noted that she said, 'we' perhaps to keep Stigr from arguing again. "For now, we will claim that you are Outlanders, that we found you boldly waiting by our outpost to request that you be given a chance to earn a place in Orn's pride."

"I'll do no such thing," Stigr said. "Like some windblown fledge stumbling for initiation. I'm a warrior grown, tested, fought through a war—"

"Then this should be an easy task for you," Valdis said smoothly. "But I understand if you aren't up to it. You can tell him how you flew down from the Silver Isles, and that you have a message from Per's kin, and we'll see what happens."

Stigr lifted his wings slightly, but fell silent. *He can't argue,* Shard realized, almost with delight. He wasn't sure he liked Valdis, but it was only the second time he'd seen Stigr struck speechless and it was just as funny as the first.

"We know our king," Brynja said more quietly. The morning wind slipped through their feathers. "Let us do it our way. Let us help."

Shard wanted to thank her, to mantle, to romp like an idiot with joy. A day in the Aesir homeland and he already had an ally. *A beautiful ally.*

Then Stigr spoke. "Why? What's in this for you, to help us? You seem very interested in what Sverin is up to."

Brynja glanced hesitantly at Valdis. Valdis lifted her head, clicking her beak once in disapproval. "You should just be grateful. Didn't we say we saw a starfire sign? That we believe bright Tyr sent you?"

"I think she believes that," Stigr said, tilting his beak toward Brynja, though his gaze remained on Valdis. "But not you. What about you? Why would you help us?"

"You should be grateful," Valdis repeated, and flung her wings open. "Will you go along with our plan, and wait to reveal your true story until you have earned the king's trust?"

Shard was ready to agree, but he waited for Stigr to think, for Stigr had the experience and skepticism to think of things that Shard didn't.

I trust too easily, he thought grimly.

When he gave himself a moment to think, he agreed with his uncle. Valdis didn't seem the type to believe in omens, and she seemed even less the type to help strangers unless it benefitted her in some way.

So why? He wondered. *They wanted a sign of Per. Because they're kin, or some other reason?*

"We will," Stigr said at last, glancing to Shard. "If my nephew agrees."

"I do," Shard said too quickly. He could sort Valdis's motives later. If they needed permission of the native pride to roam the Winderost, then he would gain it however he had to. Valdis inclined her head to seal the agreement.

Brynja turned to the younger huntresses who stood, staring and silent. "My friends. This is to remain between us. Huntresses, sisters, your oath, or your life."

"My oath," agreed Lisbet.

Sigga glanced at Valdis, then Brynja, and lowered her head. "My oath."

Valdis looked to Brynja. "Your wing?"

"Much better this morning," Brynja murmured, stretching it out.

"Then fly!" Valdis ordered. "Bright Tyr stands at first quarter already."

"Fly!" Brynja agreed.

The young females keened into the dawn and leaped up to fly. Shard and Stigr followed them into the air. Shard worked his wings in smooth strokes, stretching out the aches of his long flight. The night's rest had done him well. His ankle where the painted wolf bit him throbbed dully, but no longer bled, and he doubted he would need a healer.

The air smelled of warm rock and some tenacious flower still blooming. A line of pale cloud ringed the horizon and Shard peered out toward distant silhouettes of rock towers and arches.

Brynja glided a leap's length from his flank, but didn't speak. He admired her smooth flight, like a bright russet hawk. Her wings were long and broad, the wings of a full-blooded Aesir, but there was something of a falcon's grace in her, and, he noticed, a mesmerizing, subtle pattern of darker stripes down the underside of her long flight feathers.

"Mind your staring," Stigr's cool voice grated next to him. "Or you might run into a cloud."

Shard fluffed and focused his gaze away, heat rushing under his feathers. "I was thinking how she…she reminds me of Sverin." He clenched his talons. That hadn't come out right. But there was a faint familiarity in her build, in her face. Valdis had seemed so interested in Per, had called him kin.

"Keep eye on your prey, nephew." Stigr folded his talons together, voice low in the warming, quiet air. It was hard to speak privately with the females flying in a close diamond around them. "You're here to learn how to win back your Isles and follow your vision. You aren't here to court. Not here. Not an Aesir. Not *any* kin of the Red King."

Shard twitched his tail and it sent a bump through his flight. "I'm not."

"Good."

The Winderost looked endless. Endless, solid land stretching out before Shard just as the ocean had. Higher now, his head clearer, Shard took in all he could. At their backs lay the coast. They soared toward the distant rock formations and the farther nightward and inland they flew, the more broken and craggy the land became.

"Brynja," Shard said, floating closer to her. "You said you'd point out the boundaries."

She cast a furtive look at Valdis and then flapped once to angle in toward Shard. "Behind, of course, is the Dawn Reach. Those rolling hills. Where it flattens out ahead and windward of us is lion territory. See the coast curving round there?" She stretched out talons and Shard peered behind them, noting how the shoreline just out in a fat, wide curve. "Where it curves back in is the Vanheim shore. A rogue gryfon clan lives there, not allied with the Dawn Spire."

"I see," Shard murmured. Valdis had asked him if he was from the Vanheim Shore. "What sort of gryfons?"

She looked back at him, gliding smoothly along. "The sort that don't answer to a king."

"Mm. And your starward boundary?"

She studied him a moment, and looked forward again, squinting. "You can't see it from here. The Ostral Shores are a great, salt lake. Also overrun with rogue prides."

"So many," Shard said thoughtfully, wondering what reason they might have not to answer to Brynja's king.

"It's a big land," Brynja said. "You have only one pride in the Silver Isles?"

"Yes, just one. Though I suppose we could break into more, if there were reason."

"Reason?"

"Reason," he said. "I'm sure these rogue clans have reasons for not following King Orn?"

Brynja searched him with a piercing look and for a moment he feared he'd said the wrong thing. Then she broke into a cool laugh. "Yes. I suppose they must. Anyway, the final boundary is the Voldsom Narrows, nightward of us, part of a long canyon—well, you can see it there." She pointed again, and he admired her neat, sharp talons before looking.

Nightward, perhaps a half day's flight away, the land broke into a massive, serpentine gorge. It stretched for leagues and leagues starward and windward as if great Tyr himself had gashed a talon across the face of the earth. Smaller canyons spidered off from it. Shard chirruped quietly, impressed.

"We do much of our hunting in the Narrows, though sometimes we hunt the Reach to make sure the lions and the rogue clans aren't trespassing."

"I see." Shard angled in closer to Brynja, twining his talons together to keep from fidgeting. "And there, on the other side?"

Beyond the large gorge a haze cloaked the land. The earth there paled to gloomy, infertile brown and gray. "What is that place?"

"The Outlands." She didn't even look toward it. "Where there is no hunting. Where the enemy lives. Where the exiles go and die."

Shard felt a chill. Valdis ordered them to silence from the front of the group, and another withering look from Stigr quelled any more questions Shard had. He squinted toward the Narrows, staring at the dark, desert land beyond.

Where the enemy lives. Where the exiles go and die.

Shard wondered if any Vanir had tried to flee to this land during the Conquering. He wondered, with a sudden, leaden sense of responsibility as prince and heir of the Vanir pride, if any of them were lost and suffering as exiles in a place not even the Aesir would fly.

If they were, he vowed silently, he would find them. He would find them all, and bring them home.

20
THE DAWN SPIRE

TYR SOARED HIGHER ABOVE THEM, then low toward the nightward horizon as the land below changed from grassy plains to drier, scrubby, broken earth.

If I'd flown this long in the Silver Isles, Shard mused, *I'd be out to sea.*

Below, the landscape of the Aesir stretched on and on in all directions. Stigr broke the last sunmark of silence. "Tyr's wings," he whispered, and Shard shook out of his thoughts to peer forward.

The aerie of the native Aesir towered up from the earth before them. A scattering of stacked rock columns, ribboned red, ochre and brown sprawled for a league. Shard's gaze traveled up rock towers that met each other by impossibly delicate bridges of stone. Spires balanced precarious boulders on their crowns and the whole place formed a maze of tower, canyon, gorge and spire. A sparkle of water caught Shard's eye, a stream darting and splashing through one of the shallow canyons between the red arches.

Some miracle of the First Age had created this place, Shard thought wildly. Ancient wind, the First Wind, and vast ocean, and Tyr's mighty talons had fought each other and carved this place from the earth.

The smell of juniper smacked his senses with the feeling of home, for it smelled the same as the trees of the Silver Isles. The scent of gryfons overpowered everything. Shard couldn't fathom how many must live in the red maze of rock.

This is where my wingbrother was born. Where Sverin was born. Where Per the Red was born, who killed my father. He wondered if Kjorn remembered it at all, then he tightened his talons, narrowing focus again. He couldn't let himself be distracted.

Brynja glanced at him furtively and Shard looked directly at her, trying to summon an intelligent response. "It's beautiful."

She looked away and keened a greeting toward a sentry standing on one of the high, rock-crowned towers along the outskirts. A sentry stood on every high post of rock. So many sentinels. Shard thought of the Aesir's unconquerable terror of the night and wondered what enemy, other than darkness, they feared.

Each sentry post had what looked like a large matted nest atop it along with the gryfon guard. Every few moments Shard saw young, barely fledged gryfons adding long dry grass or chunks of dead wood to the pile.

"What are those?" he asked Brynja. She shifted her wings to swoop ahead of him, almost in challenge.

"You'll see."

They flew through the arches and towers of red stone and the ancient weight and presence of them sent exhilaration through Shard's veins. It took all his reserve not to plunge ahead and dive in wild, acrobatic spirals around the maze.

Ahead, the maze ended to reveal a central clearing of rocky plain. In the center of the little plain, another rock formation jutted out of the earth like a leviathan fin, massive and slightly twisted to form a peak like a horn. Gryfons soared all around it and dwelling-caves pocked its red face.

"Dawn Spire?" Shard asked lightly.

"How did you guess?" Brynja replied, and called a third ringing cry into the wind. "Summon our Lord Orn!"

Shard's feathers prickled to hear her molten voice ringing back from the Spire.

"Summon the chiefs!" She flapped hard to gain altitude and Shard lifted his wings to follow her, but Valdis hissed a warning for him to remain low.

Brynja circled high, calling. "A meet! A meet! We bring Outlanders to speak with the king!"

Gryfons stopped their business to turn and stare. Sentinels watched from their quarters, gazes trained on Shard and Stigr as they glided in toward the Dawn Spire. One broad flank of the Spire faced dawnward. Shard imagined that morning light must pour into it the moment the sun touched the horizon.

A bright call answered Brynja's announcements and a bolt of dark brown shot toward them from under one of the arches.

"Sister!" cried Brynja, and the bolt of brown collided with her in a tangle of happy trilling and playful shrieks. Shard blinked twice and squinted, finally managing to see the new gryfon's face when she broke from Brynja. She was as brown as fertile earth, dark and shimmering with bronze highlights where the sun touched her feathers.

"My grounding has ended!" declared the new gryfess as she and Brynja flapped and regained proper flight position. They hovered, wings beating, forcing the rest of Brynja's group to do the same. "The queen and Asvander agree that my, hm, how did they put it? My *enthusiasm* might have been out of place, but that hunting eagles is not a crime. Next time you travel to the outposts," she declared, "I shall be at your side again. Who's this now?"

"Outlander wreckage," Valdis offered introduction before Shard or Brynja could speak. She was rewarded with a growl from Stigr.

The brown gryfess, whose quick eyes and bright voice Shard was beginning to enjoy, glanced to Shard. "Well met, Outlander." She tapped her beak playfully toward Stigr. "And Wreckage, I presume. I am

Dagny, daughter-of-Jor, third huntress and so on and such. Wingsister to the finest huntress of the Dawn Spire. Are you joining our pride for the winter?"

Shard's beak slipped open and he almost laughed. Before Stigr could mutter something rude, Shard quickly replied, "That's what we hope."

"Breezy," she declared. "Then I look forward to many fireside tales. Sister, I must fly, before my father starts squawking about proper tier."

She and Brynja laughed before Dagny flipped down and dove fast toward a narrow alley between rock columns, swooping toward the Dawn Spire.

"My wingsister," Brynja supplied at Shard's struck look. Her eyes sparkled as she studied Shard and he could tell that being around her wingsister made her feel more at ease.

"What did she mean, fireside?"

"Oh," Brynja said, "That's—"

Valdis chattered her beak impatiently. "Brynja."

Brynja flew to her and Shard knew he shouldn't listen, but he tuned an ear their way as he and Stigr hovered.

Between the growing excitement of the gryfons around them and the wind of many wing beats, all he managed to hear was, 'watch them,' and 'speak to the queen.' Then Valdis flew up above Shard and Stigr.

"You two. Mind my niece. I have other business."

"We're glad you could spare the time for us," Stigr said. From his tone, Shard wasn't sure if he was being honest or rude, and from her expression, neither could Valdis. She left them without answering, though Shard thought he heard her mutter something about winged boar, just as Stigr muttered, "Insufferable harpy."

"This way, friends," Brynja called.

She led their group in a small spiral to the nightward flank of the Dawn Spire. There, it curved to form a thick crescent of rock layered with ridges and shelves of red stone. They landed in a line on the flat ground in the center of the crescent and Shard stared up at the curving wall of red rock, clutching at the earth. His talons barely glazed the dusty rock. He missed the cushioned peat of the Sun Isle, the carpet of sweet pine needles on Star Island, the smell of evergreen trees.

Those are sitting places, he realized, staring at the tiers. *This is a meeting place.* Like the King's rocks back on the Sun Isle, but so much larger. He tried to fathom how many gryfons lived there. How many gryfons lived there and saw him as a stranger, a threat, a possible enemy.

These are the cousins of my wingbrother, Shard told himself, reminding himself why he loved Kjorn—for his honor, his courage, his strength. Those were the supposed values of the Aesir. He must respect them to work with them. Surely, not every Aesir was as arrogant and willful as red Sverin. Brynja was a perfect example, and Dagny seemed friendly enough.

He stared up, and up, at the gryfons making themselves comfortable in the layers of rock ledges above. Gryfons poured in, curious, though Brynja had only called for chiefs and the king.

Shard glanced at Brynja. "What will happen?"

"You'll meet the king," she said, also eyeing the gathering crowd. "You can speak your piece, but please remember what Valdis said."

Shadows rippled over them. Gryfons, circling above and diving in to land. In the shadow of the towering rock, the fire of Brynja's feathers dimmed. Shard thought again of their coloring, and as he peered once again at the gathering throng, he realized that none of them possessed the jewel-bright feathers of Sverin's pride either.

"Thank you—"

"Speak well," she said quickly. "I have to go to my tier."

She pushed back into the air and flapped up to the sixth highest shelf of rock from the top. Shard cramped his neck staring up at the high tiers. He saw Valdis fly in to land near Brynja, and they conferred. Now her introduction made sense. Sixth tier. So, whoever sat highest was of the highest rank. Closest to the king.

"There's so many," he whispered, looking to Stigr for guidance.

"I see that." His uncle swung his tail in a low arc, his black feathers standing out as foreign as a snowflake in the red desert. All the colors before them were of the desert, russets, duns, grays and golds and some pale, sage green.

After a moment Stigr added some wisdom. "Don't say anything stupid."

"But what do I say at all?"

"Remember what they said. We're from the Outlands." Stigr swiveled and Shard swallowed his own fear, staring at his uncle's one good eye, then the scarred one. An Aesir gryfon had taken that eye. Blue Caj, during the Conquering. Shard's nest-father. Now they were surrounded by the enemy.

But are they my enemy?

He waited, tail swinging slowly as more and more gryfons flew in. Chatters, mutters and shouting clamored through the crescent of rock until Shard thought the echo would break his skull.

One wing stroke, he bid himself, *then another. One foot in front of the other.* Stigr's lifted wings and ruffed neck feathers made him look ready to fight the first gryfon who sneezed in his direction.

"Peace, Uncle," Shard said. "We have friends here."

"I'm glad you think so," Stigr rumbled, settling his wings slowly. Shard pressed his talons against the red ground.

A shadow swooped over the tumult, and a booming roar rolled down the face of the rock. Beside Shard, Stigr tensed again, looking up. Shard followed his gaze. A normal beast would've strained to see who circled above, but Shard's sharp gaze showed him a well-built gryfon of later years, tan in coloring with just a hint of iridescent green where the sun hit. It wasn't a flashy green like Shard's old rival, Halvden, but subtle, like a desert plant.

Coloring more like a Vanir, Shard thought uselessly. *Like all of them.* But that was the only similarity. The build, carriage and voice were Aesir.

Tawny colored, with handsome, rangy spots along his flight feathers and sleek golden haunches, the final gryfon landed and stared down at Shard with light brown eyes in a face paled by age.

"I am Orn, son-of-Throsver," he declared. "King of the pride of Dawn Spire and the Dawn Reach of the Winderost Plain."

Orn had the look of wisdom, of strength, and Shard saw none of the hard, wild edge that Sverin carried in his face. He stretched into a low bow, splaying his wings over the ground in a mantle of respect. After a short huff, Stigr did the same. Shard straightened and waited, uncertain, taking a moment to settle his wings. He felt very small. Rock towered over him. At least a hundred gryfons peered down at him, rustling, judging, each half again as tall as he.

"Speak, strangers," said the king in a deep, easy voice that the rock carried down to Shard in a soft echo. He looked at Stigr, the elder. "If you are friends, you're welcome here."

Shard tried to swallow his fear and a rock lodged in his throat. Stigr swatted him with his tail. "Go on," he whispered, inclining his head to Shard so that all could see who was considered in charge of their pair. More rustles. But no one spoke, not under the eye of King Orn. Shard stepped forward.

"Mighty Lord Orn," he called, opening his voice so it would carry. The echo spat back at him and he jumped at the booming call. A few chuckles rippled through the gryfons. Shard laid his ears flat, gaze flicking to Brynja, on her tier. She didn't laugh, but looked at him a little wide-eyed, as if he were mad. Hadn't he noticed how Orn's quiet words carried, she seemed to ask. Shard drew another breath, and tried again, lowering his voice.

"My lord." That was better. His own voice reflected back to him, smooth and light and distracting.

Is that what I sound like? He sounded weak compared to Orn. He tried to imagine Sverin speaking in the crescent and knew the Red King's voice would rattle the stones. "I am Rashard, son-of-Baldr." *Conquered king of the Silver Isles.*

For a moment he planned to defy Valdis and simply declare who he was and what he wanted.

But he couldn't say it. Suddenly, he realized they might consider him an enemy. Valdis had hinted as much. Now he knew she'd done it on purpose, keeping her own information secret so she could keep control of Stigr and him. There was so much he didn't know. *What if they weren't friendly with Per and his clan? What if Per's family denied Orn's rule, like the other rogue clans?*

He would have to stay with Valdis' plan, Valdis's advice, until she was willing to tell him more. *I've lied before,* he thought grimly. *I'll lie again until I learn the truth of things here, and then if I need to reveal myself, I will. What do these hundreds of gryfons care for my problems at home?* Saying he was from the Silver Isles would probably amount to the same respect as saying he was from the Outlands, and Valdis had seemed so adamant that he not mention Per.

"I fly with my uncle, Stigr, son-of-Ragr." Before anyone could rustle again at their names or shift, Shard forced himself to go on, striving not to let the sound of his own nervous voice distract him.

"We've come from the Outlands to ask a place in your pride." The murmurs rose into a wave of disapproval and shouting. "You'll find us capable warriors," Shard raised his voice above the din, "skilled hunters…" The chatter grew into shouting and demands and swelled, and Shard couldn't quiet them.

I followed a starfire, Shard thought to say, and almost laughed as nerves crawled up his throat. One elderly female on the second tier shoved a scatter of rocks off the ledge and hissed as Stigr and Shard trotted aside from them. They were only pebbles, but the gesture was large enough.

"Out of here, Outlander filth!"

Another, younger male on a lower tier took up the rock throwing idea and spun around to kick a chunk of rock down, striking Stigr in the shoulder. "No more rogues in our nests!"

"Here now!" Stigr crouched, ears flat.

"No, don't," Shard said, whirling around as more shouts rose against them. He looked desperately up to Brynja, who stared around, eyes wide. She turned and spoke pleadingly to Valdis, who watched calmly. Then, after Stigr had to dodge another rock, Valdis looked meaningfully toward the king's tier, as if to signal someone.

"Silence!" A female voice whipped against the stones. It was not Valdis. The shouting died.

The speaker stepped forward from behind Orn. It could only be his mate. She stood tall, tawny gold, and with eyes so blue and familiar Shard gasped.

"Uncle," Shard breathed, and Stigr growled low to silence him.

"I like the look of these two," the queen declared, and her voice rang against the stones. As tall as the king, bright, sleek and beautiful, she looked a good deal younger than Orn, but older than Shard by many years. His mother's age. Orn didn't interrupt her, but watched with interest how Shard reacted.

Shard couldn't find his voice, and at last Stigr said for him, "We seek a chance to prove ourselves to you and your lord."

The queen crouched, tail lashing like a huntress, to peer at Stigr and Shard with eyes of ice-blue. *Kjorn's eyes.*

"Y-yes," Shard managed, staring at the queen, who hadn't bothered to give her name. "With your permission—"

"Winter comes," said the queen to Orn, her eyes on Shard. "What harm could two extra sets of talons do, my lord? I trust the lady Valdis and her niece to bring us worthy gryfons."

"Very well," agreed Orn, and the quiet words sent relief through Shard's heart, even as he stared at the queen's familiar face and bearing. Chatter erupted at once, some curious, some grim, until a young, ringing male voice broke above them all.

"A moment, my lord! A moment, my queen!" The chatter slipped down to murmurs and then quiet. "With your permission, I have questions for these Outlanders."

Shard spied him on a wide, red ledge just below the king's perch. The gryfon looked Shard's age, his broad, falcon-colored wings open in easy arrogance, his face the color of raw, blue-gray iron.

He met Shard's bewildered look with one of keen intelligence and skepticism. "If that's who they really are."

21
First Sentinel

Once the young Aesir warrior said he had questions, it seemed others did too. The great tumult of gryfon questions and voices rose so that Orn the king flared his wings and dismissed all but the heads of the leading families in the pride. Long sunset light cast the inner tiers of the Dawn Spire in shadow. Heat rippled up off the stone but Shard smelled the night chill trickling in, and the sweetness of foreign autumn blooms still drifting.

Shard and Stigr watched as dozens of gryfons took wing or silently paced out of the red-rock crescent. The echoes still dripped off the stones.

Orn waited until the rest silenced. Shard watched him quietly. Then he narrowed his eyes, studying the king's feathers. Again the ordinary color of the Aesir there struck him, and as the last of the low-ranking gryfons took wing, he leaned in to murmur to Stigr. "Have you noticed, about these Aesir—"

"Now," boomed the Aesir who'd spoken before. "That's better."

Shard jumped back to attention when the speaker glided down from his tier below the king's. Closer up Shard saw the detail of his falcon coloring. Ruddy brown coated his long flight-feathers and haunches, and his face gleamed rich gray and black with hints of iron blue. Something about his face and his heavily muscled build reminded Shard of Caj, and he wondered if they shared any family tie.

Sigrun had taught Shard as a kit ancient lore telling that long, long ago, gryfons had once been more like the lesser eagles and falcons. Their clans, markings and breeding had been more pure, but travels and alliances in the Second Age had muddied those lines. It was nearly impossible to tell heritage by color markings alone, though Shard could still tell Aesir from Vanir by build and beliefs.

The gryfon before him was an Aesir to the core.

Guessing by his tier, Shard supposed this was a gryfon of some importance, so he inclined his head. "Thank you for coming down here to speak with me face-to-face." He met the other's startled eyes directly, and beside him, Stigr covered a chuckle with another disgruntled huff. "You honor me."

In the moment it took the gryfon to recover his intentions, the other leading gryfons flew down, weary of the shouting back and forth, Shard presumed. Orn himself stepped up to Shard, and Shard bowed low again. To his relief, so did Stigr beside him. He wasn't used to his uncle being so silent, and it unnerved him.

Does he mean to show them that I'm leading? He didn't feel like a leader. *I am a prince. A prince.*

Still, just being told he was a prince didn't make him better at speaking, or facing this tall, old king and the ten gryfons with him.

Behind Orn stood the queen, whose wild gaze had calmed as the larger group of gryfons left. To one side of the queen and behind Valdis, Shard caught sight of Brynja. She blinked to see him looking at her, and quickly glanced away.

"Well?" King Orn asked quietly, once all had flown down and gathered, sat or paced, circling behind Shard to peer at him from all angles. He wished he'd preened his tail more thoroughly.

"Your Highness," said the falcon-colored gryfon in front of Shard. "They look too sleek to be Outlanders to me."

"We're just better hunters than the rest," Stigr said, sizing up the young warrior with his single eye.

Shard set one hind paw back, then at Stigr's huff, stood proud and lifted his wings. "I don't know why you're questioning us. The king has already offered us a place with the pride."

I am a prince, Shard repeated in his head. The more he thought it, the truer it felt. *I am a prince. A prince among my pride. Son of a king who was killed by a king. I am a prince.*

His challenger looked to Orn. "My lord, surely you don't believe them!"

"Believe us," Shard cut in, before the king or the challenger or even Stigr could say anything else. He had to prove himself. "Respect your king's decision."

The challenger's eyes widened. "You give me orders?"

The king said nothing, nor did the queen, as if waiting to see what would happen. So Shard's gaze darted to Brynja, then Valdis, who watched him, eyes gleaming with approval. So, he was to act like an Aesir and prove himself.

"I challenge you," Shard corrected the other, and slapped his talons against the stone, hunching his wings over his shoulders. "If that's what it takes."

His challenger laughed in disbelief. Shard could see why. He stood almost as tall as Orn, his hindquarters and shoulders defined by thick muscle, his feathers and coat shining and healthy. Shard doubted many of the gryfons there would have challenged him even if they matched him in size. When Shard only met his laughter in silence, his gaze flickered to Orn. "My lord?"

The king's expression remained mild if even a little impatient, and the others present appraised Shard with a kind of pitying excitement. "You've been challenged, Asvander. Do you accept?"

The gryfon, Asvander, looked at Orn, and then Shard again. "You're not serious."

"Afraid?" Stigr offered, and a female near the back of the group chuckled. Shard thought it was Valdis.

"I accept," Asvander snarled. "First blood, or yield."

"First blood, or yield," confirmed Orn.

Before Shard could speak, Asvander lunged with talons splayed. Shard dodged aside and felt talons scrape his tail. The rest of the gryfons scattered, including Stigr.

Shard whirled and leaped at Asvander with a shriek, all while his mind screamed—*madness!* They slammed into each other and Shard, stunned by Asvander's weight, relaxed his muscles in a practiced fall, letting Asvander roll him over. *I have speed, I have speed and surprise, he won't expect me to be a challenge…*

Shard's back hit the ground and he shoved his hind paws into Asvander's stomach. Asvander coughed and fell forward, his talons and chest dipping toward Shard's face. Shard caught Asvander's front feet in his own, jammed his hind paws into Asvander's stomach again and used the other gryfon's falling weight to launch him over into the dirt.

Dry red dust clouded up around them. Shard hopped to his feet just in time to discover that Asvander, despite his size and muscle, was fast too. He'd already recovered and lunged.

He smacked into Shard again, shoved him to the ground and reared back to his hind legs with a challenging shriek. Shard scrabbled up and beat the air with his wings, scattering dust toward Asvander's face as he kicked up off the ground. Two wing beats up and he dropped again onto the Aesir's back, hooked talons around his wing joints and pumped his wings hard, dragging Asvander backwards but careful not to puncture skin.

He didn't want first blood. He wanted the haughty warrior to yield.

As Asvander wrestled forward, trying to keep his feet, laughing calls reached Shard's ears.

"Looks bad for ours," laughed a male.

"Two rabbit pelts on Asvander," called Dagny.

"I'll meet that bet," said another. Shard would have sworn it was the queen. He wrenched back, twisting until Asvander lost balance and crashed backwards. Shard shoved up to keep from being crushed, spun mid-air and dropped hard, straddling Asvander's chest and shoving talons to his chest.

"Yield!"

Asvander snarled and kicked both hind paws into Shard's stomach. Shard coughed and black lights flashed in front of his eyes. Talons dug into his shoulders, his world swung and crashed as Asvander lifted him and threw him to the ground. Shard's head smacked a rock and he groaned, blinking hard to clear his vision, thrashing his wings to try and shove Asvander away.

"First blood!" Stigr shouted. "It's done!"

But Asvander wasn't done. Talons grabbed the long muscle of Shard's right wing and he felt a searing strain, but he couldn't seem to move fast enough to break away.

A baleful yell broke through the dull ringing in his ears. Asvander released him, swearing. Wild commotion blurred before Shard's ears and eyes. He lurched up, shaking his head hard to clear it.

After five breaths of confusion, everything fell quiet.

As the dust cleared he saw Stigr, crouched back on his hind paws, the talons of one forefoot gripping Asvander's foreleg to hold him back, the other clenched around Asvander's throat. Shard stared, swallowing dust, and shame swamped him.

"Do you yield?" Stigr's voice dripped ice. "Or shall it be blood?"

Asvander gurgled something. It must have been, "I yield," for, with an expression of disgust, Stigr dropped him and trotted to Shard.

"Nephew," he breathed, meeting Shard's eyes, then, seeing he was coherent, searched him for injury. "Are you well?"

"Fine," Shard muttered. "You shouldn't have done that."

"He was going to break your wing. I saw. Foul fight," he growled louder for all to hear. "Shard had thrown him down. Wing breaking? Is that respected here?"

"No," said Valdis, stepping forward from the group of observers. She didn't look amused. "It isn't. You drew first blood, Asvander. That was uncalled for."

"You'd won," rumbled the king.

"I was angry," Asvander argued, ears flat. Then he realized he'd snapped at the king, and lowered his head. Seeing all eyes on him, and unhappy looks, he slowly smoothed his feathers down. He looked at Shard, and his expression was entirely different than Shard had expected. His eyes still sparked with anger, but in his face was also an honest measure of shame. "Forgive me, Outlander. I lose myself in a good fight."

"A *good fight?*" Stigr rasped.

Shard decided, in order to keep the peace of those present, to believe Asvander for the moment, though he still felt the strain in his wing. "Don't call me Outlander," he said. "My name is Shard."

"Very well then, Shard. And you?"

"Stigr. You didn't hear before?" Stigr's tail switched back and forth in irritation. "And you are?"

Asvander addressed them both, undeterred by Stigr's sharpness. "I am Asvander, of the Ostral Shores. Second tier," he lifted his head even higher, "of the Dawn Spire. Captain of the King's Guard and First Sentinel to his Majesty Orn."

Shard hesitated. They had so many names and titles. Suddenly the Silver Isles seemed so small. So simple. But there was one name he hadn't heard in the introduction.

Asvander hadn't named his father. Until that summer, Shard had always been son-of-Sigrun. Fatherless. Son of a nameless, conquered warrior. Now he knew his father had been a king. Asvander was also young, Shard's age, maybe a year older. For whatever reason, Asvander hadn't named his father and for a brief breath, Shard saw himself in his challenger, and was able to relax, and incline his head in respect, despite Asvander's foul play.

"Good fight," Shard said quietly.

The surprised expression on Asvander's face was worth the moment of humility.

"So," said Orn. "You've met the head of my Guard. I respect his judgment. You lost the fight. Do you have an answer for him?"

"Yes," Shard said, carefully stretching his wing. A little strained, but not broken. He'd be able to fly in the morning, and that was all he needed. "My answer is that what we've said is still true."

A strange smell drifted to Shard, woody and sharp. He'd only ever smelled it once before, when skyfire struck dead timber on the Crow Wing isle, and the forest burned. He didn't have time to wonder about it.

The queen sidestepped Orn and strode up into Shard's face, lashing her tail to clear others from her space. "Enough of this feather fluffing, with darkness coming on. Has everyone proven themselves satisfactorily?"

Shard met her clear, hard gaze, so like Kjorn's. He felt, for a wild moment, that he knew her. He didn't dare look away before she did.

"My queen," Asvander pleaded. "Surely you can see these two aren't all they seem."

"Perhaps," purred the queen, searching Shard's face with narrowed eyes. "But I see no ill in them. And clearly they're fine warriors." Abruptly, she turned and walked back to king, tail flicking in Shard's face. "Even you have to admit that, Asvander."

"This is folly," growled Asvander. "Taking new blood just before winter—"

"Calm yourself, Lakelander," Valdis said, but Asvander ruffed opened his wings wider, drawing more attention.

"As First Sentinel, Sire, I insist you let me run them off. They fight too well, look too well fed, too alert. I've never seen Outlanders such as these. I name them spies and liars."

Shard wanted to ask for whom Asvander thought he might be spying, but that would make him look like more of a stranger. Surely even Outlanders knew of the enemies of the Dawn Spire. Brynja had mentioned rogue clans and those who didn't pledge loyalty to Orn.

"You windblown fledge," Stigr snarled at Asvander. When he stepped forward, six other gryfons stepped forward in turn, warning 'enough,' and 'the challenge is done.' Asvander turned to face Stigr, unafraid.

"Undisciplined and foul-mouthed," Asvander said. "Not good to have in our ranks at all."

Stigr tossed his head in disbelief. "I'm undisciplined, wing-breaker?"

Shard glanced to the king, who made a low, quiet cough. "Your style of challenge does bring that out, Asvander. But I trust your instinct."

"Your Highness," Shard said firmly. He curled his talons against the rock, grounding, trying to gain strength from the desert wind, to remember how strong he had felt, soaring over an endless sea. This couldn't be harder than that. The smell of wood smoke filled the air now and drove him almost to distraction, but none of the others seemed worried. "You've seen us fight. Let me prove myself in your pride. Let my uncle prove himself. Even if you aren't glad of me, you will be of him. He's the finest warrior I've ever known."

Silence.

They couldn't contest it, not after seeing Stigr beat the head of their Guard in less than ten heartbeats, and even Shard had managed to get him on the ground. Orn didn't argue Shard, but his expression was almost worse. Pity. *He does think I'm a poor Outlander desperate to gain entry into the pride. I suppose that's good for now.*

Shard locked on the king's eyes. He didn't seem an unreasonable gryfon. "Let me prove myself, let me guard for you, hunt for you, patrol, prove myself."

"Let him," the queen said, overlapping Shard's words. He wondered why she was so eager to have them join the pride, and recalled that Valdis had left earlier to speak with the queen. Shard was wary of being drawn into whatever tangled loyalties there might be at the Dawn Spire, but he wouldn't argue with the queen just then, not when her apparent desire aligned with his.

"My mate," she crooned to the king, "at least it will be interesting."

Another silence full of evening wind and the disconcerting scent of smoke fell on them.

"Very well," Orn said at last.

Asvander angled his head high. "Well I won't have him in my Guard."

Before Shard could think up an argument, a quiet voice offered, "He may hunt with us." Brynja stepped forward from behind the queen, and Dagny beside her. Shard looked at her gratefully, but she didn't meet his eyes.

Asvander whipped his head around, looking betrayed. "Brynja!"

She tossed a quick, annoyed look to him, but the king clapped his beak together and they fell silent again.

"Very well. And you?"

With a blink, Shard realized the king addressed Stigr. The older black gryfon lifted his head, met the king's stare, then turned a challenging look to Asvander. "Your Highness, I *will* serve in the Guard."

Asvander looked ready to argue, but something about Stigr's stance and the dangerous tilt of his head made him nod, once, instead. Shard wished he had some of his uncle's ferocity.

"Very good," Orn said, looking around for any more objections. There were none. "Valdis," he called. She walked to his side. "You brought them here. Show them to a dwelling on the low tiers. Night falls, and we must be in."

"Wait," Dagny piped up, and to Shard's surprise, even the king and queen looked to her patiently. "Shard lost to Asvander, but Asvander lost to Stigr. What does that mean?"

"It means you owe me two rabbit pelts," said the queen. Dagny scoffed, scowled at Shard, then Asvander in disbelief, then bowed to the queen. With that, the queen, the king, and most of the elders took wing to find their dens. Dagny followed them up, muttering.

Brynja gave Shard a furtive glance and Asvander looked imperiously toward Stigr. "Outlander. Report to the Wind Spire at daybreak."

Stigr inclined his head as Asvander pivoted and shoved into the sky, leaving them.

Shard looked at Stigr. "What's the Wind Spire?"

"How should I know?" Stigr grumbled. "But I wasn't about to ask that fluffed up jaybird, was I? I'll find it. Don't you mind about me. You stay on your own wind, nephew, and remember why you came here."

As soon as he'd said that, they both realized that Brynja was still standing there. Valdis had already begun walking and an older gryfon followed her, arguing about the whole thing. Shard could hear his beak grating and tapping as he mumbled to himself about the days when they simply dispatched Outlanders and didn't worry about discussing it in committee. Valdis talked him down and sent him off, and Shard looked at Brynja.

"Thank you for your help," Shard said hesitantly. "Where should I report tomorrow?"

"I'll fetch you." Brynja looked from Stigr to Shard and one ear slanted back in skepticism. "You two will be all right?"

"We will," Shard said before Stigr could say something crude. He fixed his gaze on Stigr's narrowed expression. "We have good practice lying."

Stigr growled low. "Nephew."

"Hopefully you won't have to lie all winter," Brynja soothed, though at Stigr's growl she stepped a hind paw back defensively. "This was the best way. I promise, once you've proven yourself, Orn should grant you whatever you need. And, you have friends here."

"What friends?" Stigr's gaze rolled up and around the rock cliffs. "You're making a lot of half promises."

Shard followed his look and cocked his head, squinting. A strange orange light pervaded the whole nesting colony of the Dawn Spire, as if it were still sunset. Strange, bobbing shadows filled the crannies and shivered along the walls—but since Brynja didn't jump and spook at their movement, Shard forced himself to stand still.

"The queen," Brynja said firmly. "Valdis. Me. Even Asvander. The queen will be most glad to know that her sister, Sverin, and their kit made the flight across the sea."

So I'm not crazy. The queen is the sister of Sverin's mate. That's why she looks familiar. Shard and Kjorn had grown up hearing that Kjorn took after his mother, but Shard had never realized how much—or that Sverin's mate had a sister.

Shard met Brynja's eyes. "Will the queen still be our friend when she learns that her sister is dead?"

Brynja hesitated. "If you are Kjorn's wingbrother as you say, then yes, she will be your friend."

"What is this light?" Stigr hissed, and Shard felt relief at knowing that he wasn't just imagining it.

Brynja blinked, then laughed and opened her wings to indicate they should look up again. Shard tilted his head, gaze traveling up the high walls, ribbons of rock covered in strange, flying shadows. A low, uneasy thrum sounded from Stigr's chest.

Patches of fire flickered at the top of every column and spire and along the rocky crest of the Dawn Spire itself. Pyres burned along the ground every ten leaps or so, shedding light throughout.

"Tyr's beak," Stigr muttered, ears flattened in plain fear. "What is this witchery?"

Shard didn't understand his uncle's reaction. They knew of fire from Pebble's Throw, from skyfire strikes that split pine trunks and sometimes burned in the heavily treed areas of the Silver Isles. That kind of fire was dangerous, wild, and uncontrolled, a nameless force of the First Age like the wind and the sea.

The fire in the gryfon aerie of the Winderost, contained on burning stacks of wood, lighting the rock walls and towers and stream, delighted Shard's heart.

"No witchery," Brynja said, her voice warm with adulation. "Tyr's greatest gift. His light, his warmth, all through the night. Years ago a terrible storm ravaged the Outlands, and we saw the fires burning. They burned for days and days and my father and others finally knew that Tyr had given it to us. We harvested the flames using the same branches it burned, and we've learned more of its ways ever since."

"It's incredible." Shard stared. He soaked in the perfect heat of a summer's day, though through the wood and smoke he smelled frost gathering in the areas beyond the aerie. The possibilities reeled his mind if they could harness skyfire for the Silver Isles.

Then they need never fear the long, dark, icy winters.

"We don't know how to make the fires," Brynja said. "So they must be fed."

"To what end?" Stigr demanded. "This is unnatural. Darkness and light, that is the way."

Brynja turned to him, closing her fanned wings. The orange light cut dramatic angles against her lovely face, making her appear more stern and distant, the way Shard imagined eternal Tor. He shivered, eyes locked on her face, as Stigr's were.

"When you truly know the danger of the darkness in the Winderost, you'll begin to love the fire." She looked lovingly up toward the torches and bonfires and patches that filled the aerie. "The sun never sets on the Dawn Spire."

"Daughter-of-Mar," snapped a withering voice. All three startled, looking askance. Valdis strode back to them when she'd realized Shard and Stigr hadn't followed. "To your nest. You needn't worry about these two until the dawn."

Brynja squinted in amusement, but without a word she spun on her heels and loped twice before flying into the air. Shard watched, mesmerized as the firelight shivered over her russet wings and cast her in dramatic shadow.

"Enough now," said Valdis. "With me, you two. This way."

She turned and Shard and Stigr fell into step behind. While Stigr's gaze traveled warily along the walls, watching the shadows, Shard studied Valdis' feathers. He thought of Brynja's wings, their coloring russet and rich with the slight iridescence of a higher creature. Then he thought of red Sverin, and how the firelight would have made his feathers look.

"Uncle," Shard whispered as low as he could. Valdis's ears didn't twitch. If she listened or cared, she was pretending not to. Stigr dragged his gaze from the fires. "Have you noticed…have you realized how none of these Aesir are as brightly colored as Sverin's pride?"

Stigr slowed, then twitched his head. "I'm only half blind, you know."

"I just mean, I wonder what it—"

"Will knowing gain you your kingship?" Stigr's fierce mutter threatened to rise to shouting. "Will knowing help you to rid the Silver Isles of the Aesir?"

"I don't—"

"Stay on your wind," Stigr warned. "We have only one reason to be here. Your vision. And we never should have had to come at all, nor prove ourselves to this pride."

Shard's belly tightened and his wings tensed. Before he could respond, Valdis stopped and gestured her talons toward a dim crack in the stone wall. It looked just large enough for a gryfon to squeeze through.

"You may nest here." She said it as if she presented a wide den laced with the scent of pine and piled with soft furs. Stigr swiveled to eye the dark crack, and sniffed twice. Shard had already caught a whiff of old rat bone and plant mold.

Stigr coughed. "Tell the king his generosity is overwhelming."

Valdis studied him calmly. "I will." She turned to go and then paused, looking over her shoulder at Stigr. "Not many impress me, son of Ragr. If that means anything to you. Rest well."

She left them, and they stood there, eyeing the den and the shadows from the fires bouncing on the rocks.

"What is that supposed to mean," Stigr demanded, feathers ruffling.

"I think it was a compliment," Shard said, growing tired of Stigr's attitude.

"As if I need complimenting. From an Aesir. From her."

"I think she admired the way you beat Asvander," Shard added, just to rub it in. He had never seen his uncle so belligerent or quick to anger. He tried to be understanding, for he needed Stigr's support and strength, tried to remember that he'd landed Stigr in the middle of his sworn enemy. "Uncle..."

"Rest well," Stigr said as he stepped forward to work his way into their den. "I have a feeling tomorrow's going to be a long day."

Freezing winter winds gusted through his dream, knocking him from a star-filled sky into a blizzard of blowing snow. He couldn't figure out if he was back on the White Mountain, or if the snow filled the Winderost, but he rolled to face it on his feet. Something locked his talons and hind paws to the ground, and he couldn't move.

He stood shivering, wings open, staring at a wall of white.

A shadow loomed forward in the white flurry. Something stalked forward through the storm. Shard's heart beat hard.

For a moment he expected to see the owl, or Catori, or even a raven, and he was ready to call the name of a friend.

But he had no name for what exploded out of the storm.

A dark, screaming creature burst out of the white gloom, knocking him flat before he got a look at it. Shard hit the ground gasping, his limbs locked, unable to block out the creature's hateful, grating roars. It was gone, leaving him in cold dark, but the roars went on and on.

Someone called to him. He strained to the voice.

"Shard. Rashard! Wake up!"

Shard surged out of the dream. Brynja jumped back when he leaped to his feet, wings knocking the rock walls on either side of his cramped den.

"It was a nightmare!" Brynja ducked her head to avoid his wings.

"What is that sound?" Shard asked, breathless, barely understanding that he was no longer dreaming. The chilling roars from his dream hadn't left him. They remained, echoing from afar, in the real dawn wind beyond the Winderost.

"The enemy," Brynja said quietly, her gaze averting to the entrance of Shard's den. "You needn't fear them during the day."

No sentries sounded an alarm, and it seemed that Shard was the only gryfon to have awakened to the sound. Whatever beast roared in the pre-dawn light, it wasn't an immediate threat.

But it was a threat.

"Tell me what it is," Shard demanded, settling his wings. "And where is Stigr?"

"He was gone when I arrived," Brynja said, ignoring the first question. "Probably to meet Asvander. It's dawn. Time to go to the hunt." Brynja turned to leave, tail twitching.

Shard didn't move. "I'd like to be friends," he said. "But if you don't tell me who or what this enemy is, I will find out myself."

Brynja paused, looking over her shoulder. "For one who claims to be wingbrother to the great grandson of Kajar…well, I'm surprised you don't know. We don't speak of it. Ask me again and I'll find a more suitable duty for you."

Shard narrowed his eyes but followed her out of the den into the morning light. Sunlight glowed orange on the horizon, and the roars had faded, leaving only the sound of waking gryfons and twittering birdsong in the breeze.

22
First Frost

The howl of wind against rock pulled Kjorn from a vague dream of his first nest, surrounded by red stone and an elusive, sweet, grassy scent. He lunged up, tail flicking, and sniffed the air. The sweet smell of grass was gone, replaced with frost and sea. Beside him, Thyra burrowed deeper into their nest with a huff. Frosty cold deadened the air, and the wind sang against the riddled face of the nesting cliffs.

Kjorn walked to the entrance, head cocked. "Did you hear something?"

"Yes," mumbled Thyra, tucking talons over her face. "A great boar is shuffling around my den."

Kjorn leaned out, listening. Dawn tapped at the sky in light grays, a long rosy line under a blanket of cloud. He shuddered. Thyra and others with Vanir blood had already grown in winter feathering—long, soft feathers that nearly covered their talons and brushed down along their necks like manes. Kjorn had always thought it looked beautiful on the females, enviable on the males, but some muttered among themselves that it only made the half bloods stand out.

"I heard something."

"Mmh."

Kjorn slanted an ear to her, then, irritated, leaped from the cave into the morning. The cold air swept against Kjorn and he worked hard to gain lift over the bronze-black faces of the cliffs. Rising over the edge, he entered a world of white.

Hoarfrost caked the ground and the rocks and the trees as far as Kjorn could see. The rolling plain above the nesting cliffs stretched white and silent, broadening into frosted hills around the Nightrun and the White Mountains beyond. Kjorn's breath drove small clouds before his eyes and every wing beat needled cold under his feathers.

Voices echoed softly off the rock and water. It was difficult to keep secrets around the nesting cliff. Kjorn perked his ears and saw his father, unmistakably red and large, and Halvden, vivid green against the thick frost. They were speaking.

And *eating*. The torn carcass of a caribou cow reddened the ground between them.

Like a falcon Kjorn stooped, silent, until he smashed in between them. He ripped the caribou haunch from his father's talons and flung it aside.

"*Father!* What is this? You eat fresh meat while the pride goes hungry in exchange for wolf hunts?"

"Calm yourself, Kjorn," Sverin warned, his scarlet hackle feathers lifting. "You don't know—"

Kjorn whirled and bore down on Halvden, lifting his wings, tail lashing. "And you. You should be taking food to your mate, who carries your kit. Soon she won't be able to hunt at all."

Halvden's gaze slid to the king. Kjorn spun back to Sverin, who opened his wings to greet Kjorn's threat.

"Kjorn. Stop."

"Soon *none* of them will be able to hunt. Only the old females, and us, and none of us have any fat to guard against the winter. Although now to look at you, Father, you seem sleek enough to me."

From the corner of his eye, Kjorn saw gryfons gathering. Young, and elderly, and some flying in from the air.

"Are you quite finished?" Sverin growled.

Kjorn flattened his ears. "Yes. Explain this."

Halvden yawned and examined his talons. "My lord, may I carry on while you give the honored prince his explanation?"

"Yes, Halvden." Sverin didn't take his eyes from Kjorn. "Thank you."

Halvden cast Kjorn a smug, amused glance, then continued breaking apart the carcass. "You should consider trusting your father," he muttered, then shouldered by Kjorn, dragging the meat away.

To Kjorn's surprise, as fledgling gryfons and elderly approached, Halvden handed out offerings of meat.

Heat lanced up Kjorn's face and turned his belly. "Father?"

"Einarr's mate advised us of a herd low in the foot hills," Sverin said, his voice cold. "And select huntresses left early this morning to bring what kills they could."

Kjorn sunk into a low bow, hanging his head. "Why didn't you tell me?"

"I didn't have a chance. The plan happened late in the evening. I thought it would be a pleasant surprise for you and Thyra this morning. She's seemed overly tired these last days and so we didn't include her in the plans for the hunt."

Kjorn tucked his feathered tail low and pressed his head into the frost, sick with himself.

"Did you really think I would eat before feeding my pride? Should I have to explain myself to you?"

"No," Kjorn whispered, though he had. "I just…when I saw…"

"Don't stutter," Sverin said. Kjorn flinched, then, taking the hint, shook frost from his head and stood tall again, meeting his father's gaze with the small measure of pride he could muster.

"Forgive me." Kjorn looked around again, and noticed gryfesses soaring in with meat clutched in their talons. A good hunt. Thyra *would* be surprised and pleased. If Kjorn had waited a few moments more before assuming the worst, it would have been a wonderful morning indeed, despite the cold. "Father, don't shelter me. Include me in your plans. I do trust you. You just haven't seemed yourself since the summer, and I know winter is hard on you. And Father, I don't entirely trust Halvden." He hadn't planned to say the last part but it burst out, and he was relieved to say it.

Sverin watched him a moment, then cocked his head, indicating that Kjorn should follow as he walked farther from the gathering pride. "If I haven't seemed myself," he said quietly, "it's because I was betrayed. As you were betrayed, Kjorn. Shard lied to all of us. The deceit of his mother and Sigrun and his own lies have torn us apart."

Kjorn walked slowly, muscles stiff in the cold. "I know."

"It is difficult to trust again after such a thing," Sverin said, looking toward the leaden sky. "I know that Halvden can be arrogant at times, but he is young. Remember he lost both of his parents this summer. You know what it is to lose a parent."

It was a blow. Kjorn narrowed his eyes, forcing his ears to remain forward, not wanting to look hostile.

"Consider," Sverin said after giving him a moment to feel sympathy for Halvden, "That you will want a new wingbrother at your side one day."

Kjorn narrowed his eyes. *Is that Halvden's scheme? To become my wingbrother? He doesn't even like me.* He forced his expression to relax, and dipped his head. "I will consider."

Sverin gave him a sideways look. They'd walked to the edge of the cliff and stood there, listening to the crash of icy waves. Soon, chunks of ice would roll in along with the water. Soon, more cold than Kjorn could bear to think of. Kjorn thought of Shard, falling into the sea, and shuddered.

"Do you remember her?" Sverin asked, his voice changed and quiet. Kjorn looked over furtively. Sverin's gaze fixed firmly on the sea.

"Remember…" Kjorn paused, feeling foolish. It was not Shard who Sverin thought of when he gazed out to sea. "Yes, of course. A little. I would know her scent, and her voice."

"Good," Sverin whispered, and turned abruptly from the waves.

"Father…"

But Sverin's expression turned stony and Kjorn saw that he was watching the division of meat. There among the huntresses and those flocking in for food stood Ragna, like a phantom in the frost.

Kjorn loosed a hiss. "Why do you let her stay, if you hate her so?"

"Such an early frost," Sverin muttered, his talons sinking into the white. "It seems unnatural." Kjorn heard the crunch as the powerful claws broke through the frozen ground, clenching peat and earth as if it were flesh.

"Father—"

"Go make sure Halvden is fair," Sverin said. "I have things to tend to."

Before Kjorn could ask what things, Sverin loped away and jumped up into the sky, flapping away in the gray air. Kjorn shivered in the cold rush from his wing beats.

"Because I'm healer to this pride!" Sigrun snapped when Halvden asked her why she demanded extra meat. "You arrogant buffoon. Will you question me when your mate is whelping, too, and needs my help?"

"Don't threaten me on account of my mate," said Kenna, sidling in between them. All around, fledges and elderly stopped to stare at Sigrun's outburst. Sigrun, normally so quiet. *Don't they notice that no ravens or crows are flocking to this kill? Even they know we will need the meat and take pity.* Soon, she feared, the Isles themselves would turn their backs on Sverin's pride and they would find no meat at all.

"Halvden," Kenna said, "Surely as healer, Sigrun knows what she'll need later on."

"Fine," Halvden muttered, throwing the disputed sheds of meat at Sigrun. "How long until it rots though?" He strutted off toward another argument.

"Thank you," Sigrun murmured to Kenna, who fluffed her violet wings.

"I meant what I said, that's all. Do you have all you need?"

Sigrun dipped her head in answer. The only challenge would be finding a time to salt the meat with no one seeing. Kenna walked off to help see to other arguments, and then with relief Sigrun saw Kjorn approach to mediate. She took her own stash and turned, nearly bumping into Ragna.

"Sister," Ragna greeted, out-of-place amusement on her face. "How goes all?"

"I'll need time at the shore tonight."

"I can help make a distraction," she said, gaze roving the pride. It settled on Kjorn. "I think Sverin's son resents me."

"Of course he does. Ragna..." Sigrun glanced to both sides, but no one listened to them, all concerned with getting their share of the meat. "I know why Sverin tolerates me, but why did you come back? Why does he let you stay? I couldn't believe this summer when he said nothing about you returning."

Ragna's ears twitched back and her gaze grew distant. "He said nothing, because to him, I am nothing. To him, my heir is dead. Killing or exiling me would cause rebellion."

"Would it?" At the question, Ragna's expression quirked and she peered at Sigrun, who dipped her head, chagrined.

"I only meant, he's exiled others. So many others. Are you telling me the truth?"

"I'm telling you all I can," she said quietly. "Honor binds the rest." She met Sigrun's eyes. "You understand."

Ablaze with curiosity of the new knowledge that Ragna had a secret from her, Sigrun could only say, "Yes." She did understand secrets, but it almost became too much, and she blurted, "I wish none of this had happened. Sometimes I wish we'd secreted Shard away as Stigr wished, to let Stigr raise him, gather the other Vanir and..."

"And?" Ragna prompted, voice dropping low. "Come storming back in on the wings of war to challenge a conqueror who'd already beaten us? To lose more lives? To tear apart a pride of half-bloods and friends?"

"Conquered friends."

"And if Stigr flew in, and he and Caj battled once again?" Ragna tilted her head, and Sigrun tightened her wings to her sides, knowing full well she had argued the opposite scant weeks ago. She sympathized with Shard's plight, torn between two prides. *Or are we one, damaged pride now?* Ragna nodded slowly at her expression. "Who would you cheer to win? Your first love? Or your true mate?"

Sigrun couldn't answer, and she knew Ragna had meant it that way. "But even Shard's heart is torn. And Kjorn's. Sometimes I want to tell him, just tell him Shard lives and that he'll return and…" once again she couldn't finish. *What would Kjorn say, to know that Shard plans to return and claim his islands?* "Why did we do it this way?"

"Because," Ragna said, her gaze flicking to the sea. "It was Baldr's vision. It was his hope that we would have peace, that through his son there would be balance. He asked if I could do it, to raise Shard among the Aesir. It was his hope and his dying wish."

Sigrun blinked at her. "Per killed him over the water. He died in the sea. How do you know his last wish?"

Ragna's look was wistful. "Oh, Sigrun. We couldn't have won. Something had to end the fighting, and you knew Baldr. He knew himself. Do you think he really believed he would survive a fight against Per the Red?"

Ragna shook her head and left Sigrun then, left her standing in snow with caribou meat steaming at her feet. She stood there blankly, imagining the humble gray king on his final night of life, speaking in secret to his mate, then going forward into a fight he fully knew he wouldn't win.

It was then that Sigrun realized, for the first time since the Conquering, that rather than force his pride to flee or draw out the fighting into a sad and bloody end, Baldr the Nightwing had sacrificed himself to end the war.

23
The Voldsom Narrows

Morning wind suffused with sweetness buffeted Shard's face and pushed under his wings. He soared with Brynja and her band of huntresses toward their hunting grounds for that day. His dream of the roaring beast from the night before still haunted him, and waking to find that the nightmare sounds had been real.

"Hunters!" Valdis called over the wind. "Today we raid the Narrows for goat. Keep alert for eagles!"

Valdis divided the group into two parties, assigning Brynja to lead her hunters in from the windward side of the canyon.

Shard peered forward at the smaller series of canyons branching off from the massive gorge that separated the Winderost from the Outlands. He had never had enmity with an eagle of the Silver Isles or truly spoken with one. Perhaps they were larger and more intelligent here. He looked over to ask Brynja and found that she had already banked toward the dawn wind.

Shard ground his beak and turned sharp to catch up. "What sort of eagles live here?"

"The sort that fly and hunt. What sort do they have in the Silver Isles?" She scanned the horizon and added, "Stay alert. Prove yourself here and Orn will give you more freedoms and acclaim."

Shard clenched his talons, feeling like a fledge on his first hunt all over again. His gaze swept across the canyon. Far in the distance he saw circling motes. Eagles. Surely they wouldn't fly all the way over to harass a gryfon hunt.

"On the windward ledges!" called Sigga, the gray gryfess Shard had met his first day. Shard looked, and missed the sharp, formulated turn that Brynja and Sigga made toward the windward edge of the canyon.

Brynja loose a frustrated sigh as he caught up. "Pay attention," she ordered. "I know you're male, but I still expect you to keep up."

Shard flattened his ears in consternation. "I'll keep up." He was the best flier in the Silver Isles. He could stay in a formation.

Brynja growled low and Shard saw the twitch of her tail as she formed into a dive. That time, he anticipated the dive and kept up, neatly mimicking her wing movements. Valdis, Dagny and a third huntress Shard didn't know dropped below, to keep the goats from scattering down.

Shard, Brynja and Sigga dove in a tight wedge, straight at the far canyon wall. The wind slapped him, smelling of sage and the elusive flower. Then warming rock. The scent of water wisped up from far below, a tributary of a larger river that had worn down the layers of rock into canyons.

Looking to the wall again, Shard spied the goats. Compact and stout in the shoulders, they boasted thick, curling horns that reminded Shard of seashells. Their ruddy coats blended with the canyon walls and Shard marveled at how they held themselves nearly flat against the steep rock face.

"Shard!" Brynja called, and a thrill slipped through him to hear her call his name. "Drive in from the flank!" She shouted similar instruction to Sigga. They broke their wedge and dove in from three sides to keep the goats from scattering up the rock face.

Hunt-thrill woke in Shard's chest to see prey so close and he stretched his talons, ready for Brynja's word to close in.

An eagle shriek broke his concentration and pain lanced his back. Talons caught his wing joint, wings thrashed in his face and he barely had time to smash his beak against the attacking eagle's beak to protect his throat.

"*Eagles!*" Brynja's screech bounded down the canyon walls. They'd come in from high, silently.

If he hadn't been under attack, Shard would have laughed. Surely the eagles were outmatched. A fourth the size of a gryfon, with no forepaws, they had distinct disadvantages.

He squirmed against the female who clung to his wing joint as she slashed her beak toward his throat. A smaller male eagle swooped from below to attack Shard's belly, and yet another male slashed at his hind-quarters. His urge to laugh died when he understood their strategy.

They attacked in threes.

Valdis swooped in with her hunters but they all focused on helping each other, with none to spare for Shard. No time to help a foreigner like him. Harried and unable to defend all points, Shard folded wings and dove, while Brynja shouted directions that he couldn't hear.

The female eagle clung to Shard's shoulder though he sped past the males for a few seconds. Talons caught Shard's ear. He grabbed the she-eagle's foot. The wind swallowed her cry and Shard yanked her from his shoulder and held her, flapping wildly, in his claws. A young male caught up and dove in at Shard's face.

Shard flared to a hard stop, clapped his wings together and flipped backward to kick the male's face with a clawed hind foot. Then he snagged the male's wing and held tight, satisfied at the sound of crunching feathers.

With both struggling eagles in his grasp he spiraled back into a dive. The third male eagle hung back, calling alarm to the others above. Distantly, he heard Brynja shout his name.

"I am Shard, son-of-Baldr!" he shouted into the wind. Witless screams answered him. The ground and the roiling, muddy river leaped closer. "I know you understand me! Leave our hunt alone!"

He hadn't heard them speak, but any creature that attacked hunting gryfons with such strategy had to be more than witless animals defending territory. They were intelligent. They were Named.

The female slashed with her free foot, wings wild and slapping Shard's face. They hurtled toward the river.

"*Poachers.*" A word formed out of the she-eagle's beak at last, and Shard flung his wings open, falling into a swift glide just above the water. He raced the river downstream, so close to the water that the eagles stopped struggling for fear he would drop them in.

Poacher, Outlander. Trespasser. Everywhere Shard went in that land, it seemed someone had claimed the territory, and he couldn't see where they drew their lines. It was easier in the Silver Isles, with territory divided by the sea.

"Tell me your names," Shard demanded, carefully working his wings against the competing canyon winds and the eddies of cooler currents above the river.

"Release me!" ordered the she-eagle.

"As you wish." Shard dipped lower, loosening his grip so that her sprawling wingtips brushed the river.

"Hildr!" She flapped hard, smacking Shard's face again. "I am Hildr of the Brightwing aerie, daughter-of-Brunr. My consort is Arn, son-of-Arn."

They named themselves like gryfons. Surprised, Shard banked hard around a jutting rock, and just managed not to make a fool of himself by saying his thought out loud. For all he knew, the eagles might consider that gryfons named themselves like eagles, rather than the other way around.

More rocks broke out of the water ahead, forming white, foaming rapids. The male, Arn, hung loose in his grip, either wary of being dropped or deferring the situation to Hildr. Either way Shard was grateful that he held still.

"Fly higher, Outlander." Hildr laughed hard, breathless. "You're in dog territory now." Shard held her upside down and kept a grip on Arn's wing, not truly wanting to drop him in water. Little paw trails, caves and tracks marred the canyon wall, but he saw no painted wolves.

"Why do you call me Outlander?"

"You're not of Orn's pride. That's clear. The Vanheim Shores perhaps, but not the Winderost. Release me now."

"Do we have a peace?"

She only swore in defiance. Shard dipped lower. "This day," she cried. "This day, we will leave your greedy hunters alone."

Shard flapped hard to gain height and give the two eagles room to correct their flight, then released them. The male sped off toward the other eagles in crooked flight on his damaged wing. Hildr corrected to a dignified glide and glared over at Shard.

"Gryfons ruin our hunts and trespass without thought to our rituals or territory. They won't hear us. They think us witless."

Shard couldn't decide why she would tell him that, or what she expected him to do. "I know you aren't."

"Who are you, graywing?"

"I told you my name."

"But who *are* you? You don't smell of the Winderost. You smell of fish and evergreen and the sea. On the Halfnight our seer said the great starfire was a sign of something coming from the top of the world. Is that where you flew from? What is your true name?"

Shard stared at her, and it felt as if someone else answered. "I am Rashard. Son of Baldr the Nightwing. Prince of the Silver Isles in a sea far starward. I followed the fire in the sky, though I don't know yet to what end."

She loosed an amused twitter, a motherly sound, then angled her wings to catch an updraft. Maybe she had expected a different answer. "I'll remember your name, Shard of the Silver aerie. And our fight this day."

Shard couldn't tell, the way she said it, if that was a good or bad thing. She called a word into the canyon and her band gathered to fly upriver. She turned to follow.

Thinking of his vision, Shard called, "Wait! Do you know of a high, solitary mountain peak anywhere in the Winderost?"

"A high mountain?" She circled him once, keening a laugh in to the wind. "Not in the Winderost. A hard flight starward, beyond the end of the great gorge, beyond the Ostral Shore and the Forest of Rains. You seek the Aslagard Mountains. You seek the Horn of Midragur."

With that she caught an updraft and soared out of earshot. Shard craned his neck to peer after her, then movement on the shore caught his attention.

One of the strange, painted wolves padded along the canyon wall, watching. When she saw that Shard looked her way, she broke into a run.

"Wait!" Shard turned off the river. She stopped, bared fangs to warn him off, then sprinted toward the canyon wall. Before Shard could say another word, she disappeared into a narrow hole.

Shard landed in front of the cave, wings still lifted, panting, and peered into the darkness. It would be madness to step inside, but he had spoken with eagles. Maybe he could speak with the painted dogs.

Why would you? He could just hear Stigr, chiding him for being distracted.

But the Summer King listened to all who spoke. His mother had sung the song that summer, on the Daynight. She had sung to tell Shard something, to call him out. She believed he was the Summer King, born to bring justice and peace.

He couldn't do any of that without knowing what he faced. Maybe the dogs would give him the information that Brynja wouldn't. Or maybe Hildr or another eagle would. They, too, lived in the Winderost. They must face the same enemy that roared in the night.

And they must also wish to be rid of it.

Above, Brynja shouted for him. He peered again into the darkness of the den in front of him, thinking he saw movement. Brynja called again.

Shard hesitated, then turned and flew up to rejoin the hunters in the sky. He angled into formation quietly, his mind awhirl. No one suffered major injuries and so the hunt continued. They ranged down the canyon, searching for the goats that had scattered and fled during the flight.

It took him awhile to realize that Brynja was staring at him. He laced his talons together uncomfortably but let her speak first.

"How did you do that?"

"Do what?" Shard's thoughts loped back to grabbing the eagles, diving, the glide over the water, unsure which part she referred to.

"Do—all of it! I've never seen a gryfon fly like that."

"Oh." Shard relaxed his talons, shifting his wings as the wind shifted under them. A furtive glance ahead showed him that an ear on each gryfess slanted his way, though they tried to look as if they were only hunting. A flush of pride crept from the tip of his tail to his face, and he was glad for his dark gray feathers.

"I'll show you some time."

She loosed a light sound, half laugh, half breath. Shard kept her gaze, waiting for a true answer. She glanced half away, then perked her ears forward, looking as if she was trying not to laugh. "I look forward to it."

Shard trilled and then chuckled, looking away before he said something stupid. They resumed their hunt for goat and felled three beasts to haul back to the Dawn Spire. Shard learned about the precision of their hunting and the group-thought of it. It was almost like hunting with the wolf pack on Star Isle. He noticed, but did it all through a cloud of pride and happiness and a distracted habit of checking to see if Brynja was watching him.

When they returned to the aerie that evening and Shard found his crack in the wall that Valdis had called a den, Stigr had plenty to say about his first day in the Guard, and Asvander, and what he thought of the Aesir.

Shard made appropriate listening noises, until finally Stigr asked, "And how was the hunt?"

Shard curled up on the ground, nudging away a rat skull. "It was fine."

Stigr made a low sound of disapproval at Shard's vagueness but didn't press him, and as he curled up, Shard drifted toward sleep. His thoughts drifted on buoyant winds. Knowing that Brynja respected his skill in flight, he was sure she would tell him more about the Winderost and the enemy soon, if he asked.

At first dark the horrible roars broke again in the distance, but since no other gryfon roused, and no alarm raised again, Shard found them easier to ignore. The nightmare beast of his first evening didn't seek him out in dreams again.

Instead, in his dream he flew with a gryfess, a huntress who matched him for wit and skill, a gryfess who could become his queen.

But in that dream, her feathers were not the color of violet twilight.

24
Blending In

After the successful hunt and fight with the eagles, the gryfons of Dawn Spire grew less wary of Shard and more curious about him. The hunting never ended. It took a dozen bands of hunting gryfesses and the occasional male, like Shard, trying to earn a place, to feed the massive pride of the Dawn Spire. Unofficial hunting was not outlawed, Shard learned, but other than the occasional rabbit or small game bird, generally not encouraged. The king and the huntresses were to approve game hunts and make sure no one was crossing out of their territory or taking more than their share for their own clan.

A stretch of days passed as he learned the laws and unspoken routines. The nightmare beast of his first evening did not come again. Each night Munin brought him vivid dreams of the Silver Isles. He had to trust the raven, though Catori and even Stigr warned him that Munin was a trickster, that raven dreams were their own message, on their own timeline and meaning and not necessarily to be believed.

When he could call Catori to him in the dream, Shard had her confirm anything she knew. Kjorn and Sverin had an unsteady truce, though in his dreams, Shard could see the Red King growing edgy and tense as winter drew in, dark and cold.

His daylight hours at the Dawn Spire found Shard receiving more recognition for his work than he ever had from his own pride in the Silver Isles. Random gryfons found reason to trot by his and Stigr's den, pause, and size Shard up, as if to gauge his true size and coloring and the measure of his wings for themselves.

His fight with the eagles found its way into more than one conversation even as the days passed.

"Two eagles," Brynja recounted again to one of her many cousins, nearly a fortnight later as they gathered for a morning hunt. She sat close to Shard, and her warm scent distracted him from stopping her telling the tale again. Dagny sat at the back of the dozen huntresses, counting heads while Brynja told the tale.

"He held them both in a spiral dive, straight down toward the river, then a leap's distance from the water…" she popped her wings open and the others jumped. "Just like that, he opens to a glide. I wouldn't have thought it was possible until I saw it. I've never seen a gryfon fly like that."

Stigr, walking by on his way to the Wind Spire, paused near the gathered hunters. "Nor will you. At our home, he is the best flyer known. At home, they call him the Stormwing."

Heat swept under Shard's feathers when the gryfess hunters swiveled to peer at him, unbelieving, and Shard tossed his head back in disagreement. "My uncle's being kind."

"Stigr's never kind," Dagny chirruped, and all the females laughed.

Stigr bumped a wing against Shard and he straightened, remembering that he had to let Stigr build him up if they were to prove themselves to the pride.

"I almost hope we run into eagles again," Brynja said to the gaggle, "So you can see what I mean."

"I don't think we will," Shard said, thinking of Hildr. "Not in the Narrows, anyway." Before Brynja could ask why, a shadow swooped over them and Asvander landed, feathers ruffled, and trotted forward to stand in Stigr's space.

"You, Outlander, you're late."

"Show respect, fledge," Stigr rumbled, rustling his wings. The huntresses fell quiet, watching the exchange. Stigr made a show of fluffing his feathers. "We frail elders take a little time in the morning."

Shard noticed Dagny shift and straighten when Asvander paced nearer. Asvander narrowed his eyes, then flattened one ear in amusement. "By the time you get to full speed, the dogs will be whelping in our dens."

Shard looked between them, surprised. Asvander's taunt sounded more like a jest than an insult. Maybe Stigr was carving a place for himself in the Guard, after all. He and Shard had barely had time to speak the last fortnight, to regroup and form plans, so exhausted from the hunts and the visits from Aesir gryfons.

Brynja swatted Asvander's tail feathers. "Leave Stigr alone. You're lucky to have him."

Stigr coughed but Shard noticed a pleased gleam in his eye. Asvander turned to stand closer to Brynja, but looked at Shard. "And you, more bird catching today?"

"Maybe," Shard said. "If there's anything worth catching."

Brynja chided, standing. "Show respect, Asvander. Shard is proving himself well."

"As a hunter." Asvander didn't take his eyes from Shard, and Shard didn't like how close he stood to Brynja. Close enough to flick his tail lightly against hers, which nearly distracted Shard from his next words. "How will you fare on the Wild Hunt, I wonder? Brynja, should we have him hunt with the clans of Oster?"

"I'm claiming him for En!" Dagny declared, springing forward, but it was Asvander she bumped against, like a playful kit. "You can fight me for him."

Asvander chuckled, nudging her off with a wing, though he gave her a fond glance.

Shard looked between them. "The Wild Hunt?"

"The midwinter feast," Brynja said, moving away from Asvander to face Shard. "The first chance at initiation for our young warriors, huntresses, and—"

"And Outlanders?" Shard guessed.

"And Outlanders," Asvander said. "And you."

And you. Why did he say it that way? Shard tilted his head, glancing from Asvander to Brynja. *Did she tell him who we truly are?* "I'll just hope to prove myself well then."

Asvander chuckled. Shard braced himself for an insult, ready to exchange wit or talons with Asvander if he challenged again.

"If you hunt and fly as well as Brynja says," the big gryfon said instead, with no trace of mockery, "then I just might fight Dagny to have you hunt with our groups. Son-of-Ragr," he said to Stigr, "we're late. Good hunting, Brynja." He dipped his head to her before loping off. The gryfesses scattered to make room for his large wings as he jumped into the sky.

"Good hunting," Stigr said unhelpfully to Shard, and followed.

Shard, his blood up, wings tensed, could only stand a moment and stare after them.

Brynja laughed at him. "What did you expect him to say?"

"I thought he didn't like me. I expected..." He'd expected someone more like Halvden. Incurably arrogant and boastful and cruel.

Dagny chuckled. "Asvander will surprise you. Of course, he wants to be the best at everything, but when he's not, he'll admit it."

"You'd do well to make a friend of him," Brynja said quietly. Shard met her gaze, searching, trying to see what she might have told him, or her wingsister for that matter, or anyone else, about where he'd really come from.

Dagny stretched her long forelegs in front of her. "Anyway it's two moons still until the Wild Hunt. By then I imagine you can hunt with whoever you like."

"I'll remember that." Two moons. Two moons was too long. Shard couldn't wait until midwinter to gain Orn's approval to roam. He had to seek his vision, seek the white mountain peak and whoever called him, he had to remember why he'd come.

Dagny called the huntresses back to attention and told them the hunt plan.

Brynja walked back to Shard and tilted her head in close to murmur, "I truly hope you'll choose to hunt with me."

Warmth flushed Shard's face again. "Oh, well…"

Brynja bumped him fondly and pushed off the ground with the others, and all he could do was follow.

Dagny flew in close to inform him that pronghorn deer grazed on the plain, since he hadn't yet had opportunity to hunt there. The danger lay in the vast herds and their aggressive, protective nature, and the great prides of grass lions who competed with gryfons for meat.

As they flew and narrowed in on a herd for the hunt, Shard noted the heavy scent of lion in the grass, and paw prints the size of gryfon hind paws in the dusty earth. No lions showed themselves, but Shard sensed their heavy presence. Even as the gryfons felled five plump deer, no challenged rose. Perhaps the lions were less aggressive than the eagles.

Shard wondered if they really were arrogant or Voiceless or Nameless, as Brynja suggested, or if nobody bothered to speak with them, as he suspected. The eagle had been willing enough to answer his question about the mountain peak, the Horn of Midragur. If he'd gotten to speak with her longer, she might have told him about the enemy in the night.

What might the grass lions of the Winderost know?

Shard looked over to Brynja as he worked with others, tearing the pronghorn carcasses to carry back to the Dawn Spire. She wouldn't tell him about the mysterious enemy, or what it meant to Kajar in turn, Kjorn.

There was a reason the Red Kings had forbidden flying at night, a reason the gryfons of the Dawn Spire retreated to their fire lit dens after sunset. But the beasts must affect all of the Winderost, too. If the gryfons wouldn't tell him, perhaps another creature would. He would wait until the moon grew full, to have as much light as possible in the strange land.

The laws of the Aesir and their fear of the night were not Shard's laws or fears.

He could blend in at the Dawn Spire and live as an Aesir as needed, but now it was time for him to resume the forbidden, Vanir art of flying at night.

25
The King's Decree

A cloud of black crows alerted the King's Guard to the body. Vald discovered the dead gryfess at first light, washed up on the shore, her flesh swelled from the sea and feathers soaked in salt water.

Sigrun was in her den when the young orange gryfon landed, eyes wide and feathers on end, to tell her. By the time she flew down, a crowd of gryfons gawked and whispered in a ring around the dead gryfess. Sigrun shouldered through them, but there was nothing left for her to do.

"Her spirit flies with Tyr," she said calmly, lifting her gaze to those around. There was no cry, for the old gryfess had no family left, her mate and grown offspring all slain in the Conquering. Caj's big, warm presence loomed up beside Sigrun, and he draped his wing over her shoulders. Before anyone else could speak, Sverin's voice cut the chill air.

"Have I not spoken on the danger of the sea?"

"She was out of practice," Sigrun whispered. "Out of practice and hungry." The last fortnight of hunting gained slim results, a deer here or there, but the game of the Star Isle was going to ground.

"Have I not spoken of the dangers of flying at night?" Sverin said, striding forward.

The gryfons parted in waves around him. He stopped and stared at the dead gryfess, and an old pain flashed in his eyes. Sigrun watched him closely, watched as he thought, she was certain, of his own drowned mate whose body had never washed up on the shore. "Let us bear her to Pebble's Throw to burn the flesh and release her to bright Tyr."

"She was Vanir."

Sverin's head flew up, eyes narrowed.

Gryfons stepped aside to reveal Ragna, standing at the edge of the group. As they had for Sverin, the gryfons parted again for the Widow Queen. "Let her body rest among the dead on the hallow ground of Black Rock. She was Vanir."

"Black Rock?" Sverin scoffed. "Where the dead and the exiles go?" He stretched open his wings and cast the group in a shadow of red. "So you can bear her body there and meet with the last dregs of your kind? So you can form new plans against me?"

Those gathered held a collective breath, staring at the open accusation. *Why?* Sigrun wondered wildly. *If he hates and fears her so, why does he let her remain?* The question lay on everyone's face.

Ragna inclined her head. "No more Vanir but those in your pride dwell in the Silver Isles. At least none I know of. Let her rest on Black Rock." It was the first time she had ever spoken up over a Vanir death, the first time she had asked for a proper burial.

Chill wind and the slip of waves across the pebble shore whispered while the king stood silently, eyes locked on Ragna. Something passed between them, though what, Sigrun couldn't say. Sverin broke the stare, looking windward.

"Very well. Leave her on your cursed rock, and hope that Tyr can find her there."

Ragna lowered her head in thanks, though Sigrun watched her ears lay flat. As the Red King turned to go, she raised her head high.

"Who will help me bear her?"

No one volunteered. Propelled by duty and pity for her wingsister, Sigrun stepped forward, feeling the heat of Caj's stare at her back.

"I will."

"And I," called Einarr, slipping around other staring gryfons to stand over the dead gryfess.

"And I," said Kenna, and Halvden hissed in surprise.

"I will," whispered Vald, still staring at the body.

Sverin stopped, tail twitching once. As he turned, Caj walked to Sigrun's side.

"I will help," he rumbled, and at Sverin's betrayed expression said only, "Brother, she was starving."

Tension pulled the air taut as a feather vein.

"She flew at night and died for it," Sverin said. "The night, as I've implored you to understand again and again, is our deadly enemy." His gaze burned the gathered gryfons. "Any gryfon found out of their den after twilight will be considered in defiance of my law. The King's Guard will enforce this." Low murmurs grew, but that law was hardly new, even if the hour was now earlier.

Sverin stalked away and leaped onto a boulder, raising his voice to proclaim, "The sea, too, is our deadly enemy. From this day on, no one is to go nearer than ten leaps to the shore. There is no reason," he said sharply at the shocked expressions before him. "To venture closer. No reason."

No one argued, no one offered agreement. Caj pressed his shoulder reassuringly against Sigrun's before he walked over to stand beneath the king, and supported him by stating, "Any gryfon seen within ten leaps of the seashore will be considered in defiance of the King's Law." He sounded weary, unable to meet the eyes that stared at him in disbelief. "For your own safety," the blue gryfon reminded. The dead gryfess felt huge in front of them all.

"My den is only five leaps from the shore!" cried an old female.

Caj's eyes found her, hard and cold. "Find a new one."

Sigrun stared at him, torn, knowing he had to support the king, but feeling betrayed. She would have to sneak out at night to salt more meat for winter. She would have to break two of the king's laws, under the very eyes of the captain of the King's Guard. *I'll have to drug him,* she thought dismally, staring at Caj. *Betray my own mate.*

She sneaked a look at Ragna, but the pale gryfess had locked eyes with Sverin. By their hot, challenging stare, Sigrun feared this would only be the first of many new laws they would see that winter.

26
NIGHTMARE

THE CREEK SPLASHED AND LAUGHED, rolling through a cedar forest in the mountains of the Star Isle. Larks twittered and starlings chattered gossip among the higher branches. Summer sun glowed in lances, spearing the shadowy woods with pockets of warmth. Shard stretched on his belly in front of the stream, a talon dipped in the water.

"Wait quietly," he told the gryfess snuggled under his wing. She watched intently, though it was his face she studied, not the stream.

"I like this form of hunting," she said, and yawned, rolling to her belly in the lazy sun. Shard laughed, frightening the first trout that investigated his talon.

"Brynja, I like—" a roar cracked the summer day and the woods shattered into a cloud of gray dust.

Brynja shrieked, fighting an enemy Shard could not see. Dark wings that first looked like raven's wings and then monstrous bat wings swept between them, knocking Shard away.

He landed in a snow drift in the woods. Brynja was gone. Summer was gone. Snow pelted him and he lurched to his feet, staring. Deep winter cloaked the Star

Isle in snow, and he looked down to see a dripping trail of red glimmering in the twilight. He raced it over a hill and stopped, stunned.

At the bottom of the hill he saw a large blue gryfon, sprawled broken and unmoving in the snow. Ravens swooped and circled, laughing, and wolves gathered around the body.

"No!" Shard tried leaping but couldn't move. The snow dragged him away and down like water. "Caj! Nest-father…Catori! How could they?"

His friend's mournful howl sang through the winter woods, but he couldn't see her. "Shard, beware of raven dreams…"

Shard cried out again but sank into the snow, and through, and dropped until he was in the sky again, gliding over a high mountain peak. The song called him again but at his back he felt heat, and hate, and fear. He whirled to face it…

And woke, hissing defiance in Stigr's face.

The black gryfon blinked calmly. "What did you see, my prince?"

Shard caught his breath. The first dream raced back, of Brynja by the stream. The enemy who plucked her away. Then, Caj.

He shook his head, face hot, and looked away. There was no way to tell Stigr that he feared the death of his nest-father, the very gryfon who had taken Stigr's eye in battle, and took Stigr's first love for his mate. But the image of Caj lying bloody in the snow hung between them, and he wondered if he had called the blue gryfon's name in fear, if Stigr heard.

"Just a nightmare. A raven dream. Probably…probably not real." He said it to Stigr, and to himself, though everything else Munin had shown him was true. And if that was so, it meant bleak winter was closing on the Silver Isles.

It meant his nest-father would die, and wolves would be the ones to kill him.

It couldn't possibly be true.

"Well," Stigr said. "We've overslept."

Shard shook his head again and followed Stigr out of the den.

"Ah, there's my finest hunter!" Brynja loped along the canyon wall to meet them. She and Stigr bid good morning before Stigr left them, and Brynja met Shard with bright eyes.

"I'm not your finest," Shard mumbled, recalling the dream and her, tucked snugly under his wing. He hoped the embarrassment couldn't show in his eyes.

"What it is?" Her expression fell and she cocked her head, searching his face. "You seem—"

"Race you," Shard said quickly, and bounded away, jumping up to fly toward the tower where Brynja's hunting band met each morning. Behind him, her laughter only made the memory of his dream flare brighter. He had to remember why he'd come. He had to accomplish his purpose soon. As soon as the full moon brightened the Winderost, he would fly.

That day they hunted in a distant, windward portion of the Narrows. A vicious flight of eagles attacked them there, though they were different then those Shard had met on his first hunt. They refused to speak to him, and fought savagely.

Their numbers were great enough to harry the gryfons out of their territory and the retreat ended with all the hunters but Shard in the healer's dens for gashes and bruises. Now that he understood the eagle's fighting strategy, he'd been able to fend them off and out-fly them to help others.

Sigrun would have marveled at the number of healers, not even counting the apprentices. The Vanir in the Silver Isles had one trained healer, sometimes two but often that was a healer and an apprentice. Sigrun, with her two apprentices, made up the largest healing force the pride had enjoyed in many years. The healer gryfons, upon learning that Shard's nest mother was a healer, promptly put him to work treating the smaller injuries.

Shard had done well by chasing off the eagles that harried Dagny, probably saving her eyes from their talons. She made a point of telling any gryfon within hearing, and boasting with grateful awe that she had never truly appreciated her eyes until she almost lost them. She made sure everyone knew that she owed Shard her life. And her eyes, of course. It was all very dramatic, but any time Shard tried to play it down, Dagny smacked him with a wing.

That same day Stigr and his small patrol of gryfons had run off a large pack of painted wolves from gryfon hunting grounds in the pronghorn plains. The younger guardians couldn't speak enough of Stigr's fighting skill despite his handicapped vision, and his fine leadership when their younger captain panicked under the onslaught of wolves.

That evening, Shard followed Stigr toward their crack of a den, both tired and aching, but proud of what they'd done. When they arrived at the den they found Valdis blocking their way.

"King's orders," she said, eyeing Shard. Stigr began to growl but Shard nudged him with one wing, waiting. "You're to nest in a higher cliff." She stretched her broad wing up to point across the canyon floor to a neat row of more artfully carved dens, each facing dawnward. "Take your pick of those, one each. Well done today."

"We only did what was necessary," Stigr said.

Valdis appraised him. "Stigr, please consider joining my clan on the Wild Hunt. And you, Shard, though I'm sure Brynja has already asked. Rest well."

She left, and Stigr narrowed his eye, looking to Shard. "The Wild Hunt?"

Shard laughed, and flew up to claim a new den.

The half moon swelled toward fullness. Shard worked as he never had to be the best hunter in Brynja's band, the best male hunter of the whole pride of the Dawn Spire. When gryfons spoke his name, they spoke of great skill in flying and his wit when facing and fighting other hunting beasts. Shard had only encountered the eagles and wolves. The lions of the plains remained a mystery, and most warned that he was better off not knowing much of them.

"All breezy from here," Dagny said one morning as they flew toward the plains to hunt pronghorn. "Do well on the Wild Hunt, and the king will accept you as one of his own."

And then, will he let me roam freely? Shard wanted to ask. But it was a question for Brynja or Valdis. If Dagny knew of his real origins, she hadn't said it out loud. Shard thought she must know, for otherwise, Brynja was keeping a big secret from her wingsister.

But who of us have never kept something from someone?

"Thanks," Shard said belatedly. "I hope I will." He tilted his head as she just laughed and soared off into formation. Shard flapped to catch up to Brynja. "Brynja!"

She cast a look over her shoulder, wings working smoothly against the chill dawn air. Shard caught an odd look in her eye, but he couldn't name it. "Shard, stay in formation."

He blinked at her tone, then chuckled. "Brynja, did you know we moved to a higher den? You should show me where to find some pine bows so it doesn't smell like old gryfon."

"Shard—"

"I think the last gryfon to live there must have been ancient. The scent is—"

"Shard! This isn't the time."

Shard angled away and stared at her. The last fortnight they had always talked and laughed before a hunt. He tried to catch her eye but she looked away with a stern expression.

"Sorry," he mumbled, and fell back, straightening his wings to fly in line with Sigga.

"Serves you right," the gray gryfess said under her breath. "She's too high tier for you."

Shard ignored the barb. All the talk of tier and rank and clan wore thinly on him after awhile—truly, it wouldn't matter to him once he was safe and secure in the Silver Isles. Safe and secure, and king. Something else must be worrying Brynja for her to act like that. They'd been growing closer, and Shard's whole world seemed better when she was near. Later he would find a time to ask what it was, and they would laugh again.

But he didn't find a time to ask her during the hunt, or the butchering.

At the end of the day as they bore the meat home, Shard tried to catch up with her, but she only glanced at him with another strange expression, as if she was nervous. "Shard, please. I'm very tired."

"I only wanted to say good hunting today."

"Thank you. You too."

Shard kept pace with her a moment and then fell back when she said nothing, the deer haunch in his talons feeling five times heavier than it was. Something was different.

Did I do something wrong? He wracked his mind and came up with nothing. Something else was troubling her. He could help, if he knew what it was, but she wouldn't talk to him.

By the evening when they were done distributing the spoils of the hunt, Shard brooded. He returned to his den and kicked dirt and nesting material around, trying to rearrange it again and drive out the old scent.

A female voice hailed Stigr from outside the neighboring den. Shard, feeling nosy, trotted out, ears lifted.

Valdis flared and landed on the rock ledge outside the dens. "Stigr! Out you come, you stubborn crow. I've promised everyone."

Stigr emerged, with a strange expression when he saw Shard, as if he'd been caught at something. "Valdis. You're early."

"I'm perfectly on time. Come on then, I suppose you're cleaned up enough."

"Where are you going?" Shard stepped forward, noting the distinct lack of enmity in the air between the two older gryfons. That evening, they appeared more bemused by each other than hateful.

"Apparently I'm to be the amusement for Valdis's kin tonight."

"What he means," Valdis said, "is that I've asked him to come tell us tales. Whatever tales he can without giving you both away. Although they'll suppose anything strange you know will be some sort of Outlander thing."

Stigr flattened one ear. "What sorts of strange things do you think I know?"

"I couldn't begin to imagine."

"I'm sure you've thought of a few things," Stigr said. Shard stood there, watching, until Stigr noticed him again. "Shard. Would you like to come?"

"No." If Stigr was joining Valdis's kin for the evening, then Brynja might well be there, and if she didn't want to be near Shard, then he didn't want to be near her either. He had plans to make.

Valdis grated her beak. "All right. Let's be along then, before the lighting of the fires."

Stigr gave Shard a look, as if to warn him not to do anything stupid in his absence, then he flew off with Valdis, down through the towers and spires toward the creek.

Shard sat down where he was to watch the lighting of the fires, trying to shake a sense of foreboding. Brynja wouldn't talk to him. Stigr was befriending Aesir, or making a good show of it. He hadn't dreamed a vision again and so he knew it was the same. Seek the mountain. He had to know what he faced, and to do that he had to ask someone other than a gryfon of the Dawn Spire.

Shard watched the gryfons who bore the torches toward the great pyres on top of the towers and canyon walls. He admired their flight, the careful, slow wing strokes that kept their feathers from catching the flames or putting them out. The shadows grew deep around him, the light warmed to orange.

A gryfon landed heavily behind him, drawing him from his reverie.

"Shard!" Dagny declared, as if surprised to see him there, in front of his own den. "I've come to help you."

"Help me?" Shard stood and fluffed the dust from his tail.

"I heard you tell Brynja that your den has a *special* smell. I know a good spot to get some pine and juniper. And herbs. We'll get it fixed up tonight."

He leaned forward, sniffing the air around her. "You smell like—"

"Smoke? Yes." She flapped her wings a couple of times, sending up dust. "A hazard of the duty."

"Duty?"

"Flame-bearer." She eyed his wings. "You could do it, you've got the skill. It's a high honor. A good way to earn respect. Anyway, I'm here about the smell in your den. You want that cleared out…in case you have any gryfon visit."

"Who would visit?"

She laughed so loudly it rang off of the rock. "You are a lark, aren't you. Come with me!"

"Oh, well…" Shard had to skip forward and hop into the air to keep up with her. He would be grateful to freshen up his den, and it was best not to spend the night brooding or wondering what Stigr was up to. "Thank you!" he called again, and she only laughed over her shoulder. Shard took the opportunity to glance at the moon, and felt a thrill.

The next night, it would be full. The next night, he would fly.

27
Kajar's Legacy

The grass plain stretched ghostly pale beneath Shard, washed in moonlight and rippling with silver when a wind caught the grass. He glided low, breathing in the sweet grass and frost scent. The Dawn Spire and the Outlands lay a half mark's flight behind him, and from where he flew, he couldn't even hear the roars of the enemy.

He hunted lions.

He hadn't told Stigr.

Sneaking away from the Dawn Spire had taken longer than he'd thought, for the sentries never slept. At last he'd discovered a darkened corridor between the arches where he could slip away into the night, but he'd gone on foot at first to avoid attention.

Far ahead of him, he made out the ghostly mass of a pronghorn herd, grazing, sleeping, some on watch. Not wanting to startle them, he landed and walked through the tall grass, ears twitching to and fro, beak lifted to scent the air. Where there were pronghorn, there would surely be lions.

A sensation more than a sound made him turn, and through the grass, moonlight flashed green in night-seeing, feline eyes.

"Greetings, huntress," Shard said, rumbling the words in the language of the earth. The lioness turned her ears first back, and then forward again. She crouched only two leaps' length from Shard, still and silent as stone. Then her eyes moved to something behind Shard. He turned, breathing slowly, working himself to stay calm, for he hadn't come for a fight.

A second lioness walked up behind him, and she matched him for height and build. He'd never seen a lion so large. The mountain cats of the Silver Isles were smaller and lithe, and the spotted snow cats of the high mountains so rare they might as well be spirits.

Her sleek, pale hide shone in the moonlight, sheathing rippling muscles on her shoulders, back and haunches. A long tail like a mountain cat's hung low and confident with an extra tuft of fur on the end, and the faintest hint of spots freckled the backs of all four legs. Shard met her eyes, then was surprised by a familiar sight.

Long, tapered feathers hung like a bird's crest behind her ears, around the back of her neck like a collar, braided roughly into the fur. Gryfon feathers. He wasn't sure if the feathers meant she was a friend of gryfons, as it did with the wolves of the Silver Isles, or if they were trophies of battle. Shard checked movement on either side of him, and from the flickering eyes and the flash of fur, he knew he was surrounded. Here and there he saw a lioness with a feather or two, but none like the one before him, so to her, he bowed.

"Great huntress," he said as he straightened. "I am Rashard, son-of-Baldr, prince of the Silver Isles in the distant Starland Sea. I wanted to speak with you about the gryfons of the Dawn Spire."

The lioness regarded him with the intelligent, measuring look of a Named creature. Low, warm rumbles came from the surrounding huntresses. Shard shifted his talons, trying not to be impatient, for just when he thought Brynja was right and the lions were Voiceless, their leader spoke.

"I am Ajia the Swiftest, the third daughter of Badriya, Who is Pale." She walked forward, her paws silent through the grass. She might have been a ghost in front of him, except that if he concentrated he heard the brush of grass against her fur. The ring of lionesses around him held perfectly still. Ajia stopped three steps from Shard and stretched her head forward to sniff delicately. Her nose and whiskers wrinkled and her gaze rolled to the moonlit sky.

"Yes, he is the one! He is the one great Tor has led to us. He is the Star-sent, who bears the fire of Tyr." Again she smelled him, as the words sank in for Shard. "You come from snow, from the dark, from far away."

"I followed Kajar's Sign."

She chuffed, nose wrinkling again but this time to reveal long, thick fangs. "That is an eagle-cat name. We the oldest know it was a sign for all, and bears no true name." Her gaze leveled on him. "I am singer and healer and story keeper of my pride. I have waited for you since the starfire came. I wanted to hunt for you, but the winds said wait, the Star-sent will come to you. Wait for the Summer King. No gryfon of the Dawn Spire would come to us, not under the light of Tor, not speaking the words of the earth. So I know it is you. Welcome to the First Plains, young prince."

Shard sat down in the grass, struck dumb. Catori had once told him she thought all creatures had a song of the Summer King, but he hadn't believed, or he'd thought she meant only creatures of the Silver Isles. But truly, it must have been an ancient song, a legend for all.

"Tell me how we may help you, for surely it is you who will lift the darkness from the Winderost."

"You mean the enemy," Shard said softly. "The enemy of the gryfons of the Dawn Spire, who they won't even speak of or name."

Ajia loosed a low, disgusted roar. "They will not? Then the enemy is winning. We of the earth know they wish only to spread fear." Her eyes gleamed in the moonlight. "Do you truly think it is the fire that keeps them from the Dawn Spire? No! They delight in filling every creature's heart with fear, for their hearts are filled with hate."

"How do you know they hate?"

"Can you not hear it in their cries?"

Shard could. He remembered his dream with a chill. It hadn't been Nameless hunger or fear that filled the creature's screams. It was hatred. And to feel hatred was the burden of a Named creature, a higher creature who felt pride and fear and sorrow. Shard thought of the gryfons and wolves of the Silver Isles and the hatred between some of them and its cause. *Where there is hatred is anger, is injustice. But surely these creatures are too powerful to have experienced injustice.* Shard couldn't fathom it. They had to be angry over Kajar, over their lost treasures. That had to be the source of their hate.

"Who are they?" he whispered. "What are they?"

Ajia dipped her head low, her eyes lifting once again to the moon. "They are the First children of the earth, born of the earth and of fire."

Shard shook his head, not understanding. "Are they…are they dragons?"

Ajia looked to one side, as if consulting the night. "You should know with your own eyes. You should see. They might have been great beasts once called dragons, but now they are only their hatred, wicked wyrms in a dying land. Come. You should see."

She slunk past him and picked up to a trot. As one, the circle of lionesses rose to follow her, and Shard turned to catch up before he ended up alone in the grass.

"Where are you taking me?"

"To the border," Ajia said as Shard caught up. "To the home of the enemy."

Grateful for his time running with the wolves, Shard fell into a traveling pace at her side, and she cast him a look of approval. Her gaze settled forward, and Shard felt the heat of the lionesses around him. "We go to the Serpent River Gorge that separates us from the Outlands."

"You don't have to go there. I can fly there alone, and faster."

"No. They hunt gryfon above all else. Alone, they would kill you or drive you to Nameless terror. Travel with us, and our scent will mask you."

Shard fell quiet after that. It was what he'd wanted, after all, but a raw fear crept through him at her warning. He kept pace with the lions and noted the landscape changing under their feet and around them. The moon slipped lower from her midnight perch. His muscles clawed and protested but he kept up as the grass plain changed back to the rough ground closer to the Dawn Spire, and when that flattened into long, barren slopes of desert far windward of the Dawn Spire. Shard knew if they turned and walked starward, they would end up in the Voldsom Narrows.

They swam a wide, shallow river. Shard had flown over it when he left the Dawn Spire but he swam, in respect for the lionesses. Ajia said nothing of the ability nor seemed surprised by it. Shard hadn't seen Brynja or any other Winderost gryfons swim, but he hadn't heard or asked if it was forbidden, as it was in the Silver Isles. At least under Sverin's rule.

"You called your home the First Plains," Shard said as they shook themselves dry. "Is it a hallow place?"

"All places laid by Tyr and Tor are hallow places, but some are older than others." Ajia paused to wash, and made sure that her collar of feathers laid flat. Shard had yet to ask her about it, afraid he wouldn't like the answer. She shook again and watched Shard a moment. "Just as all creatures are worthy. Named, Nameless, Voiced or silent. Because gryfons rule both earth and sky does not make them better than others."

"I know," Shard said, feeling edgy, though her lecture didn't seem directed at him.

"For we know," she said, low, a warm purr in her voice, "we know that we walk in the image of Tor, who first walked the earth as a great cat."

Shard looked at the moon, surprised. He had never heard that particular version of the mother goddess. "But, she is mother to gryfons…"

"Yes." Ajia turned and trotted on and Shard followed, ears perked to her tale. "She first made us in her image, and then she saw the great, bright eagle in the sky, and fell in love with him and his winged children."

"Tyr?" Shard whispered. Stigr had never told him any legends that cast Tor as a great lioness, and Tyr as an eagle.

"And he found her beautiful, and called her to join him in the sky. And she bore him many children. So, Rashard, gryfons may be the favored children of Tyr and Tor, but they are not the first, nor the oldest. Tor lives high with her eagle mate most nights, but we know the holiest time is the time of no moon, when she returns to us and sets her paws on the earth again."

So wrapped up in the tale, Shard barely noticed where they were.

The scent of sulfur and rotting flesh slapped him. Another league ahead he discerned the sudden drop of the wide gorge that formed the edge of the Winderost, the dank, deep canyon that separated them from the Outlands. Shard couldn't force himself to take another step, and even the lionesses stopped. They clustered around Shard and he remembered what Ajia had said about masking his scent from the enemy.

"The wind is good," Ajia murmured, curling her lips in a grimace, ears flat. "We will have to smell them before we see them, but it means they won't smell you."

Before they saw or smelled the enemy, they heard them.

A roar shook the dry earth beneath their feet and Shard fought the urge to cower. They stood a long distance off from the gorge, and Ajia didn't look afraid.

The roar split into discordant notes, a wracked cacophony like an eagle and a shrieking boar.

A rush of wind hit them and Shard braced, shocked, sucking a breath. Ajia was right. The stench of old blood, dung, and under it all a waft of reptilian flesh overwhelmed Shard.

He held his breath.

The first of them launched out above the canyon rim. The full, dark wings of Shard's nightmare swelled against the night. Silvered by the moon, he could only tell they were dark, but whether black or brown or some other murky hue he couldn't see.

Roars cracked against the rock walls and bounded along and along, unending, echoes of fury. Shard flattened his ears, crouching down despite himself and pressing himself to the nearest warm lioness, who did not pull away, but offered a reassuring purr.

The gloom of the gorge exploded into five worming, shrieking forms, each ten times the size of a gryfon.

The largest swept up high into the air. Shard caught his breath, his talons spread and clenching against the ground, tail whipping to either side as he fought to control his terror and comprehend the monsters he saw.

A head at least the size of Shard's body, reptilian and wedge-shaped and crowned with a thick, sweeping crest of horns. The long, thick neck broadened into a body as stout and muscled as a boar, with a serpent's sinewy grace, forepaws and hind legs tucked up for flight. The forepaws clenched against a deep chest, each boasting four thick, curving talons like an enormous cat.

Something niggled at Shard at the sight of those claws. Then his gaze caught movement and the thought fell away as the creature's tail swept out like a serpent tail. It ended in a sharp spade.

Veined wings blocked the moon. Membrane that stretched taut across the wings turned the white moonlight to muddy brown and green. As the monster opened its jaws to scream again, Shard beheld rows of shark-like fangs.

That was the beast that stalked his dreams, the beast he had seen burst through the snow in his nightmare. The monsters that screamed in the night.

The four others flew up to join the first, gazes casting around the ground below them. Shard hunched lower among the lionesses.

"Do…" his chest clasped tight as if he were underwater and he struggled for words. "Do they fly during the day?"

"Never," said Ajia. "They seem to fear Tyr's light."

"Or perhaps they're too ugly to face the light," offered another huntress, trying to make Shard laugh. Shard could only make a soft sound of acknowledgement, still struggling for breath.

They only flew at night. They only screamed their hatred into the dark. As Ajia said, they lived only to drive terror into the hearts of other creatures.

So this was Sverin's nightmare.

Shard thought of Kjorn's great-grandfather and the glorious tales of his war and his victory and his gold. Then he thought of Per the Red fleeing his own homeland. He thought of Sverin's fear of the dark, his tyranny of the Silver Isles, and the mighty aerie of the Winderost gryfons brought low each night the sun went down.

And last, there in night, Shard understood that an epic war and great treasures of gold were not Kajar's legacy at all.

"We should leave now," Ajia said calmly, and Shard's gaze darted up to see that one of the creatures had spotted them, or at least turned attention their way. They must have the vision of eagles, or owls, to see in the dark. As one, the lionesses turned and walked calmly away, as if they only searched for prey. They shouldered Shard into their center.

"Be calm, gryfon prince," Ajia's low voice was the only thing connecting Shard to his body. He felt the monsters' stares at his back, felt the heat of their hatred. The Nameless, animal part of him screamed in every muscle to flee, to fly, but that would bring him a swift death, and the lionesses with him.

"They don't care for lion kind," said the other who'd tried to make him laugh. "Think of your name. Think only of things you love, don't let them frighten you into darkness."

Shard took slow, gulping breaths, grasping to follow her suggestion. His name. Son-of-Sigrun. No, Baldr. Son of Ragna, the white Widow Queen. He scrambled for all those who loved him, those he loved, and walked as if he were only another lion on the hunt. He thought of pronghorn deer and grass and the scent of frost in the air.

Then he was swimming. They'd reached the river.

The roars faded behind them. Shard fell gasping on the opposite bank of the river and Ajia nuzzled his neck with a motherly growl. "Stand up. Walk."

He dragged himself up and followed. Soon it was easier to breathe, the animal fear slipped back like a wave and he felt like himself.

Ajia stopped him and with surprise Shard recognized the First Plains again. "They haven't followed this far. We must leave you now and hunt. You are safe to fly to the Dawn Spire, and you should. The dawn comes." She considered him for a moment, then tilted her head. "Know this, Star-sent. If you choose to fight the enemy, we will stand by you if you ask."

As they slipped away Shard bid a quiet farewell, thanking them again, promising to do what he could for the Winderost. He blinked slowly. Dawn. It had been just after midnight when they found the dragons. They had walked hours again and he, so wrapped in fear, hadn't noticed.

As he took to the sky, muscles tight and heart fearful, he searched the horizon like a nervous sparrow. The dragons, as they must be, were nowhere in sight, and faint gold shone in the dawnward sky.

His mind turned over and over the thought of the dragons' blunt, powerful forepaws. Something bothered him about the thick, sharp claws beyond their impressive danger. Something. Something was missing, something wasn't right.

He landed a distance off from the Dawn Spire and slipped past the sentries by way of the creek, making it look as if he'd gone out for a morning drink of water.

When he at last crawled back into his den, Stigr was waiting for him.

"Well," said the black warrior, face hard with anger. "Since you couldn't be bothered to take me along wherever you've been, maybe you'll be good enough to tell me the tale."

28
A Gryfon Mother's Lament

Sigrun huddled in her cave with as many pregnant females as could fit, rubbing the little fresh meat available with herbs to calm and warm them.

We could be fat and sleeping if the king let us fish, she thought bitterly, and perked her ears toward the crashing of the sea.

Ragna remained stubbornly with the pride, and was at that moment crooning a lullaby to the youngest of the bunch, Einarr's mate Astri, who quivered with fear and cold. Einarr and three others had been gone for three days, hunting.

The sound of male voices and calls turned every female face hopefully toward the entrance. It was a long, tense, cold wait. Then males streamed in and out with small offerings. Rabbit, a fox, half a deer carcass. Sigrun supposed the males had been unable to keep from eating some themselves. No one could blame them, and she saw shame on one young male face when he presented his own mate with the pathetic offering of half a rabbit. He left, his face dark with determination to control his hunger next time.

Sigrun watched Ragna's face as each of the males left their pitiful bounty. Her expression was cold, unforgiving, and growing angry, but Sigrun knew she wasn't angry at the young males. It was Sverin. Always Sverin.

If only we could fish the sea, Sigrun thought vaguely, as if it were a distant, unattainable dream, as if her talons had never touched saltwater. Next to Ragna, young Astri's pretty, delicate face suddenly lit with the light of a thousand stars and Sigrun swiveled to see Einarr dragging in a large, strange carcass, with the help of two other sturdy males.

"What is *that,*" demanded Kenna. She stood near Astri, and Sigrun wondered idly if the meek little female and the brash one might make good wingsisters. Sometimes it was good to have a close friend who evened out one's weaknesses. Kenna had somewhat adopted the younger gryfess, chiding her for being too quiet, while Astri, when she got her nerve up, could sometimes soften Kenna's edges.

"Sea lion," grunted Einarr's friend.

"Where did you get it?" Kenna eyed the large carcass warily, but with a raw, hungry edge.

"We flew to the starward edge of the Sun Isle," Einarr said. "Beyond the mountains to the shore. There's a colony there, but they'll move after this we think. Share it," he said gently to Astri, tilting his head to indicate Kenna and the other, wide-eyed females. "There's plenty."

Sigrun had seen Einarr change slowly over the autumn and winter. Once timid and soft-spoken, he had become a leader among the hunting males. Still soft spoken, he usually said correct and wise things, and his face was set with a firmness and strange, distant quiet. Sigrun wasn't sure how faithfully Einarr prayed, but his demeanor as the winter grew darker reminded her of fervent followers of the distant god Tyr, reminded her of a gryfon who sees not the night, but the gleam of stars or the distant dawn.

Of all the gryfons in the pride, she saw in him the light of hope. She couldn't help but wonder at its source. Ragna had the same look about her, but Sigrun knew that was because of Ragna's faith in Shard's return. She didn't know what lit Einarr's hope, but whenever he came, it filled the den.

Kenna sniffed and looked as if she might refuse—but everyone in the cave knew that Halvden would bring her no meat. He hunted wolves.

Little white Astri wriggled out from under Ragna's wing and cuddled up to Einarr as if the meat wasn't there. Slowly, the other males greeted their mates but then squeezed out of the den again. It was too crowded, and they had to hunt more before the Long Night, which stalked ever closer. In the days of darkness, there would be no flying, no hunting. Einarr lingered a moment, dipping his head to preen at Astri's ears.

"Eat," he whispered.

She nipped at him but turned to fall on the sea lion carcass. Kenna joined after with a grudging word of thanks, and others, even Ragna at Einarr's quiet encouragement. All of them were keenly aware of the scent of blood and seawater—but surely even Sverin wouldn't grudge a hunting male keeping his mate alive by whatever means necessary.

After another look around, Sigrun was certain no one in the den would be telling Sverin of the sea lion, anyway, or the smell of salt water. She caught Einarr's gaze and he raised his head, shrugging one wing, as if he couldn't have cared less for the king's new law.

It didn't take the pregnant females long to strip the carcass and begin gnawing on the bones. Sigrun didn't even have time to try to salvage the pelt. They ate it all.

Ragna helped her clean the blood while the females, at last feeling full, settled into their usual corners. The lingering scent of seawater put several of them on edge, the thought that Einarr had hunted near the forbidden shore. All the edicts and rules drifted silently around the den.

"The trouble," Kenna said to no one in particular and yet to everyone, "is that the king isn't mad. We do have traitors among us."

"Quiet," whispered another, ears flat. Sigrun lifted her head, glancing to Ragna.

"Let her speak," said Ragna, still and white as the gray and white world outside. "But know this. A traitor is only a matter of the current king."

Soft hissing greeted that statement. Kenna, particularly, was unsympathetic to Ragna's ideas. Unrest grew against the Vanir, and Sigrun feared Ragna's plans would turn against her in the end. But she remained still and calm, and presented an alternative to fearful, ranting Sverin. Still, Sigrun couldn't leave her wingsister to fly this wind alone. She stood, speaking quietly to all of them.

"All we did, we did to save the life of Ragna's son." Sigrun stared hard at the young faces in front of her. "All of you carry lives in your bellies now, sons, daughters, your own legacy, the kit of your chosen mates. Would you have done less?"

In the silence they all heard wind moaning along the rocks, and the fierce crash of freezing waves far below.

"Well Shard is dead now," Kenna snipped, though she wouldn't meet Sigrun's eyes again. "Was it worth it?"

"Oh, yes," whispered Ragna, and some of the softer females grew looks of sympathy. Violet Kenna lashed her tail and lowered her head in disgust. Sigrun happened to glance at Einarr, and he was staring hard outside the den, as if he might see something fly in from the sea.

A few stood to help Ragna and Sigrun finish cleaning the den of bones and blood, as if to say that they weren't on Kenna's side, though none pledged undying allegiance to Ragna either.

Once the den was clean and all settled in for a nap, Einarr, who had remained silent during Kenna's accusation, turned to go.

"Einarr stay," Astri whispered. "My mate, please."

"It'll be dark soon, we won't be able to hunt."

"Stay," Sigrun said quietly, watching Astri's desperate face. There were some medicines not even the greatest healer could deliver without help. Astri needed love. "For a few moments more."

Einarr looked askance, but he wouldn't argue with a healer.

"Sing us a song." Everyone turned to stare at Ragna. She sat pale and quiet at the back of the cave, demure, as if she knew she'd stepped a talon too far the last time she spoke. "Einarr," she clarified, her gaze quiet and admiring on the young gryfon. "You have a fine voice. Do you know any appropriate winter songs?"

For a moment his silence was filled with the heartbeats of the gryfesses in front of him, Ragna's quiet request hovering in the air. He glanced to Sigrun and she inclined her head just slightly. Some things were more important than food. He walked back to Astri and sat, ears slipping back into a shy expression Sigrun hadn't seen since the summer.

"A song my mother sang me…" It remained quiet and he hesitated. His mother was full-blooded Aesir, distant kin to Sverin, a gryfess Sigrun rarely spoke to, a gryfess who had lost her Vanir mate and her oldest son to exile. Einarr glanced to Astri.

"Will you help me? It's really for a female to sing."

She looked pleased and pushed herself up to sit, recognition lighting her eyes. Einarr nodded and turned to his audience. "Then, I sing you the Gryfon Mother's Lament."

Chill wind dusted into the cave and Sigrun smelled the dampness of snow. Then music was there as Einarr warmed his voice into the first notes. Sigrun nearly melted. She had never heard Einarr in full song, only spoken tales, and his clear, gentle speaking voice became like lark song.

> *"Eyes wide, heart full*
> *Stand my nestling, tall and proud*
> *Stand my nestling tall and proud."*

Astri sang the refrain with him, the song meant to show the hard difference between what a proud gryfon mother would say to her kit, and what she felt on the inside.

> *"Stay my young one*
> *Stay with me*
> *The world is dark and harsh and bleak*
> *Don't fly, don't fight, just let it be*
> *And stay, young one, with me."*

Einarr sang the next verses and each time Astri joined him for the chorus, and Sigrun found herself yearning to sing along, yearning to say it to all the young warriors, to Caj, even to Sverin if he would only relent, to keep them all safe in her wings and never speak again of war.

> *"Wings wide, heart free*
> *Fly my fledgling, far from me*
> *Fly my fledgling, far from me.*
> *Claws wide, heart cold*
> *Fight, my warrior, fierce and bold*
> *Fight, my warrior, fierce and bold."*

Together Einarr and Astri sang the refrain, their voices dipping in a chilling harmony, her voice hopeful, his determined but grim, the whole chorus a mixture of love and fear.

The last verse began and Sigrun's chest tightened, for she knew it.

> *"Eyes closed, heart still*
> *Rest my young one…"*

All the gryfesses in the den leaned forward, but the two didn't finish singing. Silence trickled in. Sigrun blinked out of her listening trance and looked up to see Einarr staring at the entrance of the den. Sigrun turned.

So wrapped in the song, none of them had heard a gryfon flying through the snow, landing, standing there and watching for who knew how long. Sigrun's heart, which had seemed to pause to listen started up again, hard and nervous.

"In Tyr's bright hills." Caj's low, rough voice touched the back of the cave. He stepped forward, watching Einarr and Astri expectantly. "Rest, my young one…"

"In Tyr's bright hills," Einarr finished, raising his head.

Sigrun gazed at her mate.

"I've heard it's ill luck to leave a song unfinished," Caj explained to the staring females. They watched him like a riddle, as if something they knew for certain had become uncertain. He stood too wiry thin those days, watching over the Guard, over Sverin, and Sigrun herself. Finally the females offered quiet respect, breaking their trance, though many feared him as much as they feared the king. He was the king's wingbrother, after all, and supported him. Sigrun pushed forward through the females and shoved her face in the feathers of Caj's neck.

"My mate."

"The king calls a meeting."

"But it's so cold," whispered Astri.

Caj didn't look at any of them. "Anyone who doesn't attend will be considered—"

"We know," Kenna saved him the trouble of saying "traitors" yet again. The King's Guard and Sverin himself threw down the word at the slightest provocation as the days grew shorter. Kenna looked around to the others and, as if she instructed them, added, "And we will be proud to listen to the king's words." She walked to the entrance, slipping past Caj, gave the others a challenging look, and shoved off to fly crookedly up and out of sight.

Ragna walked to the entrance. "I'll help anyone who doesn't feel up to flying."

"So will I," said Thyra. "Let's go."

They stood, chirruping wearily, and followed. Ragna paused, catching Sigrun's gaze over Caj's shoulder. Sigrun inclined her head just slightly, to show that she still supported Ragna.

"It was good of you to sing for them," Caj murmured to Einarr as he passed, just as if he'd fought an admirable spar. Einarr paused in surprise, then continued out with Astri, to help her climb the cliff.

When all had gone and her large den felt unnaturally empty, Sigrun lowered her head and said again, "My mate."

"My mate," Caj breathed, relieved to be alone with her. In her mind, Sigrun couldn't help but feel like a traitor to him, thinking of Ragna and her talk of traitors. Shard lived, and as far as she knew, he planned to return, but in what way she couldn't fathom. The last time she'd seen Shard he had been among two exiles who promised to seek out other Vanir and return. Sigrun couldn't say what would happen to those who served Sverin now, if Shard managed to wrest the Silver Isles away from him.

Caj had always stood by Sigrun's side, and so she would stand by him. Whatever happened she would remind Shard, if she had to, that Caj had also been instrumental in saving his life so many years ago.

"Eat something before we go," she whispered. "It will take a while for the females to climb, and everyone to gather."

Usually he argued. That afternoon, he lay obediently on his belly and perked his ears. Sigrun stepped to the back of her den and clawed a flat rock away from the wall to reveal a deep, dark cubby carved into the rock. Usually it lay empty, one of many storage spots in her den. Sigrun had stuffed it full over the fall.

"What is that?"

"Protection against winter," Sigrun said, heart beginning to pound. *He would have found it eventually.* It was best to show him while they were alone. "Our store for the Long Night. And ration for the pregnant females. How do you think we've been keeping them healthy, with this poor hunting?"

Caj stood, wings opening. Sigrun brought him a long, dry strip of venison and he looked at it as if were a writhing serpent. Slowly, he bent his head to tear a bite, swallowed, and rasped.

"*Salt?* Are you mad? Everything I do is to protect you and you flaunt Vanir ways in my face? In the king's face?"

"Vanir ways?" Sigrun crouched, ears flat. She'd known he would react this way, but it still broke her heart to fight her chosen, her mate, her protector. "You told me yourself that in the greatland the pride would preserve winter meat with salt!"

"Salt from the earth," Caj whispered. Then he slapped the meat back to her. "You've used salt from the sea! Sverin will…" His eyes had pinpointed like a savage eagle, scarcely believing what he saw.

"What?" Sigrun demanded. "What will he do to me, for keeping the son of his son alive in Thyra's belly? For keeping his pride fed and alive through winter? I wasn't fishing. I wasn't even in the water. How will he know the difference between salt from the earth and sea when he can't even tell the difference between his enemies and his friends?"

"He sees you." Caj lashed paced away. "He isn't half as mad as everyone whispers, and you know that. He has been betrayed. His own son barely heeds him. The wolves mock us from underground."

"It was for our daughter," Sigrun said. "For all of us."

"When have you done this? The sentries see everything."

Sigrun was silent. Caj's eyes widened, he looked at the cave entrance, then her face again.

"At *night*? You've gone out at night and down to the shore? Why didn't I know? Why didn't I wake when..." He looked breathless, Sigrun fought the urge to cower. "You've put sleep on me somehow. Some herb. Something in my food. I can't eat my own food, now? Sigrun, where am I to stand, with you and Ragna scheming behind my back?"

Sigrun's voice cracked. "I *scheme* to keep this pride alive through winter. We will eat salted meat or we will starve."

They stood, feathers on end, tails lashing.

Sigrun met Caj's pale gold eyes and saw their whole history–the moments after the Conquering when she knew he would make the gentlest mate of all the Aesir, the moment when she saw the nobility in him. The moment she began to love him, and chose to fly with him always. The moments he spent teaching their daughter and the son he'd tried to raise as his own.

In that heartbeat, Sigrun ached for nothing more than to go to ground with him and wait for one king or another to rise and rule, to live peacefully with her mate. That was all.

"I'll rub the meat with herbs," she whispered. "Heavy enough that he won't taste, that you can tell him it was those that preserved—"

"More lies," Caj rumbled. *Noble Caj*, had been his nickname.

"Only until spring."

"What happens in spring?" He lifted his ears, eyes narrowing in suspicion.

Sigrun glanced away, closing her wings tightly. Spring was when Dagr and Maja had vowed to return to Shard, bringing whatever Vanir they could gather.

"In spring," she began again, trying to smooth the irritation from her voice, trying to think what to say. Then, for the first time in their history, she lied to Caj.

"When we can hunt again. After the whelping. When we can have fresh meat."

Caj stared at her. Sigrun stared back, trying to discern in his face if he knew she was lying, and if it mattered. If he would still protect her.

"Let's go," he said, turning his back. "Sverin will be looking for us at the gathering."

"Please eat," Sigrun asked. "I've made a special batch too, with sleeping herbs, to soothe Sverin during the Long Night. I know how it haunts him."

Caj hesitated, glancing back. "Oh, the same herbs you gave me?"

He huffed in disgust and jumped out of the den into the whirling, freezing winds.

Sigrun stared at the yawning mouth of her den. Exhaustion clawed her heart. She looked at the piece of meat on the stone floor and for the first time, the sight of it filled her with shame.

I should have told him.

Caj barely heard Sverin's words during the meet. More rules, stricter and particularly harsh against the Vanir. He could hardly argue the points, still seething over Sigrun's deception.

He sat still on one of the lower levels of the king's rocks, trying to lock his muscles against shivering. The gray sky pressed low and dampness clung to the wind.

With a quiet, creeping dread, Caj watched as snow at last began to fall.

The first snow of the winter punctuated Sverin's warnings about the night, the sea, the cold, the importance of keeping Tyr in their hearts.

Eyes darted away from the king to the snowflakes that grew thicker and faster by the moment. At last Sverin drew to a close, bidding the hunters good luck, and those tracking wolves all haste and safety. By the time those gathered had stood and stretched their cramped muscles, a blanket of white covered the ground.

Caj stood, shook snow from his feathers and climbed up to the top of the rocks to meet Sverin.

"Only another moon until the Long Night, Sire." He drew a slow breath as Sverin looked at him. Weighing truths, weighing his honor against his friendship, his mate, his own heart, he quickly chose a side, as he had the last ten years. "Sigrun has prepared special meats, preserved with salt from…flats on the Crow Wing Isle. Some are rubbed with herbs to aid sleep, if you—"

"No." Sverin stood like a red stone in the falling snow, watching every gryfon stand and walk, or fly, watching Kjorn and Einarr gather their hunters, and Halvden and the Guard taunt them, lightly under the king's eye, before setting out. "I will remain awake for the Long Night."

"If you change your mind—"

"Is there a reason I should sleep, brother?" Sverin eyed him, tail twitching.

Caj dipped his head. "Whatever you wish, of course. But I know the dark troubles you. I know…Elena's memory troubles you."

It was a risk to say her name, but Caj had to draw attention from the salted meat. Sverin shut his eyes at the name and a low growl built in his throat. "*They* stole her from me. The widow witch convinced her she could fly as the Vanir do, tempted her to the sea, and she died for it."

"Exile her," Caj growled, knowing it was a betrayal to Sigrun, but he also saw Sverin's pain, and it would solve many problems. With no Ragna, Sigrun's heart would not be so split. "Be rid of Ragna for good. She has no place."

"Exile your own mate's wingsister? Don't think I don't know." Sverin looked away from Caj, found Kjorn among the departing hunters and watched as the golden prince soared starward with Einarr and the others. "Did you know that Shard wasn't Sigrun's kit, when you mated?"

Caj's voice froze, and only after a moment was he able to answer, whispering, "Yes. I knew."

Sverin barked a cool laugh. "Don't worry. I guessed that you knew. I just wanted to see if you would tell me the truth, this time."

"Forgive me." Caj hunched down, mantling, bowed his head. "My wingbrother, my king. I didn't know what your father would do. Shard was only a kit. There'd been so much death already. I planned to raise him as my own."

"You failed." Sverin moved at last, ruffling snowflakes from his wings and pacing away. Slowly Caj raised his head. "The exile Stigr took him out from under you. The wolves. The Vanir. His father's ghost. Then he tried to kill me. Do you mourn his death?"

Caj could barely answer, but Sverin would've sensed a lie. "I… mourned losing him."

"Hm." The Red King's tail swung back and forth. "Go, lead the wolf hunt."

Caj stood straight again, surprised at the quick dismissal. He murmured farewell and jumped from the rock into the cold air.

Would I have mourned Shard's death? He remembered the seconds, the awful seconds of seeing Shard and Sverin falling together toward the waves. He couldn't have said then, and couldn't bear to think now, whose death he feared the most.

Then he narrowed his eyes, realizing something else. Sverin had completely diverted him from the question of exiling Ragna.

I've hidden things from you, Brother, it's true, Caj thought grimly. *But what are you hiding from me?*

He peered down and back toward the king's rocks. Sverin had walked to the edge and stood staring out at the sea, as the snow fell down and tried to mask his red feathers with white.

29
A Painted Wolf Speaks

After Shard told Stigr all that he'd seen with the lions, the old warrior advised him to silence. He reclined on the floor of Shard's den, looking grim, while Shard paced and told the tale. Morning light suffused the air and Shard knew they'd both be late to their posts if they didn't leave soon. His limbs quivered and threatened to collapse from exhaustion.

Stigr's tail dusted the floor. "I'm sure if King Orn gets word of your little night flight, that will be the end of the Dawn Spire for us. If you go again, I'm coming with you. Even if it means I have to stay in your den to make sure you don't sneak out again."

Shard resisted the urge to lower his head, chagrined. "I had to go."

Stigr shook his head, ears slipping back. "I came here to help you. To protect you. How can I do either if you won't tell me your plans? Even Baldr let me advise him."

"I know. If I leave again, I'll tell you."

"Fine." He stood and stretched, sliding his talons across the dirt floor. "Shall I tell Brynja you're ill?"

"No." Shard yawned, then shook himself. "I can hunt."

Stigr made a gruff sound and trotted out of the cave. Shard followed. He had a feeling Brynja wouldn't notice his condition, one way or the other.

And she didn't. He hunted that day, and the next and next, watching the full moon wane. He had to go out again, but not to the Outlands.

He wanted to see what the painted wolves knew of the enemy, if they could tell him more to settle the nagging questions he couldn't put name to. He pictured the beasts over and over again soaring up out of the black canyon, their great jaws full of teeth, the powerful wings, the thick, curving talons on the end of blunt forepaws.

On the night of the talon moon, Shard planned to sneak out again and seek the painted wolves. He told Stigr, and the warrior was waiting for him when Shard slunk out just before midnight.

"Not leaving me again," he growled. Shard lifted his wings in assent, and showed Stigr the path to sneak out of the Dawn Spire.

Feathery clouds drifted high above, masking stars and the weak moonlight. Between them, Shard and Stigr had enough experience with the painted wolves to know their hunting routes and track them through the night. Farther starward than the First Plains, back toward the Dawn Reach where Shard had first arrived.

They flew low, in silence, Stigr just behind Shard. Distantly, dragon roars cracked the night. Though they grew farther away the longer Shard and Stigr flew, instinct chilled Shard into landing, walking, when they reached painted wolf grounds. He kept his breath slow and didn't speak to Stigr, who landed and walked beside him without question, as if he were only Shard's shadow.

The scent of wolf came to them on a rising wind. Together, they turned to follow it across the broken, grassy hills.

Shard's ears twitched, seeking the sound of warbling barks in the night. No sounds came. The dogs were hunting. Shard crept forward, trying to determine how many and how far. He knew he shouldn't plunge in while they hunted, that they'd think he was trying to steal their kill. He loped forward after determining their direction, ears perked, head lifted to scent the wind. There was no trace of lion there, or dragon.

"The kill," Stigr said quietly, and Shard halted. Wind brushed grass against his hindquarters and he smelled blood. The wolves had brought down prey, and their triumphant growls and warbles filled the night.

He and Stigr remained where they were, resting and waiting for the wolves to feed.

Wind sang by. The growls died down.

"Enough," Shard said. He raised his head loosed his imitation of a wolf howl.

The last of the happy snarling and cavorting ahead of them fell dead.

Shard flicked his tail, and howled again. *"I'm here, earth brothers,"* the low song proclaimed through the night, "*no threat, earth sisters.*"

"Well done," Stigr murmured, but didn't raise his voice with Shard's.

Rough paws scuffed through the grass. The wind was wrong to bring the dogs Shard's scent.

"Who hunts here?"

A female voice. She spoke in the low, growling language of the earth. A gryfon who wasn't listening would hear only witless noise.

"I am Shard. Son-of-Baldr. Prince of the Silver Isles in the starward sea. I've come to meet you in fairer winds than we have before. This is my uncle, Stigr, son-of-Ragr."

Words disintegrated into snarls. Shard made out their faint outlines in the dark and tried to get a count. They would see him clearly now and know he was a gryfon.

"You trespass here!"

The female circled around him, sniffing, trying to gain a scent. Shard stood still, as a wolf would, to let her. Stigr likewise stood still, though tilted his head to keep her in his field of vision. If they had to, they could fly.

At least she trotted back, baring her teeth. "This plain marks the border of gryfon claim."

Shard mantled. "Then we ask your leave to stay and speak with you."

Stigr inclined his head and added, "Do you lead this pack, great huntress?"

She stopped in front of Stigr. "Do you know why I lead this pack?"

"No." Stigr watched her, and Shard tensed, sensing the pack moving around them.

"Gryfon filth killed my mate. My hunter, Kuruk."

Angry yips and howls met her declaration. Wind drove against them with the scent of icy rain. The moonlight dimmed but Shard caught the glint of her eyes.

"He went to speak with them as you speak to me now, but they wouldn't hear him." Her teeth gleamed through the dark. "He was a hopeful fool. What do you want?"

Shard answered. "Only to speak with you. To ask you about the dark creatures who terrorize the Winderost. I'm not from this land."

"That much I can see."

"Will you tell me your name?"

She dipped her head and paced, gnashing her teeth once, then stuck her nose near Shard's face. He had seen Catori do this to the wolf cubs, to establish her dominance over them. Shard moved his head away and lifted his wings, respectful, but not accepting her dominance. She bared her teeth, first to Stigr, who met her gaze, head tilted respectfully, then Shard.

"You see me as your equal?"

"If not my better," Shard said quietly. "You know this land and hunt at night when the dragons fly. That makes you braver than any gryfon in Orn's pride."

Wild, surprised laughter and howling met his words. She leaned in to sniff his wings, then raised her head. "I am Nitara. I lead this pack now with my brother, Ilesh. He hunts tonight by the Little Serpent River in the canyons that gryfons call the Voldsom."

Shard dipped his head. "Thank you. May I ask you questions?"

"Ask me questions? What must a gryfon learn from a wolf?" She studied him, head cocked, and licked her muzzle thoughtfully. "You're strange."

"I know."

"He gets it from me," Stigr said, and she loosed a curious *yawr* sound, as if she gnawed on a laugh.

"You both smell strange." She looked from Stigr to Shard. "You smell of winter and the sea, like the gryfons of the Vanheim Shores."

Stigr looked interested at the mention of that, but only shrugged his wings. "We're from a bit farther away."

Shard took a chance. "Ajia the Swiftest said I am the Star-sent. I followed the starfire here, and I'll help you rid the Winderost of the Enemy, if you help me."

Nitara held still, then tossed her head. Shard caught the glint of white around her eyes. "We do not share signs with the hunting cats of the First Plains."

"But you know Ajia."

"We arrange our hunting borders." Again she showed Shard her teeth, as if years of anger with gryfons had to release in snarling at him. "We can meet and talk, as gryfons will never meet and talk. I talk with lions, with eagles. I would talk with dragons if I thought they could hear, but they…"

"All that's left in them is hate," Shard whispered. She *whuffed* in agreement. The scent of rain grew stronger and the wind icy cold. They had to speak fast.

"How would you get rid of them? They hear nothing. They say nothing. They are witless and dead in the heart. They're too large to fight."

Shard had heard it said so often from one creature that another creature was witless, Nameless, without reason or honor—yet he'd found that the opposite was usually true.

Could it be so, for the dragons of the Winderost?

Shard wondered, with a shock, if that could be the true meaning he was supposed to gather from the Summer King song Ragna had sung. It claimed such a king would speak to all.

Am I meant to speak even to these dragons?

"We don't know how, yet," Stigr said, when Shard failed to answer Nitara.

Shard shook off his thoughts, apologizing. "But we will. Ajia said she would stand with me, if I chose to fight."

Nitara studied him. "And the gryfon pride?"

"I don't know yet," Shard said. "Tell me all you know of the dragons."

Like him, Nitara was aware of the gathering storm, and she spoke quickly. "All we know is that they do not belong here. No dragon was born in the Winderost. They came after Kajar's war, they came seeking gold. Then the cursed clans fled, and the dragons didn't follow them over the sea."

"But they might," Shard whispered, fear tingling up his chest. "If they regain their wit and understand that the son of Kajar left."

"What do you mean, cursed clan?" Stigr asked. Icy drops of rain splattered against their backs and Shard heard the greater part of the storm rumbling toward them over the plains.

"The cursed clan," Nitara repeated. Dark murmurs coursed through the wolf pack who milled around them. "Those who followed Kajar to the dragon land. Those who made war and who stole dragon gold. Cursed," she bared her fangs around the word, "as my dam'a taught me, their feathers burned bright, we know not how. Like adders, their bright feathers warn of their poisonous natures."

"But Sverin never fought dragons, nor Per before him," Stigr said.

"Or Kjorn," Shard said.

Nitara huffed and shook herself as heavier rain fell. "It's as my dam'a told. They are cursed, blighted, by the deeds of their forebears."

Before Shard or Stigr could respond, the rain struck. Frosty wind lashed them and curtains of sleet battered down. Nitara yelped and wheeled about.

"Away, away, my pack! Strange gryfons, strange allies, come to shelter. Shelter with us, and we will talk more."

Neither of them questioned. They turned and ran like fellow wolves in the rain, toward a rock outcropping where they could shelter together.

There Nitara told them the history that she knew. Kajar had seen the starfire as a young initiate, Shard's age, and led the young warrior heirs of all the Winderost clans to the realm of the dragons. They made war, took spoils of gold and gems, and returned to the Winderost.

Then the dragons came.

Shard tried to reconcile what she told and what he had seen of the dragons. Somehow, they didn't match. Nitara's story was missing something critical, but he didn't want to question and insult her and break their new, tenuous truce. Every piece of information would help.

"They fought over gold," Nitara said. "Per and the others tried to keep the gryfon clans together, but we watched as they splintered, returned to their homelands." Freezing sleet poured around their rock shelter, and Shard huddled close to Stigr. The musky, rich scent of the painted wolves was almost comforting, for it reminded him of Ahanu and Catori. "And then the dragons came, and the gryfons could not fight them."

"So Per and Sverin fled," Stigr said, fluffing his feathers. "I knew it all along. The cowards fled their own land, left them to the dragons, and came to wreak havoc on our home instead."

"This is what we know," Nitara agreed.

Stigr broke into grim laughter. Shard watched him, knowing it filled his uncle with dark glee to hear that everything he believed about the Aesir was true.

An ache began behind Shard's ears, crawling forward. It seemed too simple. Something was missing, something was not right. Nitara couldn't know everything that happened, and possibly Brynja and the others didn't even know. There was no one left alive who had fought the dragon war, no one who knew the truth. If Sverin and Caj and the Aesir of the Silver Isles actually knew the truth, then Shard now suspected they covered it with tales of glory and war.

"If the dragons hated Per," he said slowly, "Why didn't they follow him to the Silver Isles? Maybe he actually hoped to draw them away."

Stigr's gaze slid to him, but he offered no guess.

Nitara chuckled. "A question I'm sure the gryfons of the Dawn Spire ask every day."

"Cowards," Stigr spat again. "Thieves and cowards, I knew it. They flee one fight and then declare themselves king of a different land."

Shard remained quiet. Stigr had not seen the dragons in the night. Shard couldn't say if he would've stayed to fight.

Stigr ruffled his feathers. "Maybe the dragons fear the sea."

"Maybe," Shard said doubtfully. He thought of Ajia. "Or maybe they don't care about the gold or Per anymore, or who started it. Maybe nothing is left for them but to hate."

Nitara whined, low and soft. "Maybe this is true, Star-sent. Maybe… if so, then our future is dark indeed."

Beside him, Stigr grumbled, then shuddered, and they said nothing more.

They sheltered the rest of the night with the wolves and flew back only when gray dawn touched the sky. Overnight the falling sleet softened to slushy snow. Frost and drifts of white pocked the Winderost. Shard and Stigr slipped undetected back to their dens, slept a half mark and rose again to start their days.

They didn't fly at night again. Stigr was ready to leave, Shard could tell, thinking that the mystery of the Aesir was solved. But Shard still had questions, even if he couldn't articulate some of them. He still needed to earn King Orn's esteem so that he could roam freely as a true member of the Dawn Spire pride. He needed to find the mountain from his vision.

Though Brynja still spoke to Shard with only courtesy, as if she were avoiding forming deep friendship with him, he still enjoyed his days hunting. Dagny assured him the Wild Hunt, their mid-winter celebration, would be his chance for initiation. He need wait only a little longer.

Part of him was happy for the days to stretch out, to know that every morning he got to wake and fly with the same gryfess who filled his dreams.

Soon he would be initiated, he could fly freely, fulfill his vision and answer his questions. Shard woke each day with purpose and a strong place in the pride. He fell to sleep each night thinking of his accomplishments. He'd rarely felt so proud in the Silver Isles, where his only true accomplishment was being Kjorn's wingbrother, and a botched attempt at running Sverin's colony on Star Island.

In the Winderost he had a warm, fine nest of his own, more positive acclaim and curiosity from the gryfons of the Dawn spire and even grudging respect from Asvander.

It was as things in the Winderost improved that Shard's dreams began to change.

30
The King of Star Island

Snow flurried through the great pine forest of the Star Isle, blurring Kjorn's vision, deadening the scent of any creatures that might have passed by. The only advantage they gained was spying fresh tracks in the white powder. Kjorn, Einarr and the rest of their band had split to each follow a game trail through the woods, prepared to summon others if they detected a fresh scent. They mimicked bird calls—an invention of Shard's, that summer past.

Kjorn trotted through the woods almost like a wolf, head bent as he stared along the game trail, wings tensed and ready if a threat arose. The worried faces of his pride, his father's warnings about the Long Night, the sea, and all else faded in the face of the hunt. He had found, over the last weeks, that he enjoyed his time on the Star Isle, losing himself in the woods, in the chase and the kill. He wondered if it would be un-kingly if he continued hunting once Thyra whelped.

Not that it matters yet.

The deer trail before him split and he paused, looking up, tail twitching. Tall cedars ringed around him, the sweet scent of moldering fern filtered from under the new snow. Under that, cold wet earth. And deer. He turned his head, studying the paths for freshness. Then he spied the distinct, round outline of a wolf print in the snow.

A snarl built in his throat. *How it would ease Father's mind before the Long Night if he had a new wolf pelt!*

It wouldn't do to plunge ahead alone. It could be a trap. Kjorn lifted his head and loosed his chosen call—the mimic of a pine jay—then clawed a distinct mark in the nearest cedar trunk. He was confident Einarr would understand that he'd turned off to track the wolves. The others had ranged far, but with the light, fresh snow, they would easily be able to follow him. He called again, a quick *she-ay she-ay* that carried through the woods to his hunting band, and loped down the wolf print trail.

Chuckling at the thought of Halvden's face when he saw Kjorn and the other hunters hauling wolf carcasses, Kjorn slipped quickly through the woods. Snow slacked in the heavier undergrowth and he lost the trail in places, but the scent grew strong enough to follow.

Maybe I should find Caj...he dismissed the thought. The wolves were elusive. If he left the trail now, they would likely cover it, or the snow eventually would, and he would miss the chance.

Rowan mingled with the cedar and a twinge of familiarity slowed Kjorn's steps. He knew the place, though he had seen it in spring and now winter pied it white and brown with snow. He emerged from the woods into a clearing and shivered against the sudden wind. Snow pelted his face, and his throat tightened when he realized he had, indeed, been led.

This is where we killed Lapu the boar. Kjorn held very still. In the distance, a red-tailed eagle called—but he hoped it was actually Einarr mimicking, responding at last.

From the trees on the opposite side of the woods stepped a lupine form.

Kjorn's blood leaped and he raised his wings in challenge, ready to meet in battle. But he couldn't make himself move. As if in a dream, he only stared at the creature that had eluded all of them for so long. For some reason he had expected the female wolf who'd warned them of the attack on the Sun Isle that summer, who had befriended Shard, bewitched him, taken him away.

Before him stood a tall, hulking male. Black fur blended into gold and a pale chest and belly. Thick muscles roped his neck, back and shoulders under his heavy winter coat. He stood proud, ears erect, tail fluffed out behind, but he didn't bare his fangs. Wary eyes scrutinized every feather on Kjorn's head. An out-of-place movement caught Kjorn's eye, and then his breath.

A long, storm gray feather flicked against the wolf's neck, braided roughly into the thick fur behind his ear.

"Shard," Kjorn whispered. *Is that some kind of battle trophy? But I thought they were friends.* In that moment, he remembered that he'd seen the wolf before. This one had stood with the red female and a third, had not attacked the nests of the Sun Isle.

"He lives."

Kjorn shook his head. He could've sworn he'd heard words in the muted growl.

"Do you understand me, brother-prince?"

Kjorn backed a step away, hunching his wings.

"If you understand the language of the earth," the growling, rich words settled and sounded more normal as Kjorn twitched his ears forward to listen, "then we may have hope."

"You stole my brother from me and he died for it!"

The wolf tilted his head. "No. We opened his eyes, as your eyes are opening, your ears, your heart."

Kjorn's breath came harder, he panted as he battled with himself. He should be attacking, his talons soaked in wolf blood, at least, to prove to his father…*to prove what?* he thought desperately. *To prove that I think he's right and that we should annihilate the wolves and claim all the islands?*

And only in that moment, thinking that, did Kjorn realize he did not agree with Sverin.

But, the wolves had turned Shard from Kjorn. He had his own grudge to settle. He stalked forward, snarling, and a gleaming expression grew on the wolf's face.

"Are you angry from grief, brother? I know this feeling."

"I'm not your brother," Kjorn said. "I have no brother."

"What if I said that you do?"

Kjorn paused, only two leaps from the wolf now. If he lunged, took him off guard, he would stand a chance to win. The wolf stood as tall as an average gryfon, but more muscled, and Kjorn had the advantage of wings.

I could kill him. Kill him for my father. For Shard.

Yet…

"What do you mean?" Kjorn demanded.

"I have a secret." The wolf lowered his head, almost as if he bowed, though he kept his eyes level with Kjorn's. His voice dropped. "Rashard, son-of-Baldr, my friend and brother and yours, is alive and well and treating with your kin in the windward land."

Kjorn curled his talons into the mud and dead grass beneath the snow. A war of hope and then anger battled in his chest. He had to be lying. It wasn't possible that Shard not only survived, but flew to Kjorn's homeland…but such a strange lie.

"Einarr!" he shouted. He called for the others, then, in desperation, Caj and even Halvden, knowing they, too, hunted somewhere on the Star Isle.

"They're busy," the wolf said quietly. "My family leads them on a merry chase."

"You did this on purpose. You probably even made the deer trail somehow. You've turned this whole isle against us so we can't even hunt!" Kjorn crouched, stalking closer. One leap…"Who are you?"

"Ahanu," he said, not denying Kjorn's claims. "Son of the Great Hunter Helaku."

"Great Hunter?" Kjorn scoffed. "Your king? That wolf my father killed?" Confusion tempered into solid anger. This wolf had separated his hunters, herded the deer from them and driven away even the smallest of game. Now he lied about Shard, even while he wore a feather as a trophy.

"Yes," Ahanu said, his brow crinkling. His muzzle twitched, showing fang, as if he, too, struggled to control anger. "That wolf your father killed. I should have known you wouldn't...very well, son-of-Sverin. Be blind, and deaf, son of the glorious Aesir. I told my sister you wouldn't see reason. I wouldn't let her come alone. She had a message for you from Shard, but I see you don't want it."

He stretched his forelegs and bowed his head while Kjorn stood in shock. He rose, a mocking glint in his eye, and sprinted into the woods.

Anger drove caution from Kjorn's mind. He dove into the woods after Ahanu, tripping and sliding on patches of mud and snow, barely able to keep pace. The ground rose steadily and the trees fell back to reveal patches of bare rock.

Boulders scattered the area ahead, and a short cliff jutted up from the forest floor. Stacks of snow-covered rock loomed in the falling snow. Ahanu darted around the boulders and under a fallen tree. Kjorn, excited with the rush of a hunt, squeezed between the rocks and under the tree—and faced the dark entrance of a narrow hole in the ground.

He stood a moment, panting as the snow thickened to a blizzard around him. A laughing howl mocked him from deeper down the tunnel.

Anger dissolved his last shred of doubt and he gave a final jay's call into the trees before he plunged into the dark.

They'll track me, he thought, wedging himself down the narrow tunnel, his wings scraping rocks and mud. He'd forgotten Ahanu's warning, that his family led the others on another hunt. He could think only of the chase, of catching the wolf who dared to use Shard against him. *I'll kill their new king and end this, my hunters will track me and we'll rid ourselves of wolves at last.*

Kjorn followed Ahanu under the earth as a blizzard smote from above, burying his scent, burying his tracks, cloaking the entire Star Isle with white.

31
Winter Strikes the Sun Isle

Raven wings carried Shard visions of heavy snows. In the dreamland of Munin's creation, he saw visions of what happened in the Silver Isles. He called to Catori to confirm if the dreams were true, but she never came, or didn't hear. Shadows darted through his dreams, wolf or gryfon, he couldn't tell.

The days of hunting wore Shard down, for his dreams gave him no rest.

He turned restlessly at night in the warm red rock of his Winderost den and dreamed of winter in the Silver Isles.

Sverin's fear showed itself in earlier and earlier curfews. Gryfons had to be in their dens by twilight, not dark, and Sverin banned the pride from venturing at all near the sea shore.

Wolves ran tirelessly through the frosty white pine forests of the Star Isle, leaving fresh trails to drive Halvden and his wolf-hunters mad. Shard's nest-sister Thyra and her hunters grew too heavy and round with kits to hunt. Young Einarr led bands of hunting males into the woods, seeking deer that had gone to ground, then hare, then birds. Then anything. Desperate for food, they even followed boar tracks into the deep dark of Star Island, but all the animals disappeared like shadows.

As the days passed, his dreams followed the days, though what happened as he watched and what had already happened or what might yet be changed was unclear to Shard.

He begged for Catori to come to him, but he couldn't find her in his dreams, and so he followed ravens through the dark.

"The isles themselves turn on the War King," whispered the old Vanir to each other, and fell silent as others walked by. But the old songs rose.

"The Long Night is coming," Sverin boomed from his rocks, while gryfons who should have been hunting and females who should have been nesting huddled against each other in the cold. "The Long Night is coming, and the sea rises against us."

Trapped by raven wings that held him aloft over the king's rocks, Shard watched all the happenings of the Silver Isles with the eyes of a thousand birds, over the course of days he couldn't catch his breath to count. It stretched into a single long nightmare.

"Where is Kjorn?" Shard shouted in silence, in the dark.

Voices that might have been birds echoed back, "Where is the Summer King?"

"No gryfon will hunt alone," Sverin announced. "Not even on our own isle. No female with kit will travel without a member of the King's Guard, even to the river for water. The wolves will be upon us, they will take us alone."

Shard heard whispers as if he sat next to each gryfon. The War King. The Mad King. With Kjorn missing, Sverin's fear ruled him now.

Young males wove in and out of the assembled, snapping them to silence. The King's Guard. There had never been a King's Guard in the Silver Isles but there was one now. Haughty young males, eager to prove themselves by killing wolves, could find no wolves to kill, and so they proved their strength by bullying their own.

To his relief, Shard saw that Caj was head of the Guard. He cowed any young gryfon who got too big for his wings, and escorted the young, harassed females himself. He took them to the river, or on walks when their restlessness or aches got the better of them. But he couldn't be everywhere.

Shard watched, appalled, as any gryfons with Vanir blood were harassed by the King's Guard and the full-blood Aesir. He watched, infuriated, as the pregnant females began to feel safer alone than with a member of the King's Guard, unless it was Caj.

Except for Thyra. His nest-sister, tall, proud, pearly lavender against the winter snows, showed no fear, and kept the other females close to her when she could. Future queen, Shard thought proudly.

"But where is Kjorn?"

A raven laughed at him. "The wolves, the wolves have taken the prince alive."

Shard called again for Catori, but again she didn't come. "Has this happened yet, or is it something to be?"

Munin laughed. "Who could say, my lord? Time is not a line, but falling leaves...here, catch these." He flung a wing, and his black feathers exploded into blustering leaves, more visions, flashes, moments, and Shard grasped for them.

Hunts split between searching for food and wolves and searching for the missing prince. Thyra remained unusually calm despite her missing mate.

"I'm sure he is hunting wolves," she would repeat to anyone who asked, as if they were pestering kits. "Why would he return unless he found them?"

Rather than feel grateful for her calm, Shard feared his sister was slipping to madness. With Kjorn missing, the king's suspicions wheeled and stooped on every Vanir and half Vanir in the pride, including Thyra.

"Why would I dispose of my own mate?" she demanded when the King's Guard milled around to question and spy. Half the time Caj ran them off, though he flew himself to exhaustion most days, searching for Kjorn.

"Any gryfon found hunting near the shore, or after twilight, or before dawn will be in defiance of my law," Sverin proclaimed. The words, the king's voice and the visions of huddled gryfons, hunting gryfons, frightened, hiding gryfons

overlapped in Shard's mind until it was a blur of Sverin's voice and blowing snow, a blur of days and nights and evening rants.

The days passed, and with them, more laws. Falling leaves. Falling flakes of snow.

"Any gryfon seen alone on the Star Isle will be considered in defiance..."

"...any gryfon seen consorting with lesser creatures will be considered a spy..."

"Any gryfon suspected *of..."*

The words rolled on but now it was Halvden, strutting on the top of the king's rocks.

Once, twice, Sverin made as if to leave the Sun Isle to search for Kjorn himself and it was Halvden who stopped him, Halvden who begged him not to leave the pride, who swore they would find Kjorn or at least his body.

Now while the king brooded, Halvden spoke to the assembled pride.

"For your own safety," he called, green wings stretched wide in imitation of the king. "Now is the time for real action. Real hunting. Real work. Not songs. Any gryfon heard uttering strange incantations or rhymes considered dark magic or Vanir witchery will be considered a traitor in defiance of the king, and Tyr's law."

"Tyr's law?" a shocked voice echoed.

When Halvden's bright, hungry gaze swept the assembled for the speaker, no one spoke again.

"Hunters to me!" he keened.

"Bring us meat!" begged a female.

"We'll bring you a wolf pelt!" replied a member of the Guard.

"I'll skin you myself!" snarled a brilliantly violet gryfess, but two females leaped in front to hold her back. Vaguely Shard knew her, but couldn't bring a name in the dream. The laughter that followed from the males swept rage under Shard's skin.

"They're starving!" he shrieked, and clattering ravens called over the assembled gryfons. "Your own mates!"

He struggled against the invisible wall that silenced his voice, stayed his talons, struggled against the thousands of leagues of sea and wind between him and these crimes. Even Caj stood cowed, in shock over Kjorn's disappearance and unwilling to stand against Sverin when the prince was missing. There was no one.

"Help them!" he pleaded to the raven, Munin. "This can't be real!"

Munin's eyes shone dark as a sky without stars. Staring into them, Shard realized he was seeing things that had already passed. There was nothing he could do. There was nothing anyone could do. Catori didn't answer because she wasn't really there.

The caribou Aodh's hooves thundered across the sky. "Winter stalks us. Find the summer in yourself." Hooves rang, echoing, "find the summer, find the summer…the son, brother, father…"

"I waited too long," Shard whispered. "What of Einarr? He knows I live."

"He hunts," Munin said. "He survives. He watches the War King and weighs him against the memory of you."

Munin turned so that Shard could see through his eyes again, could see the heavy snow and Sverin on his rocks.

"The Long Night is coming," the king warned again, on a new day. It was silent. Gloomy afternoon. Clouds crouched low over the Silver Isles and fat, silent flakes of snow fell.

"These laws are for your own safety."

The King's Guard wandered among the silent, shivering, huddled gryfons, and now, no one spoke or questioned.

"For your own safety!" the Red King boomed. "All I do, I do to protect you. In these dark times it is easy to turn to suspicion, to superstition and fear. Some of you," his gaze landed on Einarr, Sigrun, others, "come from families who have betrayed me. Some of you have betrayed me yourselves. But the cold winter is on us, and I know that none of you would put the pride at risk in this time. My laws are in place to remind you of the law of bright Tyr. Those loyal will be rewarded and protected."

The pride held its breath, staring up at the king, harsh red against white snow.

"Anyone in defiance of even one of my laws will be considered a traitor." The king lowered his head, his gaze searching hearts and eyes.

"Any traitors," he said quietly, "will be exiled."

Shard found himself standing next to a beautiful, older, snowy gryfon.

"Mother," he whispered. An ear tuned his way. Shard realized that he didn't actually stand next to her, but a raven did, and he could speak to Ragna through his strange friend. Even if it was only a dream, he had to say, "Help them."

"All I do is for the pride," murmured the widow queen, in a way so different than Sverin. "There are strengths in the Vanir Sverin does not know." She looked at the raven, at Shard. "Stay on your wind, my son. Do what you left us to do."

Then Munin had to take wing or be seen, and Ragna be seen speaking with a "lesser creature."

"Where is Kjorn?" Shard shouted at the dead, pale sky.

"He hunts for the king's heart," the raven said, though now it sounded like wind on the rocks, and he smelled the sage of Winderost and the smoke of a thousand fires.

"Where is the prince?" demanded Shard.

"Where is the Summer King?" cried all the birds of the Isles.

Stigr's voice called and Shard knew he was waking. Grateful, he plunged away from Munin and the nightmare. But he was stuck. Again he saw Sverin on the rocks, then he saw blood, saw Caj still and bloody in the snow.

"Munin, let me wake!"

The raven laughed and laughed, holding Shard in the dream. "You didn't follow Kajar's starfire far enough, little graywing! Your father never dreamed of the Dawn Spire. Is it a pretty gryfess who holds you captive there?"

Whirling in the black dream sky, Shard slashed talons at the dark feathers tangling his thoughts.

Raven wings flung apart to reveal twin suns that became serpent's eyes, staring at him.

Shard did not have time to put together the creature's face before he heard a familiar voice. The voice of the storm, of the unknown song, the voice he'd heard over the sea.

It was female, and wisped, "I wait for the Summer King."

"Where?" Shard breathed.

"You know."

Wake up.

"*Shard.*" Stigr cuffed his ear. "Wake! Something's happening and you should probably look alert."

Shard lunged up, wings flaring to smack against the rock walls. His heart lanced about like a sparrow, and he stared at his uncle, dusty black in the early morning.

Stigr's feathers sleeked down with tension. "What is it?"

Slowly, Shard closed his wings, tried to smooth his feathers. "A dream."

"Another dream," Stigr growled. "All these nights, you dream, I hear you."

"Raven dreams," Shard breathed. "I think—I don't know. There's nothing I can do now."

Stigr's eyes widened. "Tell me what you saw."

Before Shard could, a commotion outside drew their attention, wild shouts and the rustle of many wings. "I will," Shard had to promise before Stigr would lead them both out of the den.

32
THE WILD HUNT

"WHAT'S ALL THIS?" STIGR DEMANDED of a young fledge bounding by. She stopped, blinked at him, then ran toward a mottle of other fledges, who screeched and laughed when she said Stigr had spoken to her.

A familiar faced winged by above and Shard called to her. "Brynja! What's happening?" The red huntress didn't hear, and flew on. Another gryfess glided by, and deigned to land in front of them.

"Valdis," Stigr greeted. "What's all this?"

"Come and see. The Wild Hunt. The chance for you to prove yourself to the king." She tensed to fly again but Stigr lifted his wings.

"We have proven ourselves. Tell us what this hunt's all about, what manner of beast, and what's expected of us. No more speaking to us like fledges. No more secrets."

Valdis checked, flexing her wings, then laughed. The husky sound surprised Shard, and, he saw, Stigr. "Oh, a proud member of the King's Guard now and he thinks he has the wind of things? Think of it as a surprise, instead of a secret." Her stern gaze traveled down the length of him and up to his eyes again. "Don't you like surprises, Stigr?"

With that she shoved off, keening for them to follow.

Stigr flattened his ears. "Belligerent fish-hawk."

"Actually," Shard said, "I'm becoming fond of her."

Stigr swiveled to glare at him.

Shard gave him the most innocent look he could manage. He had few chances to run his uncle's feathers the wrong way. "I just mean that she reminds me of you." Stigr's feathers pricked up and he peered at Shard suspiciously. "As a matter of fact, I think she likes you. A mysterious foreigner turned prestigious member of the guard. It's dashing, like a song."

"A song indeed," Stigr muttered, just as Shard began to warm to his idea of how Valdis must see him. He'd never thought of his uncle as a target for admiring females, but surely there was plenty to admire.

From the right angle, Shard thought wryly. And if Shard could encourage Stigr to respond with affection to even one Aesir, it might change him for the better and help Shard in the long run.

"There's a reason that one's not mated, I'll tell you that." Stigr began to walk, muttering, and Shard followed him. A stream of gryfons and fledges walked the same way, through the rock maze toward the perimeter of the Dawn Spire.

Stigr's gaze tracked Valdis's flight through the sky. "And as if I would fly with an Aesir. As if it would do either of us any good, too old for kits." He shook himself. "As if I weren't old enough already, and needing a female to harry me."

Shard chirruped, stifling a laugh. "But she is a fine huntress. Besides, you would hate a meek, submissive female, I know that much—"

"Stay on your wind, nephew," Stigr warned. "Everything I do here is to make you look good. And when are you planning to get on with... all this?"

Stay on your wind. His mother had said the same thing in his dream. In his vision. *It couldn't be real.* It had felt so hopeless, but Shard felt a sliver of suspicion that Munin toyed with him. A raven dream.

Not even Sverin would fly to such wild heights. Banning all those things. All that suspicion and fear. Barely hunting for game in winter. If it was real, Shard feared what the king would do next if he couldn't calm himself. Vividly and with a stroke of fear, Shard recalled that nowhere in his dream had he seen golden Kjorn.

He hunts for the king's heart, Munin had said, and remembering that, Shard feared all he had seen was too real.

Shard pulled himself back from his thoughts, back from the cold sinking into his belly to answer Stigr quietly. "After this hunt," he promised, eyeing the gryfons walking around them. "Brynja and Dagny told me this is our chance for winter initiation into the pride. I'll have a voice with Orn, we'll be free to travel the Winderost and seek…"

The large golden eyes from the dream came back to him.

The single, snow-covered peak.

I wait for the Summer King.

"And seek what you came for," Stigr finished for him, also wary of speaking too much with others around. "Good. You have my support. I'm weary of everyone thinking we're pitiful exiles from some mud-water crack in the ground. It's a waste of time playing their tier-climbing game. Time to move on." His gaze skirted upward though, and Shard suspected he might be looking for Valdis.

That was a conversation for another time, and the crowd of gryfons was too great now to speak more.

Fledges leaped around, bowling each other over. "The hunt, the hunt! The Wild Hunt!"

A whirl of commotion fluttered above and around them. A member of the Guard called to Stigr, and he left Shard, promising to meet after to plan. Shard loped along with a group of gryfons toward the towering rocks that formed the nightward border of the aerie.

"Welcome all!" King Orn's voice leaped over the stones and Shard peered around, squinting against morning sun toward the tops of the rock towers. He saw the tawny king standing tall on a far spire and lifted his ears.

"Our scouts tell me the herds of greatbeast have reached the border of the Winderost."

Greatbeasts? Shard's heart pounded harder. Those were something Brynja never mentioned. A small part of him wondered if it was the dragons, but knew that couldn't be. A danger they refused to even speak of could not be the target of a yearly hunting ritual.

Orn spoke on in the rhythm of a reverent song, for the benefit of the kits and fledges who didn't know, and, Shard thought, for him and Stigr. "Each year the greatbeasts migrate from the Horn of Midragur, windward to their wintering home. Great Tyr guides them with the lowering of his wings, urging them down through the Winderost to give us game enough for winter."

Shard lifted his wings unconsciously. The Horn of Midragur.

A warm scent pulled him from further thoughts of his vision. Brynja had walked up beside him and any thought of distant mountains or even his horrible dreams fluttered away like starlings.

Her gaze was bright, and energy bunched in every muscle from her tail to her ears. He hadn't seen her look so intent and friendly since after their first hunt together.

"Are you ready, Rashard?"

"To hunt?" Shard managed not to sound confused that she was speaking to him suddenly, was proud of himself for being calm. "Always."

"To hunt the greatbeast. They stand three times as tall as a gryfon, and twice as wide."

"If I ask, I suppose you won't tell me what they are?"

She looked at him ruefully, and fluffed her wings. "Shard, listen, I'm sorry I haven't been...well I'm sure you've noticed. I've just had a lot of things to think about."

Shard's heart quickened and he shifted a little closer to her. "That's all right. Is—is it anything I can help with?"

Her gold eyes searched him and he saw a spark of doubt that seemed out of place. "Oh, no. No I don't think so." She took a deep breath. "I just want you to know I consider you a good friend."

"Me too," Shard said, bumping his wing against hers, happiness rushing to fill in all the holes of doubt and fear left by his dream. "We'll hunt together today?"

"Yes. I'd like you to hunt with my family."

Shard inclined his head. "I'm honored."

Far above, Orn was still speaking of hunts past, of the dangers, of the traditions of the Wild Hunt, and the feasting that would come after.

Midwinter feasting.

The time had flown. In the Silver Isles, it would almost be the Long Night. No wonder Sverin was growing more fearful.

"The greatbeasts are hoofed," Brynja explained, for Shard's benefit, pulling him back from his thoughts. Orn finished his history of the hunt and sent the heads of families out to divide up the hunters into groups. Talk rose and comrades called to each other.

"Hoofed," Brynja continued, to get Shard's attention, "and horned, and stupid. Their meat can feed a whole family of gryfons. We store their meat in the salt waste windward of the Ostral Shores, and it sees us through winter, when the herds are sparse, and the—" she checked herself and corrected, "when the hunting is more dangerous."

Shard reeled back to his initiation hunt, when Caj had lectured that the boars of Star Island were stupid and dangerous. "Are you sure they're stupid?"

She blinked at him, tail switching. "Of course they are. Witless, lesser, just like the deer, the goat, the eagles—"

"The eagles aren't witless." Shard stretched his wings, opening space for himself, nudging away a rollicking kit who was chasing grasshoppers and calling them greatbeasts. Brynja had no answer but to stare at him, as if reconsidering her choice to stand by him.

"They have names," Shard said. "They name themselves like gryfons."

"Well," Brynja said, narrowing her eyes. "It doesn't matter for hunting the greatbeasts. But you might've told me sooner. Perhaps you can tell me more after the hunt. Any knowledge can help us, Shard."

Shard flushed under his feathers, realizing that he shouldn't have kept his knowledge of the eagles to himself, that their intelligence was important and possibly dangerous to the Dawn Spire. "I will. I didn't think you'd believe me, or care."

"Why wouldn't I?"

Shard considered that. "I'm not used to gryfons being interested in my opinion."

She gave a short laugh. "After everything you've done here? Of course I'm interested in your opinion, and the things you know, and the tales of your homeland." She stopped, beak grinding a little as if she'd said more than she meant to.

"Then spend time with me," he urged, feeling hopeful.

She had no answer for a moment. Then she spoke carefully. "Shard, it's been difficult, getting away."

"Away from what?" He gained some satisfaction from her exasperated expression. "I thought we were friends."

"We are," she whispered, and something flickered in her eyes that sent Shard's heart pounding.

"Then?"

She stared at him, a strange expression growing in her face, then shook herself and twitched her wings as if to leave, but someone called her name. She and Shard looked up at the same time to see Asvander gliding in.

Shard suddenly wished he'd remained with Stigr.

"Brynja!" Asvander landed gracefully and Shard had to admire that, at least. "Hunt beside me?"

"Of course," Brynja said, with a glance at Shard. A breath of silence passed before Asvander spoke again, and to Shard's surprise, Asvander addressed him. "You've had enough time to consider, Shard." He held his iron-gray head at a proud angle, but watched Shard with a spark of respect. "We hunt in fours. I've already asked your uncle. Will you join us?"

It would've been foolish to refuse him, Shard knew, to give in to his pride and seek another group. He had hunted with Brynja and Stigr and knew he worked well with both of them. He wanted nothing more than to pivot tail and to prove himself alone. But that would be stupid, and he would only prove himself stupid.

"Thank you," he ground words out of his beak. "I'm honored." He dipped his head and relaxed his wings in a very casual mantle. Asvander was, after all, First Sentinel. Seeing him stand close to Brynja ran Shard's feathers the wrong way, and he turned. "I'll find Stigr."

"No need," Asvander said. To Shard's surprise again, he sounded pleased. *He's probably looking forward to an opportunity to make me look bad.* "He already waits at the meeting rocks."

"Then let's fly," Brynja said, shifting her hind paws. "I've stood still too long."

Asvander laughed. Shard, feeling heavy, shoved into the sky with them.

Morning sun spread long golden wings across the red desert, the grassland toward the sea, and even tried to pierce the hazy gloom of the Outlands. Long shadows lanced the ground where rock towers rose.

Rising on a cool wind, Shard stared out across the plain. He couldn't see the Horn of Midragur. *How far did Hildr say it was? How far to fly, how far on foot for a greatbeast?* All around him, dozens of gryfons rose into the morning, falling into bunches grouped by family.

"Brynja just told me you've killed a great boar?" Asvander winged up beside him. "I've heard of them in legend, but I thought they'd left this land long ago."

Braced for mockery, Shard saw with surprise that he seemed genuine, ears perked, talons relaxed against his chest. "Yes, whatever she said was true."

Shard checked himself from adding more, and flattened his ears. He had claimed other things when he'd arrived, and wondered how often Brynja thought of that, if she did at all. She hadn't seemed to mention it to Asvander.

"I believe you, if that's what worries you." Asvander's voice drawled, confident.

I made a fast judgment, Shard thought, glancing at him, realizing with chagrin that he might be less like Halvden than Shard had first thought. "Anyway, today will prove your skills by the end, whether we believe you or not."

"Are the greatbeast like boar?"

"They're like nothing else on the earth." Asvander laughed into the wind and the thrill of the hunt gleamed in his eyes. Excitement stirred Shard's breast.

If only Kjorn could see it all. This hunt was more his birthright than Shard's.

"Hunters!" roared King Orn himself from the front of the lines. Shard straightened to attention, falling into a diamond formation with Asvander, Stigr, and Brynja leading on point. He noticed groups of three males with a female to lead them, and then groups of only females, all in fours, but no males hunting alone.

As a group they were over three hundred strong, and flew in a giant wedge built of the small diamonds of four. *Such precision,* Shard marveled. *Such discipline and skill. How could they fear anything at all?* He shuddered at the memory of dragon wings stretched taut across the sky.

"Prove yourselves!" challenged the king. "My blood kin, we will harry the front. Blood of Ingmar and En, to the dawn wind! Blood of Maj and Oster, to the windward flank! Let each clan show their strength today!"

The names flew by. Arranged by family, diamonds of gryfons banked with talon-tip precision, drifted into new wedges and soared away, ready to circle around and pen in the greatbeast herd from the sides. When he called Maj and Oster, Asvander and Brynja led them to peel off windward.

They flew sometime in silence and the ball of nervous energy rolled tighter in Shard's chest.

At last as the sun reached its first quarter mark, a cloud of dust lined the horizon. Shard squinted, straining to see through. "Is that the herd?"

"Yes," said Brynja, her voice husky with hunt-thrill. "Our kin will harry in from the side and drive them to the king."

Shard's heart began the slow, thrilled beat of focused hunting, his wings taut against the wind, the rising sun warming his flanks. He saw with awe how many gryfons claimed kinship to each other, however thin the bloodline.

Mind awhirl, he found himself looking for those who might be kin to the Aesir conquerors in the Silver Isles. Brynja, Shard still theorized, simply had to be a cousin of Sverin, no matter how distant, which made her kin to Kjorn. He wondered at the name of Oster, and Asvander's link to it, and if that land and family had any link to Caj. The bloodkin of King Orn himself reminded Shard very faintly of Hallr and Halvden for their heavy builds and the faintest flicker of olive green that showed itself in the tawny feathers under sunlight.

"Are you with us?" Brynja had glided in close to murmur to him. "Shard? I see a look in your eyes often, as if you're staring across the sea."

"I'm with you," he managed, and she tipped one ear back in amusement.

"Where do you stare?"

"Home." For a moment it felt as if he was alone with her in the sky. She gazed at him, curious, questioning, a little frustrated, he thought.

All she said was, "I need you here, today. Hunt well."

"And you," he whispered, before his tongue went dry.

King Orn's triumphant eagle cry filled the air. The greatbeast herd had seen them and began to turn.

"Down!" called Brynja, and ahead, in another small diamond, Valdis echoed her, then another.

A female several formations to Shard's left ordered, "Down, down, hunters to the windward flank! Drive them from the side!"

The formation shifted again. Shard caught Stigr's eye and together they fell into a new, large wedge. The satisfaction of hunting at full pride-strength was like nothing Shard had ever tasted before. To feel his own muscles and mind working full tilt and then to know he was only part of a larger, living, hunting thing, with every gryfon as a vital organ, flooded his mind with delight.

Valdis flew at the head, directing the quartets of hunters, and Shard caught Stigr casting her an admiring look. He laughed into the wind and Stigr slashed his talons through the air.

"Mind your flight!"

"Mind your own," Shard muttered, and chuckled. Stigr was unimpressed.

"Stay alert. I won't see you survive wind and sea and Aesir just to be trampled by a witless hoof-beast."

Valdis shrieked the cry to dive in.

Wind slapped Shard's face as a hundred gryfons turned their wings and the air slipped around them. He laid his ears back, stretched his talons forward and closed his wings to a dive. He possessed longer, slimmer wings than the native, broad-winged Aesir, and had to open his feathers to keep from diving too fast, from shooting ahead of the formation. Tempted to sweep ahead, to roll and flip and turn, to show Brynja again every flight move he'd ever perfected, Shard caught a breath and focused.

Through the dust and the thundering of the earth, he saw the greatbeast herd. He saw that Asvander was right.

They were like nothing else he'd ever seen.

Hulking shoulders sloped down steep backs to form mountain-like creatures with short, powerful legs. Their black and brown fur glimmered with a strange red iridescence. Witless panic shone in their dark eyes and they threatened the gryfons by shaking their curved, black horns.

Mad bellows bounded through the herd as they stormed across the plain. Shard tried to discern if they were speaking. He hadn't understood earth language at first, when he first met Catori and then fought the boar, Lapu. Only when he listened closely could he hear it and speak it.

Torn between twin desires of the hunt and curiosity, Shard decided it was wise to remain in formation with Stigr and Asvander. The hunt-thrill was too powerful. He wanted to slam into the nearest greatbeast and fight to his or the other's death. He clenched his talons.

"Just drive them!" Brynja ordered when Asvander and Shard both leaned into the wind, targeting the same older, hobbling beast near the edge of the herd. "Drive them to the king!"

Shard exchanged a quick look with Asvander and they both loosed a nervous laugh, regaining themselves.

As one, the clans of Oster and Maj harried the massive herd from the side. Far across the mottle of dark, galloping beasts Shard saw distant gryfons swooping at the other flank of the herd. *Those must be the bloodkin of Ingmar and En,* Shard thought, recalling the king's directions, trying to remember names, ranks, things that were important the Dawn Spire. He might need the information some day.

They harried the beasts until the broad-ranging herd formed into a narrower stream, and ran them across the plain.

Like tiring out a massive fish, Shard thought, his mind reeling. Twice he flew in too close to drive a beast back into the herd and another nearly gored him with a thrust of its horns. It was easy to lose the buoyancy of the flight wind, so low to the ground. It took quick wing strokes like a hawk, quicker thinking, better flying to stay aloft.

"Shard! Look at this!" Asvander's whoop caught his ears and Shard looked around, peering through the dust. There Asvander crouched, clinging to the back of a mountainous female greatbeast. Wings open, haunches low, he looked for all the sky as if he were riding her.

Shard laughed breathlessly, annoyed and awed at Asvander's nerve. The beast bellowed and Shard blinked, staring at her dark, bright eyes. Fury burned there. Shard's amusement twisted to shame. These were Named creatures. He knew it. The hunt-thrill and amusement drained from him. He tried to catch Stigr's gaze but his uncle had somehow found his way to hunt closer to Valdis.

"Get in formation!" Shard called at Asvander instead. "To the edge! Don't be stupid!" To his surprise, instead of questioning, Asvander shoved up, slapping the beast with his wings as he rose.

"Stop that foolishness." Brynja's clear voice rang through the thunder and dust. Too many gryfons had seen Asvander's trick, and wild laughter and shrieks battered the line of greatbeasts, and others tried Asvander's trick. The neat edge of the herd grew ragged as beasts broke through the undisciplined hunters.

"Shard!" Brynja called desperately. "Asvander! Stay with the plan."

Shard looked around and saw Stigr, finally aware of the problem and calling to the nearest gryfons to bring them to themselves.

"Wild Hunt!" Stigr spat. "Wild my foot, stupid is more like! Back in line and drive them on. I won't be trampled by a mudding beast today!"

The combination of Brynja and Stigr brought the hunters back to the serious work. Swooping hard, Shard worked to keep driving the greatbeasts in a stream toward the king and his kin, who poised leagues away, waiting to attack. Female gryfons shouted instructions to each other, reminded each other of the plan.

The herd shifted and for a moment Shard couldn't figure out why their direction shivered just a tail's breadth in the wrong direction. Then he knew.

They had heard the plans.

Every word, Shard thought. "Brynja!" He glided in close, pumping his wings hard to stay aloft so low to the ground. "Don't you see, they understand. They're trying to turn away!"

"Then those on the starward flank aren't doing their job! Ingmar's line are ever lazy, fat fools…"

Shard wheeled away. He knew it wasn't his place to correct them, or to even touch the delicate family squabbles, but he could see clearly how the hunt might fail. He looked around and saw a surprising face tuned in to him. Asvander.

The big gryfon flapped in next to him, his expression hard. "What's the problem?"

"They understand," Shard said, and Asvander eyed the herd as it continued shifting, pressing toward the far line of gryfons to avoid being driven to the king and others.

"What do we do?"

Shard curled his talons, gaze searching the herd, the gryfons, and others. Before he could answer, a young male greatbeast stopped, forcing others to flood around him. A gryfon warrior stooped low to goad him on. Shard tried to shout a warning but the greatbeast lunged up, horns thrashing. He caught the gryfon's wing, knocking him off balance. Before the gryfon could correct flight, another beast ramped up, flailing hooves and horns to knock the gryfon from the air.

One quick eagle cry cut the air, then all they heard was hooves.

The line of En broke in surprise and the herd shifted, the lead male bellowing triumph.

"Shard," Asvander breathed. "This has never happened…"

"I'll fly ahead," Shard said. "I'm fastest. I'll tell the king we need all his warriors."

"And me?" Asvander asked.

"Tell Stigr. Tell Brynja." Shard worked against the air to rise. "Try to turn the leader!"

"Yes brother!" Asvander laughed. "This will be a day for songs, Shard!"

Brother, Shard thought, feeling slightly crazy. *Here I fly with the Aesir, hunting among them*…but he had no time to dwell. He spiraled high, turned and soared with all his speed to find the king.

33

THE SONS OF LAPU

KJORN DRAGGED DOWN THROUGH COLD, black stone. Wolf scent clouded his nose. At first his anger had driven him to pursue Ahanu down. Then the passage narrowed and he slowed to a scraping crawl. His body blocked the scant daylight. He rounded a bend and faced blackness.

Fool, stupid fool, letting that beast anger you…Kjorn forced a steady breath and tried backing out. His haunches squeezed against the rock walls and no matter how he pushed, he couldn't force himself backward.

There would be no turning, and the rock wall scraped and broke feathers when he tried. A lump hardened in his throat. *Stupid. Stupid.* He lifted his ears, holding his breath to hear. A wolf howled, mocking him. The passage had to widen ahead. Either he'd have his chance to face Ahanu, or be able to turn around and return to his father.

He berated himself for panicking like a kit off its nest. *I am prince of the Silver Isles.*

So he crawled through the dark, crouched, ears pricked forward. As he stalked forward, the tunnel opened a little, stretched by deep tree roots. All around him lay smooth, pocked rock that might have been carved by water or, in the First Age, molten earthfire. Now it was black, silent, cold. Wolf scent ran fresh through the tunnels.

Kjorn paused when the scent wafted like a wall in front of him. He had room to turn. He should turn, go back to his father, settle with Thyra for the Long Night. Still, he hesitated. No wolf had attacked him yet. Indeed, Ahanu hadn't even attacked or defended himself in the woods. He'd only run.

And he'd said he had a message from Shard. He'd said that Shard was alive. The things Shard had tried to tell him descended on him in the damp, cold tunnel. The wolves had been there first. There could be balance, there could be peace.

And Shard might be alive. There was only one way to know for sure.

After a moment of indecision and thinking of light, Kjorn realized he could see, however faintly.

He took a step forward, heart thrusting up in his chest. It wasn't fire, nor was it an enemy, or chance sunlight peeking through. After another moment of sniffing and staring, Kjorn figured out the source. Lichens grew thick on the tunnel walls, the roof, and the edges of the floor, and cast a soft, muddy glow.

Even in the darkness of the earth, Tyr brings me light. Kjorn wondered how long Shard had known of this place and kept it from him.

Any amount of time was too long.

Kjorn crawled forward, trying to maintain his bearing underground. He could find this Ahanu, or the sister he'd spoken of, and learn the truth about Shard. If they lied, he would kill them and bring a wolf pelt to his father. One wolf pelt, to appease his father, to prove they weren't ghosts, that there were tunnels that led to the island and that the wolves hadn't flown to the Sun Isle by dark, secret magic. They were only flesh and blood. One wolf pelt, Kjorn was certain, would restore his father's sanity and show the pride that Sverin was not leaping at shadows.

One wolf, a softer thought echoed, *could tell me if Shard is really alive.*

And then what, Kjorn couldn't say. He couldn't think that far ahead, there in the gloom.

"Show yourselves!" Kjorn barked into the gloom. His voice bounced lightly a leap or two and fell dead. He ruffed his feathers, shook off dripping water, and crawled forward, hoping the way opened enough for him to walk soon.

If he met wolves in the cramped space, he would barely have room to fight.

"I don't fear you!" Kjorn stalked forward, then stopped. The cave widened enough for him to stand a little taller, but then it branched into different tunnels.

Appalled, Kjorn loosed a hoarse laugh. He didn't deserve these tests. He realized now that he had imagined a neat, single tunnel leading from one island to the next in a convenient trail. If it branched much more, he could easily get lost.

He paused to peer back over his shoulder, then lifted talons to claw hard against the rock, leaving long scratches to mark the way he'd come. He did this every several steps, checking back to make sure that his trail looked clear and obvious for as far as he could see.

Three tunnels branched in front of him and he almost took the largest out of relief, then paused. He took time to scent the air, to examine the stone for wear, to think. He wasn't a mindless beast, he was Kjorn son-of-Sverin the king, a prince, a hunter, a warrior.

As it was, the largest tunnel turned out to have the freshest scents.

He trotted down into the dark, hesitating only when the glowing lichens dimmed and thinned. Ahead, the way brightened again and so he renewed his pace, still pausing to scratch the walls. Even though it was a single tunnel now, he had a feeling he would want to see the reassuring mark of his own talons on the way back.

It felt like hours.

It *was* hours of nothing but dim, greenish dark, dripping water and the scent of moss and far off, stagnant water. He wasn't sure he was even going the right direction. Ahanu did not laugh or call again. But there might be others. He followed wolf scent, however stale, though it was weak on the stone.

"I am Kjorn son-of-Sverin!" he declared into the dark, and his own voice comforted him in the dead, cold silence. "And I fear no creature born on this island." He paused, tail lashing. "Show yourselves!"

Surely the caves didn't really extend under every single island. If so, the wolves could be leagues and leagues away, happily unable to hear or smell him, and have no idea Kjorn was even underground. Or they could be all around him, silently laughing.

A scuff drew his ear.

Kjorn stood rigid, ears straining forward. Another soft scuff on the stone, far ahead. He paused to claw the wall, and trotted forward. That time, he didn't shout. More sounds were definitely paws falling on stone. Kjorn fell into a quick crawl as the cave narrowed again, stifling a snarl that built in his chest.

Finally.

Faint movement ahead. Light caught on fur, a wolf tail rounding the bend.

A mix of excitement and anger tightened Kjorn's chest. At last. He would have his answers or he would have blood.

Kjorn paused once or twice to mark his way, but it cost him precious time and the flitting phantom of a wolf ahead of him was too quick. After a time he only glanced back, sure he would remember that twist, the strange curve of rock, and the little trickling stream.

At last the way opened enough for him to run. The air felt drier, fresher. A whisper of pine floated to him.

I'm still under the Star Isle! He paused, then caught movement in the dark and plunged forward, wings folded tight to make it through the narrowing passage. Stone gave way to frozen, pungent earth. Tree roots tangled his passage and Kjorn realized he had lost his quarry as quickly as he had found it. Somehow, whether through sheer speed or some quick turn Kjorn had missed, the wolf was gone, and all was silent. Dim, pale light filtered from somewhere.

The cave entrance.

Kjorn wriggled through ancient tree roots, covered in mud and flakes of glowing lichen. He must look like some sad, mudding, rock-bound thing of the earth. No matter, he could preen later, for ahead was sunlight and fresh air, and the desire to be free of the caves cast all else from his mind.

What would it be like to be lost down here? And to think he almost hadn't marked his trail.

As he reached the top of the tunnel where it broke into a cave somewhere on the Star Isle, a heavy, sour scent drenched the air. Kjorn lurched to a stop, gagging, every feather on end. He knew that scent. He had smelled it once before.

Boar.

The cave led to a tunnel that became a boar's den.

Caution froze him. It had taken an entire hunting party and the teamwork of Shard and himself to bring down a single boar last spring. It felt like an endless time ago, and now he was alone.

The scent nearly blinded him, but he forced himself to remain still, breathe and think. There was no movement. No sound. Just the scent. He crept forward. The den must lie under ancient trees, roots gnarled the way. In one spot, they were bent and broken. A massive boar had slept there.

If I can get to the entrance, I can fly. Then I will lead a hunting party into the caves. I shouldn't have come alone.

Kjorn thrust one foreleg out of the den, clawed at the tree roots, and hauled himself forward.

The curve of his wing joint caught in a tree root. He flexed, trying to force his wing around the root, but it held and crunched his feathers and muscle.

"Mudding, windblown…" He wriggled, only able to strain forward enough to thrust his face into the light and fresh air.

A quick glance around showed him a dense thicket of pine and nettle brush. Beyond the thick trees, sunlight on snow dazzled his eyes. Pine filled the air and he never thought it would smell so sweet.

If he could untangle and escape from the hole, he would have to crawl through the woods to the field before he could fly.

Underneath the pine a heavy scent clouded the cold breeze. Kjorn's heart jolted and he lifted his ears, slowly turning his head. Three leaps away in the shadows of the ancient pines, stood a red-eyed beast. Kjorn knew the bristled back, the stone-hard skin, the tusks, the hooves like jagged ice. He curled his talons against the roots, half pinned in the earth.

The boar lowered his head and shook its curved tusks. Kjorn could have sworn he heard a squealing voice.

"*Your wingbrother called my father Brother, and knew him as a prince of this isle.*"

Kjorn shook his head, hard, straining one last time against the tree root. When he realized the voice belonged to the boar, he broke into mad laughter. The first time he'd known a hoofed creature to speak, and it insulted and lied.

"Your father—that boar we killed, a prince?"

The wet, baleful red eyes fixed on Kjorn's face, alight with hatred. Alight with intelligence. "You will rue the day your forefather set talon to this isle."

He pawed the snow, challenging. Snorted, stamped and bellowed. The raw, split note sound raked Kjorn's ears and shook his bones.

The boar stamped again, and lowered his head to charge.

34
Shard's Victory

SHARD FOUND THE LINE OF the king's kin and folded his wings, diving fast. He swept in front of the line, calling the warning as startled gryfons ramped and shuffled back.

"Orn—your Highness!" He spied the king and landed hard in front of him. Orn sidled back, eyes narrowed, but he listened as Shard explained breathlessly. "The herd rebels, we can't make them turn. You must come to us or we'll lose control of them."

Orn angled his head, studying Shard. "It is tradition," he said slowly, "that each clan has its part to play. And my family have the honored task of the slaughter. The others are failing. It isn't our fault."

Shard met his gaze evenly—he'd expected argument. "Then the hunt will fail. Forget bloodline, Sire, you are a pride. If you want to succeed you have to trust me, and fly now. We need reinforcement."

Orn glanced down the line of gryfons, all fresh, hungry, read for the fight. One heartbeat, another, another, and Shard thought he might remain stubborn.

Then, backing away from Shard he called, "Hunters! The forward lines need our help. Fly! Follow Shard!"

Shard dipped his head and turned to lope away and push back into the sky.

They soared high. Shard glanced behind him only once to see the giant wedge of nearly a hundred gryfons flying behind him. A rush of confidence and power lifted him more strongly than any wind. He angled up, taking the highest point, ready to lead the Aesir to the final battle with the greatbeasts. A cloud of dust on the horizon showed him their target.

Shard's gaze lifted past for a moment and he saw something else.

Far on the rim of the world he saw it. A low range of mountains on the horizon. One peak thrust above the rest, a black fang against the sky. It was black, there was no snow, but Shard knew it as the mountain from his dream. For a breath he faltered, every instinct urging him to turn, to abandon the Aesir and turn to follow his quest.

The time isn't right, he argued himself, catching a slow breath. *There is no snow on the mountain peak*. Every time he'd seen the vision, the mountain was white with snow. He could not ignore that sign.

"Shard!"

Orn's voice brought him back. He had to finish what he'd set out to do. He had to win his place among the pride of the Dawn Spire, to earn a place and a voice and the right to wander freely in the Winderost. Far below, he caught the unmistakable form of Brynja, darting around the herd and trying to re-form their hunters into an effective, herding wedge. He had to win his place—and possibly one thing more.

With a sense of purpose, the mass of gryfons at his back and Orn's trust, a new, strange confidence welled in his breast.

For the first time, for a moment that burned like starfire, Shard felt like the son of a king.

"Down!" he called to Orn, pointing his talons at the points with where line of greatbeasts frayed into confusion. "We must turn the leaders!"

Orn repeated the order for the line and they soared down. Like a rhythm in the wind, Shard felt the panic of the herd, the disorder of the gryfons who tried to run them back into a line. Having seen the disorder from above, he knew where they needed to drive pressure, where they needed to give the herd its head. He glided fast above the hulking greatbeast herd, shouting instructions to the gryfons on either side of the line. Orn's hunters divided to either side, repeating Shard's orders, joining those driving the herd.

Three of Orn's own kin fell in behind him, repeating, pulling the gryfon hunters back into order. It didn't matter that the greatbeasts understood Shard's instructions—those who even listened—if they wanted to avoid talons and beaks, they fell into line. Slowly the herd reformed into an orderly channel of giant, galloping bodies.

As soon as order restored, Orn's kin pulled away, flying ahead to try to reform their own line and wait for the honored task of the kill and slaughter.

Indignant at their sudden departure, Shard wheeled and flew hard back to the front of the line to find Brynja and the others.

Asvander reached him first, laughing. "Well done, Shard! I never thought anyone would pull old Orn from the final line."

"I don't think we're done," Shard said, eyeing the front of the herd. A disruption broke out again. The lead greatbeast fought against gryfons and other members of his own herd to try and break away, to try to turn the herd again.

"We have to stop him," Shard said.

"That's an honor for the king—"

"No time!" Shard called, turning to whip ahead of Asvander. If Orn wanted to slay the greatbeast leader, he should have done it sooner. If they couldn't stop the leader, the herd would break again. Shard saw Orn and tried to summon him to the front, but the king shook his head and flew high, calling his kin back and away.

Asvander called to Shard. "He still means to have the final kill! It's an honor for the high families."

Now Orn was out of ear shot, letting his own kin rest while the other clans of gryfons tired the herd. Shard stared— "Can't he see the herd is angry? If they break again, we'll tire before the herd does!"

Asvander looked from the king's kin, flying fast ahead of the herd to ready for the final kill, then back to the tiring lines of gryfons still pushing them on. He saw what Shard did, that the beasts meant to break again.

He curled his talons and met Shard's gaze. "Then let's make sure they don't."

"With me!" Shard shouted. "We have to stop the leader."

Asvander whooped and Shard dove in close to him. They curved their wings and raced the herd, straining to outpace the leader again. When Kjorn and Shard had killed the boar it had only taken the two of them to get the beast off its feet. The greatbeast outsized the boar many times.

Shard winged higher now so they were out of earshot. "I'll get his attention!"

Asvander nodded and caught Shard's gaze. Shard realized, with a jolt, that the young First Sentinel was ready to help however he could. Shard laughed and they split, flying fast.

Shard sped over the heads of the greatbeast herd, calling warnings and snarls. They galloped hard, ignoring him, bellowing rage and fear. He targeted in on the leading male, angled sharply and swooped in his face with a half-mad shriek.

The beast's long, thundering bellow shook the ground and he swung his massive head, threatening with curving black horns. He didn't slow a step. Shard veered hard before two charging female beasts could rear up and catch him.

"Great one!" Shard soared higher and swung down again, flying in an achingly controlled glide next to the leader's shoulder.

Another witless bellow. His rage went so deep, his instinct to run so strong, that Shard couldn't understand his words, even in the language of the earth. Shard pictured pine trees, loam soil and peat under his talons, the stiff wind through the rowan of the Star Isle. His hind paws, rooted to the earth. He was lord of the sky *and* earth.

"*Hear me*," he said in the language of stone, of hoof and paw. "Some of you will die, but not as many if you stop fighting"

Understanding gleamed in the beast's huge, black eyes, but he shook his horns again.

"The red-rock king killed my sire and my son." A low, hot bellow. "I will kill him. I will fight and kill him before I die."

"Stop this," Shard shouted. "Break again and more will die than need to. We will only kill what we need unless you fight again—"

"So be it."

The beast veered to stab his horns at Shard, nearly trampling a female of his own. She lowed and attacked Shard in turn. Shard stole Asvander's trick, swung up with a hard wing stroke and flipped sideways to land on the she-beast's back. Then with a roar, he lunged into the leader's flank just as Asvander slammed into him from higher air. The greatbeast staggered to the side, hollering rage. But he did not fall.

"Tyr's beak," Asvander panted, as he and Shard clung hard to the woolly pelt of the beast's shoulders. "What now?"

The king and his line of hunters came into view. The leading beast veered, bellowing at his herd to scatter, to fight.

Shard clung hard, riding the side of the mountainous beast. "*Push.*"

The beast plowed forward. The thunder of the hooves buried all other sound. The front of the herd bore down on the king's line and the sides pushed against the gryfons all the way down the line.

Together, Asvander and Shard forced their wings open.

Shard saw that the gryfons in the king's line didn't flinch, hovering ahead and waiting. They would realize too late that the herd was about to plunge into chaos. More gryfons and greatbeast would die than anyone had planned.

Shard and Asvander thrust their wings back, then forward, shoving all their desperate, tiring might against the mountain of galloping muscle and bone. The beast leaned into their claws, loosing a mad, frothing wail.

"It won't work!" Asvander swung one wing closed and almost slipped from the beast's back. Shard slapped talons to his shoulder and hauled up until he got a grip again.

"Again!"

Shrieks from behind them warned of the herd about to break through gryfon lines again. With all the dust and bodies it would be impossible for Orn to see that the gryfons were about to lose control.

Asvander leaned in to Shard. "We have to warn the king!"

"We tried," Shard growled, and shoved again.

The gryfons who had herded the beasts that far finally saw, too late, that the herd wouldn't slow. They shoved to the front, desperately trying to turn the beasts, but the beasts followed the leader as a body follows the head.

Shard and Asvander had to take the head.

"Again!" Shard shouted, opening his wings. Asvander shrieked, flaring his wings, and pushed. The beast bellowed, staggered—

And another gryfon smashed into the haunch on Shard's flank. Another into his shoulder. Russet and black.

Brynja and Stigr.

The greatbeast toppled hard into the one next to him. She smashed into the ground and he flipped over her. Hooves lashed the air. Horns slashed at anything near.

Brynja, Stigr and Asvander shoved free but Shard's tail feathers caught under the heavy shoulder when the beast first flipped and they rolled together, Shard tucking his neck and scrabbling to stay on top. He lost track of the herd and the hunters, focused only on not getting crushed. He clung to the leader's shoulder as they skidded to a long stop in the dirt.

Dust swirled in a storm, churned by wings and hooves.

Shard allowed himself a breath, then leaped up to the greatbeast's face before more hunters could descend. "You ran well, great one. You fought well. Brother." The language of the earth would sound like gurgles and growls to the other gryfons.

The great ribs rose and fell hard in defeat. "Thank you for my good death." His eyes closed, accepting his fate.

A shadow fell and Shard looked up, panicked.

The dust whirled away to reveal King Orn landing hard in front of him, wings wide.

Shard staggered back, muscles quivering, as Orn lunged in to deliver a killing bite. Shard looked quickly behind him. The gryfons, including Orn's hunters, had at last cowed the herd. With the leader fallen, the rest of the greatbeasts fell into order. All around, gryfons brought down beasts enough to feed the pride through winter, while the rest of the greatbeast herd in the back fled.

Orn raised his tawny head, streaked with blood, and narrowed his eyes at Shard, wings open in amazement.

"Very well, Shard, son-of-Baldr."

It dawned on Shard that those simple words were the king's acceptance. In the middle of the dust and blood and with gryfons lunging to and fro to fell the last of the greatbeast, Shard was initiated.

He was now a member of Orn's pride.

35
Kjorn's Mistake

Kjorn strained against the earth and roots that pinned him half in, half out of the ground. The boar, young, lean, not quite the size of the one Kjorn had killed with Shard, pounded toward through the white snow and mud.

"Keep coming!" Kjorn shouted. "I challenge you!" With a strangled lion snarl Kjorn surged up, tearing roots, clawing, and came rolling out of the hole. He ramped to his hind legs, flashing his wings wide against the tight undergrowth and tree trunks. It would be impossible to fly out. He had to fight, for the boar would reach him before Kjorn could run to the meadow if he tried.

Kjorn slapped his talons to earth and roared. The young boar bucked out of the charge and sidled, squealing, hesitating. Kjorn crouched, growling low. His checked the sides, trying to see the easiest path through the brush. "I killed your sire, you stupid beast. And I need meat."

The boar stamped with an angry shriek, but hesitated.

"Coward," Kjorn snarled, his heart winging up to his throat. He had the beast's attention, but he feared if he moved to flee, it would charge again. When they'd killed the boar before, Shard had worked to make it so angry it couldn't see straight. Kjorn wasn't sure he could do it alone.

Help, help, great Tyr. He knew he was a fool, trying to stand down a boar. Caj had warned that no gryfon could manage a boar alone, even a young one. But Kjorn had no choice, and anger coursed through his muscles after his fruitless, underground hunt. Hunger lanced his belly.

He snarled another challenge and an insult. At last the boar stamped, lowering its head to charge again. Kjorn braced. Shadows beyond shifted and for a moment he thought he saw something impossible in the trees beyond. Not impossible. Real.

A second boar.

"*Fly fly fly,*" called a magpie from the trees, echoed by the cackling of a raven.

The second boar emerged from the trees, snorting steam. It stood taller and thicker, a shaggy bristle of black fur standing up along the ridge of his back, his small, stupid eyes gleaming. A strange, gurgling rumble rolled from its throat and Kjorn shook his head, again hearing strange words.

"This is not your fight, little brother. I will kill the eagle cat."

The first boar tossed his head in defiance. The elder stamped and slashed his tusks with a squeal. They butted hard, squealing and locking in argument and for a moment Kjorn hesitated, wings tensed and raised. His chance. He turned slowly to creep toward the meadow.

At his movement, the beasts broke apart and their attention locked on Kjorn, small tails swishing, heads low.

Kjorn found he'd lost his roar.

He might've fought or outrun a single boar. Not two. He lowered his head, hackle feathers ruffed up, and hissed. The larger boar squealed. The smaller swung its tusks, and together they charged.

Kjorn's courage drained. He could not fly. The meadow was too far to run.

Like a kit, like a coward, he whirled and crammed himself back down into the tunnel.

The boar's den, idiot. As if they can't follow you here! He shoved, clawing, squirming to get back down into the earth. Tusks slashed at his heels, his tail, and he shrieked.

With a last shove through the narrow entrance, he collapsed in a heap on the muddy floor of the den. After a breath he staggered up to worm his way back through the tunnel. The boars stamped and clashed again at the mouth of the den, as if arguing who should pursue him.

Kjorn heard them come rooting down. He sped until he emerged from the earthy den into the colder stone tunnels.

Down, down, back under the island. He could lose them in the tunnels. He saw claw marks on the wall and followed them mindlessly, panting, speeding up every time he heard the boars behind.

Soon they fell away. Lost, or drained of the anger to attack.

Kjorn slowed to a crawl, then a stalk. He stopped when the tunnel opened into a small cavern, and lifted his ears, scenting the air. Something wasn't right. There were claw marks on the wall, but he had no memory of the place.

He walked to the edge of the cavern where claw marks slashed the glowing lichens, and sniffed. The scent wasn't his own, but it was familiar. Kjorn backed away slowly, tail twitching.

Wolf.

He spun around and saw that in his panic he had missed a simple sight. Slash marks marred *every* wall. Wolves had come behind and destroyed his trail.

Maybe, if he hadn't panicked, if he'd noticed sooner, he could have gone with caution, searching for his own fading scent. All the slashes looked too similar now, and wolves had marked the walls to bury Kjorn's own scent.

Tension lumped tight in his throat. His wings flared and he crouched.

Kjorn, locked in a gloomy cavern deep under the earth, released an eagle's scream that dropped to a lion's roar, and he was answered through the stone by distant, laughing howls.

36
A Matter of Pride

"YOUR HIGHNESS," SHARD SAID TO Orn. "I need to speak to you—" Gryfons plowed into Shard from all sides, knocking him back to the ground. He rolled in a surprised, laughing tumble with Brynja and Asvander. Orn stepped away to deal with the butchering. Shard would have to ask him permission to explore the Winderost another time.

"See what I told you?" Brynja asked Asvander. "Now you wish you had him in the Guard, don't you?"

"I think he's been waiting to show me up." Asvander laughed, nipping at Shard's wing as if they were kithood friends.

Then Dagny piled on top, declaring she had seen it all from the far line. She had hunted across the herd with the bloodline of En. Shard laughed, reeling with the sudden, strange joy of belonging, as three gryfons crushed him with their weight and their admiration. He had never felt so strongly part of a pride even at home, except with the wolves and his very few friends. All around the news flew, it was Shard, Shard the Outlander who had seen that the greatbeasts meant fight to the death, meant to kill the king. More gryfons milled around, congratulating, and a familiar voice made its way through Shard's joy.

"Just like I promised," Stigr was saying to Valdis as they approached more sedately. "I promised you he would do something magnificent, and stupid."

"Does he get it from you?" inquired Valdis, dusty and proud.

"Doubtful," Stigr said.

Brynja went still, watching with bright eyes. Shard realized how close she was, one wing draped companionably over his back. Every nerve felt on fire and he resisted the urge to preen the dust from behind her ears.

Others called Valdis' name to help with the division of meat, with driving off stray beasts. Valdis invited Stigr to help. Shard's heart leaped. Stigr, exiled from the Sun Isle at home, might have found acceptance there too. And maybe something more.

Shard balked. For all his talk, he feared some part of Stigr might like it in the Winderost, might want to stay. He had a growing reputation, he was warming to Valdis and other hunters had called his name with respect during the hunt. He had gained the respect he'd once enjoyed as Baldr's wingbrother, Shard knew, and wondered how hard it would be to give up. And there was Valdis. If he took a mate late in life it would surely bind him here in the Winderost, unless Valdis decided to fly with him to the Silver Isles. Somehow he couldn't see that happening, not with the long winters, and so far from her kin.

He shook his head of the doubts, determined to be happy for his uncle either way. He swiveled to ask what Brynja thought about it all—but his words fell when he saw her.

She had dipped her head low while Asvander spoke quietly in her ear, then he nuzzled under her beak.

A block of ice froze Shard's chest.

I couldn't possibly have been so blind. They don't act mated. Friendly, but not…

He untangled himself from Brynja's wing and strode several steps away. Asvander and Brynja watched him, surprised.

"Are you all right?" Brynja stood and shook herself, and Shard noticed at last how close Asvander stood to her.

Are they mated? he wondered in wild silence. It hadn't seemed like it. As far as he knew, they didn't nest together. He caught Dagny's gaze and his face must have looked truly shocked, for she flattened her ears in dismay at his expression, eyes wide as if to warn him that he should act calmly.

It doesn't even matter, he insisted to himself at once. *I've been a fool either way.* He hadn't flown to the Winderost to find a mate. He had sought truths that would resolve the war in his own islands. His vision haunted forward and with shame Shard recalled the flooding images of his dreams, the events of the last weeks in the Silver Isles, the tyranny of Sverin.

And here I am, romping in the red desert with new friends and not a care…

Bitterness over wasted time and wasted thoughts about Brynja soured the victory of the Wild Hunt.

"Shard," Brynja said firmly, stepping away from Asvander. "Are you all right?"

It was too much. Shard could barely think for all the regret and worry and thoughts of the past. He had to clear his mind.

The only use in looking back, Caj had instructed Shard and Kjorn once, *is to learn from what has gone before. Aesir don't dwell in the past.*

For the first time since he had learned his heritage as a Vanir and begun to forsake the ways of Sverin's pride, Shard firmed his will, refused to look back, and put himself firmly in the moment. He met Brynja's gaze.

"Of course. Just tired from the hunt." He looked to Asvander, biting back a claw of jealousy. "What's next, brother?"

Asvander laughed and at last peeled himself away from Brynja. Shard's heart beat a little easier. "The butchering. Then the storing. We will fly half the meat to salt waste, bury it for winter, and take the rest to the Dawn Spire for the feast."

"Good," Shard said. "Let's get on with it."

They agreed and shook themselves of dust. As they walked toward the greatbeast carcasses, Dagny slid up next to Shard, speaking softly. "Well done. Don't worry. You'll have your chance at the feast."

Shard looked sternly ahead. "I don't know what you're talking about."

"Ha. All right. Don't worry, Shard." She bumped her wing against his. "I like you. I've decided to help you."

"Help me?" Shard wrestled away from a thousand other thoughts. "With what?"

Dagny's breath slid out in a slow, measured sigh. "Help with Brynja," she answered, after a struggle for patience.

"Oh," he mumbled.

"She does ruffle your feathers, doesn't she? Or am I wrong?"

"I…"

"It's what wingsisters are for," Dagny assured him. "Tomorrow night will be feasting, songs, plenty of opportunities for an eligible bachelor to declare himself. I'll help you."

Shard stared at her. His mind overflowed with his fears for the Silver Isles, feeling he'd betrayed the Vanir with his brotherhood to the Aesir, fearing he'd waited too long, still trying to untangle the riddle of his visions.

Then, close by, a sparkling laugh broke his muddle. Brynja's laugh. The white mountain drifted through his thoughts—but the time was not yet right. Tyr had led him to the Dawn Spire. Surely there was a reason.

"All right," he said to Dagny, pushing aside ten other doubts. Dagny laughed and bumped him roughly with her wing again.

"That's the spirit. You survived the hunt and outshone even the king. We can't let all that acclaim go to waste can we?"

"No," Shard agreed, not sure what else to say.

"Now," Dagny said, leaning in, "I'll find you before the feast. Pretend we haven't spoken."

Before Shard could nod agreement, she bounded away.

The enormous hunting band returned to the Dawn Spire at dusk the following day, loud and bragging and weary.

Shard and Stigr had helped to drag half of the greatbeast carcasses to a salt waste along the border of what the Winderost gryfons called the Ostral Shores. Though Shard had seen gryfons flying distantly on the border of that land, they didn't approach and no one but Asvander spoke of them.

"Independent clans," he said, averting his eyes. "Who swear no loyalty to the king of the Dawn Spire."

Shard watched him while they turned the meats in the salt ground, burying and caching it like mountain cats. After a moment of silence, everything settled into place and made sense to him. "That's where you're from, isn't it? But you do swear loyalty to Orn."

Asvander chuckled and lifted his wings in a shrug. "I do. My mother says I was born old. I feel a sense of loyalty. We were all united once, years ago when I was a newborn, my mother told me that the Dawn Spire, those of the Ostral Shores and the bordering rim of the Outlands, the great plains windward of the grass cat territory, and beyond, all were represented at the Dawn Spire, all answered to the king there…" he trailed off, his gaze drifting up to the horizon.

"The most powerful alliance of gryfons under Tyr's eyes. I still wished to honor it. My family didn't. They won't see me now."

The sheer number of gryfons living at the Dawn Spire overwhelmed Shard. He tried to imagine an even larger alliance than that, and wondered what in the world any such pride would fear, or what could break them apart.

"What changed?" Shard whispered.

They'd finished their work and as they leaped into the sky to join rest, Asvander said simply, "The king."

They split then, Asvander called away, and Shard to Stigr. He pondered Asvander's answer and realized he didn't know if he'd meant that Orn himself had changed in some way, or if a different king had ruled before, and the clans didn't support Orn. He would ask the next chance he had.

They left the salt grounds by afternoon, and when they neared the Dawn Spire the whole sky glowed rose with evening light. Warmth rushed up from the ground to speed their flight.

The hunting band splintered off as they reached the Dawn Spire, some still bearing meat for their families and the great feast, and others, like Stigr and Shard, glided in toward their dens to rest and preen. From what Shard had gathered by eavesdropping, this was one of the greatest events of the Aesir's year, second only to the first day of summer when they, like the Vanir of the Silver Isles, chose their mates. That made him think of Brynja, and he wondered exactly what Dagny intended to do to help him.

Shard and Stigr landed just outside their dens, and Stigr broke Shard from his thoughts. "Valdis told me that after the feast they have a meet to plan the winter, the guarding, and division of meat. Since Orn has recognized you, she said you may speak there if you like, and ask what questions you will."

"All right," Shard said absently. All around them soft evening light fell gray on the red rock maze. Stigr eyed him skeptically.

"What is it?"

"Nothing," Shard lied, "I'm just tired. I think I'll rest before the feast."

"My prince," Stigr began. "Before we left for the hunt, you said you'd dreamed."

"Just dreams—"

"You are Vanir," he said firmly. "Son of a seer. You've had visions of your own. Tell me what you saw."

Shard took a deep breath and looked toward the highest, distant red spires. The unbelievable acts of Sverin's rule winged forward, but he hesitated to tell Stigr everything.

"Things we could have guessed without the help of raven dreams, Uncle. Sverin is playing the tyrant, and we must get home as soon as possible."

Stigr ground his beak. "I knew it. I knew this would happen. We never should have left."

Shard faced his uncle fully, surprised the argument had taken so long to arise. "Even my father's vision showed him the Winderost."

Usually mention of his father cowed Stigr, but not this time. Baldr's wingbrother snarled and lifted his wings. "That was his vision. I thought you came here to follow it, but we've been here through autumn and it's winter now."

"We had to make allies here, Uncle."

"Yes," Stigr said, keeping his voice low as gryfons winged by above. "But you don't belong here, and I see you getting more comfortable every day."

"Not like you I suppose!" Shard burst out. "Winging with Asvander as if he was your own kin, consulting Valdis, you look to be getting along with the Aesir fine. Or am I wrong?"

Stigr looked stricken. Then he narrowed his eye and lowered his head in threat. "I fit in here because I must. I do it for you."

"I have to know the history of my enemy, the history of my brothers, Uncle, I can't betray Kjorn again. It will split the pride."

"The pride is already split," Stigr hissed, fighting to keep his voice low as Aesir romped and laughed around them, trickling toward the Spire for the great feast. "Those who belong, and those who don't. Shard, be a king. Declare yourself, reclaim the Isles, get rid of Sverin, keep those who are loyal, and exile the rest."

Shard stared at him, unable to believe the words, or that Stigr couldn't truly hear himself saying them. He wondered how long Stigr had wanted to say those things, if his hatred was truly that strong.

"I will be a king," he managed after a long, tight moment. Stigr nodded, satisfied, and turned to go. Shard finished quietly, "But not a king like Per."

Stigr stopped, tail twitching, but he didn't turn, and without a word he stalked into his den.

Shard fought guilt. There was a time when he'd told his uncle nearly everything, when he'd taken Stigr's advice and listened.

But how can I talk to him about the kind of king I want to be when anger rules him, or ask his advice on Brynja when he hates Aesir, or hearing the dragon's song in my dreams, or what I saw at home? Why can't he see my side?

The other possibility, and Shard was keenly aware of it, was that Stigr was right. Perhaps Shard was being weak, and he should have followed the way of the conquerors and simply killed Sverin when he had the chance. Even now, they could have been mending the pride, striving through winter, and none of it would be a question.

He told himself all of that, but the thought of killing Kjorn's father made him balk. Glad he had kept the description of Sverin's manic rule somewhat vague, Shard walked into his own den.

A gryfess sat there waiting for him. Shard started, glancing over his shoulder, then back to her.

"If you're done dallying," Dagny said, a strange and frightening gleam in her eyes.

"I don't think this is a good idea after all," Shard said, glad his den was tidy.

"Why?" She stood and stretched luxuriously, scraping her talons along the floor, then hopped forward to examine him. "Because of your uncle? I wouldn't worry about him."

Shard huffed, wondering if she had eavesdropped, and swiveled his head to watch as she circled him. "Why not?"

"He's being two-faced, that's why. In case you haven't noticed him swapping purrs with Auntie Valdis here and there, you can take my word for it, even if he pretends otherwise." She stopped in front of him and Shard watched her, amused and grateful for her cheer.

"So," Shard began slowly, "Brynja has told you who we are."

She tilted her head. "Of course. She's my wingsister. Don't worry. Your secrets are safe."

"Thank you," Shard said, and she circled him again, examining.

"Anyway, if he disapproves of you courting Brynja, let him know that you know about Valdis. Listen, I don't mean to be crude, but you need a rinse in the stream. Nothing to worry about, just two days of hunting and dust. Go on and come back and we'll begin."

Shard blinked, then let himself laugh, relieved by her attitude. "Yes, my lady."

Ready for distraction, for anything to take his mind from his trouble, Shard bounded out of his den and flew to the stream. Many other gathered there already, bathing and swapping stories of the hunt. To hear Dagny openly say the word "courting" in reference to Brynja brightened his heart, let him know that she approved. As Brynja's wingsister it was critical that she did, and gave him a glimmer of hope.

He needed a night of hope. He needed to answer his own heart, to clear his mind, to not worry for a little while what Stigr thought. High above, someone began singing a ballad, and from there the song caught and carried through many voices throughout the spires and dens, all in celebration for the feast about to begin.

Laughing and recounting the tale of the hunt with others bathing in stream, Shard let his heart be light. Tonight, he would tell Brynja how he felt, he would speak reasonably to King Orn, ask openly what they knew of Per, and he would show Stigr that the issue of his kingship could be solved with reason, and without further bloodshed and hate.

37

IN THE LONG NIGHT

"BROTHER," CAJ HUFFED AS HE landed inside the king's den. His fore claws overflowed with strips of long, dried meat. Sverin paced near the back wall, stopping to watch Caj. "Meat, for the Long Night, since you won't sleep." He paused while Sverin stepped forward, then added, "Preserved with salt from the flats on the Crow Wing isle."

Sverin chuckled wryly and tried to meet Caj's eyes. Caj kept his gaze on the wall. If Sverin met his eyes, he would surely be able to tell that Caj lied. "You aren't happy with me," Sverin murmured. "Why?"

"You've quartered off my mate and daughter," Caj growled, and dropped the meat at Sverin's nest.

The Red King didn't answer right away, but walked to the nest to sniff the meat. Gold and gems flowed over the sides of the nest, long, intricate chains of dragon craft, gauntlets thin enough for gryfon forelegs.

The sight of the treasures used to fill Caj with awe, now everything about them struck bitterness into his heart. They were too heavy. Too bright. They caused the young males of the Guard to squabble.

Wolf pelts bunched among the gold. Caj eyed one massive fur that lined the bottom of the nest in indigo black and pale cream and gray. The pelt of Helaku, dead wolf king of the Star Isle.

"I only quartered off your mate," Sverin said when he was done examining the meat. "Thyra chooses to stay with her and the white witch. Don't pretend you don't see them talking behind my back—and yours."

Caj ruffled his feathers in displeasure. "Winter is driving everyone mad. I won't choose between you. Sigrun would never do anything to endanger the pride in winter."

"The *pride*?"

"Or you," Caj amended, finally meeting Sverin's eyes. Outside, winter wind howled against the dens that riddled the nesting cliffs. "This half," he laid his claws over several strips of the meat, "are rubbed with an herb to help you sleep. If you desire."

"So your mate would have me think."

Caj rumbled deep in his chest and lifted his wings. "I trust my mate. Do you trust me?"

Sverin dipped his head, but gave no more answer. "Will you settle? The sun is setting."

Caj looked away, hesitating before he answered. "I'll spend the Long Night with my mate. With the pregnant females who shelter with her."

Sverin raised one forefoot, surprised. "Why?"

"In my place, you would do the same." Caj hesitated, then stretched out his wing, prepared to renew his wingbrother pledge, to remind Sverin of his loyalty and friendship. Sverin watched him, hard, then opened his red wing to cover Caj's.

"Wind under me when the air is still," whispered the Red King.

Relief filled Caj's heart. "Wind over me when I fly too high."

"Brother by choice." Sverin studied Caj closely.

"Brother by vow," said Caj, and together both began, "By my wings—"

"My lord!" a voice called from outside the cave, and Halvden swooped in to land, his emerald wings dusted with snow. Caj tried to hold Sverin's gaze, but Halvden sauntered in, eyed their joined wings and dipped his head.

As if he ever feels like an intruder, Caj thought, stifling a growl. *The arrogant jaybird.*

"Forgive me. I didn't mean to interrupt."

Sverin folded his wing though their vow was incomplete, and lifted his head. Caj felt the chill settle over his wing when Sverin moved away to speak to Halvden. "What news?"

"Everyone is settled in their dens." Halvden glanced at Caj, then the meat, and mantled low to the king. "The Vanir are quartered in the old starward dens, the sun turns down, and we are prepared for the Long Night."

"Any sign of Kjorn?"

At that quiet question, Halvden only bowed his head lower. Sverin loosed a soft noise and paced away to his nest. Caj stepped forward to comfort him and the king's tail lashed, warning him away. "Caj, be well my friend. Watch over them. I will see you…at dawn."

Caj blinked at the dismissal, murmured respect and left the den. Halvden did not follow.

Caj launched up, hovered for a moment and landed in silence to the side of the entrance, careful not to stir the snow. Watching Shard fly, he had learned some graceful tricks. He crouched near the entrance, ears lifted to Halvden and Sverin's voices.

"…provisions, my lord?"

"Yes."

"From the Vanir witch?"

"From Caj's mate," said the king, with too much patience, Caj thought. *Can't he see how every word out of Halvden's beak is to turn Sverin against me?*

The light dimmed as clouds thickened over what was left of the sun.

"Preserved with witchery," Halvden said loudly. "My lord, since Caj would rather be with others, I would be honored to guard the entrance to your den over the Long Night."

Caj dug his talons against the rock

"Oh?" Sverin's sounded relieved. "You won't spend the Long Night with your mate?"

"She is with the others. How could I leave my king alone?"

Without prompting Sverin said, "The meat is preserved with salt from the flats on Crow Wing."

Halvden spoke hesitantly. "My lord…"

"Speak openly," Sverin growled impatiently.

"There are rumors — that the meat is preserved with sea salt."

Caj's tail twitched and he glanced around to make sure no one saw him listening. Halvden added quickly, "I'm sure Caj meant well. I'm sure sea salt has no effect on a Vanir, but…"

"I trust my wingbrother," Sverin said.

"Do you trust his mate?"

Curse him, Caj thought. *Curse his mudding, tier-climbing, dead father. I hope he lives forever in a land without sun.* Something kept him from plunging into the cave, from challenging Halvden, from ending his slimy, dangerous charade.

Guilt. And fear.

If he fought, Sverin would know that Caj was defending Sigrun, that they'd both lied. He might have faced Sverin alone, but he would lose a fight to Sverin and all of the Guard who were loyal to the king. They would kill him—but not before they killed Sigrun.

Caj shut his eyes, listening hard, but silence stretched in the cave. Sverin didn't answer, which meant he did not trust Sigrun. *Which means he doesn't trust me,* Caj thought. *And he shouldn't. I'm a liar and traitor.*

At last Halvden spoke again. "I would be proud to taste it for you, to test—"

"No," Sverin whispered. "No, leave it. I will fast the Long Night as I have before."

A soft scuff would be Halvden bowing. The light was almost gone, Caj knew he had to fly soon, or be accused of breaking the king's law.

"Of course, my lord. Shall I leave you?"

"No," said the king again, through the gloom. "The sun is gone. We mustn't fly in the night."

Darkness loomed. As silently as he had landed Caj leaped from the cliff again and glided to Sigrun's den. Her worried expression as he made his way through the clumps of pregnant females only hardened his heart. He couldn't speak to Sverin now, or he'd know Caj had flown in near-dark. He couldn't speak to Sigrun. He couldn't do anything.

"Father," Thyra whispered, coming up beside him. Her warmth steadied him, her strength filled him with pride. Sigrun joined them, they curled up together and listened to the wind and snow.

It was only a quarter mark later that the first of Sverin's tortured screams broke the night.

"There's nothing you can do," Thyra said, when Caj made to move. Caj looked out, silent, and knew that she was right. Sverin's nightmares were his own.

His family was all that mattered now.

Warbling howls and wolf song rolled off the damp stone. Kjorn lay on his belly in the middle of a tunnel, peering through the gloom. Something moved at the edge of his vision and he twitched, peering around. It felt as if ants crawled just out of sight, drawing his attention. His belly cramped with hunger.

He didn't know how many days he'd been underground.

The wolves led him on a distracted chase through the tunnels and now there were no marks on the walls, either from wolf claws or his own talons. He was lost. A wolf's laugh echoed down the tunnel.

"Silence!" Kjorn shouted.

Laughter answered him. He scraped his talons against the stone and shoved to his feet. Weak with hunger, he trembled and wove a step to one side. He forced himself to walk forward, drawn to the scent of water.

Ahead lay a small cavern, smooth and round, carved by earthfire long ago. A subterranean stream trickled into a thin waterfall down the far wall, splashing into a black pool of water a wingspan long and round. All glowed misty green and gray from the lichens and fungus clumped in rock shelves all around.

Kjorn had no concept of how long he'd been underground, and knew only by his hunger that it had been days and days. At least he'd found water, and he was reluctant to leave it.

Things he wished he'd said and done, harsh regret welled in him, then anger. An image of his mother swelled before his eyes, though it was vague. She'd died their first winter there, when he was only a kit.

Then the only other living kit of the pride was put into his nest to comfort him.

Shard.

I'm a fool. My wingbrother is dead. My father is witless with anger. I have a mate to feed and cannot hunt.

"I won't die down here," he whispered. He'd walked to the pool without thinking. For a moment he thought he saw his mother in the water, then realized it was his own dim reflection. His face, stern but softer in angles than his father, looked haggard. His eyes, bright blue, were his mother's.

"Eyes like the sky," he whispered hoarsely at the water, "his heart burns like the sun." The words of the Widow Queen's song. A Vanir legend. A stupid, mudding song of the Vanir, and his father had tried to take the name of the Summer King and make it Kjorn's.

Now Kjorn knew why Ragna had sung that song, before their war with the wolves began. To call out a hero. To call out Shard.

Shard, prince of the Vanir.

Kjorn loosed a broken laugh. His wingbrother, scrawny, quick, full of wit and no sense. If it thought about it long enough, it didn't feel as odd. His wingbrother, a fellow prince.

A dead prince.

"His heart burns like the sun," Kjorn muttered at his reflection. "He brings justice to the wronged—"

"They will call him the Summer King," a smooth, female voice lilted off the stone. Kjorn staggered back from the pool and reeled around. "And this will be his song."

A female wolf stood before him. Her ruddy fur glowed with silver iridescence in the dim green of the lichens.

"You." Kjorn knew her. She had stayed at the wolf den that summer to warn Sverin of the ambush. Ahanu's sister. She hadn't attacked their dens. But she had led Shard away from him. "You took my wingbrother from me!"

"He flies in the night," she said, her head still high. "And in the day."

"Shut up!" Kjorn lurched toward her. She sprang away into the tunnel, nimble and healthy.

"Do you listen to all who speak?" She twisted away, darting past Kjorn back into the cavern by the pool. "Do you speak to all who hear?"

Kjorn blocked the entryway, opening his wings. He had her cornered in the cavern, if he could only catch her.

"Is your voice the song of summer?"

A low, kit-like keen tore from Kjorn's throat. The last time he had heard those lines he'd felt called, felt something stir in him. The last time he'd heard that song was when Ragna sang it in high summer. Surrounded by his friends, his family, his pride, prepared to go to glorious war, and his father had named him the Summer King.

Now Kjorn knew it was a lie. He was no special king. He was the son of a mad ruler. He had no wingbrother, he'd gotten himself lost underground by his own stupidity, a wolf's plaything.

"He comes when he is needed," uttered the she-wolf, in a low singsong. Her voice in the dark cave was strangely soothing. Kjorn crouched in front of her, staring, empty as a pelt. He should kill her. Or force her to tell him the way out.

"Who is the Summer King?" he whispered instead, and hated himself for asking her a question.

"He comes when he is called," she sang, eyes glowing off-amber in the dimness.

"They will call him the Summer King," Kjorn said dully, remembering. Any strength he'd had to attack her out of anger seeped out of him and he only felt cold.

"Shard was called," she said softly. "And he answered. Will you?"

"Why are you doing this to me? Just kill me if, you that's what you want."

"That's not what I want," she said, and Kjorn found that he almost believed her. She stepped toward him, unafraid. Kjorn had the sense that she was some kind of spirit, that he couldn't touch her if he tried. Still, she stood so close that he could smell her. His talons seemed numb, empty, useless.

"You've wandered for days on end, son-of-Sverin. In this place that challenges you." She stood tall. "Weak and empty as a kit, and just as ready to learn?"

"What would you have me learn?"

"I have a message," she said quietly. "A message from Shard."

"Oh yes, your brother said. I'm supposed to believe that he lives?"

"Yes." Her nose crinkled, exposing the points of her teeth. Somehow, Kjorn thought she looked amused, not aggressive. "When last you saw him, Shard had just come into his full powers as a Vanir. Do you think he feared the sea?"

Kjorn stared at her, and at last he understood. "He *dove*."

"He dove," she confirmed. "He released your father rather than kill him, and he dove. Even now he seeks an answer for peace and balance that doesn't involve turning on you."

Kjorn shook his head, feeling heavy. "What…what message do you have from him?"

"He forgives you," she murmured. "And hopes you will forgive him for all that passed."

Kjorn couldn't even laugh. He didn't know what to do. "Everything used to be so simple."

"Simple," Catori said, "because you didn't know all there was to know about the world. Now that you can listen and see, it may be much harder for you to be as you once were. Come, golden prince, look into the pool with new eyes."

Kjorn met her eyes, searching for lies or mockery.

Then, as if another force lifted his limbs, Kjorn stalked to the black pool. His head slumped and his beak touched the water, sending a ripple. As he tasted the mineral bite of the water, images played across the strange lights of the ripples.

"Show him," Catori whispered to someone Kjorn couldn't see.

Black wings seem to glide under the water, and Kjorn followed them back through the autumn, seeing through raven's eyes.

They slept a little, but at midnight, another cry broke out.

Caj winced, looking toward the entrance. A few females shifted nervously, but many slept on through, as if the sound were part of a nightmare.

"I should have stayed with him," Caj whispered.

Sigrun answered with a growl, tightening her wing around him. "He's done this to himself."

"Have you no pity?" Caj stared through the dark. "He dreams of Elena."

"The Red King is alone by his own devising," warned a low voice from the back of the cave. Caj's hackle feathers pricked when he turned to try and see Ragna through the dark. She spoke quietly, a pale shape. "He has quartered himself off alone, and he must live with it now."

"Fine advice from you," Caj growled. "You above all should have sympathy."

"I mourn Baldr, but I have no pity left for Sverin."

Another nightmare cry echoed down nesting cliffs. Caj wondered how many other gryfons remained awake to hear their king's sorrowful, angry dreams. The same every winter, every Long Night since his mate's death, only this was the first year Caj had not been there to wake and distract him.

Let Halvden comfort him, he thought bitterly. *Let him see what a brother is truly for.*

The sound cut off, as if Halvden had heard Caj's thought through the dark and pulled Sverin from his nightmare.

"The only way you could help is by flying in the dark," Sigrun said, her voice frosty. "So he would throw you out for rule-breaking before you had a chance to help."

Caj feared she might be right, that the loss of Kjorn had driven Sverin so far into rage that he wouldn't see reason. He could do nothing until after the Long Night, nothing but wait in the long, cold black.

"Caj," Ragna said, and he forced himself to listen, for Sigrun. "You're his wingbrother. You're supposed to know all of his secrets."

"Yes?" Caj kept his voice measured and calm, for the sake of his mate, and all the females in the den who were afraid. "Is there something you know that I don't?"

"Perhaps." She shifted, leaning forward so that he could better see her face, and her expression was grim. "But I have promises to keep. You should know though, before the dawn, that something far more dangerous than sorrow haunts the king, and I fear it will drive him mad by the end."

Caj took a slow, patient breath. "And what's that?"

Through the dark she said quietly, "Guilt."

38

BRYNJA

GRYFONS GATHERED WITHIN THE WALL of the Dawn Spire and on high ledges and along the stream, laughing and singing and listening again and again to tales of the hunt.

Some of the older warriors spent their time feasting on fermented fruits and juniper mash that made them grandiose, adding details that had not happened and increasing the size of each greatbeast twofold.

By the time Shard had washed and gotten a swift tutelage on courting from Dagny, it felt as if the hunt had happened years before. The sun lay low, just about to slip under the horizon and leave them in cold dark.

Clean and smelling of juniper that Dagny had insisted on rubbing behind his ears and under his wings, Shard trotted confidently toward the Dawn Spire. He hadn't seen Stigr since their argument. Either his uncle was already out feasting on his own, or had sequestered himself in his den.

He can molt for all I care, Shard thought, feeling giddy. He was going to tell Brynja how he felt. He had to trust Dagny's ideas and suggestions, for if a wingsister couldn't help him, then no one could.

On the dark, nightward side of the Dawn Spire, he found a group of gryfons preparing torches to light the fires. A little fire burned in a pit between them, near a stack of materials that they used to build their firebrands.

"Hail," Shard called. One fledge recognized him.

"Hail, Shard, son-of-Baldr."

Shard drew a deep breath, trotting forward, wings open, ears forward. He must look confident. "I stand in for Dagny. She's ill this night."

The fledge who'd greeted him exchanged a look with an older, tawny female. She eyed Shard up and down, fluffed. "The lighting of the torches of Tyr is a great honor, son-of-Baldr, reserved for the higher families of the pride."

Shard stretched into a respectful bow, not so much to the female, but the mention of Tyr. Dagny had prepared him for all of this. "I ask for that honor tonight. His majesty Orn has recognized me and I wish to serve."

The older female studied him, then nodded to the fledge, who Shard gathered was an apprentice of the fire.

"Two torches please," Shard asked, and all of them blinked at him.

"It isn't safe."

"Would you argue," Shard asked, careful to keep from sounding arrogant, "that I'm not the best flier of the pride? I can carry two."

The older female chuckled and shrugged a wing to her fledge. "Very well. But you'll hear me laugh when your feathers are what lights our feast tonight."

Shard dipped his head in respect, and waited while the fledge selected two long brands and wrapped the ends in a combination of grass, thin strips of hide and old feathers. Then he rolled the ends in a shallow trench filled with pitch from juniper trees. Warily, the fledge lifted both brands and handed them to Shard. He was grateful to see that the fledge had selected two especially long torches.

"Light them," said the female gravely, and they all watched in silence while Shard pressed the two branches together, gripping them as he would a large fish, and lowered the ends into the fire.

The flames licked up, caught and crawled over the ends of his torches. For a moment Shard stared, awed at the power in his talons. Tyr's flame, the heat of the sun, the power of skyfire, dancing tamely on two sticks. He dipped his head low, gave thanks to the flame tenders, and crouched back on his haunches.

"You may light the seven pyres in the nightward quarter between the stream and the Wind Spire," the female told him. Shard inclined his head to her, bunched his muscles and sprang from a sitting start into the air.

"Don't fly too fast!" shrieked the fledge after him, "wind can kill the fire, or blow it on your feathers! And the torch will only burn until darkness falls! Don't take too long!"

"Thank you!" Shard called down to them. Then he was distracted with managing his flight while neither drowning the flames in wind from his wings, or catching his feathers in the flame. The challenge thrilled him. Soon he found a gentle soaring, flapping rhythm that brushed the flame from his wings but didn't kill the fire. That mastered, he sought out a certain nest Dagny had told him of.

Gryfons stared as he flew through the arches and spires with two dangerous torches in his claws. He reached a series of dens carved high off the ground, in a beautiful red wall of a dawnward facing cliff.

Hovering outside Shard called, "Hail Brynja, daughter-of-Mar!"

A moment of silence fell. Shard flapped carefully, holding his position, watching the flames of his torches and the horizon. He had just enough time.

Then Brynja appeared. Washed of dust and blood from the hunt, she appeared like an apparition of red from the red stone and as the firelight touched her face, Shard almost forgot his plan. Then she cocked her head.

"Shard?" Her eyes widened at the sight of the torches. "What are you doing?"

"Brynja!" He laughed, angling his fires carefully. "I've been honored with lighting the evening fires. Fly with me."

Don't make it a question, Dagny had said. *Brynja is kind, but she is from an old, proud, powerful line. Carry the fire to impress her family. Be strong to impress her.*

An older pair of gryfons peered out from behind her. Relief filled Shard, though he trusted Dagny, he'd had doubts—but if Brynja still nested with her parents, then she truly wasn't tied to any other.

They eyed him skeptically.

"Honorable Mar and Byrja!" Grateful Dagny had passed on the name of Brynja's mother as well, Shard lowered his head in a flying bow. He'd practiced the sentence over and over so he wouldn't stutter. "I wish for your daughter to help me light the fires."

"I don't—" began her mother, and from her Shard saw where Brynja got her beauty, but Brynja leaped from the mouth of the den.

"It's a good honor, Mother."

"Be careful!" warned Mar, her father, his gaze trained on Shard. "You've never flown with the fire before."

"Shard will teach me," she called. Circling around Shard once, she met his gaze and asked, "Won't you?"

"Of course." He cast one look around, wary of what her parents must think, and of seeing Asvander.

What about Asvander? Shard had asked Dagny as she advised him on Brynja's favorite songs, scents, and choice of meat from the greatbeast.

I'll keep him busy, she'd said. It wasn't entirely what Shard meant, but Dagny hadn't given up more information. The last thing Shard wanted was to be accused of stealing a mate, but Dagny had tutted, assured him they weren't mated and that Asvander could handle a little competition. Shard had to weigh the worry of losing a new friend against the possibility of pledging to Brynja.

You're an honorable gryfon, Shard, Dagny had assured him finally. He ran her words over and over again as Brynja watched him expectantly, her eyes glowing with admiration at the way he held the torches.

Declare yourself to Brynja, fight for her if you want her, and let her decide. That's the way. The strong endure, she'd added flippantly. *Asvander has plenty of options. How could you live the rest of your life not knowing if she feels the same?*

It was that last sentence that set Shard on his course without doubts. Surely it was his right to at least declare his feelings. Then Brynja could decide for herself. He thought of his single, bumbling attempt at speaking to a female of his own pride in the Silver Isles, and how Halvden had snatched her away at the end of the very same conversation. It hadn't been right, anyway. Shard hadn't really wanted to fight for her, couldn't really seem himself with her.

"Show me," Brynja whispered, her gaze flicking to the end of the fire. Shard met her eyes, and almost told her everything. He did want to fight for her, even if it meant putting himself against Asvander. He could see himself flying with her for the rest of his days, as he had never pictured himself flying with anyone except his wingbrother. This was how Thyra and Kjorn had felt, he was sure of it. He wouldn't bow out easily.

"Take it carefully," he instructed. "Keep your wing strokes higher, short, as if you're just hovering."

Cautiously, he turned the brand so that the flame almost licked his face but his wing beats kept it pulsing back. Brynja gripped the end before the flames burned Shard, then laughed nervously. Shard let her experience the moment of awe of holding the fire.

"Do everything just a little slower. Wind can put it out, but you can also protect it with your wings. Careful—there, you've got it." Shard studied her wing beats, nodding. "Well done!"

Brynja's face shone at him like the sun. "This is amazing, Shard."

"If you scoop your wings a little, you can dive without putting it out. Do you think you can do that? And point it down. The flame likes to burn up, toward Tyr."

She practiced, dropping a little, wings cupped to protect the fire, holding it out far enough that it wouldn't burn her. "Yes!"

"Good," Shard said, confident she had the rhythm of it. Then he turned without warning and dove.

"Wait!" Brynja laughed behind him.

Marveling, Shard enjoyed the moment that she chased after him, then slowed so she could catch up.

Dagny was right, he thought. She'd promised him that a little adventure would be just the thing to catch Brynja off guard.

"We've been assigned the nightward quarter," Shard said. He gauged the sunlight left, while Brynja watched him in quiet curiosity.

She won't ask questions right away, Dagny had promised, *she'll try to figure out what you're up to. That's the secret of most females, you see. We actually* do *want you to come after us, to court us.*

Unless she blatantly said no or hissed in his face, Shard had retorted, and Dagny agreed. But Brynja hadn't done that. She'd followed, laughing, and mimicked the way Shard flew to keep her feathers safe from the fire.

"Should I teach you some of my tricks now?" Shard asked. It sounded arrogant to him, but Dagny had told him to show off a little. Brynja had to know he was worthy of her, that he had something to offer, that he could be exciting and worthwhile.

"Not with the fire!"

Shard almost laughed at her panic. "Then just watch," he said, amazed at how well Dagny knew her wingsister.

"Shard, wait!"

He rose higher, folded one wing and fell in a spiral, stretching the torch out so that it formed a swirl of fire, a tunnel that he flew straight through. He heard someone yell in amazement below. Brynja shouted breathlessly for him to stop being foolish, but there was laughter in her voice.

Shard winged up again, closing his mind from everything else but flight. Lowering the torch, he soared up again so that he flew like the starfire over the aerie. The first unlit pyre came into view and Shard wheeled hard to the side, grazing the dry brush just before he flipped upside down, his torch gusting sparks above him.

The sentry at the post shouted at him for his foolishness. Shard only laughed, and peered back to see Brynja, face determined, pumping her wings to catch him. Shard slowed so that she could. She smacked his head with a wing and he expected her to tell him to stop being foolish.

"Show me," she demanded. Shard laughed.

"Yes, my lady.

He'd taught Kjorn a few tricks and so he knew what she had to do to make her broader wings function like his. He caught her around the wrist joint and, pelting each other with their wings and holding their torches out with care, Shard dragged her higher into the sky.

"You have to give yourself room," he explained. She hadn't pulled from his grip, though it was awkward to fly together.

"*Shard—*"

"Tuck a wing!"

She obeyed, trusting him so instantly that his heart glowed, and he thrust her away hard. When he released his grip she fell spinning away from him in a fancy roll, the torch sputtering and showering sparks on the gryfons staring below. She corrected in time to realize Shard had flung her toward the next pyre and, laughing in surprised triumph, she swept her torch across the dried grass and soared away as the fire sprang to life.

"I did it!" she cried. Shard laughed and winged in to grasp her tail. She blinked back at him, feathers fanning and closing again.

"Flap hard!"

She did and Shard lunged below her, tugging her tail so that her wing beat pushed her into a graceful back flip while he spotted. He echoed the flip and they fell together, touching their torches to the next pyre at the same time. Shard caught her gaze as the flames surged to life, then laughed and flapped away.

So they danced across their quarter of the aerie, flipping around the last of the pyres, laughing at friends below, until darkness fell and only firelight drove back the dark. Below, a singer's voice rose in a ballad.

"Shard!" Brynja called as he broke from her to flap high again. "We've finished! Come down!"

"Catch me!" he challenged. Laughing, she flew after him.

After the fires, Dagny had said, *you have to show her something only you can.*

What's that? Shard had asked, and remembered Dagny's blank stare.

I don't know. You do have something special, don't you? Something you haven't shared with anyone? That's what we want you know, to be let into your secret world.

Brynja called from below. "Shard, wait, it's dark!"

Something he hadn't shared with anyone, Dagny instructed. His secret world.

"Shard, my torch!"

For as the apprentice fire keeper had promised, the torches would only last until darkness fell. Shard's torch guttered in his talons, dying to dim blue in the cold and the wind of his wings. Brynja caught up to him, breathless. Below them the aerie flickered and glittered with firelight, but they flew high enough that they felt only the frosty cold of desert winter and the darkness cloaked around them.

Shard tossed his cold brand away. Before Brynja could speak, he gently pried hers away too and dropped it. Their breath clouded the air between them. Shard's heart rolled like a thunderstorm and his talons trembled.

"Shard," she whispered, ears flat with fear. "The dark..."

"Look."

They flapped, hovering in the chill dark, and he tilted his head back. Brynja watched him a moment, her gaze flickering down to the warm glow of the aerie. Then, taking a deep breath, she turned her face up.

Shard watched as the starlight spread over her face and filled her eyes.

"Oh," she whispered, her gaze roaming across the sweep of stars above. By her expression, he knew she had never seen the stars so bright, not since the gryfons of Dawn Spire lit the flames of Tyr. The sun might not set on Dawn Spire, but that meant never seeing the stars.

Shard murmured, "Have you ever seen them so bright?"

"No." Her voice quavered.

"There is light in the dark," Shard said. "See those stars there? That is Sig, the swan who flies ever starward. And there, Bjorna, the First Bear, and her cub. That cluster, the First Pack, the wolf stars..."

He saw her eyes trail along the great, bright river of stars that wove in the brightest band across the sky.

"And that is Midragur," he murmured, his wings sweeping cool wind between them. "The star dragon who coils around the earth as a serpent around its egg. The egg will hatch one day, and that day will be the end of the world."

Slowly Brynja's eyes found Shard again. His heart pounded.

"I wanted to show you," he whispered, not sure how he found the words, staring in the dark shine of her eyes. "This is how it is the Silver Isles, Brynja. I fly at night. There's nothing to fear, no place we couldn't go, no where we couldn't fly and explore," the words tumbled out of him and he didn't realize how strongly he'd imagined showing her his home.

"We?" was all she asked.

"If—if you fly with me," he managed, reaching forward to slip his talons through hers, where she'd tucked her foot in the warm down of her chest. She didn't pull away, but she looked away from him to the stars. The slow, steady rush of wind from their wing beats sent chills through him.

"It's beautiful, Shard."

"Brynja." He tightened his grip. It would be so easy to leave it at that, to savor the moment forever, not to take the risk. He forced himself to say more words. "I have so many things I want to tell you." For a moment she grasped him in return, then her grip loosened.

"We have to go back," she said. "This isn't safe, this…" her gaze dropped from him and the stars to fall toward the Outlands. Shard sensed her fear was taking her from him, even from his secret place.

"Just a moment more." Shard kept his voice firm as Dagny had instructed, trying not to sound apologetic or too shy. Brynja looked to him, quiet curiosity in the dark.

"It's getting cold."

I'll keep you warm, he thought, wondering if she could hear his heart, but even with his pretend confidence he couldn't say that. He fluffed up his feathers with a chuckle. The scent of smoke and juniper wafted from him and his wing beats and suddenly, before he could say more, Brynja sneezed. Shard started, releasing her talons.

"Juniper?" She sniffed. "Is that you?"

Mortified heat flushed under Shard's feathers. "Dagny said…well, yes."

"Dagny," she echoed, then tilted her head back and looked at the stars, the fires below, her own wings as if remembering the wild way they'd flown. "I see now."

"Brynja," Shard tried to call her attention back.

"It's nice." She didn't meet his eyes. "The scent I mean. It just surprised me. You didn't seem like the kind of gryfon to do that. So it makes sense that Dagny helped you." She sighed and mumbled, "It makes perfect sense." Between them, their wing beats chilled the air, and Shard began to feel the strain of hovering.

"Let's land." The stars were losing their magic, he could tell, and he couldn't talk to her if they were both growing weary and distracted by cold. Silently she followed as he stooped to land on an empty rock tower just outside the ring of fire light.

For a moment they stood in silence and Shard settled his wings uneasily, sensing that she wanted him to say something.

Stubbornly, though he knew the moment had passed he said, "Brynja, I like you more than I've liked any other huntress, ever. I like you the way I would a wingbrother—I mean, but a female. I want you to be by me always, I want to fly with you."

It sounded so stupid when he said it aloud. He persisted, even though she looked a little amused. "You make me feel stronger than I am. And you're smart, and you're kind and you listened to me when I first arrived here. Not many would do that. And…"

When he finally met her gaze, he couldn't go on. He didn't need to.

There was a light in her eyes that took the breath from him. As if another force controlled him, he stepped toward her, as if he might drag her back into the sky into a pledge flight right then.

She pulled away and he realized with a tremble that some of the brightness in her eyes was sadness. The faint firelight that touched her face traced vivid lines along her delicate beak and the wide, watching circles of her eyes.

"You're one of the most amazing gryfons I've known, Shard." She drew a shaking breath and let it out in a cloud of steam. "And I care for you. More than I should, much more than I should."

Shard hesitated, because while he could have back-flipped off of the tower, she didn't seem happy. "Then what's wrong?"

"Don't you see? It can't be, Shard."

Somehow the words didn't quite make sense, and he tried to hold all the bits together. He'd led her on a breathtaking flight, shown her a beautiful secret, had managed to confess himself without sounding like too much of an idiot and, if he'd heard her correctly, she felt the same. He didn't think he'd missed anything.

"Is it because I've claimed to be from the Outlands? You know that's not true." *I'm a prince,* he wanted to shout, but kept his peace, eyes narrowing slowly. Females thought differently than males, he knew that much, and he waited to let her explain herself before he said something stupid.

"No," she said quickly, and suddenly her eyes were on him again, wide and pleading. "That's not it, you must believe me. I care for you, Shard, for who you've proven to be, for your skill and your humility and your kindness and...your laugh," she tapped her beak shut and crouched back a little, as if horrified at her confession.

"Then?" he asked, cautiously joyful at her words.

"Don't you see," she whispered, ears laying back, eyes widening as if she couldn't believe he didn't understand yet. "I'm promised. To Asvander."

Slowly, proud of himself for remaining calm, he said, "I don't understand. If you haven't pledged, how can you be promised. You make it sound as if someone else promised for you."

The joy in him at her confession sat behind a wall of dread, behind a rising wall of fear that even though he'd been brave, done his best, found the most perfect female for him in all the world, he couldn't have her.

She watched him. Songs drifted to them, laughter, it sounded worlds away. "Shard, I think things are more complicated here than they are where you're from. In the Silver Isles."

"This isn't complicated."

"It is," she said gently, and Shard took a step back. "Sometimes we mate to form alliances, to bring families closer. You know that Asvander abandoned his family to come to the Dawn Spire?"

"I know," Shard said, hollow.

"His family and mine are old, old allies. Orn hopes that if we mate, it will bring his clan back to the Dawn Spire."

"*Orn*?" Shard burst out, finally. "In the Silver Isles, not even the *king* can choose another's mate! Not even Tyr! It's—it's not about that, Brynja, it's about—it's about..."

"Love?" she offered, her voice very soft.

"It's about love," Shard said firmly, and took a hard breath. "Brynja, I—"

"Please stop," she said, one ear tuning toward the feast, as if others might hear. Suddenly, Shard didn't care.

"But you do care about me. That's why you've been avoiding me?"

She blinked at his tone and he realized it was the wrong thing to say. It sounded arrogant and forceful and not like him at all. *But it's true,* he thought desperately.

"You don't have to do anything you don't want to do," he insisted.

"I want the Dawn Spire to be strong," she said evenly. "If a match with Asvander—who is dear to me, too, by the way—makes it so, then that is what I want."

Would a match with a prince make the Dawn Spire strong? he wanted to ask. *Would making you a queen?*

He wondered if she would laugh. He wondered how much his little kingship in his little islands in a distant sea even mattered to the gryfons of the Winderost.

"Orn wants to be stronger," he said quietly, "so that you can fight the dragons?"

That surprised her. "The dragons? No...no. So that we can defend, if need be. So that we can begin reuniting the families and reclaim the glory that was."

"Glory," Shard echoed. "I see. Now you sound like Sverin's kin after all." He lifted his wings, restless, and she looked stricken. He shook his head at the scent of juniper on his feathers, feeling sick. "This is stupid. I can't believe Dagny let me think any of this would do any good."

"Shard—"

"Never mind," he said sharply, embarrassment and anger flooding out before he could stop himself. "You and Asvander can have each other. Stigr was right."

Before Brynja could say another word Shard shoved up from the rock and beat his wings hard, soaring away over the feast to find some dark corner to sit alone. He thought of how he'd planned to find her a perfect cut of meat, a singer to lay her favorite ballad, how he'd rubbed his feathers with scent…

Stupid, stupid, stupid. He must look like a fool. And Dagny had let him. *Why would she do that?* He'd thought they were friends.

What stung the most was knowing Brynja felt the same about him and would still turn him down.

Shard flew to the very edge of the Wind Spire, away from the stream and the feasting, laying his ears flat against the sound of singing and drunken boasting. He stared into the night.

I flew here on a different wind. I've wasted time. I've let my family down.

It was time to do what he'd come to do.

A gryfon soared overhead, calling out to everyone within hearing.

"Hail all! His majesty Orn, son-of-Throsver, calls the Wintermeet! Let all with grievances come forth. Let all with news. We will meet, and hear, and speak! Hail chiefs, warriors, huntresses! Meet at the Dawn Spire in a quarter mark."

For a moment Shard watched as other gryfons left their circles to stream toward the meet. Then he pushed himself up and trotted toward the Dawn Spire, eyes narrowed.

He had a grievance.

39
Wintermeet

The crescent that formed the inner curve of the Dawn Spire teemed with gryfons. Shard thought every gryfon in the Winderost must be there, even the fledges. Fires waved from the highest ridge of the crescent and from torches set within the tiers, sending smoke and orange light.

Shard trotted to his tier, but found a fledge there, who gazed at him nervously. Stigr hailed him from above and Shard peered around until he caught sight of his uncle—the only black gryfon in the pride.

We've been moved up again, he thought. *Good.*

He hopped into the air and landed by Stigr. "Fair winds, Uncle."

Stigr only inclined his head. After a moment of silence that buzzed with the voices of other gryfons, Shard drew a sharp breath.

"Forgive me, Uncle. For before. You were right. I've forgotten my purpose here and betrayed the trust of those who wait for me. Thank you for trying to remind me."

He dipped his head and saw that Stigr looked surprised. "Forgive me too. I was harsh, and spoke out of turn." His voice was odd when he added, "Shard…we should talk."

But before they could, Orn landed and hailed all present. Shard sat, shifting his feet and tail twitching, while Orn spoke of the hunt and gave news. Others on higher tiers gave reports on the activities of their families and Asvander spoke about the state of the borders and incidents of eagles and dogs attacking. Shard watched the First Sentinel, trying to keep his expression impassive as he tried to figure out what Asvander possessed that Shard himself didn't.

"And now." Orn stood again when Asvander had finished. "Any with news, any with grievances or matters of importance, speak now. Any initiated warrior may speak their mind this night."

Shard stood. "I have something to say."

Stigr looked at him slowly as excited whispers arose. "My prince," he murmured, low enough that no one but Shard heard. "What are you planning?"

"Stand by me," Shard said quietly, "that's all I ask."

"Always," Stigr said.

"Shard," Orn acknowledged. "Son-of-Baldr, my new pride member and friend."

All fell silent, then rustling cheers rose. Shard's belly fell to his claws and he looked up slowly, staring at the king, who spread his tawny wings wide as if to embrace Shard from afar.

"You have more than earned your right to speak here. What say you?"

Expectant faces watched him. Hundreds and hundreds, so many more than the pride at home. Shard tried to imagine them all as enormous sparrows, so that it wasn't as intimidating. Rather than stay on his high ledge, jumped off his tier to glide down and stand on the rock platform in the center of the crescent, where everyone could see him, and he could see everyone.

"I came here with many questions," he said in even voice, and waited until the echo of it faded against the rock. "And the hope of becoming your friend and brother. I even…wanted to court a certain one of you. That distracted me from my purpose, and I shouldn't have tried to disrupt your pride. But there are things wrong here. Things I should have realized—and now you need to know the truth."

A face distracted him. Brynja, on a high tier with Valdis. She stared at him, and Valdis gave a quick, negative shake of her head. *Don't do it,* they both seemed to shout silently. *Not here.*

Shard turned and saw Stigr with almost the same, horrified expression.

A slow, rolling anger began at his talons and heated his chest. *Who is Stigr to recommend what I do? And Brynja, and Valdis? My father was a king. If I want to be a king, I must make my own way.*

He took a deep breath, holding the last image of his father, of Sverin, of Helaku, the old wolf king. He held them all and pictured himself among them. Strong, a prince. A king. Finally, he thought of Kjorn, of the many lies he'd told, and he found his voice.

"I didn't come from the Outlands."

A slow, surprised murmur rolled through the assembled, and those who might not have been listening turned their faces toward Shard. The bobbing firelight cast them all in strange shadows, a single, curious beast with a thousand eagle eyes.

"I came from a place in the Starland Sea called the Silver Isles. It won't mean anything to you until I tell you that it's now the home of the son of Per the Red and all who flew with him."

Shard expected another outburst of murmurs, but it was silent. His tail twitched with rising nerves and he glanced at Stigr—but his uncle was watching the crowd with a wary eye.

They could have heard a feather touch rock.

"Per?" Orn demanded. "What is this?"

Shard knew he had to hold strong, that Valdis had said Orn wouldn't like to hear Per's name for some reason. Perhaps, like the outlying clans, Per hadn't been as loyal to Orn. Shard wondered if it was that simple, if that's why he'd flown to the Silver Isles.

"What game?" Orn glared down at Shard. "I've offered you honors—"

"Hear him," said the queen, from behind Orn and to Shard's surprise. "He has earned his place here. He hasn't acted as a spy. My honored lord," she said to Orn. "Hear him."

Shard bowed to the queen and Orn made a rough noise. Shard continued, looking around but letting the faces blur as he spoke, afraid to meet too many eyes too closely. "I flew here to learn why they came to my home, and I think I understand now. They fled the enemy here that you don't talk about."

Uncomfortable shifting began and Shard took a steadying breath, trusting his words to Tyr and to Tor, who'd guided his visions and dreams. Expressions darkened all around him and Shard forced himself to go on. He had to finish what he'd started, or everything was for nothing.

"And I had to learn why. Because Per and his kin didn't just *escape* to the Silver Isles. Rather than take my father's offer of friendship, Per turned violent, and he and his followers conquered and killed my family. They took our land. Members of my pride, the Vanir, were killed or driven away."

The crescent filled with restless, dark muttering. Shard turned a half quarter so that he addressed King Orn and his fierce mate. Sister to Sverin's dead queen.

"Thank you for speaking up for me, my lady. I understand you loved your sister. I'll tell you what happened to her. You deserve the truth, for welcoming us here." She watched him with her cool blue eyes, so like Kjorn's, and he could not read her face.

"The Aesir's first winter in the Silver Isles was the harshest in many years." Shard had been too young to remember, but Stigr had told him the tale that autumn. "The hunting was poor. The pride was starving. The females of the Vanir tried to teach Sverin's mate to fish from the shallows, but she flew too far. She tried to dive. But Aesir wings aren't made for the sea." Shard took a breath, holding the queen's gaze. "She died."

A soft, mournful gasp swept the onlookers. "She died," Shard said again, almost apologizing to the gold gryfess above him. The briefest sorrow flashed over her face and was gone, hidden, behind a cold, regal expression.

Shard looked around, eyes narrowing. "But Sverin and Per didn't blame her inexperience. They blamed the Vanir. They blamed the winter and the sea and they forbid fishing. That started a war with the wolves of the next isle, because we forced ourselves onto their hunting ground."

They weren't happy. Shard knew he stood on dangerous ground, accusing their missing kin of violence and ignorance. He didn't care. He was done pretending to be a begging, grateful Outlander.

"Last summer Sverin's plan to slaughter the wolves was turned against him. The wolves attacked us on our own ground."

Dark murmurs of 'dog' and 'treacherous.'

"But," Shard called, and his voice bounced hard against the stone, deeper, harsher with his growing anger. "Sverin brought it on himself. I called him out. I challenged him."

Slowly he raised his wings. He expected to hear chuckles and snorts at the thought of him challenging Sverin, but it was silent. Even Stigr stared at him as if he was a strange, foreign thing.

"I could have killed him." Shard stared around, eyes narrowed at the angry faces. "I could have dragged him with me into the sea. But I didn't." He drew a slow breath, flexing his talons against the grounding red stone. "I didn't, because Sverin's son is my wingbrother. Kjorn, prince of the Aesir in the Silver Isles."

"This is boastful treachery!" shouted an old male on the high tiers. "He's clearly an enemy and a spy. Send him to the Outlands!"

"Hear him," Stigr countered. Voices rose in argument. Wings flared, talons slapped the rock and Shard flapped his wings for attention.

"I came only to learn the truth of the Aesir's coming. I can help here!" Shard raised his voice against the rising noises of dissent. "I forged a peace with wolves of the Silver Isles. The painted dogs of the Winderost are no different, and not your enemy! The same for the lions, the eagles! You share this land!" Laughter, shouting, argument. Shard turned in a circle again. "Don't you see, if you all came together, you could fight the dragons, you could drive them away, and claim the Winderost without fear!"

"The dragons?" shrieked an ancient female.

"Peace with wolves?"

"Fight the dragons indeed!"

"Witless Outlander!"

"Why did you come here?" King Orn's smooth voice fell on the din. "Why did you come here, really? You speak the names of cursed exiles and throw out suggestions of war? Foolhardy, wild suggestions for my pride? Who are you?"

Shard noticed that the queen remained silent, and stared at him with the intensity of the sun. He glanced to Brynja, Valdis, even Asvander, who watched him with an odd, keen look. Finally Stigr, who only lashed his tail, wary. Arguments stifled to low chiding and restlessness.

"Who are you?" demanded a female of Orn's tier.

Shard held his head high.

"I'm Shard. Rashard, son-of-Baldr the Nightwing and Ragna the White." Shard dug his talons against the rock. "Rightful prince and future king of the Silver Isles."

40
SHARD'S OFFER

THE CRESCENT EXPLODED. SHOCKED LAUGHTER and enraged shrieking rattled off the faces of rock. After his tale of Per, it seemed that to claim he was king of a foreign land was too much. Stigr leaped off his tier to glide down and stand protectively at Shard's side, a solid black rock of gryfon.

"Fancy you getting better at speaking to large groups," Stigr muttered, his wing pressed to Shard's wing, "at a time like this. Now what?"

"That's up to Orn," he muttered, still feeling raw over Brynja, over wasted time, all of it.

"I will hear no more!" Orn's voice silenced all. The gryfons stilled, ears perked toward their king, suspicious glances sliding sideways to Shard.

"Go, all of you, back to the feasting. This is a mockery. The family chiefs and I will discuss this. And you." He swiveled to stare at Shard. "I offered you shelter, safety, good hunting, and a chance for a place here, and you return the favor with slanderous tales and insulting suggestions for ruling *my* land. If I find that you are a spy from the clans beyond, here to cause unrest, I won't wait for the beasts of the Outlands to kill you."

"I helped saved the hunt," Shard reminded him. "I won my initiation fairly."

"That is why I give you a single second chance to live in peace here. No more of these tales. You will be silent." He raised his voice again. "Everyone, to the feast. We enjoyed a great victory at the hunt. Forget the tales this Outlander has told to shock us, and feast!"

Shard stared as the gryfons leaped down from their tiers or flew up and away to the scatter of boulders where the feast would be held. Brynja and Valdis began to fly, and Orn's voice cut the air.

"You two. Stay. And you," he said to Stigr and Shard. "Valdis, did you know of this?"

Shard watched Valdis closely. She exchanged a look with Brynja, then bowed low toward the king, mantling. "I did."

Orn's hackle feathers ruffed up and his gaze darted to Brynja. "You?"

"Yes, my lord."

He stared at them. "You bring friends of Per into my very nest? Into the pride? What were you thinking? I could slap your families to the lowest tiers or into exile for such a thing."

"We thought of the queen," Valdis said. "Who would wish to know of her sister."

Orn looked sharply to the queen and Shard wondered, suddenly, if she had known since the first day of their arrival and simply bided her time. *If Valdis told her that first day, why? What game are they playing here?*

"Valdis and Brynja acted for us," Stigr said to Orn, his voice calm and grave. "Everything my nephew says is true. And we're no friends of Per."

"I wish you no ill," Shard said to Orn. "I don't want to cause unrest here or hurt your pride. But *my* pride is hurting. Valdis said you might not give me a chance if you knew my tale. I needed answers here. I have them. I didn't wish to lie to you about who I am any more."

Orn measured him, tail swinging back and forth, then eyed Valdis, Brynja, Stigr, and his queen. "No more talk of these Silver Isles, Per's kin, or war with the dragons. That is too dangerous a proposition, and the thought will distract my warriors from their current duties. If you abide by that, then you may remain."

"Thank you," Shard said, then, "I have another favor."

Stigr made a low, warning noise.

"And that is?" Orn said, staring.

"I need to explore the Winderost to search for missing, exiled Vanir of my home pride. I ask your leave to travel unhindered."

"No." Orn glowered. Shard lowered his head, eyes locked on the king's face, and bit back argument. "An unnecessary privilege in the face of the unrest you've caused tonight."

"My lord—"

"If I find," Orn growled, "that you have been traveling for any reason other than to hunt or fulfill your duties as a pride member, conversing with rogue clans or venturing near the Outlands, I won't stop at exiling you." He snapped his beak in warning. "Asvander."

The First Sentinel snapped to attention. "Your Highness."

"You and the Guard will make sure Shard and his uncle heed my instructions."

Without even a sideways glance to Shard, Asvander bowed and murmured assent. Orn excused Shard and Stigr and kept the others back, his voice rising in anger.

"Now what?" Stigr muttered as they left the crescent.

"Now," Shard said, feeling rebellious, "I'll just have to try talking to someone else."

Stigr looked toward the sky. "I was afraid you'd say that."

The celebration lasted almost until dawn. Shard and Stigr sat alone on the outskirts and ate little. Bits of conversation floated to Shard, songs, the laughter of romping kits.

"And they won't even look at us now," Shard muttered, pacing. He eyed Stigr, lying on his belly close by, picking apart the leg bone of a greatbeast bull. "They won't even talk about it. Or us. The Aesir like to forbid things, don't they?"

"You will be a different kind of king?" Stigr offered. It was more of a question than a statement.

"Yes," Shard said.

Stigr watched him, his single eye hard and bright. "Finally starting to think of yourself as a king? That was something, your little speech. I'm glad to see you won't need me as much anymore."

Shard felt uneasy. "That's not true, I don't feel that way. You're my father's wingbrother. When we return home, when Sverin is gone, you'll help me…"

Stigr stood and stretched. "Shard, I've taught you all I can about flying, about fighting, and the sea. What I know about being a king could fit on the tip of my talon."

Shard sat down, feeling hollow. Somehow, he'd always had a vision of his uncle guiding him, telling him what his father would have done.

As if in answer to that silent thought, Stigr said, "You'll be your own kind of king. I know your father would be proud. And your mother will be there."

"But you'll be there too."

Stigr inclined his head and glanced toward the Dawn Spire. "What are we going to do with this bee's nest you've stirred?"

"I don't know," Shard whispered. "I couldn't lie anymore. I was angry. Maybe it was stupid."

"Very stupid," agreed Valdis' smooth voice from the shadows.

Stigr and Shard startled, turning to see the gryfess appear from the dark around the corner of a towering stone spire. She trotted up with Brynja and Asvander behind her. Shard stepped one hind paw back. He didn't want to see any of them.

"What did you think would happen?" Valdis looked from Stigr to Shard. "I thought you were going to wait, to let us help you. Now not only did you mention Sverin and Per in one breath, but you've suggested that Orn is a poor leader and a coward."

The way she said it made it sound as if she agreed, but Shard didn't dare interrupt her.

"Be still," Stigr said, lifting his wings, as if she were a hunting female in his own pride. To Shard's awe, Valdis lowered her head a little, watching Stigr warily.

Unease tightened Shard's belly at the display and he wondered how much things would be different if Valdis was not an Aesir, if that was the only thing Stigr held against her. He realized Stigr hadn't answered his question about returning to the Silver Isles. He wondered, feeling hollow, what Stigr had wanted to talk to him about, before the Wintermeet.

"Is that all true?" Asvander asked Shard. "About Per, and his family, and you, fighting Sverin?"

"Of course it's true," Shard said wearily, feeling ill toward Asvander only for the way Brynja stood at his side. "If I were going to lie I would've thought of something that wouldn't get me exiled."

He noticed, in that moment, that Dagny wasn't there. *I'll keep Asvander busy*, she'd promised, to give Shard time to court Brynja. He couldn't figure out before why she would do it if she knew they were promised. Finally it dawned. *Why would she have told me not to worry unless she thought she could win Asvander herself? She must have had as much luck as I did.*

His bitterness toward her eased only a little.

"I've told Orn for years," Asvander said quietly, with a sideways look to the festivities, "that we must take the offensive. That we must fight the dragons. They don't belong here."

Shard stared at Asvander, at the gryfon that he wanted to hate, but couldn't.

"But Shard, you haven't seen them fighting and hunting. Even with all our numbers, it isn't enough. You don't know what it's like. You lose yourself in fear. We can't keep ourselves together. If we could, it might be different..." He lifted his wings in a shrug.

The night chill seeped in, a cold wind rising to sing between the red rock towers. The faint scent of smoke and sage stirred Shard's imagination.

Maybe they could speak to the dragons. Maybe, like gryfons and wolves, they just misunderstood each other. Or, if they couldn't make peace, maybe there was another way.

Shard studied Asvander quietly. "What of help from the painted wolves?"

Valdis tapped her beak in a laugh and Brynja snorted, "Unlikely."

"What of the eagles?" Shard looked over at Brynja, challenging. "What if the wolves did fight with you? And the grass cat prides? What if all the Winderost rose against them? What of my pride? What if you had help from the Silver Isles? Everyone says the dragons don't belong here. They haven't been here forever, have they?" A thought hit him and he look around at each gryfon. "Only since Per's father claimed dragon treasure."

Valdis nodded.

So not only had Per and his kin and friends stolen dragon treasure, they'd brought doom on the Winderost and then fled. Shard's view of them as conquerors darkened to something much worse.

He nodded once, completing his own thoughts while the others watched him. "They don't belong here and you can send them back where they came from!"

Stigr stared at him. "Shard, this isn't our—"

"You said the lost Vanir would return to the Silver Isles in spring. In what numbers, Uncle?" Shard paced in a tight circle. For half a breath, he felt like a prince, and he stopped pacing to look at Stigr. "What if I sent a message through the winds and the birds for the Vanir to fly to the Dawn Spire? Can it be done? Can you help me?"

Before Stigr could respond, Shard whirled to face Asvander, Brynja and Valdis.

"How many dragons are there? Does anyone know? A great pride of them, or only a few?"

"No one knows," Brynja whispered, trying to meet his gaze. "No one has ventured into the Outlands to find out."

"Then the exiles may know," Shard said grimly. "If any survive. Exiles, living in the Outlands."

The wind picked up, carrying away sounds, and the smoke of the fires gusted between them. Shard faced the gryfons before him, drawing a breath.

"What if we banded together? Made new allies, re-forged the ties of the Dawn Spire? What if you were free of the dragons, not for a season, but forever?"

They stood, staring, then exchanged glances. Shard saw their hope, the bright light of the hunt in their eyes—then saw it die.

Brynja lowered her head, ears flat. "Orn would never agree."

"You forget who has the loyalty of the Guard," Asvander said, fluffing.

Brynja flashed Asvander an admiring look and an ugly creature wriggled up in Shard's heart. He looked away.

"There are enough loyal," Brynja said uncertainly after seeing Shard's expression. "Loyal to Orn, and afraid of the enemy, who would keep their kin from fighting."

"The Lakelanders would follow me," Asvander insisted. "And those most loyal to them. We could fly to the Ostral Shores, and to the plains, the Vanheim shore, to the scattered clans that don't nest at Dawn Spire!"

"You're speaking of full rebellion now," Brynja said quietly.

"Orn is an old coward," Valdis muttered, and Shard and Stigr looked at her in surprise. She lifted her head proudly. "A pathetic replacement for the line of Kajar."

Kajar.

Shard took a deep breath. "Kajar and his line ruled the Winderost?"

"Once." Valdis lashed her tail, and eyed the violet sky warily.

Shard perked his ears. Kjorn's great grandfather. With Valdis' words Shard realized Per hadn't simply styled himself a king when he conquered the Silver Isles, as he'd always thought. He *was* a king. He'd wondered what tier Per and Sverin held before fleeing the Winderost.

It wasn't tier at all, but the very crown of the Dawn Spire.

Once, all of the Winderost had been united.

What changed? Shard had asked Asvander.

The king.

"It became clear," Valdis continued, "that the dragons hungered for the blood of the red kings. Per took all who bore the curse of the dragons, and fled starward. We don't know if he fled from fear, or because he thought it would rid us of the scourge. But they stayed, and he left." She blinked at Shard as if making sense of it for the first time. "And discovered the Silver Isles."

Stigr spoke at last. "As he wasn't in a hurry to get back and help rid you of the scourge, I'd say he was a coward."

Valdis slanted one ear, looking uncertain. "Perhaps. But their bloodline still has loyalties here."

"I see that," Stigr said, and Valdis shot him a dark look.

"Tell me about the cursed families," Shard asked before they could argue. The painted wolf Nitara had said the same thing.

Valdis glanced at Stigr, but spoke her answer to Shard. "Kajar didn't fly alone to the land of the dragons. His wingbrother of the plains went with him, and others, warriors, representing clans of the Winderost, and they began their war and stole treasures. The dragons tracked them back, so they are cursed by their greed."

"And brought this curse on you," Stigr reminded.

"We can lift it," Shard said quietly. "We can rid the Winderost of dragons if we plan it right."

Silence fell. The answer burned as brightly to Shard as Tyr's first rays of light. He wanted to fly, to soar and leap for joy. It was all so simple.

"This is madness," Brynja whispered, crouching low, looking out nervously into the dark.

"I know," Shard said. "We must go in. But before you sleep tonight, consider." He lowered his head and his voice, and they leaned in as the night sentinels flew overhead, changing posts with those of the evening watch.

"What if I offered peace with the painted wolf packs, an alliance with eagles, and lions, and an end to your war with the dragons?"

"I'm with you," said Asvander.

"It's impossible," Valdis sighed. "The king will never agree."

"What if," Shard glanced to one side and dropped his voice, "I offered you a *new* king?"

41
In Stillness the Wind

Kjorn didn't know how long he crouched at the dark pool, the scent of mineral water and strange, distant sounds echoing through his senses, staring at phantom images.

The raven wings carried him back through the days of red rowan and he saw all that had passed.

The wolves lived on as if they'd known their whole lives underground and he saw it all. Laughing, happy, hunting at night and bringing their kills home. None of them planned attacks on the gryfons as Sverin feared in his waking dreams. They didn't fear or hate gryfons. In fact, they barely spoke of gryfons at all. They sang winter songs and lived underground, waiting for Sverin's anger to cool. At the sight of fresh deer kills, warm saliva pooled under Kjorn's tongue, though he smelled only water and stone.

The wings tilted him away, bringing him something new.

On the Sun Isle, gryfons huddled in their caves, eating salted, secret meat from Sigrun. Kjorn saw it all as if he were a bird that could flutter in and out of each den.

Sverin lashed out against wolves, the Vanir, the evils of darkness. But everyone knew that as the nights grew longer, dark and full of ice, it was the king's fear that drove him, the memory of his mate's death. The Long Night approached and it was the only monster in the world that set a chill down red Sverin's back.

When Sverin declared any Vanir half bloods were to be quartered in a separate section of dens, Kjorn curled his talons against the stone.

"Would that include my mate, Father?" he snarled at the water. "And Halvden, who poisons your ear? Is this true? Has this happened?"

Beside him, the wolf witch was silent.

Then Kjorn's vision reeled, across the black tossing waves of the sea.

And he saw Shard. Impossibly, he saw his wingbrother stalking alone through the night, in a sleet storm across a desert of red stone.

"Shard," he whispered.

In the vision, Shard's head flew up, startled, speaking in disbelief. "*Kjorn*?" echoed Shard's voice in his mind. It couldn't be real. Kjorn couldn't have seen him all the way across the sea, spoken to him, heard his voice in turn.

"What is it?" asked a black gryfon beside Shard, but their voices muddied and fell away as Kjorn saw something else.

Something dark coiled along the edges of the vision. Something horrible and huge and dark on the edge of the world, stalking Shard and the black gryfon beside him, and Kjorn had no voice to warn him.

"What is that?" Kjorn whispered desperately. "What is that creature?"

A strange, coarse male voice answered like a raven call. "Kajar's legacy." Black wings tilted him away from the shadow so that he saw Shard clearly, alive and real.

"Shard, be careful."

The world around Shard grew dark and Kjorn watched monstrous beasts forming out of the night, all strange wing and fang and talon. A horrible scream ripped in the air, as if the very rightness of the world was torn by black claws.

Kjorn fell among them, and saw Shard far away, battling against another shrieking monster.

"*Shard!*" Kjorn shrieked in the midst of the writhing, deadly blackness. His wingbrother didn't answer, or didn't hear, or was gone.

Kjorn fought free and flew up, away from the creatures and their shadow talons, up away, landed suddenly hard on a stone floor...

And he realized he stood in the silent cavern. Catori watched him. He panted, the horrible vision whirling in his mind before fading like a dream, only he had never slept.

Furious, Kjorn slapped talons against the water. "Witch! Mud-covered, lying wolves! How dare you call up my wingbrother's memory! How dare you plant nightmares in my mind?"

The she-wolf lunged back when Kjorn leaped at her, and he nearly crashed into the wall.

"He's no memory! What did you see? You've been granted visions for your sacrifice here. This is a hallow place you've found, carved by the earthfire of the First Age, cooled by Tor's sea, blessed with fresh water. Whether you saw Shard now or in the past or the near future isn't sure. But it is true. What nightmares you might have seen are warnings, are signs for what you may soon face, for your destiny. You've had a vision. What did you see?"

Kjorn, out of breath, trembling with hunger, could only stand and stare, unable to decide what was true. If it was real, he wasn't afraid. He could fight the raging beasts from the nightmare. If that was his destiny somehow, he didn't fear it. The vision had revealed something more important to him. He watched Catori warily.

"Shard really lives?"

"Of course," she yipped merrily.

"Did he really fly to the home of my fathers, as your brother said? He lives?" Kjorn saw a flash in his mind. Kajar's Sign. The starfire, soaring windward across the night sky. It was his guide to travel across the sea, and he should have followed it.

"Yes," Catori answered after seeming to watch those thoughts pass over his face. "He lives."

"Who are you? How do you know these things?"

"I am Catori." She dipped her head almost in true respect. "Sometimes I see. I only guided you to your own path. Where will you fly?"

"I don't know," Kjorn whispered. "I'm lost in here."

"Do you believe your vision?"

Kjorn stared at her, every instinct telling him to attack. No. Not instinct. That was hunger, anger, blindness. His true instinct guided him to trust the wolf before him, to know what she said was true. His deep heart longed to know that Shard was alive.

It's not longing. He is alive. We never found a body or saw one in the sea. The Vanir gryfons of the pride schemed and whispered of something. Now Kjorn knew, it had to be Shard's return.

"Yes. I believe it." Instead of worrying that his wingbrother planned an overthrow, for a moment all Kjorn felt was joy, and regret for the way they parted. Catori seemed to see it shining from him.

"Then you're on your path."

"Please," he forced himself to utter, and lowered his wings to a mantle, bowing his head. "Will you guide me out?"

"Not yet." The words fell deep on the stone. Kjorn fought a snarl and didn't raise his head, to hide his anger. *She's still toying with me?*

She stepped forward and touched her nose to the top of his head between his ears. Kjorn shuddered and his muscles twitched to flee or fight. She could bite his neck, crunch it like a branch. He forced himself to remain still and she spoke before he could question her.

"You've wandered for days. It is not a good time now, to begin a journey. Come with me and eat good food. Come with me and celebrate your strong vision with my family. It is long past time they should know that you're so different from your father. Wingbrother to the prince we love."

"I have to leave," Kjorn argued, fighting his temper. He couldn't find his way out without her. "I have to face my father and set the pride right." *And then find Shard,* he promised himself. *Find Shard and fight those shadow beasts, if that is my destiny.* He would follow the starfire as his great-grandfather had, even if he was late in doing so.

Catori only shook herself.

Kjorn opened his wings, pleading, "Don't you see? They're all in danger."

"Not yet," she said firmly, ears set forward. "The time isn't right."

Kjorn's tail lashed. "Why? Who are you to decide?"

Catori's ears swiveled uncertainly. "Very well, you decide. But, gryfons believe that all things are best begun under Tyr's light?"

"Yes," Kjorn said.

"Then you must wait."

Kjorn felt suddenly cold. "The Long Night."

Catori dipped her head. "It has begun."

42
From Ice the Flame

"More waiting," Shard burst out when he and Stigr were safe in Shard's den. "I have the perfect answer and it's more waiting, more talking."

"I thought you liked talking," Stigr said, and when Shard glared at him added, "Shard, perfect answers aren't always *easy* answers. They have a lot to contend with here."

"Kjorn is the rightful king of the Winderost."

"Maybe, once, but his coward father and grandfather lost him that birthright."

Shard ruffed, pacing to the back of his den, then turning to face Stigr again. "He would fight beside me. We could win it back!"

Stigr sighed. "This was never our fight."

Shard walked to his nest, straightening the long dried grasses and juniper bows. "It is. It's all our fight, because it's tied together, don't you see? If we win back Kjorn's kingdom, then we won't have a reason to fight in the Silver Isles. It's all tied, Uncle. All of it. You can't teach me that we're all linked and then say, all of us but the Aesir."

"Hm." Stigr huffed, and ground his beak to stifle a yawn. "Fair enough, my prince. But please. Listen to Valdis this time. Let her get sight on what she thinks the queen will do before you say anything else to Orn."

"Oh, it's listen to Valdis now?" Shard chuckled and Stigr growled in warning. Shard dipped his head. "All right. I won't say anything else to Orn."

Stigr nodded, turned, then paused at the mouth of the cave, looking over his shoulder at Shard. "What are you planning?"

Shard whispered, "*He speaks to all who hear.*"

"Shard…if you're saying what I think you're saying, it's madness. From all I've heard…"

"Don't try to stop me."

Stigr took a slow, measured breath. "When? You'll have to go at night, or Asvander's guards will stop you."

"Tomorrow night. Rest well, Uncle."

"Shard—"

"No more waiting," Shard said quietly. "This has to be done, and if I am the Summer King, then I must be the one to do it. You can come with me, or not. Either way, I'm going."

Stigr's tail twitched. "Leave without me, and you'll have worse than dragons to worry about."

Shard managed to laugh. "Thank you, Uncle."

"Tomorrow night," Stigr confirmed, eyeing him, and Shard nodded. While Valdis and the others negotiated, it was time for Shard to do what all of the creatures in the Winderost said could not be done. Before they declared war, before they fought, before anything else.

It was time to speak to the dragons.

The next night, freezing damp wind swept across the Winderost. Shard and Stigr watched the lighting of the fires, let themselves be seen entering their dens, bidding good night. Then they waited. Shard dozed. It was Stigr who woke him at midnight.

Sleet and thick darkness covered their leaving. Sentries and fire keepers kept busy lighting their backup flames as the rain drove against the bonfires on the high towers. Lower pyres under overhangs and within empty caves cast pale light through the Dawn Spire, but it lacked the brilliance of the usual fires. Together, Shard and Stigr crept out of their dens and into the shadows.

Cracked hunting roars boomed through the downpour. The enraged, mindless calls of dragons in the night. They sounded closer that night, as if the beasts reveled in the gloomy dark of the rain. Or maybe it only seemed worse because of what Shard planned to do.

"Let me strongly discourage this once more, my prince," Stigr said over the wind, once they were far from the Dawn Spire.

"Stand by me," Shard said as he had at the Wintermeet, and Stigr could only bow his head in the rain.

"Always."

They took off, gliding at a mid-level above the earth toward the Outlands. The rain slid from Shard's wings and he fluffed his feathers against the cold. No moonlight made it through the storm, but he wasn't afraid. Stigr had taught him long ago how to walk and fly in the dark, his birthright as a Vanir. He knew that Sverin only feared the dark because of the dragons, the beasts his grandfather had brought down on them. Sverin and the Aesir believed their danger made the dark unholy and dangerous.

But Shard knew bright Tor guarded his back even from behind the clouds.

"I'll make it right," he muttered into the dark, talons closing. The wind answered him, blowing hard from starward and pelting him with rain.

An owl or bat shot overhead and in the wind, Shard heard his name. It sounded like Kjorn's voice. *Shard?*

"Kjorn?"

"What is it?" Stigr asked, startled. Shard worked his beak for a moment, staring up and around in the dark, wings working hard in the rain.

"Nothing. I thought…nothing."

A familiar scent slivered through the rain—not dragon. Shard followed it, angled down and swept fast along the ground, calling out.

"Nitara! Hail, painted wolves, hail friends!"

Stigr followed, Shard's shadow.

Skyfire raked the clouds and revealed the wolf pack sprinting through the rain. Shard picked out Nitara and landed, running hard beside her. She panted, flashing fangs at him. Thunder boomed and after it echoed a dragon roar, closer than Shard had ever heard.

"Why must we always meet in the rain, graywing?"

"Why do you hunt in the rain?" Shard asked, laughing. The wolves streamed around him, and he sensed Stigr at his side in the dark. A murky scent crawled through the night and Shard's skin prickled.

"Why do you?" Nitara asked.

"I hunt dragons."

She stopped and circled and Shard stopped quickly before he ran over her. Tendrils of skyfire lanced above, and a moment later the crack and roll of thunder. "Don't be foolish."

"I must."

Nitara tossed her head, and looked to Stigr. "Your pup is mad! Take him home. Let him dry off."

"I tried," Stigr said in hollow voice. Shard laid his ears back.

"I've spoken to creatures before that others thought were witless."

"It isn't their wit that worries me," Nitara said. "It is their hate. If they smell gryfon on the wind…"

"Then why haven't they attacked the Dawn Spire? Why didn't they follow Per?"

Nitara turned in a nervous circle with a whine, and lifted her nose to the air. There must have been a rotting carcass nearby, for the next rush of wind brought the smell of decay. "I don't know. Perhaps they enjoy causing fear more than killing."

"If they enjoy it," Shard said, "then they can feel and think, and hear."

Rain pounded. Shard flexed his talons, squishing them through the mud.

The thought struck all of them at once that it had been moments since they'd heard a dragon's hunting roar.

A rotting scent filled the shifting wind, dead flesh and something metallic like sun-baked stone. The familiar scent of reptilian flesh.

Shard blinked as a slow, alien panic rose in his chest in reaction to the scent. Nitara's eyes slid away from him, falling to an eerily blank expression.

"Shard," Stigr said, dangerously soft. Shard watched Nitara.

"Nitara," Shard whispered. The dogs milled and panicked whines filled the air.

Shard tried to hold Nitara's gaze fear crowded out her strength and wisdom.

"Stay strong," Shard urged, though sudden terror grasped his own chest. "It's only a beast, only another creature, fight this!"

"We must run," she whispered, her voice rising, mouth hanging open in a nervous pant. "They've scented gryfon in the air."

"Stand strong, we'll fight with you!"

"No, we must run! Run!" She pivoted in a circle, loosing three wild barks. "Run!"

A roar shuddered across the earth in answer. It lanced up the marrow of Shard's bones and he clamped his beak against a witless shriek. The dogs broke and scattered into the rain.

A strobe of skyfire revealed the dragons only fifty leaps away and stalking closer.

There were four. The skyfire showed their colors—dull mixes of earthy brown and black, stone gray and worn, dull green like moss root. Huge, boney scales shielded their chests, plated their faces and legs like armor. The rest of their skin was leathery as a boar hide. Horns crested each thick head.

Skyfire crawled again and in the instant Shard managed to grasp his wit and study them, talons clawing the mud to keep himself from flying.

Two held their leathery wings close to their sides, their heads low and scenting at the ground. The other two held wings open as if to shield themselves from the rain. If Shard stood on top of four gryfons, he might touch the shoulder of smallest of them, and their long serpentine necks arched up further from there.

For half a breath, Shard thought they were beautiful—the way a shark or serpent or other deadly foe was graceful and horrifying all at once.

"Great Tyr's wings," Stigr moaned, crouched back, staring up. A new surge of panic struck Shard.

He'd never heard fear in Stigr's voice before.

"It will be all right," Shard said, and realized that Nitara had circled back, and stood, quivering, but bravely, just behind Stigr. Shard forced himself to take a step toward the dragons.

"Shard," Stigr gasped, as if struggling for his voice, "this is folly."

"I have to believe," Shard whispered. "I have to believe that they too are sons and daughters of Tyr and Tor."

He walked forward, Stigr and Nitara and her cowering wolf pack at his back.

Another flash lit the night. The dragons spied him, and stopped. Shard stopped. Thunder rolled and the sound went on and on until Shard realized it was the leading dragon, roaring.

Shard's hind legs quavered but he raised his head.

"Greetings!" He spoke as deeply, as loudly and as firm as he could without shrieking or letting his voice crack. "Great—Hunters! I'm honored to—"

A witless, hollow roar buried his words. He flinched back, ears flattening against the echo. Then he stepped forward again.

"I am *honored* to meet you." Grinding snarls responded. But they hadn't attacked. Shard forced a shallow breath. "My name is Rashard, the son of Baldr, from the Silver Isles far in the Starland Sea. I am…a friend to the descendants of Kajar, who—"

A raw bellow seemed to cut down Shard's very spine.

Their heads lashed up and wings flared. Biting shrieks broke the night in anger. Not a witless reaction. An angry one.

The name of Kajar, it seemed, was known to them.

The lead dragon stamped forward and the steps quaked the earth.

"*Shard,*" Stigr yelled. "Enough!"

"Stop!" Shard shouted at the leading dragon, which another flash of skyfire revealed was rich sable, the armored scales a lighter earth brown. The same dragon, Shard knew on instinct, that he had seen flying under the moon with the lions. Something, something deep in him urged him to speak, urged him that the wrathful creature was Named, had a family like him, had a reason she was filled with such poisonous hatred.

She, he realized, locked and staring as the dragon pounded through the mud, wings flared in warning, tail lashing. Nothing told him the dragon was female but his instinct.

"Mighty, mighty huntress!" he shouted, his voice cracking high. "Sister, daughter of the earth and sky, like me, listen. Tell me your name, say *something*, I know you have a voice—"

Something knocked into Shard and fell skidding to one side in the mud as the dragoness leaped. She whipped low over the ground, claws gouging the earth where Shard had been a moment ago.

Stigr had knocked him aside.

"Now," he barked, "can we run?"

Shard scrambled to his feet. The other dragons loosed triumphant shrieks and stalked forward, flapping their wings to whirl up tempests of sleet toward Shard, Stigr and the painted wolves.

The pack scattered again, their courage drained.

The dragoness wheeled back around and landed hard, huge claws and bulk slithering through the mud toward Shard.

Behind him, Stigr challenged the other dragons with a weak eagle's cry. They moved slowly, as if they enjoyed causing terror.

The female opened her jaws, showing every fang. Shard knew now the terror of a vole under an eagle's shadow. He could not move.

They are only flesh like me! Flesh, fang and bone.

Shard refused to fear what Sverin feared.

"If you kill me," his voice rattled in his own ears, "I thank you for my good death."

The dragoness shook the ground with her step, and her roar chorused across the plain like a herd of raging boar. Shard realized he'd sunk to the sodden ground, clinging to the earth. Wet grass whipped his face in the wind.

The dragoness stamped again and he whimpered, unable to move.

Nitara darted in front of him, barking madly. Her pack streamed around her as she, blind with fear, bared her fangs at the terrible monster before her. She stood to give her pack enough time to flee. She tried to distract the dragon from Shard.

Her courage snapped Shard back to himself.

He tried to shout her name but he couldn't move, couldn't bring air to his chest.

The dragoness loomed up, head arcing back, and displayed her enormous jaws. Nitara crouched back toward Shard, a pained, grating growl scraping from her chest.

The last of the wolf pack escaped into the dark.

Nitara leaped away as the dragon swiped claws forward—*too slow,* Shard's mind screamed. Dragon claws plucked her from the earth. Her dying yelp rang out.

Shard lunged to his feet and forced himself to shout her name so at least she could take that to the Sunlit Land. Sorrowful howls sounded from the dark in response to Nitara's last cry, and dragon heads whipped around, tracking the noise.

No more, Shard thought.

"Shard!" Stigr bellowed, and shoved into the air once the wolves had escaped. "Fly! now!"

The dragons looked toward the wolves that sprinted away into the dark.

"No, not them!" Shard shrieked. "You hunt me!" He spun and shoved from the ground. "You hunt me! Wingbrother to the son of the Red Kings who stole your treasure!"

The dragoness roared and the others followed, flared their broad, bat-like wings, and launched up after Stigr and Shard.

Stigr met Shard in the air, both of them battered by sleet and wind. Shard tried to say his uncle's name, staring through the dark, but couldn't bring the word. They locked eyes, then turned as one and soared higher as the dragons flew after them.

Terrified, mindless, he veered away, up higher into the storm.

The dragons' roars lashed discord through the night sky. One veered off, and a tiny part recognized that it must be chasing Stigr. The rest of him only knew he must fly to live.

The leading female swept up to his level with a single wing stroke and Shard yelped in surprise, folding his wings to drop below her. Her claw slashed the air where he'd been. She bellowed rage. Two dragons circled below, smaller than the female, one muddy green and the other gray as bone. Shard shot down between them.

The gray dragon whipped around faster than Shard thought possible and snapped its jaws. Pain darted up Shard's tail and he shoved hard, breaking free. A few tail feathers broke away in the dragon's teeth.

The green had risen above and stooped, diving toward Shard. He heard the female to his left and he hovered, panting, until they were both almost upon him. At the last moment he kicked into a back flip, falling out of the way. The dragons collided, wings thrashing and jaws agape. They managed to untangle, and turned to find Shard. He'd already flown high.

Tight fear began to cloud his mind. Their scent overwhelmed him. Their hateful roars. Their size. He couldn't outmaneuver them forever.

A sound drew him. A gryfon cry. His mind couldn't pull together to bring a name, but he knew it.

He wheeled, dodging dragon claws and gaping teeth, to find his uncle in the storm. Skyfire flashed. He saw a black gryfon, high above. He soared toward it, dragons a wing's length behind him.

A dragon paw swiped, catching his tail, and he wrenched down and away, almost smacking into an armored, reptilian chest. Letting himself fall, he slipped below a slashing paw and then winged up again, dodging under a lashing tail. He tried to become one with the night wind and the storm that lashed his face.

There were too many. Their writhing bodies and slashing claws and horrible screams became his sky. He had to flee.

His plans and thoughts dissolved into nothing but the sense of the dragons. They crowded his entire field of vision. Dragon stench coated the air, filled his lungs with reeking fumes and rot. He lost track of Stigr. Any words, any faith, any knowledge of his own soul or Tyr's protection or any courage he'd ever felt in his life crumbled in the heat of their hatred.

Seized by terror, his instinct guided him toward a faint glow of light.

Toward Tyr's horizon.

Toward the Dawn Spire.

43

THE DARK OF NIGHT

DRAGON SCREAMS BROKE THE DARK.

He tried to shout a warning to the sentinels on the towers, tried to make any sound at all. Roars and eagle screeching answered him.

"Shard!" shrieked a sentinel. Shard couldn't answer. Everything was flight, fast flight, dodging sweeping talons and fang-lined jaws.

"Warriors to me!" roared another male with a deep voice. Overhead, thunder echoed him and rain lashed against the fires. "Sentinels to me!"

Asvander, Shard wanted to yell, but had to swallow the shout and dodge the green dragon that chased him.

He wove around the rock towers, gasping for breath against his terror. He glanced up to see what was happening. At least he had one dragon distracted. If he could keep his fear in check, keep hold of himself, he might be able to lead it away again…

Twenty gryfons gathered in a wedge and drove against the first dragon—the female, the one Shard had spoken to.

Tried to speak to.

Fool, fool, fool—

The dragoness stopped midair and roared. Rocks shuddered down from the towers and Shard's wings seemed to turn to water for a moment. The wedge of gryfons dissolved into panic.

Except for Asvander, who hovered until the last moment, roaring defiance. The dragoness swooped forward and Asvander dropped down below her.

A female voice commanded, "Don't let them pass the outer towers!"

Shard veered to one side as his own pursuer dove in fast, jaws agape.

Talons swept the air above Shard's back and he shut his wings to drop out of reach.

"Stigr! Uncle!" He cast around, but couldn't make him out in the madness of wings and battle.

"FIGHT!" shouted Asvander, to anyone who could hear, Shard thought. "Don't flee! Remember yourselves! Your families! Only the strong endure!"

The battle cry drowned in witless terror and cries. The Dawn Spire had exploded into chaos. The brown dragoness landed hard, swiping her spade tail at gryfons on the ground, screeching challenges. The rain seemed to lessen though it hardly mattered then.

As Ajia had said, it was not fire that kept dragons away from the Dawns Spire.

It's my fault, Shard knew, looping around a high spire as he tried to lose the green dragon. *I goaded them into this.*

A volley of warrior gryfons launched toward Shard, led by Asvander. They slammed into the green dragon and fell together, a thrashing mess of talon, wing and writhing dragon.

Shard swooped around and back to help, then caught sight of the female.

She's leading them, he realized. *If I get rid of her…*

"You!" Shard yelled. She seemed to know his voice, and whipped her head toward him. "I tried to befriend you! Now, I challenge!" he flared his wings, loosing a lion call.

She reared up to her hind legs, knocking away gryfons with her wings and tail. She shrieked, a strange, clattering sound. It wasn't a challenge.

Shard realized, as the gray, male dragon broke away from harrying the sentinels on the towers, that it was a command. She didn't pursue Shard, but the gray male did.

He dove fast, twisting his body and wings like a falcon to gain speed. The dragon's roar sang through Shard's bones and he banked hard, leading the creature back away from the gryfon towers.

He soared low over the plain, his tail bumping brush and rocks, then flapped hard to gain height as a desperate planned bloomed in his mind. The dragon caught his tail feathers in his teeth. Shard flapped wildly, twisting, straining, his shouts drowned in the dragon's roar.

He couldn't fly. He had to fight.

He shut his wings and twisted, dropping on the dragon's face with talons splayed. The dragon's head alone was the size of Shard's body and he clamped talons against slick, bone-hard scales. Scrabbling, he found leather hide between the scales, and dug in.

The dragon's eyes filled Shard's vision. Black. Black and empty as a serpent's gaze.

But then the distant firelight caught a yellow gleam deep in the dragon's glare. Yellow, like the light before dawn, like Tyr's first rays...*I have to listen,* Shard thought strangely, staring deep. The light flickered within, and he heard a guttural roll as if the dragon might actually speak. *I have to wait, to be still—*

"Shard!"

Stigr's voice made him blink. In that second the dragon's jaws yawned open and it flicked talons up as if to grab him. Shard raked his talons across the gleaming eye.

The dragon screamed.

Searing dragon's blood ran down Shard's foreleg and into his feathers and it was like thrusting his flesh into a lava flow.

Shard writhed off the horned head and slid, bumping and clawing, down the long, scaled back. One wing slapped him hard and he sunk talons into the dragon's tail. Shard clung to the tail as the dragon whipped its body and long neck around, biting the air just beyond Shard's head. He climbed higher, talons sinking in the hard leather hide, making it difficult for the dragon to bite without twisting so hard that he couldn't orient and fly.

The female, he thought wildly, looking down. The battle raged below, in the air and on the ground. Not even all the gryfons of the aerie were a match for four dragons. They fought in witless panic with no order and no strategy.

Shard had to help.

He clamped his hind claws against the scaled flesh and loosened his talons just as the dragon whipped its body and tail hard to shake him loose. Shard lost grip and slid scrabbling down its tail. A talon-sharp spade at the end of the swiped at Shard as he fell loose, barely missing.

Battered, Shard regained his wind and swooped under the dragon's hind legs, then flew high again. As he'd hoped, the dragon chased him up.

An eagle's cry followed them. Shard recognized it.

"Uncle!" He chanced a look back. His vision filled with dragon. But beneath death darted a smaller black shadow. Stigr, trying to harry the dragon into chasing him instead of Shard. "Stigr, help me drive him!"

"Yes, my prince!" Stigr's mad laughter echoed through the night.

Relieved that his uncle still had his wits, Shard worked hard to gain height. The dragon followed. Stigr wove around and flew up alongside the beast until he met Shard in the sky.

"Talk to the dragons," Stigr gasped, "indeed."

"A mistake," Shard panted, heart crumbling to hear the gryfon cries below him. The dragon screamed rage, unable to catch them.

"Yes," Stigr agreed. The air thinned and grew sharp and icy around them.

"Forgive me," Shard panted, trying to speak, to keep his mind, his name, his love for his uncle, anything to keep his reason intact. The dragons drove the gryfons to witless terror.

If they could only keep their wit, they could win, Shard thought dizzily.

"My fault," Stigr rasped, working hard against the thin air. "Should've stopped you."

The ground grew hazy and dim, the sky vast and deep. The dragon lashed talons, the giant wings stirring the only wind.

"I should've…listened to you…" Shard urged words, clinging to his thoughts. Grayish lines thinned the night at the horizon. Dawn flew toward them fast.

Stigr laughed, hysterical with the thrill of fighting and the terror of death.

"Maybe…are we high enough?"

"Yes," laughed Shard, dizzy with fear and the height. As one, he and Stigr banked sharply and wheeled fast around the dragon's head. Shard met Stigr's glance, they folded wings and dove together.

Frosty air froze the feathers of Shard's face. He clenched his talons, then stretched them out toward the distant ground. Beside him, he caught Stigr's scent and it filled his mind with the Silver Isles, with himself, and washed away his fear.

The dragon swung its massive bulk around to dive after them.

Shard closed his eyes against the stinging cold. The sound of the battle coarsed back to him. Grew louder with each heartbeat. The clouds gusted away, leaving a flat, dark sky. In the gray light he saw dead gryfons on the ground. He shut his eyes again.

Dive, dive, dive, no fear…

It was a stupid plan. He couldn't think so fast, couldn't pull up hard enough—

Don't think. I am wind. Wind, feather and bone. The ground seemed to lunge toward him. Death clawed at his hind paws. Beside him, the black gryfon he loved laughed madly at the challenge.

Ten leaps. Seven.

Five.

Two.

"*Now, Stigr!*" Shard flung open his wings and jerked up, speeding only a hare's leap off the ground. Stigr flared beside him, neat as a shadow. An impossible feat, if he'd taken the time to think about it.

Behind them, the dragon dove, its murderous gaze locked on Shard. Jaws agape and shrieking rage, it flared its wings to follow—

—and smashed head first into the ground. *Too slow.*

The shock of shattering bones resounded like cedars cracking. A shockwave plumed out in the mud as the giant body hit. Shard and Stigr's wild, relieved cries broke through the sounds of battle around them.

The dragon's muddy gray and black body thrashed once like a beheaded serpent, drawing the eyes of the three remaining dragons – the black male, the green, the brown female.

The dawn light grew.

Shard and Stigr glided fast and low, catching breath. For one moment, the fighting rang dull behind Shard, and it felt oddly quiet. The dragons didn't hunt in day. If they could just hold them back until the sun rose, it would be all right. He and Stigr wove back up, swinging around to rejoin the fighting.

"I've finally bested your mother in a hunt!" Stigr crowed, his voice raw as he and Shard regained height. "Killing a sailfish is nothing compared to—"

A dragon's spade tail slapped him from the sky.

Shocked, Shard wheeled around, and saw Stigr fall hard in the mud. Raw air lashed Shard's throat but he made no cry.

The female dragon ramped up, roaring a challenge.

Blind with fury, Shard forgot his safety and folded his wings to dive for the beast's face. The dragon's jaws yawned open wide and she swiped claws as he dove. Shard dodged under the swipe and regained height for another pass.

He stretched his talons straight toward the gleaming black eyes.

Another gryfon slammed into him from the side. Red and ragged. Brynja.

"*Let go!* Stigr!"

"No, Shard! No! You cannot win. Fly with me. The dawn will drive her off."

"But Stigr," Shard gasped, swooping with Brynja under the dragon's next swipe. The great beast lumbered around, lashing her bladed tail and swiping with fore claws sharp as chips of obsidian. They dodged and wheeled. Desperate, Shard glanced back, trying to catch a glimpse of Stigr. The dragon's jaws slammed shut a half leap from Shard's tail.

Golden light crept across the horizon. Shadows ran forward from the dawn. The storm clouds swept toward the Outlands and sunlight gleamed along the dragon's leathery hide. With a strangled roar she summoned the other dragons.

Shard climbed the air with Brynja, then glided together as the surviving dragons rose high to out fly the dawn, leaving the gryfon aerie behind them.

"Shard, don't—" Brynja tried to claw his wing but Shard banked and dove fast again toward the ground.

Sorrowful keening wrenched the morning air. One dragon carcass was no victory, not with the number of gryfon dead. Shard thumped hard to the ground and leaped through dust and bloodstained mud to Stigr's side.

"Uncle," he whispered, gently nudging one smoky, black wing. With horror he saw that his touch rolled the wing almost completely off his uncle's body. It was severed by the dragon's tail, hanging only by tendon and skin, and he bled into the ground.

"Stigr." He waited, staring stupidly, for a word, for something, for any movement. "Uncle," he whispered again. "Stigr…"

If any breath lifted Stigr's ribs it was so weak and faint Shard couldn't tell. Warm dawn light glowed over the black feathers of his face and the scar of his missing eye, spread across his wings and flank.

Asvander trotted up beside Shard, bloodied, one wing oddly bent. "Healers!" barked the First Sentinel, when he saw Stigr. "Healers here! Shard, step back, I think he might…" Asvander gripped Shard's wing in his talons, shaking him hard. "*Rashard.* He was a great warrior. If he dies, his peace will be great, in the Sunlit Land."

"Healers, here!" cried Brynja, voice breaking as she trotted up beside them. "Please, hurry!"

Uncomprehending, Shard blinked at Asvander, barely recognizing him through dirt and blood. Unable to form words, he turned and lay down next to Stigr, tucking his beak under the soft black feathers of his chest.

He must be breathing. He has to be.

Shard couldn't tell. Maybe Stigr's ribs lifted gently, maybe the wind only lifted the feathers there. Every word his uncle had ever spoken to him rose up then swept away in a frigid, inner wind.

There were no words left. No thoughts. To think meant to know that this was his doing. His fault. His stupidity. No one flew back from across the Dawnward Sea. No one returned from the Sunlit Land.

Shard lifted himself a little, crouching over Stigr as Sigrun's voice rushed into his head.

No matter the wound, if it's bleeding, put pressure on it.

Shard pressed both fore feet firmly against Stigr's shoulder where his wing used to be. Dimly he heard Asvander and Brynja still shouting for a healer. Maybe that meant Stigr would live. If he still lived. Shard scented Valdis on the wind and, through a strange roaring in his ears, heard her strangled cry. He pressed hard.

He had to put pressure until the healers came.

A movement made him freeze. His ears flicked forward. He thought he'd seen a breath. Words floated over him. Shouting, keening.

A strong tawny male, wings flared, shoved into him. King Orn.

"I know you brought this on us! I'll kill you myself!"

Shard staggered back from Stigr's body, uncomprehending. Brynja, bright and beautiful, leaped in front of him, pleading to Orn. Asvander joined, arguing. Valdis. Others. Shard backed away, tail tucking slowly, his gaze locked on Orn, then Stigr.

"Fly, Shard!" Brynja begged. "Please, fly!"

Asvander whirled. "Shard, go! We'll tend to Stig—" a member of his own Guard leaped at Shard and he dodged away, panic crawling over his reason. Orn shouted something. Shard realized the king ordered all of them to be captured and held. Brynja, Valdis, Asvander, Shard. Spies. Traitors.

Valdis shouted from the commotion. "Run, Shard, you fool!"

What would Stigr want?

Shard backed down from gryfons who circled him, their gazes dark and hunting.

He would want me to do what I came to do.

Without another thought, Shard shoved straight up from the ground and shot skyward as fast as he could fly. Exclamations and swearing echoed under him. He heard Brynja, sounding victorious. He glanced behind to see members of the Guard lifting off in pursuit. They would never catch him.

With a final look back he saw Stigr's body again, saw a healer shoving past Orn to crouch at Stigr's side.

I did this.

Cold, sharp sadness curled out like talons.

An emptiness grew and ate in his chest until it consumed him. He couldn't think. His wings slowed as his chest tightened, and he couldn't breathe. Shard grasped at some sense of strength, struggling not to fall.

But Stigr wouldn't want that. He would want Shard to fly, to go on, to find his vision and bring justice…the thought of Stigr, of not hearing his voice again, his lessons, even a reprimand, opened a hollow in Shard's heart. There was only one escape.

He let go of himself as he had over the sea.

Fleeing the gryfons of the Dawn Spire, the dragons, and the harsh judgment of dawn, he fell into oblivion.

Lost, exhausted, and Nameless.

44
A Red Dawn

Low clouds crouched at the edge of the dawnward sky. The first rays laid feathers of red low across the horizon, and relief welled in Caj's heart to see it after a fortnight of darkness.

Sigrun and Ragna led the pregnant females to the river at first light, with a number of the King's Guard walking behind.

Sverin did not emerge from his den. As the pride crept out from their dens to bow to the rising sun, Caj noted that a lingering air of relief breathed through everyone with every moment the king didn't show himself. Caj walked among the pride, talking, checking if anyone felt sick or frightened. All were relieved to see the dawn, all were shaking with hunger, but glad for the sun. All the years since the Aesir had lived in the Silver Isles they were used to the long fast, but it still put a strain on the pride in winter.

"Is the king ill?" Caj asked Halvden, who had spent the Long Night in Sverin's den. They stood in snow, and a light wind brought the faint scent of the half-frozen Nightrun to them.

"As soon as the light rose, he chose to sleep." Halvden adjusted the shining gold gauntlet on his foreleg. He looked unusually haughty and

Caj resisted the urge to throw him to the ground like a strutting fledge. "He asked not to be disturbed until middlemark."

"Then we'll disturb him with a good meal!" Caj called names and divided the males into four hunting bands. Though Einarr was a good hunter, he put the pregnant females at ease, and so Caj left him with the pride. He took Halvden with him, the better to keep an eye. As they planned their hunting routes, the females returned from the river.

Sigrun loped up to him, wings half open.

"My mate," she murmured as the other males took wing. Halvden glanced at her, flattened his ears and trotted away as if she were an exile he should ignore. Caj sighed, and looked to her.

Her eyes, soft brown like a sea eagle, searched him. "I have an uneasy feeling. It's a red dawn. I beg you not to go."

"We'll be safe."

"It's not only an uneasy feeling for you," she whispered, sidling closer.

Caj remained rigid, wings tight to his sides. He tried to be reasonable about his frustrations—she'd only wanted to feed the pride. *She means well.*

"Stay," Sigrun pleaded again. "For us. The king will wake soon."

"I trust my wingbrother," Caj said, though his muscles tensed.

"Do you?" Sigrun whispered.

"I have to hunt, Sigrun. Even you are almost out of meat."

Sigrun stared at him, ears laying back, though she spoke quietly. "Of course. My mate."

Caj hesitated, then dipped his head. "My mate."

He turned roughly when she nuzzled at his chin, and loped up to join Halvden and his band in the reddening sky.

"Come!" Sigrun barked at the next groggy, grumpy clump of gryfesses, the fledges who had nested with them, and the young males. Einarr trotted forward, looking stern and alert and ready to lead the next group. "To the Nightrun."

Feeling confident that Einarr and Sigrun had the pride well in wing, Caj turned his attention to his hunters.

The wind rose and stung them with cold on the flight to Star Isle. Caj sent a group to each side of the river, one up the coast, and led his own to the deep woods in the middle of the island, desperate to find sheltering deer.

Rabbit. Pheasant. Anything. If only Sverin let the Vanir hunt from the sea. There lies a bounty that never grows thin.

Caj huffed at himself as he tucked wing and landed hard on the forest floor. It was only hunger that brought that thought to his head. He tried to ignore his shaking muscles and the needling aches from the cold. He was getting too old to fast through the Long Night.

Halvden landed behind, the two others in his band ahead. Little snow had reached the ground there, so heavy did the pine boughs criss-cross above their heads. Dim, quiet light made the forest seem like a deep, green cave. The rowans that had blazed only scant weeks ago with fire-red berries stood bare as dark bones.

"You two, scout toward the old wolf den," Caj commanded the two youngest hunters. Each had a mate to feed, and turned eagerly nightward to seek out prey. Caj turned to Halvden, flicking his ears. "You're with me."

Halvden inclined his head.

Caj tried to fathom what might've passed between Halvden and Sverin during the Long Night, if Halvden had remained awake with him.

What new suspicions and poisons did he feed Sverin's desperate ears?

They stalked tensely through the forest for a sunmark, climbing a broken trail to follow deer droppings and then, fresher hoof prints in the mud. The trees broke and scattered, leaving large areas coated with snow.

A heavy, sour musk stopped Caj and he paused, talons lifted, staring hard through the woods. "A boar den lies close," he said to Halvden, who stood farther off, in the woods away from the deer track. The clouds pressed lower and the light faded to low gray. A storm pressed in. A red dawn.

A red dawn at morning, hunters take warning. A saying of the Silver Isles that Caj had first thought some old superstition, until he learned the way of the clouds and wind on the islands. It meant ill weather on the horizon and was a good warning indeed. The storm had flown quickly. He turned from their current path.

"Let's put some ground between us and this scent."

No answer. Caj looked up and peered around, and saw that Halvden had paused near a cluster of pine. A hole broke the ground beneath the roots and Halvden was picking around it, sniffing.

"Halvden. Leave it. We'll hunt easier game."

"I'm coming," he chirped, too airily. Caj glared at him as he trotted forward.

"Focus. Your mate is hungry, and a storm draws in."

"I know," Halvden muttered. "We're all hungry." He looked as if he would say more, meeting Caj's eyes in silent challenge. Caj's hackles prickled, his heart uneasy. Halvden had seen something by those pines, something that lit his eyes with hunting light, and Caj's instinct sparked as if an enemy stood in front of him.

Halvden's ear slanted back, and he held perfectly still. "Do you hear that?"

Caj stood silent. "No." Surely he wasn't getting that old.

Halvden's ears twitched, but he didn't take his gaze off Caj's face. Caj swiveled his ears back and around. He heard no other gryfons. He heard nothing in the dead, snow-covered woods.

Nothing but Halvden.

The green gryfon stepped closer and Caj lifted his wings.

"I heard something," Halvden whispered. His eyes grew bright, half with excitement, half with fear. "A boar, I think."

"Don't be stupid," Caj growled, chilled with understanding. Halvden advanced as if he were stalking a stag. *Maybe I am getting old. Too old for this tier-climbing. I should've seen it.* "What do you gain by this?"

"The king's ear," Halvden snarled. "You have no faith in him. You choose your Vanir witch over your king. Your wingbrother."

"Halvden, you know so little."

"I know enough."

Caj, not wanting to fight, backed toward the trees. He had to remind himself he didn't truly want to harm Halvden. He was only young and arrogant, and he had a new mate and an unborn kit.

"Stop this now."

"I heard a boar," Halvden whispered. "It will come out of the trees. We'll fight it. Valiantly. You'll save my life. The king will like that. Your mate will believe it." Halvden raised his wings in threat. "Everyone will. Noble Caj."

"Halvden—"

Halvden lunged. Caj ramped to meet him, locked talons threw him to the ground. Starlings that had sat silent and invisible in the trees raised an alarm and flocked from the trees into the iron gray sky.

"You're a traitor to your kind!" Halvden rolled to his feet, ready for attack, but Caj didn't pursue. Nothing in the forest moved after the birds fled. His other hunters had ranged wide. No one would witness.

"Halvden you are half Vanir! You're leaping at shadows just like the king!"

Caj clamped his beak. He hadn't meant to say it.

Halvden leaped again and Caj had no time to think. They clawed and wrestled deeper into the trees. Several times Caj slapped talons toward tender spots to debilitate his young opponent, and his claws scraped hard metal. Gauntlets. A collar. Dragon treasures studded with gleaming emeralds that matched the arrogant gryfon's feathers. Armor suited for battle, not just hunting in the woods.

He planned this, and I was too stupid and hungry to see.

"You want to be wingbrother to a king?" Caj hissed. His muscles threatened to cramp, his belly ached with hunger. "You have no idea of loyalty. Loyalty is knowing when those closest to you are wrong."

Halvden hissed low, and circled. They passed through trees again to a clearing. A meadow. Caj knew it somehow. Memory flashed.

This is where we killed the boar. The evidence was perfect. Everyone would believe Halvden's tale.

Halvden glanced around, pleased, then locked his gaze on Caj. "I am loyal to the king. You're bewitched, and I'll tell him so. You turned your back on us."

"Never like that."

Halvden surged forward. Caj twisted out of the way again. Hunger raked in his belly. Fight-thrill was all that kept his muscles moving, kept his blood coursing hot, and he couldn't understand how Halvden moved so quickly.

Unless…

Unless he had eaten the king's store of meat to keep strong for a fight. Halvden turned Sverin off to the food by planting ideas about Sigrun's motives, and eaten it himself when Sverin wasn't looking.

Caj ducked as Halvden slashed forward, weaving away from Halvden's advances, fearing he wouldn't have the strength to meet him full on again.

"If loyalty is knowing when someone is wrong, then I am loyal to you." Halvden's voice cut with mockery. Snow whirled down, dimming the day to strange twilight. "My teacher, mentor to the young warriors. I'll make sure your great name lives on."

Halvden ramped, flaring his wings. Something fluttered down. Something had been tucked in his golden collar. Two feathers. Two feathers blazed gold on the snow.

Only one gryfon in Sverin's pride boasted that coloring.

"Kjorn," Caj whispered, stunned. He looked at Halvden. "Where did you find those? We must tell the king!"

"Don't worry," Halvden said as he thumped back to all fours, eyes gleaming. "I will."

Caj rose in time to meet Halvden's next, vicious charge. The younger gryfon slashed and fought like a witless beast. Caj twisted and tried not to harm him.

"You can't *win,*" Caj growled, growing breathless, weak with hunger. Halvden drove him out of the meadow into the trees again, through dead, wet ferns and gnarled brush and naked white birch trees. "I taught you everything you're doing now!"

But he hadn't taught Halvden everything he knew. Some fighting moves, Caj had been wise to reserve for himself. He and Sverin had practiced them. All wingbrothers and sisters had a few. Defenses and fighting moves and hunting tricks they shared only with each other, just in case. Now, Halvden was in perfect position for Caj to use one.

"Give up, Halvden, and I won't tell the king of this."

When Halvden lunged, Caj dropped to his belly and rolled to one side, leaving his flank open. Halvden shot in, beak slashing toward Caj's belly. Caj locked his hind legs around Halvden's neck and twisted hard, throwing him down. Caj rolled and pinned Halvden, hindquarters crushing Halvden's hind legs against the ground, grabbing Halvden's forelegs in his talons. A move and pin that he and Sverin perfected, and there was only one way to break it—also a secret.

Halvden tossed his head, writhing against Caj and the ground.

"Give up," Caj growled, clenching Halvden's forelegs in his talons.

Halvden met his eyes—and laughed.

Before Caj could move, Halvden thrust his wing up and around, knocking the bent joint against Caj's skull.

Light flashed, his talons loosened, Halvden's talons caught under his wings and he shoved Caj up hard before slamming him to the ground.

"I learned something new over the Long Night," Halvden growled, talons braced on Caj's shoulder, standing on one blue wing.

He stamped a hind paw. Caj's shriek of pain hid the crack of breaking bone.

Sverin! Caj thought wildly. *How could he*...Warm blood oozed somewhere. His foreleg. Or his chest. Halvden loomed over him, wings hunched above his head, and ground his talons into Caj's broken wing, drawing a cry of pain.

"It was clear to the king that you no longer protect his back, and so he helped me prepare to defend myself. Sad," he murmured. "When wingbrothers can't trust each other."

Agony soared up Caj's wing to his shoulder and back. "Halvden," he gasped. If only he could stand upright. "You don't know what you're doing."

"I do." He knocked his gauntlet against Caj's head. Claws tore at his shoulder, another blow—Caj struggled to block, to fight, swinging talons and trying to roll away.

His weakness from fasting finally fogged across his muscles. All he could do was keep Halvden from biting his throat, or delivering a killing slash to his belly. At last he forced Halvden back by slashing at his eyes, and staggered to his feet.

Halvden darted forward again, and again as Caj limped back, blocking attacks on pure, blind instinct.

He heard a ringing. Blinking, he swung out of Halvden's way again and tried to break from the trees before remembering that he could not fly.

Not a ringing.

A low, mournful sound. Howls.

Wolves.

"Perfect." Halvden smashed into him, knocking him down again. Bright pain danced up Caj's wing and Halvden crushed him down with he tried to rise.

"Farewell, Noble Caj," Halvden said, flicking his ears to the wolf howls that grew closer. "Everyone will remember you well."

Gryfon voices, desperate and frightened of the wolves and storm, drifted to them on the wind. Halvden crouched, eyes widening when he heard the voices.

"Do it before they see," Caj snarled, panting. He searched desperately for an opening but Halvden's bright feathers and armor swam before his eyes.

But at the prospect of the killing bite, fear gleamed wild in Halvden's face. "The wolves will finish you," he rasped, stamping once on his hind leg for good measure.

"Coward!" Caj coughed and tried to move. Halvden fled, disappearing into the gray. He called the others, called alarm, warning of boar, of wolves, shouting that Caj had fallen.

Caj tried to shout. His gorge rose at the effort to move. Wolfsong. Hungry, hunting song filled the woods around him. Snow fell, settling over him as the afternoon shifted to dark.

All I wanted, Caj thought, a flicker of clarity amidst swimming nausea and pain, *was to live in peace with my mate.*

Sigrun. Thyra. They were all in danger. Sverin son-of-Per, the once powerful Red King, was truly lost to them. Caj's own wingbrother, and he had been too afraid to stop him, to bring his friend back to reason and clarity. And now Halvden would cultivate those fears with more lies.

Oh, Sverin.

Hot fear lanced through Caj's muscles. He braced talons under himself and managed to stand. He'd lied to Sverin for ten years about Shard. Too worried about his own secrets, Caj hadn't trusted Sverin as he should have.

He mourns his dead mate still, and I didn't see. He mourns his father and our homeland and now his son, and I wasn't there for him. And now I won't even be there to stand in his way.

He realized he had no plan. He couldn't fly. He couldn't swim to the Sun Isle.

The caves. The caves that run under the islands. Shadows moved in the forest around him. Wolves. Or snow. Trees. He limped, half blind from dizziness in the dimming light and swirling snow, toward the scent of earth. The sour scent of boar. A hole in the ground. That's what he needed. To get into the earth. To go underground.

A snort drew him around. A hulking form stood in the trees five leaps away. Caj shook his head, trying to slow his reeling vision.

A boar. A young boar. Caj coughed, disbelieving. Bright Tyr was surely angry with him. Maybe he truly had fallen under dark magic, and ignored his wingbrother, and bright Tyr would now show his wrath.

"I challenge," Caj whispered, lifting his good wing. The boar squealed in mad delight. Stupid beast. Caj tilted his head when the squeal twisted into laughing words.

"You will die. The wolves will hide in their holes. And I will be king of the Star Isle."

"You'll be the most foul-smelling king I've ever heard of." Caj chuckled to himself, drunk on pain and dizziness. Boars didn't speak. The blow to the head had ruined some part of his mind. "And the ugliest." He might as well enjoy a few insults before he died.

The young monster bellowed rage, stamped and charged.

"King of the sty!" Caj shrieked, and pain clawed his head at the shouting. But he wouldn't die whimpering and drooling on the ground.

The boar pounded forward. Caj crouched. It was almost too dark to see. He would die. Die in those mad little red eyes, by those tusks. A warrior's death.

No! Sigrun, Thyra!

It was too late to recall he didn't want a warrior's death. That was for young gryfons with honor to gain and nothing to lose. He had to protect his mate, his daughter. He had to fly home.

Caj braced for his final stand. "Great Tyr—"

The boar smashed into him just as Caj flung up his talons, but he couldn't throw the boar as he'd thrown Halvden. The boar drove him down and they rolled, Caj trying desperately to ward him away with a shove of his wing or talons. Tusks sliced his shoulder, squealing filled his ears and hooves pounded his ribs.

A huge, scuffling, snarling mass of fur and bodies slammed into them.

Caj screamed in eagle fury and agony. Nausea blinded him, his wing tangled to a broken knot of pain and the stench of wolf and boar rolled together around him. A heavy force shoved him, blunt paws drove against his ribs and fangs locked on the back of his neck, crunching feathers. Dragging him away.

Then it was still. The snarling and the scuffle stopped. The wolf dropped Caj and he fell with a grunt, exhausted, and waited to die.

After a moment, he realized that he was still alive.

The grim warbling and snarling sounded far away. The wolves had not attacked him. They had attacked the boar, and now, killed it.

I'll be next. Maybe bright Tyr will still accept me into his ranks in the Sunlit Land…

Caj tried to rise, wanting to die on his feet, and a furry body pressed him back down. A bloody muzzle sniffed his face. Jaws opened in a pant. A howl broke through the snow.

Paws pushed him to the ground. Caj fell from his pain into black, snowy dark, and didn't rise again.

45
THE WAR KING'S MERCY

THE HUNTERS RETURNED JUST BEFORE evening on the wings of a snowstorm, bearing little meat in their talons. Sigrun roused at their cries, ears flickering for one among them. A slow flush seeped under her feathers when she keened into the flurry and did not hear Caj's call in return.

The other females, weary of being locked in their dens, had remained outside in the brighter air, despite the cold. They trickled forward into a group near Sigrun to seek out their mates and see if they'd found game. Through the whirling snow, Sigrun peered desperately for any flash of cobalt blue.

Warmth pressed to her wing. Ragna.

"He isn't there," murmured the Widow Queen.

"He's there," Sigrun said firmly. "He's behind. See…"

But it was green Halvden who flew in last, not Caj.

"My hunters!" Sverin's voice filled the storm. He trotted forward to greet them, and then stopped. "Where is Caj?

Einarr loped up to Sigrun and Ragna, his ears flat, eyes huge and worried. Astri trotted forward behind him, her face grim.

"Caj has fallen!" Halvden's voice rang through the snow.

Every gryfon fell still. The breath left Sigrun's chest. A tremble slid up her legs. *I shouldn't have let him go. I shouldn't…this can't be happening.*

Mutters rose. Even the king huffed, "Impossible. Speak carefully, Halvden."

Halvden turned and mantled low.

Only Ragna, her wing pressed firmly to Sigrun's, kept her from leaping into the sky to fly to the Star Isle.

"We scented boar in the woods," Halvden said. "Caj told me we shouldn't hunt it, but I was so foolish and hungry." His voice dipped low, afraid.

Fake, Sigrun thought, the strange sound of blood rushing her ears. *He's faking everything.* Sigrun turned her gaze slowly to see if anyone else believed.

Ragna made a low noise. "Stay by me, sister."

"We met the boar in the woods. I…it almost killed me. If not for Caj, it would have."

A soft, low keen drifted through the falling snow.

Thyra.

She walked up on Sigrun's other side and dipped her head against Sigrun's wing. Absently, Sigrun crooned to comfort her, feeling hollow as a dried birch trunk.

"Caj saved my life," Halvden said loudly, "at the cost of his. And your Majesty," he turned back to Sverin. "Another thing."

Sverin's head hung low, but he lifted eyes to Halvden. The pride stared, amazed that Halvden could add another thing to such a loss.

He dug two golden feathers from his gold collar.

Heads lifted. Ears perked, murmurs rose, Kjorn's name drifted among them even as the darkness grew. Thyra stepped forward, her eyes locked on the golden feathers of her mate.

Halvden didn't meet her eyes, or anyone else's. "I found these near the boar's den. I fear—"

"Enough," Sverin whispered. "That's enough. Halvden, thank you."

Halvden dipped his head. The pride mumbled listlessly, staring at the feathers, heads lowering.

Then a clear voice asked, "Did you find a body?"

Sigrun switched her gaze to Thyra. Beside her, Ragna tensed, and Einarr lifted his wings uneasily. Halvden looked slowly to Thyra.

"No. But a boar that could defeat Caj--"

"Any bones? Any flesh? A fresh scent?" Thyra stepped forward, head high. "Any sign at all that our prince did other than pass by that place?"

"No," Halvden growled, and Sigrun watched as he closed talons tight, crushing Kjorn's feathers.

"Then he is alive!" Thyra declared to the falling snow, to the pride, then to the king. "My lord, he's alive. He must be. Lost, somehow, or injured, but alive."

Instead of looking just as hopeful, Sverin raised a slow, heated look to Thyra. Sigrun stepped forward beside her daughter.

"Then why doesn't he return to us? My son is dead," the king said quietly. "My wingbrother, your father, is dead. Accept that you have no place now."

That proclamation laid an even deeper, shocked silence over the pride.

"I carry your son's kit," Thyra whispered. "I carry your blood, your wingbrother's blood, next in line—"

"I will not see any trace of Vanir blood follow my rule."

Distantly, wind rattled the trees around the Nightrun like falling bones.

"Kjorn chose me," Thyra said at last, and still Sigrun heard no trace of doubt or fear in her voice.

"You witched him." Sverin's voice cut the air. "Both of you. All of you!" He raised his wings, addressing all three, Ragna, Sigrun and Thyra. "You witched him so that you and your mother and the white widow could control me once you'd gotten rid of Caj, and my son!"

Thyra growled, opening her wings in challenge. Sigrun laid talons over her hind paw but Thyra stepped forward. The fearless daughter-of-Caj.

"No witchery made your son love me, and I him. No witchery made me the daughter of your wingbrother, and we had nothing to do with his death, or with Kjorn's disappearance." She met Sverin's cold gaze firmly. "I am the most loyal left to you here, my king." Her gaze turned to Halvden. "I wouldn't feed you poison or lies just to gain your ear."

"Lies?" hissed Halvden, backing up to stand by the king, as close as if they were wingbrothers.

At the sight of that, at last Sigrun understood.

I should have seen it. He avenges his father's memory by doing what Hallr wished. By trying to become wingbrother to a king.

"I will serve you," Thyra said, ignoring Halvden now, addressing Sverin. Sigrun fought to restrain herself from clawing her daughter, pulling her back. "But not at the expense of my life or the life of Kjorn's unborn kit. I've been silent too long. Your grief maddens you, blinds you."

Sigrun could hear Caj's steady upbringing in her voice, and she was sure Sverin could too. For a moment, she hoped it would bring the king around.

But Sverin's eyes only narrowed, and Sigrun knew what he saw. Thyra's face—Sigrun's face, the soft face and coloring and eyes of a Vanir.

"My lord," Thyra said again, as if to summon him back from the brink. "My king, father of my mate. Hear reason."

"Poison and lies!" Sverin ramped up and closer gryfons scattered back, some toward Sverin to stand behind him, some toward Ragna, Sigrun, and Thyra. "First my mate, and now everything that I had left. Your Vanir ways drove my wingbrother and my son to their deaths! "

"Your fear and distrust drove them to death!"

Thyra's accusation left the king stunned for a moment.

"Daughter," Sigrun breathed, then realized she had no protection if Sverin's wrath turned on her again. Caj was gone. She was a proven traitor. She had nothing. If Sverin no longer wanted Vanir in the pride, she had nothing, not even protecting the pregnant females, to offer him. Most of them were half Vanir. He would drive his pride to death.

"In honor of my son's memory," Sverin said over the gusting snow, "I offer you mercy, Thyra. Leave, and live out your days in exile. Or remain and die. If you meet my family in the Sunlit Land, never say I didn't offer you mercy."

Thyra did not move. Gryfons ruffled uncomfortably, standing in the falling snow, some milling. Some drifted toward Thyra, as if to protect her. Sigrun wanted to grab Thyra and flee, but the king's Guard had surrounded the gathering.

"You, witches," Sverin rounded at last on Sigrun and Ragna. "Don't think I don't understand Vanir powers. You've brought this heavy winter on us, to ruin us, to ruin me."

Ragna's wings lifted slowly, but she stood solid by Sigrun. Grief and fear climbed steadily up Sigrun's back, threatening to steal her sense. She realized she was still waiting, dumbly, for Caj to appear, to speak, to protect her and the pride from his ranting wingbrother. She couldn't accept that he would not come.

Ragna spoke, firm and clear against the snow and Sverin's anger. "I can no more bring the snow than you can bring the sun, my lord."

"Leave this pride! You have blighted it long enough! You drove my mate to her death in the sea!"

At last, Ragna's expression chilled. "Is that how you remember it, my lord?"

For a moment Sverin looked breathless, as if Ragna had struck an actual blow. His beak opened in a wild pant, his gaze darting around the pride. "Leave this island!" He roared the command at all of them, at any of them who stood near Sigrun and Ragna. "You have no choice."

"That's not true!" A male voice rang through the snowy gloom.

All blinked terrified eyes at Einarr. He seemed to stand taller, wings open, head high. Terror seized Sigrun at his sudden need to speak.

"Son of an exile," Halvden sneered. "Brother to an exile. What would you say?"

"There *is* another choice," Einarr chimed in his bright singer's voice. "Another way." When he had everyone's attention, including Sverin, he spoke on.

"Shard is alive. Rashard, son-of-Baldr, true prince of the Silver Isles. Friend and brother to all of us. Vanir. Aesir. The pride."

A rumble swept the gryfons and Sverin's eyes widened to disbelieving, hunting rage.

Einarr turned his back on the king to face Sigrun and the others. Sigrun wanted to slap him to silence, but she also hungered for someone to stand against the Red King, and she didn't have the strength. No one else spoke out to stop Einarr, either.

"I met him on a hunt in autumn in the foothills of the White Mountain. He lives, he's well." A good speaker, Einarr met all the gazes that he could. "He survived the storm and the sea. He's going to return, to reclaim this island, and he said we could follow him. So there *is* a choice, you see."

He faced Sverin again, ears flattening against his skull.

"You can't banish the Vanir from this land. It belongs to them." He opened his wings and they flashed copper in the dim light. "I, Einarr, son-of-Vidar, follow Shard. I follow the Vanir, true lords of the Silver Isles, until my last breath!"

Sverin crouched. "You won't be following them long."

"Long live the gray kings! Long live Shard, the Stormwing!" Einarr's voiced cracked as he shoved up to his hind legs. "Rashard, the Summer King!"

"Silence!"

"The Vanir never die—"

Sverin lunged. Gryfons screeched and scattered as he met Einarr in a clash of tearing beak and talon.

Sigrun whipped around and shouldered hard into white Astri. "Run! Now! To the trees!"

Astri's scream ripped the air. Sigrun turned wildly to see.

Einarr lay crumpled in the snow, red staining out from his copper feathers. Sigrun's heart cracked, breaking open the grief she had sealed tight and safe in her chest. Instantly, she saw there would be no healing him. Einarr had been a better singer and friend than fighter. Sverin, like a mountain cat, went for the throat.

Sorrow tattered the edge of Sigrun's mind and she shoved Einarr's widow forward. Gryfons streamed around to escape—or attack—and the Guard drove them back. A flurry of bodies and wings and limbs squirmed and clashed into each other. Sigrun couldn't tell if others were retreating or trying to help her. Ahead, Ragna gave a battle cry and charged the line of the Guard. Sigrun whirled, seeking another way out with Astri.

A surprising streak of violet crashed through the snow toward Sigrun.

Halvden's mate, her gaze deadly.

"Kenna!" After the cry, Sigrun's voice left her, for Kenna didn't attack her. She plunged past and charged the line of the Guard with Ragna.

Few of the males dared fight Kenna, even round as she was with kit. The line broke and Vanir and half-Vanir streamed after the violet huntress.

"Flee!" Sigrun ordered Astri. "Come with me!"

"But Einarr," wailed Astri. "My mate, my—"

"He flies with bright Tyr now," Sigrun gasped, breathless. The words were automatic, and she didn't mean them to sound so heartless. "He flies victorious in the Sunlit Land and he is with you in your kit. The Vanir never die. Run with me now and stay alive for him."

A young male of the king's Guard leaped up in her face with a violent hiss. Thinking of Caj, of Kjorn, of brave, foolish Einarr, Sigrun ramped up and slapped her claws against his eyes. He shrieked, too stunned to fight back.

"We need to hide! Ragna!" Sigrun couldn't count how many had fled with them. The snow and growing dark hid many things. They ran across the plain toward the tree line, toward the river. Beyond that, Sigrun had no plan.

Behind, Sverin shouted orders. Halvden echoed them. The King's Guard pursued the fleeing pride members, harrying from above until they reached the trees. Then they scattered into chaos. Sigrun heard fighting in brush, kept Astri close, tried to find her wingsister.

A flashed of crimson warned her of Sverin, fighting ahead. Sigrun barreled in the opposite direction.

He doesn't want to exile us, he wants to kill us!

A rush of talon and feather made her turn, snarling.

Vald broke out of the underbrush, his orange feathers out of place in the snow. Long talon scars ran down one side of his face, oozing blood. Sigrun backed away, shoving a wing against Astri to encourage her to run. Instead, she cowered behind Sigrun and called for help.

"Vald," Sigrun strained her voice to sound reasonable. "I brought you into this world. Your mother is a friend—"

"Quiet," he growled, stalking close, his gaze darting to either side.

"Did Halvden kill Caj?" Sigrun rasped, crouching low, prepared to meet the fit sentinel in battle if she had to.

"I don't know," Vald said. For the first time, Sigrun noticed his expression—lost, angry. Afraid. "He split us up, and stayed with Halvden. We did hear wolves, and did smell boar. I don't know what happened…"

With his tumbling confession, Sigrun realized he was not there to kill her. He was there to help her. Astri lifted her ears to the sound of fighting.

"We have to hide," Sigrun said, letting a healer's calmness steal over her.

Vald nodded, his gaze cold. "There's one place I *know* the Guard won't go." He looked grim, speaking fast to keep Sigrun's attention. "There is an entrance to the wolf caves near the river. I found it with Halvden this autumn. If you'll trust me, I'll show you."

If he'd meant ill, Sigrun reasoned, he would've attacked. She had to trust. "Then we go underground," she said.

Astri whimpered. "The wolves—"

"The wolves are safer to us than the Red King ever has been," Sigrun growled. "Vald show me the way. Vanir to me! Ragna! Thyra!"

Sigrun gave a ringing call.

Gryfons wormed through the undergrowth to follow Sigrun's voice, but soon she fell silent. In the growing dark, all of them could see Astri, bright as a star, and they tried to put the King's Guard behind them. Fights broke along the edges of the group when the Guard found them, but steadily, they fell back as the storm cloaked the woods in early dark.

Dimly they heard Sverin's hollow shouts, calling his precious Guard back from the dark, calling a retreat for the night.

The fleeing band that Sigrun still hadn't put a number to followed Vald, Sigrun and Astri through the forest to the Nightrun river. In little meadows between the trees, the snow swirled and pelted them freely, the light strange and purple as Tor tried to glow through the clouds.

"Here," Vald called, stopping at the bank. The woods fell back there and bare rock sloped down to the river. Vald trotted up to a pile of boulders. Cracks in the rock face opened deep in the earth, and he pointed a talon down one ramp of stone that led to a dark hole. It smelled, freshly, of wolf.

Ragna loped up from the back of the line to Sigrun's side. She ordered any gryfons in fighting shape to enter the cave last, and to fan out and make sure none of Sverin's followed them. Then she looked to Sigrun. Blood stained her feathers. "If the wolves will trust and forgive any of us, it will be you. Lead us in."

Even in the night Sigrun saw her clearly, like a pale feather of Tor in the strange light, saw that she was a queen again, fearless, proud, taking charge.

Courage, bravery, all too late, Sigrun thought, turning obediently toward the dark cave. Shard would return gloriously some day with the lost Vanir at his heels and the will to rule.

All too late.

Too late for Einarr. Too late for Caj.

Sigrun stumbled, her muscles locking at the knowledge that she would never again curl up safe under a broad, blue wing. Never again would she hear his warm, rough voice teaching fledges how to fight, hear him complain of the herb stench in their den, or whisper his simple devotion in her ear. For the first time she knew Ragna's pain at losing Baldr.

Sorrow threatened to disable her, so she clung to what she had, what she had always had. She must be strong for others. Healer to the pride. Daughter-of-Hrafn. She crooned comfort to Astri and other terrified younger gryfons, repeated Ragna's commands into the dark, and gave what strength she had left to those around her.

Heart aching, her mind slipping toward witless sorrow, Sigrun forced herself to bury her anguish, once again, to survive.

46
NAMELESS

THE MOON ROSE AND SET on him many times, low on the edge of the world. The first time the sun set, he knew with surety more than he knew his own self, that he must not fly in the dark. So he landed and ran, loped, trotted, until his hind heels bled raw. When the sun rose again, he flew.

One wing stroke, then another.

The cold winter sun laid watery heat on his back. He didn't count days, only aware of light and dark.

I must not fly in the dark.

One foot in front of the other.

Checking over his shoulder for sign of gryfon pursuit, he ran. He had failed somehow. He knew that. Deaths and the anger and sorrow were behind him, and his fault, and they'd banished him from the pride. When he remembered the dragons, a pain grew so sharply in his chest that he had to bury it, to focus on fleeing, to forget.

Now he flew starward, just skirting the line between gryfon territory, and the Outlands. It seemed best to remain on the ground.

Gradually the earth under his paws faded from red to dead grayish brown, cracked and peeling from itself with dryness.

He slunk low, ears perked. A sulfuric smell seeped up into his beak and it brought flashes of another place. A sparkling bright sea, a little clump of islands, hidden hot springs that leaked the same scent…

He stopped and lifted his ears. Nothing moved but a stale, dank wind. On it curled the smell of brackish water and a rotting animal carcass. He gagged and loped forward, favoring one hind paw. A small ache flashed another memory. Two wolves chasing him up a wooded slope.

Ahanu.

He stopped, scenting the air. It was clearer there, and ahead the ground dropped sharply away into a dark, yawning canyon. Larger even than the one in which he had hunted with the others, with a red, beautiful female.

The Voldsom Narrows.

He turned from the gap and padded alongside, looking for a way across. Instinct kept him on the ground. He was near the home of the dragons, though they wouldn't fly in the day.

Ahead, vultures quarreled over the remains of a dead goat, hopping and flaring at each other. He gave them wide berth. Ache crawled in his belly, reminding him he had not eaten. Above, clouds glided in from the starward sky, heavy and as deep gray as his wings.

I am the Stormwing—

The first gruff voice to speak that name flared in his memory and he stifled it back.

He shoved to a run, whimpering at the pain in his bleeding hind paws, the ache in his shoulders. There was no way over the canyon but to fly. The idea of climbing down one side and up the other froze him with dismay. Wind rushed him, and through the haze he caught the threat of snow or rain. Pausing, he cast around for shelter.

A cluster of rocks crouched against the horizon far ahead, and stunted, bare trees clawed at the sky. Scenting carefully, he loped forward.

The rocks piled on each other to form a cave and he stuck his head inside. The scent inside should have warned him. When he walked in, a vicious shriek drove him right back out.

Two gryfons of muddy coloring leaped up challenge him. One was an older female, the other young enough to be a son. The young male leaped on him and he collapsed under the weight, fragile from hunger and thirst.

His instinct fought for him, slapped talons against the stronger gryfon's face to protect his own throat, kicked his weakened hind legs. Some odd fighting knowledge welled in him, not to bite randomly but to think, to twist like a sparrow, quick and nimble.

He writhed free of the other and backed away, wings lifted, feathers ruffed high in threat. He uttered a low growl and dangerous hiss, tail lashing. The winter wind sang around them, filling the murky canyon and the sky. The clouds pressed low, and tiny flakes drifted down, caught in the wind, to sting their eyes.

The old female stalked up, ears back. Worry buzzed through him and he turned, ramping, and forced a lion's roar from his chest.

She checked, crouching back. He caught her gaze. Something lit in her brown eyes, some awareness. Her beak opened and a strange, sorrowful sound crept out of her. When the young male moved to attack, she snagged his tail to stop him.

He didn't waste the chance to escape. Risking more dangerous enemies in the sky, he shoved straight up, flying hard.

A strange noise followed him on the wind, a strange, raw, gryfon's cry.

"Wait!"

More sounds. He didn't know their meaning.

"Wait, come back!"

"Surely I know you! Wait!"

"Son of Baldr!"

His own angry eagle scream drowned the old female's strange, meaningless cries.

Snow flashed all around him, heavy, coating his wings, then sliding free as it melted. Gray filled his world, and though his wings ached, a strange relief. This was better than running across the ground. He looked down and dimly saw the canyon. Caves and rocks dotted the landscape and now and then he would see a gryfon form darting toward one for shelter from the storm.

Outcasts. Exiles.

I am wind, feather and bone.

He needed no shelter. Gliding freely through the freezing snow, he laughed into the wind.

A dark shadow flickered ahead of him. A crow. Dusty black wings.

A talon snagged his heart.

Wait, the female gryfon's cry came to his mind. He echoed it, shouting after the crow. "Wait! Wait!"

The black bird mimicked him, then dropped, laughing, into the snowy gloom. He flared, hovering, and a dream took his mind.

A dark gryfon soared toward a white mountain.

The swirling snow filled his vision.

The white owl.

The white mountain. The Horn of Midragur.

Wheeling around, he ducked below the clouds to find his horizon, oriented himself starward, and flew fast. The canyon that bordered the Outlands cut a path starward and he followed it, wary of the scent of dragon but not wanting to stray from his goal. The white mountain peak from his dream.

Darkness cloaked over him. Familiar, venomous roars welled up in the distance behind him. He knew he had to land, that he shouldn't fly in the dark.

Rebellious anger lanced through him. *I am the Stormwing.* Instead of flying lower, he loosed a frustrated shriek and spiraled up high. Snow pelted his face. A chilling roar answered him, leagues away.

He flew out of the clouds into the clear night.

He had flown out of the storm, so high his breath fell short. Cold, cold air cleared his head and starlight dazzled his eyes. *Bjorna, Sig, Midragur...*he glided more easily as the names of the star beasts floated to him. The distant roars he'd heard grew closer, and he clenched his talons to keep from panicking. He flew high, and eventually the clouds cleared from below him.

The moon crouched at the edge of the world, sending milky beams along a bare plain that ended in a range of raw, young mountains. They broke the starry skyline like a yawning wolf's jaw.

A dream took him again. A dark gryfon, grasping skyfire, soared in a cloudless blue sky, toward a white mountain peak.

The tallest peak in front him stood jagged and hard and black against the sky, but its white peak glittered white with snow in the moonlight. For a moment he breathed relief. But it was night, not day, the sky black and starry, and he had no skyfire in his talons.

The dream in his head didn't match the outside world, and he didn't understand what to do.

A cloudless blue. A mountain peak.

Horrible roars thundered through the storm at his back. He thought of seeking shelter in the distant mountain. But something blocked him. He couldn't go there at night. He couldn't lead the dragons there. Something flickered...

Help, he thought. *I need help.*

He had to land, to hide, to wait until the dawn, but the dragons already chased him. He needed a distraction. Something to draw the dragons away from him.

Help...

Moonlight spread itself across the plain, opening out like a white gryfon wing. He looked down. A massive herd of deer dotted the ground below. Some grazed, some slept. He dove so fast his eyes streamed.

He barely thought about what he was doing. He thumped down in the middle of the herd and slapped the nearest buck with his talons. Terrified, warbling cries drowned out the sound of the wind. The herd seemed to rise up as one panicked creature, and stampeded. He leaped to one side and then the other, dodging thrashing bodies and the half-hearted swipe of a hoof or antler.

Dragons erupted from the bank of clouds. They saw the herd, angled to dive and hunt.

He hunched low, gaze darting through the moonlit plain. A gnarled stand of trees stood twenty leaps away. Grateful for dull coloring in the dark, he crept low on his belly, panting hard, eyes on the dragons. As he'd hoped, they didn't notice him through the tumult of deer.

When the herd had run past their reach, the dragons keened to each other and climbed the sky again, hunting him. Slowly, he crawled to the stand of trees, and curled up as small as he could make himself. Dragon shadows rippled across the ground in front of him. He held his breath, every feather still. One of the dragons flared, about to land in front of the trees.

A hoarse, croaking gryfon's call echoed from the sky.

He blinked, staying absolutely still. It didn't sound like a true gryfon. To him, it sounded like a raven, but they turned from scouring the ground to stare up at the sky.

Dragon wings beat the air as the closest hovered, hesitating. The cry came again.

His own breath caught as the dragon's head whipped up, searching. The moonlight only caught faint flashes on black wings.

Small black wings, or distant? His eyes were useless in the dark. Either way, it took the dragons' attention. At last they reached a roaring agreement and the little shadow led them high and away.

The gray gryfon stared after them until his eyes ached. Then he turned to perk ears toward the snow-crested peak, only a short flight away.

The Horn of Midragur.

He closed his eyes, grinding his beak against memory.

Midragur, the star dragon that coils around the world as a serpent around its egg, until the egg hatches and brings the glorious end of the world.

The legend of the earth's unmaking told itself in another's voice, gruff, ironic. He blocked it, fell away from himself, too close to remembering his name and all the pain that came with it. There was only one thing left to do.

At dawn, he would fly to the snowy mountain.

47
The Long Day Brings Rest

HOURS OF STALKING THROUGH THE damp, narrow caves left Sigrun and the others weary, aching and snappish. Sigrun squeezed back through the tunnels to check the pregnant females often, and would call halts if anyone seemed too tired. After the madness of their escape, she feared any of them might miscarry. She kept an especially close watch on Astri, who walked with her head bowed. Kenna, once she'd found Astri, didn't leave her side, and Sigrun was grateful.

Pale fungus crawled along the walls and gave them scant light. Ragna and Thyra scented the way from the front of the line. Once, Sigrun thought she caught Kjorn's scent on the rocks, but all was too damp and old to be sure.

The low, echoing call of a wolf brought the band to a dead halt.

"Be calm," Ragna called from the front. "Sigrun!"

Sigrun trilled encouragingly to the terrified half-Aesir females she had just been checking over, and shouldered through the narrow stone passage to the front. Squinting, she found Ragna had already trotted ahead.

"If they're feeling peaceful," Ragna said, "you and I have the best chance for a friendly meet."

Sigrun merely dipped her head, uneasy. Until Per the Red, she had never feared wolves. But Helaku's pack had traversed those very caves that summer past and attacked the nesting cliffs, killed fledges, killed the old, attacked the young warriors who guarded them. Sigrun knew why, but it didn't soften the hurt, nor dull her worry now.

Another low howl dipped into mournful, melodic singing. A male voice.

"Which rises first, the night wind, or the stars?
Not even the owl could say,
whether first comes the song or the dark."

A chill slipped down Sigrun's back. It was a rhyme she hadn't sung in years. To her surprise, a brittle male gryfon voice joined from the back of their ragged line. An elder of the Vanir.

"Which fades last, the birdsong or the day?
Not even the sky could tell,
Whether last stills the sun or the jay."

The old song soared through Sigrun's heart, a song of mourning, a song of the earth and moon and the Vanir. Beside her, Ragna joined. Sigrun closed her eyes, her own voice silenced from grief. The half-Aesir shifted nervously, those who had never heard the old songs, but other gryfons sang with the wolf in the dark stone hall. The Vanir, at last, unafraid to raise their voices.

"Only the long day brings rest
Only the dark of night, dawn.
When the First knew themselves, the wise will say
They took their Names to the Sunlit Land

But their Voice in the wind sings on."

"I am Ragna!" called the queen when the last echo died, and they heard the scuff of paws on stone, approaching. "Once mate to Baldr, friend of Helaku who now runs in the stars. We seek friendship and shelter. We offer peace and friendship in return."

Sigrun thought that sounded respectful enough. The steps advanced. A single wolf, but a turn in the cave ahead prevented them from seeing it yet. Sigrun shifted, lowering her head, then lifting to try and catch a scent.

"This is folly," Thyra whispered from behind, and Sigrun merely flicked her tail in dismissal.

If Thyra could stand up to Sverin, surely this can't frighten her.

"I am Ahanu, son-of-Helaku." His voice was low, smooth and rich, and he introduced himself as a gryfon would. The eerie light picked him out in pieces as he emerged from the deeper tunnel. First paws, then glimmering black and gold coat, and finally a calm, sharp-eyed face.

"Welcome, at last, wind sisters and brothers. Joy fills me to hear you sing the Song of Last Light again. We know you had losses, and we mourn with you." His gaze fell on Sigrun. "Daughter of Hrafn. I'm glad to see you here. You are needed on the Star Isle."

"This is a trick," Thyra said quietly. Before Sigrun could warn her to silence or ask Ahanu what he meant, and why, Ragna spoke.

"Be still, daughter of my wingsister. Mate and soon mother to a prince. Be calm. If you need any more proof that a friend stands here, behold."

Ragna stepped aside so that Thyra could see Ahanu for herself, Thyra took a sharp breath. Other gryfons shouldered forward to see, and Sigrun turned back, eyes narrowed. Ahanu had stepped fully into the light of the tunnel and at last she saw what she had missed before, so delirious was she with hunger and exhaustion and grief.

Neatly twisted into the heavy fur of Ahanu's shaggy neck was a long, gleaming golden feather, and like a shadow beside it, a gray.

Kjorn. Shard. The sight made them real again to Sigrun, and to all who saw. Sigrun wanted to ask what Ahanu needed with a gryfon healer, but Thyra stepped forward first, gazing hungrily at the gold feather. Sigrun knew her own question could wait.

"Where is Kjorn?" Thyra asked.

Ahanu's voice was low, but the stone carried his words to the very end of the line of gryfons.

"He has gone to face the king."

48
The Horn of Midragur

The mountain stood tall over him, black rock leaping up from ragged foothills. Snow dusted the ground, glittering in the sun, and the peak shone brilliant white. He had to tilt his head to see it. Beyond the peak, the sky blazed blue.

He leaped up to fly, soaring high, searching the mountain. He traveled along the nightward slope, not sure what he searched for, but an inner tug guided him onward.

A gash marred the face of the mountain and plunged into a deep crevasse. Drawn toward the crevasse, he plunged down, soaring along the canyon in a long, wide spiral that took him so deep into the earth that the sky became a thin line of blue above him. For many moments he flew that way, until he wasn't sure what side of the mountain he was on, or if he'd almost circled it completely.

A rock arch loomed ahead, the entrance to a massive cave. He dove under the arch. Under the mountain, into a vast, dark, underground canyon large enough for him to fly.

He marveled, winging at a steady tilt in the quiet air, feeling safe and at peace for the first time.

A low sound thrummed through the dark rock on all sides.

A warm hum.

A song.

Without hesitation, he sang out in answer. At last, the song he had longed for and thought lost. The song ceased as if in surprise at his voice, and for that moment of silence his heart ached.

Then an answering call came.

> *"Only the long day brings rest*
> *Only the dark of night, dawn…"*

Plump fungus laced the walls and its soft light caught on tiny crystalline rocks and lit his path like a river of pale blue stars.

I fly in the Horn of Midragur, the star dragon, who coils around the world, and the inside of the dragon is also made of stars…

Ahead, the starry stone tunnel narrowed. He couldn't quite tell the width, but beyond it he saw strange, dim light, and suspected it widened again into a cavern. A swift current of air filled the tunnel, air sucked through the narrow entrance by the pressure of the canyon behind him.

Taking a chance, he beat his wings hard, flying swift against the air current, and aimed for the narrow hole at the end. He just had to time it right…two more wing beats, one…he shut his wings and shot through the narrow crack. He took a risk on the passage widening before he could see, and flung open his wings once he'd passed through.

He stared.

The tunnel opened into a cavern, indeed, almost too large for him to fathom.

The Dawn Spire of the gryfon aerie could've fit inside the cavern and left room to fly over the top. He'd flown through a tunnel that opened in the middle of the rock wall between the distant roof, and the distant stone floor. He peered up, flapping slowly in the still air.

Long fangs of rock hung down from the far away ceiling, glistening with crystal and moisture. A vast nebula of stars splashed and played out on the distant ceiling of the mountain, and he stared in awe. He flew up, and up, to the very top of the cavern, and touched one of the little stars, only to learn it was a tiny, odd worm that spun a glowing thread. He laughed in delight and let himself fall back down to behold the thousands of false, glowing stars again.

He flew one long circuit around, studying everything. A freshness permeated the air that smelled of minerals and water. Tiny cracks in the mountain must let in little breezes. Far below, the cavern floor glistened abysmally dark—volcanic glass from the First Age.

He couldn't figure out what the massive cavern was. Then his mind flashed on the high, snow-capped singular peak, and he understood.

The Horn of Midragur was hollow.

An ancient volcano, he mused. *Earthfire carved this mountain, once long ago.*

He soared through the cavern, keening triumphantly, calling to whatever had called to him.

A song answered him, and he peered down. Far below at the bottom of the cavern, he spied something white. A dark rock mound rose out of the stone floor, cupped and concave like an eggshell.

Inside that rock nest perched an enormous, pearl-white serpent, such as he'd never seen or dreamed. Coil upon coil of gleaming, iridescent white scales filled the rock nest, and the false starlight light almost appeared to fall through the creature, as if it were made of snow, or rain. A silvery mane flickered around its head and down the endless serpent back. Then he spied four legs, more like a lizard than a snake. Two wings like swan wings opened to greet him.

He knew at once that the white serpent was female, that she was the one who had called to him over sea, in the storms and in his waking dreams, and that she was afraid.

He flew lower, not hesitating, and landed on the rock platform in front of her, dropping his wings to a mantle.

She was a dragon, he knew, but unlike the creatures he'd met in battle before. Some part of him remembered her large, searching, pale eyes, like twin suns before him.

"I called to you," she whispered. Then he realized it wasn't a whisper. It was her normal voice, flickering like a gentle wind on his ears. "I sang to you, but you did not come. I called the Summer King."

"I'm sorry," he breathed, finding a voice in his chest when he heard hers, remembering that he had a voice, after all. He blocked the meaning of the name Summer King, what it meant to him, the names it brought him, and the pain. But he knew she had called to him. "I'm here now."

"Welcome." Her reptilian eye ridges scrunched down in concern with wolf-like delicacy. "I…I did not expect a gryfon. The song…suggests someone greater." She tilted her large head, studying him from each angle.

He bowed lower, his beak tapping the rock, and didn't know how to answer. She slid a forepaw under his chin to lift his head. Something about her slender, articulate talons struck him with a memory.

The blunt, deadly paws of the Winderost dragons.

They couldn't have forged the treasures that Kajar stole.

As surely as their were Vanir and Aesir, he knew with sudden, sharp clarity, there were different kinds of dragons in the world.

The thoughts confused him, the names, the questions that flocked to him.

He stared at her face instead, reptilian, long and elegant and ending in a nose like a doe. A wispy mane feathered out from her jaw line and formed a crest along her neck and back. Two long, delicate whiskers drooped out from her nose, her eyes slit like a reptile but were dilated in the dark.

"What is your name?" she asked.

"I…I don't know," he whispered, tight heat forming in his chest. Tight shame.

She considered him with enormous eyes. "I see. Sorrow has hidden your name. Well." She shifted, lightly flexing her wings. "To me you shine like a shard of sunlight in this dark place, so that is what I will call you until you remember. You will only remember once you grieve. Only in grief do we honor the lost. Without grief there comes forgetting, denial, Nameless, dead hearts. We who have names and hearts *must* grieve. Do you understand, little Shard of Sun?"

He stared into her eyes. *A shard of sun.*

A shard.

Rashard.

The nightmare crashed into him and he had no time to escape.

He gasped, crumbling to his belly under the weight of it.

The battle. The dragons, the dead gryfons of the Dawn Spire that he hadn't counted. His arrogance and stupidity. The days he'd spent running, the empty, Nameless hours walking until his paws bled.

The dragons hunting him. *Still hunting me.* He had named Kajar, and so they hunted him as they had never hunted a gryfon of the Dawn Spire.

He was ravenous. He was injured, exhausted. Lost.

He was Shard, the son of Baldr—failed brother, failed son, failed Summer King.

"Stigr," he choked, and something broke inside of him.

His wild, raw keening echoed around the cavern. The dragon held still, watching him until his voice scraped and dissolved to silence.

When at last Shard only stared blankly at the roof of glow-worm stars high above them, like an impossibly close galaxy within the mountain, the dragon spoke.

"Do you remember now?"

"Yes," he said, his eyes fixed firmly above him. "I remember everything." He managed to stand, though every muscle twitched and quivered.

"Good," she said. "We have very little time."

"Time for what?" His tongue felt dry. The stars danced above him. A rush of heat flooded him from tail to shoulders and he stumbled to one side as if the cavern floor pitched beneath him.

The dragon caught him against her wing, and herded him to her side. "For everything."

Her voice sounded leagues away. Over a distant sea. Through the sky, a dream, as he'd heard it before.

"Everything…?"

"Rest," she said. "I will wake you before too long."

"Your name," Shard insisted, ashamed that he hadn't asked before.

"Amaratsu," she answered, and he collapsed into a dream of the rising sun.

49
THE FINAL EXILE

SVERIN HUNCHED, CURLED ON HIS rocks, snow weighing down his wings, and worked at cleaning Einarr's blood from his talons. A day of scraping, gnawing, and dragging through snow and he still found flecks and spots.

Snow fell on the Copper Cliff, obscuring the sea and the rest of the Sun Isle. Sverin enforced a silence of mourning to those few left in his pride. The elderly Aesir, their mates, his own kin, and his young King's Guard were all that remained. Many of their mates had left them, bewitched by the Widow Queen and Sigrun.

The King's Guard milled below him, restless, and he ignored their sideways looks.

Every warrior should know that filthy talons made dull talons.

"My lord."

Sverin perked his ears at Halvden's voice, but didn't raise his head. His new wingbrother sounded weary and uncertain.

Unusual.

"My lord, another blizzard comes."

"The witch," Sverin muttered, rasping in frustration when he found yet another bloodstain. He shook his head and ruffled his feathers, skin crawling as if he suffered mites. "The witch queen is trying to undo me."

Halvden's shadow fell on him in the dull light. "My lord. Ragna is gone as of last night, and all who followed her. Will you have us hunt for them?"

Sverin lashed out and Halvden stumbled back. "Can you not see I'm busy?"

Halvden leaned away, one wing lifted to shield himself. "Sire, your talons are clean. Please stop this. What should I tell the Guard and the hunters?"

"Tell them this winter will never end," Sverin snarled, "until we kill the Vanir and the wolves in name of Tyr. He is punishing us."

Halvden stood silently. He shifted his talons. "Sire…"

"You sound uncertain, my wingbrother," Sverin said, lifting his gaze to Halvden's eyes. "Is it because your pretty mate left you? She's a fool and a traitor and you're better off. We will find you a new mate, better, of full Aesir blood as befits your father's memory."

Doubt flickered in Halvden's gaze and he glanced toward the dregs of the pride. Then he dipped his head. "Yes, of course."

"Sire!" called a young male of the Guard. Sverin loosed a soft growl and pushed himself up to stand, shaking the snow from his feathers. "Tell us what to do! May we go in, and shelter out the storm?"

"All may shelter," Sverin called, and heard murmurs of relief. He focused on the young male who had spoken. "Except you. Leave my sight and don't return until you hold a wolf pelt in your talons, or the white feathers of the Widow Queen."

A silence fell, then other gryfons shuffled away from the unfortunate member of the King's Guard.

"Sverin," Halvden murmured, sidling closer as if to calm him before his anger grew. The member of the Guard stared at him, and didn't move.

Sverin growled. "You heard me. Fly. Hunt."

For a moment it looked as if the young male would fly, then he just stood, wings open.

As Einarr had stood before.

As Shard had stood.

Defying him.

"My lord this is madness! We serve you loyally, but you can't ask more! We—"

Sverin leaped, felt Halvden's talons try to catch his heel. "No, Sire!"

The young male cowered, bunching himself to spring away as Sverin dove. Sverin stretched his talons forward, his shriek cutting the snowy air.

Another gryfon plummeted from the sky and slammed him to the side.

Sverin hit the snow and rolled.

"*Who dares—*" Sverin jumped to his feet and turned on his attacker, flashing his wings wide.

"Enough."

It felt as if his stomach dropped out. The figure before him couldn't be real. The handsome golden outline, the broad wings, the softly angled face, so like *her* face, and so like her eyes.

"Father." Kjorn's voice sounded real, and then Sverin caught his scent. "Enough. Step down. Grief maddens you. I should never have let it go this far."

The sad remains of his pride crept forward, staring and whispering in awe as if Tyr himself had stepped down from the sky.

"You stink of wolves," Sverin snarled. "You can't be my son. You can't be the prince of the Aesir."

"I am Kjorn. Son-of-Sverin." His gaze searched Sverin's eyes, unbelieving and sad. Sverin couldn't fathom what put that emotion in his face. Here they were, both alive and well.

"My real son would be happy. You're a trick."

Kjorn shook his head. "Face what you've done and let's move on. Please, Father. There's been enough death. Enough separation in this pride."

"You sound like a Vanir," Sverin growled, his anger growing, but he was unable to attack the apparition that looked and sounded like Kjorn. "*He* did that to you."

"Shard," Kjorn said. "My wingbrother. I should have listened to him more."

"No," Sverin said. Snow flurried between them and he felt trapped, surrounded, gryfons cornering in on all sides.

Halvden glided down from the rocks to stand by him and Sverin sidled closer, pressing his wing to Halvden's. He spoke to Kjorn again. "Don't you see, don't you know what comes of that? They killed your mother!"

"They didn't," Kjorn said, his voice low and quiet. "And you know that."

For a moment Sverin panted, his heart tight at what he saw in Kjorn's expression. He couldn't tell if it was pity or loathing, each one worse enough to break his heart again.

"It's lies, Vanir lies, my son, to ruin me!"

"Halvden," Kjorn said, "you're his wingbrother now. Tell him that I'm real and let us end this."

Halvden seemed at a loss, looking from one face to the other. Then his expression darkened. "Be cautious, my king. He's clearly an apparition sent by the wolves to drive you off. You were right."

Sverin angled his head, studying Halvden sharply, then Kjorn.

He could attack neither one.

Kjorn gave Halvden a disgusted look. "The Vanir will return," he said. "Father, Shard will return. And our time here will end."

Each word fell like a blow. Sverin crouched. "No, my son, then we will have no home—"

"We have a home," Kjorn corrected, though his voice cracked. He had been raised in the Silver Isles and barely knew of his other birthright. But, it seemed, he had learned enough. "And I mean to return there."

"You have no idea what waits there, what hungers for our blood!"

"Then I will find out."

He stood in the snow calmly, the wind brushing up his feathers.

Sverin's every muscle screamed to attack, to silence him as he had silenced Einarr.

"This is not your son," Halvden hissed. "Kjorn would never turn on you like this!"

Sverin looked from Halvden's face to Kjorn's. The uncertainty and memories and shame welled up in him. The ring of gryfons pressed close, staring. Their disapproval and their fear and anger crushed in on him.

He couldn't catch a breath. He could not fight. He had to flee.

"Father," Kjorn whispered. "I see your pain. We can mourn together—"

Sverin could take no more.

He whirled, flaring his wings, slashing talons at any who approached, and launched himself into the sky, fighting wind and snow.

Wings beat behind him and for a moment he knew it was Halvden.

Then he let go of the name, fell away from himself, from the green gryfon shouting after him.

He flew, hard and fast and Nameless, away from all of it into the sky.

Kjorn watched them go, then crouched, opening his wings to follow.

"No, my prince!" An older Aesir female bounded forward. "Please, don't leave us again. Sverin has driven himself mad. He will turn on you in the end, or Halvden will. Please don't leave us again."

Kjorn hesitated.

What would a true king do?

Not abandon his pride, something in him whispered. He closed his wings, straightened, and spoke to the small ring of gryfons around him.

"What I said to my father was true. I will leave the Silver Isles to see what remains in our homeland. I will seek Shard. I think he knows more of all this than we do, now. I ask any of the Aesir elders to tell me *everything* you know of the threat in the windland. Our…our homeland.

Everything about Kajar's war, and the truth of why Per came. Then I will fly. Alone. But you need not fear any enemy in the Silver Isles any longer. I've made peace."

There were murmurs of assent, the relief sighing through those gathered so great that Kjorn felt relief in his own heart.

He tried not to look to the side, tried not to think of the red gryfon flying away from him. He had to be stronger.

I tried my best.

"There will be changes," Kjorn called, raising his voice.

The pride—his pride—gathered around him, their faces bright and hard and ready to listen.

50
LAKELANDER

He stood on the Ostral Shores, the great muddy lake glimmering before him. His home. Far on the windward horizon the peaks and spires of the Winderost and the Dawn Spire irritated the sky.

A vivid blue fledge cavorted along the water's edge, slapping at fish and water beetles. He watched, surprised to realize he was watching himself.

I always liked the water, *he mused.* Maybe it's why I never hated the Vanir.

Per the Red flew in that afternoon, to select new bachelor warriors for the Guard, and left his son near the shore.

Sverin already knew how to fly, and he spent the afternoon showing off. Then he taught Caj what he knew. In return Caj taught him refined hunting skills and secret fighting moves he had devised on his own. Sverin spoke of the glory and honor to be found at the Dawn Spire, and occasionally of his own fears and frustrations, being a prince. Caj understood, for his family was one of the leading clans of the great salt shore. They had much in common, and also many differences.

Sometimes, deep friendship was formed through battles, or courageous hunts, or a shared fear that two friends vowed to conquer together.

Sometimes it was as simple as knowing you had found your reflection, and that afternoon by the lake, they did. By the time the sun set they took the wingbrother pledge. When the long day was over, Caj left his proud parents to learn from Per the Red and remain by Sverin's side.

Wingbrothers.

Cold wind made him shiver. The Winderost turned white with snow.

He smelled the painted dogs hunting.

No, it was not the painted dogs…

Stinging cold and a sharp scent brought him awake to black, frosty night. Something warm curled next to him on each side. He felt like a kit in a nest until the heavy, dander and musk smell of wolf coated his senses.

What is this?

"You like your supper warm?" he growled. He twitched, shoving at the furred bodies all around him. "Get away from me!"

"Oh what days I have lived to see," murmured a female voice, whittled with age. "When the noble should outfly their king."

Caj weaved to his feet, upsetting the tumble of wolves around him. Agony cracked through his wing and he gasped. Stars glimmered down on them, achingly bright in the winter night.

"What do you want?" he demanded of the she-wolf before him.

"What do *you* want?" she murmured cordially in return.

He had never seen a wolf so old, her face ghostly white, her fur white, her eyes pale gold. The snow beneath them threw up light as if it were false dawn and he saw little details he wouldn't normally see in the night. Under the stars, her fur caught odd silver and blue glints, iridescent like gryfon feathers, her eyes bright yellow.

She was a snow wolf of the high mountains, of the far, frigid shores of the Star Isle. He'd had no idea they mixed with the forest wolves.

Oddly, she reminded him of Ragna, though Ragna wasn't as ancient. A sense about her was similar, a quietness, like the eerie moon.

Surrounded, he had no choice but to answer. "I want to go home."

"Which home?"

The Ostral shores, he thought, the dream washing back to him.

"My wing is broken," he growled. "So it doesn't matter. Go on and finish toying with me. A grounded gryfon is a dead gryfon."

"Yet here you stand." The other wolves rose and padded cautiously away from him, though they circled, sniffing, listening.

"I'll die here. By a boar. Or you. Or the cold."

"We have slain the youngest son of Lapu, so he is no threat. And if I wanted to kill you, Noble Caj, I could have days and days ago. I have every reason. Your wingbrother killed my mate."

Caj stared at her. Under the starry night, he wasn't even sure if she was real, or a ghost. The starlight caught strange, alien green light in her eyes. "Helaku. The wolf king." With a grim flash he recalled the wolf pelt in Sverin's nest. "So you're his mate, and mother of this cursed pack. He attacked us and chose that death."

"I know it. The king of the Star Isle," she murmured. "The dashing prince who sang me down from the mountain top and gave me seers and warriors for cubs, and fought the mad Red King." The dry edge to her tone didn't go unnoticed, and for just a breath, Caj thought she sounded like Sigrun, impatient with ideas of glory and fighting and wanting only to have her family safe. Her eyes stared through Caj as if she could see all those thoughts. "He hunts with the High Pack now."

Caj knew Helaku had been ancient. His death, it seemed, wore on his mate. He couldn't fathom how old this creature must be. Still clinging to life.

He glanced sidelong, seeking a path for escape, then almost laughed at himself. *What would I do, hobble for my life?* Still the ghostly she-wolf didn't advance, and the others only watched.

"Do you know why we named it the Star Isle?"

"It lies starward of the Sun Isle," Caj said, ears tracking the rest of the wolves. He shifted his foreleg and it throbbed. Crusted blood flaked and fell off, and he winced. Halvden's talons scored deep.

She dipped her head, ears forward, and the other wolves laughed in warbling voices.

"Not all things lie oriented to the gryfon realm. As you call yourselves children of the sun, we call ourselves children of the stars." She raised her pale muzzle and howled low.

The long, hollow, shifting note sent the night through Caj's blood. He stood firm, refusing to be intimidated.

She lowered her head, ears perked to him. "You see that cluster of stars, that lies between the two high peaks of the White Mountains on the Sun Isle?"

Hesitantly, Caj turned his gaze from her toward the Sun Isle. He could barely see the far peaks on the next isle. He must have wandered, drunk on pain, to the top of a hill, for he could make them out a little. His breath clouded the air in front of him, then cleared to show him a tightly packed cluster of stars. He counted eight.

"The First Pack," murmured the ancient she-wolf. "The High Pack. Sons and daughters of Tyr and Tor, who ran down the dragon's back of stars and dug the Star Isle up from the sea with their claws. They carried seeds from the First Forest in their coats and dropped them in the new earth, making a place of good hunting for us. When we die, it is joyous. We join the great hunt among the stars."

Caj gazed at the glimmering pack of stars, then flattened his ears, peering up and around. He didn't enjoy the idea of being surrounded each night by an uncountable number of wolf spirits.

"What do you want from me?"

"Friendship," she said blandly. "I thought it was obvious, but perhaps your injuries dull your mind."

"You'll find my talons sharp enough."

"What will you do, Noble Caj? Return to your splintered pride, tell the king he is mad, and mend it yourself? With a broken wing, you will have to pass under the isles, or swim, and neither could you do without our help. Once there, you would have to turn on your wingbrother, which you will not do."

"I'll do what I need to!"

"You haven't done it yet," she murmured. "After all the wrongs you saw. Now it's too late. I see myself in you. I saw my beloved king sliding into witless anger and I did not stop him, for I couldn't bear to see that anger turned on me."

The words chilled Caj as sure as a winter wind.

"But there are others who can help, others who can end this in a better way than brother turning on brother."

Shard, Caj thought. *She means Shard and the Vanir.* Caj considered, found that he believed her, nodded, lifting his one good wing. "Then we have a pact—"

"No," she said softly. "Not a pact. Not an agreement that will break like an old, frozen branch at the first test of strength, or once our ends are met." She raised her pale head, gaining the scent of the night air. "We must have friendship, durable, flexible, like the rowan in the time of rain and new leaves."

"Why me?"

"Because you have already opened your heart. Even now, I speak to you in the language of the earth, the language your wingbrother will never comprehend, flying too high, and you speak it back without even knowing. So many Aesir turn their backs on their second birthright, being children of the earth as well as the sky. But you, Caj, in being broken, have become whole."

Caj shifted his talons in the snow. With his broken wing, he could do nothing for anyone, and it had already begun to heal wrong. He would never be able to fly. The she-wolf, quiet, reasonable, hadn't threatened him. She had used her fellow wolves to keep him warm through—he didn't want to think of how many long, cold nights.

Everything he knew began to splinter, and so he clung to one thing. He had to survive, to save Sverin from himself, to save the pride. If he needed a new friend, if however strange, to do it, then…

"If I was winged," murmured the ancient wolf at last, "if I was a gryfon, would you think twice?"

Caj knew the answer, and suspected she did, too.

After a moment under her frank gaze, with a dozen other wolf eyes on him, he bowed his head in gratitude. There was no other choice.

"Thank you for your help. I…I'd like your friendship. And for whatever it's worth, I offer you mine."

Gleeful warbles and howls met his words. Caj shuddered and tried not to look up at the stars.

"Then fear not, Noble Caj, and hope," said the ancient wolf queen of Star Island. "We've a healer among us who knows the set of a gryfon wing."

Caj tilted his head, wary. The wolves parted to allow one through. At first he thought it was a pale wolf, larger than the others, and graceful. Then the gleaming stars picked out the edge of a wing, feathered ears, a lovely, fierce face.

Caj stumbled forward in disbelief.

"*Sigrun.*"

She leaped, and nearly broke his other wing in their reunion.

51

The Tale of the Red Kings

Shard woke from a dream of his nest-father. A foreign scent surrounded him and he held still, then remembered.

Amaratsu.

She watched him with unblinking eyes.

"You called to me," Shard said. His aches had gone, he was clean. She must have washed him in his sleep like a mother gryfon, cared for him. He didn't know whether to be reassured, or terrified, for she looked uncertain and unhappy, herself.

"I called the Summer King," she said. "But I thought…"

"You didn't expect a gryfon." Shard studied her face. Her voice sounded old and brittle, as if she were ancient, but there was an incongruous freshness to her expression, a wonder and naïve softness of the very young.

"The song has been sung," Shard said quietly, standing. "And I answered. My father saw this very mountain in a vision. Did you call to him, too?"

"How long ago?"

"Ten years."

Slowly Amaratsu shook her head. "No. No, it could not have been me. Perhaps he knew that this mountain would bring us together. It was only this autumn, when the starfire flew, that I called for the Summer King in the wind. But you flew so late."

"The signs were wrong," Shard said, battling guilt over being late for a meeting he hadn't known he was due for. "I didn't know who the dark gryfon was in the vision, I didn't have skyfire, and the mountain peak had no snow."

A tremble shook her body, a tremor he realized was a growl. "The signs? Signs? You should've flown when you knew the time was right, never mind the signs! You don't understand *signs*. Arrogant gryfon!"

Shard crouched, lifting his wings to shield himself. "I didn't know! My father died for acting on the wrong vision…I didn't want to make the same mistake."

"*I* was the snow on the mountain!" Amaratsu stretched her gleaming white wings. "*You* were the gryfon in your vision, dark with grief, and the skyfire you carry is *here*."

She jabbed a claw at his chest and Shard flinched but she only tapped him hard for emphasis. Tapped his beating heart.

Shard's skin crawled with shame and understanding. "I'm here now. What do you need from me? You sang the Song of Last Light, has someone died?"

Her whiskers twitched in the air. Shard realized he had no idea how long he'd slept, if it was night, or how long until the dragons of the Outlands found him.

"No," Amaratsu said, calming as he offered his help. "Not yet."

"Tell me why you sang to the winds."

"No," she said again, and raised her head high above him on her long, long neck. She wove to one side and then the other like a snake. "First tell me why you answered. Why a gryfon heard my song."

Shard began to answer, but a glimmer caught his eye and he looked, spying something protected within her coils. It looked like the smooth side of a large, white pearl. A light, muffled tapping made his ears swivel. Amaratsu shifted until the giant pearl was hidden again.

"Shard. What do you want from *me*? For surely you must want something too, if you followed a vision and my song."

Again that strange mix of age and young suspicion.

Shard stepped away from her, stretching his wings, his legs, testing his muscles. Everything still felt raw and sore, and he was groggy with hunger. Amaratsu watched him, then slipped something from within her coils. A strip of dried fish.

"Forgive my rudeness. Eat."

Shard leaned forward, sniffing. The fish smelled heavily of smoke and had an odd, bendable texture like damp bark. But it was food. He ate, chewing hard until the meat softened.

"Thank you." Feeling more refreshed, he stood before the dragon and lifted his wings. "You should know, the dragons are hunting me. I don't know how long until..."

Her long mouth curled in a sneer. "Dragons? They are not true dragons, but wyrms that hunt you, vengeful, greedy and thoughtless." She waved a paw in the air. "We have time. Tell me everything that you think important."

He met her gaze, and told her everything important. Everything. He told his tale from the beginning—from the arrival of the Aesir in the Silver Isles, his father's death, his own discoveries. He told her everything that had happened to him that summer, that he had answered the call of the Summer King, and all that had passed in the Winderost.

"A gryfon," she murmured when he was done. "I would never have thought...not after the Great Betrayal."

"You've met gryfons before," Shard said. "But it wasn't good?"

"Not I," she said, looking toward the cavern entrance. Shard turned his ears that way and heard distant, hoarse roars.

The dragons—the wyrms, she called them, had found the entrance to the mountain.

"We have to flee," Shard said. "They hunt me."

"Perhaps," she said quietly. "Perhaps they followed your scent. But they have also hunted me since they heard my song in this land. But we cannot flee them now. They've found the entrance. It is night. They would come upon us if we tried to leave."

"What about up there?" Shard jerked his beak up to indicate the hole in the ceiling far above, a crack that let in faint, true starlight.

"You may fit," she said. "I would not."

"Then what'll we do when they get here?" Shard demanded, anxious and growing angrier at her lack of concern.

"That remains to be seen."

She watched him as if trying to make a decision, about what, Shard didn't know.

"You've told me your tale," she said, so softly he had to walk close again. "And that you followed a vision here, though you don't know why. I'm sorry that you had to meet me, and not an answer to your troubles in the Silver Isles."

"That remains to be seen," Shard echoed her. A suspicion grew in him, and though he'd failed at the Dawn Spire, failed to speak to the Outland wyrms, and lost Stigr, he couldn't give up again. He would not forget himself, would not hide. He'd reached the mountain. He had to see it to the end.

"Amaratsu. What is *your* tale?"

"My tale," she said thoughtfully. "It begins before yours. It begins yours. My tale is of loss and fear, though I hoped the Summer King would bring…hope. My tale," she lowered her head to speak to Shard on the level, "begins with the Tale of the Red Kings."

"Tell me," said Shard.

She began to speak and Shard fell into the story like a kit, into her soft, bird-like voice, and in her eyes saw a snow-bound land at the bottom of the world across the farthest sea.

"I hail from the Sunland. A land of endless days of night in the winter, when we chart the stars and sing our songs and craft our treasures. A land of

days of endless sun in summer, when great Tyr walks the edge of the earth, and we once traveled the world. We travel no longer, not since the Great Betrayal.

"Our young cousins, the wyrms you have met in the Winderost, claimed a northern part of the world, a place I've heard is all rolling green, dense woods, rocks and cliffs and cold, crashing sea. A realm rich with metals and gems. They mined for us once, and we would take our pilgrimage to collect from them, and in turn we tried to teach them of beauty, of honor and generosity and discipline. They wanted some of the treasures that we made, but we knew they would only hoard them like witless rats. Though we tried to teach them, they fought amongst themselves, laughed at us, and learned nothing.

"Still, we needed their help to find the metals, and we hoped they would reach enlightenment, so we traveled still, and they gave us the raw metals they found in the hopes that we would craft them treasures.

"Many years ago, we saw the starfire that flew again this autumn. My father said it flies every few generations, that it is the same fire since the first dawn, that it is one of the First creations of Tyr and Tor, and it always warns of change to come.

"When the Sunland dragons saw the sign, they thought it a harbinger, not a sign to follow. They remained, preparing a great feast and gifts for whoever would come in the wake of the starfire—perhaps Tyr himself!

"The morning after the sign, a mighty band of creatures arrived, the likes of which had never been seen in our arctic home. They were gryfons. Kajar, a young prince of their distant land, led them. His wingbrother was with him, their captains and warriors who were all heirs of their clans.

"At first, dragons and gryfons alike rejoiced to meet each other, they welcomed Kajar, and he was the model of gratitude and honor. They exchanged all the songs that they knew, and the dragons were impressed to meet other creatures so like-minded, so intelligent, so focused on honor and living with a warrior's discipline.

"In their excitement, they crafted gifts for Kajar and his band. Armor, adornments, all fitted for gryfons. Kajar learned all he could of dragon ways. He learned that we are linked to the elements, the earth, sky, the water and even the fire. He learned that we have a power in our blood awakened by sacrifice, that can

give us strength for a time, and the dragons tried to teach him this power—to no avail. It is dragon blood, not for gryfons.

"When it became clear Kajar could not have a dragon's power, he grew greedy for more gold. The gryfons in his band began to quarrel. Only those of higher station should have certain treasures, and so on. It was the same as our young cousins. Greed and pettiness.

"The dragons feared they had made a mistake, that their first impressions of Kajar were wrong, or that perhaps he had even been transformed by the treasures. Before they taught him more, or risked giving him more, they wanted to test him.

"They held a great feast, inviting all the gryfons, and the dragons of many families, some who had befriended the gryfons so deeply they had even pledged as wingbrothers and sisters.

"At this feast, Kajar asked when they might see more treasures, or learn more of dragon lore. The emperor at that time posed a question to him, and all the others.

"Only one young gryfess saw that the question was a test, and she fled the feast, and as far as anyone knows, fled the Sunland, and was not heard from again.

"Kajar said he needed time to consider the question. They thought that fair, and feasted. Later, Kajar invited a dragon—his closest friend in the Sunland—to walk with him, and discuss the question, so that he might learn and answer correctly.

"But it was a trap. He led the dragon to where all of his warriors waited, and they killed her. Kajar was insulted by the test, and he thought it was a way to cover up dragon secrets. He thought killing a dragon would give him a dragon's power.

"All the gryfons of Kajar's band were bathed in dragon blood. It burned their feathers bright, stained them as a warning for all to see, stained them and their bloodline, all their descendents forevermore so that all could see the taint of the arrogance and greed.

"The dragons drove Kajar and the others from the Sunland. They took with them their precious gold.

"Our cousins, meanwhile, toiling away in their mines, waited for us to come again. But Kajar's great betrayal so scarred the dragons that they shut themselves

away. They hid themselves in the Sunland, away from the rest of the foolish, greedy world.

"When the wyrms learned that gryfons had been granted favor over themselves, and then that we shut ourselves from the outside world, it threw them into jealous madness. First, they hunted down the gryfons of the Winderost. There, they learned it was more satisfying to cause terror than it was to kill.

"Now they only seek purpose by driving other creatures to witless fear. They would see all of the greatland and the world driven to mindless, voiceless animal death and terror. It is their only pleasure now. To bring others to where they are.

"This summer past, my mate flew here to try to speak to them. I'm certain they killed him. When he did not return, I pursued him.

"As I flew, I heard the Song of the Summer King in the wind, and I thought he would be the one to bring me hope. Perhaps he would help my witless cousins find their voices and hearts again. Perhaps he would draw my kin in the Sunland out of isolation and back into the world.

"That is why I've come..."

A grinding shriek and a pounding like falling boulders woke Shard from the tale.

"The dragons—the wyrms..."

"They've come," Amaratsu agreed curtly. They couldn't fit through the entrance Shard had, but the pounding and roaring was them throwing their bodies against the stone. They had moments, perhaps, before the wyrms broke through.

"Now what?" Shard demanded, his feathers on end, his body prickling in anticipation of a fight. He could probably escape through the hole at the top of the cavern, but she...he wasn't sure why she was there, what she wanted of him, and why she didn't seem worried about escape.

Unless she's with them, he realized, feeling suddenly cold. Unless her tale was a distraction to keep him there.

"Son of Baldr," Amaratsu said. "Now you know the true tale, and why the gryfon Per fled his own land."

The cavern shuddered with the force of another blow. Above, the thousands of glow worms rocked as the ceiling shuddered.

Shard nodded. "I know your tale. Tell me, what question did the dragon emperor ask Kajar? What question drove him to kill his closest dragon friend?" There had to be more to it than she said. Perhaps she'd only stalled, holding him in the cavern until the wyrms came.

Her eyes crinkled as if she were delighted for him to ask. "The emperor asked if he wanted power. If he wanted gold, treasures, armor for all of his aerie and adornments for his mate and their kits and their descendents forevermore."

"And this drove him to kill a dragon? That doesn't make sense." Shard lashed his tail, looking toward the entrance.

"No. It was the insult that followed."

Another dragon pummeled at the opening, clawing. Rocks bounced loose and tumbled to the floor. Amaratsu said those dragons mined in the earth…it was only a matter of time until they dug through…

Finally Shard wrenched his gaze to Amaratsu. He had the feeling he stood on brittle, testing ice. "What insult?"

"They asked if he wanted power…or friendship."

Shard cocked his head. "But that seems foolish—if he was a friend to dragons, wouldn't they help him if needed? Wouldn't their friendship be power?"

She reared back in surprise and Shard leaped away, startled. Her great, booming laugh reverberated around the mountainous stone hall.

"It does seem a simple choice!" She lowered her head, whiskers floating, feeling the air. Her long, doe-like ears lifted to the sound of the dragons breaking in, then she focused, entirely, on Shard. "The same choice I will offer you now."

She shifted and Shard looked over his shoulder, high up where he'd entered, as more boulders scattered down. He turned back, narrowing his eyes at her.

"You're testing me, as Kajar was tested."

"I am."

"Now? Why?"

"I need to know," she whispered. "Prince. Summer King. I must know your heart. For some reason, the wyrms hunt you. They responded to you. Your voice woke them from mindless rage and put them back on a quest for vengeance."

"How lucky," Shard whispered.

"But they're *thinking*," she said. Shard didn't answer, his mind spinning.

She watched him.

Power or friendship.

That couldn't be all. *What if she is only tricking me?* If she had brought him there only to throw him to the wyrms of the Winderost, and they were in league, then Shard counted himself already dead, unless he chose power.

If whatever power she offered him gave him enough strength to fight off the Winderost dragons, to win over Sverin, to reclaim his home, he had to take it. There had to be something more, something she wasn't telling him. If she truly wanted his friendship, then she might help him fight.

But why the test?

He thought of Kajar and his greed, of Sverin, of the wrathful monsters breaking their way in.

"Rashard of the Silver Isles," said bright Amaratsu, and the jolt of his full name yanked Shard from his questions. "Power? Or friendship?"

Outside the cavern, the dragons of the Winderost clawed and shoved violently against the small entrance, breaking rocks to force a way in. Shard stared at her as dragon roars shook the mountain and doubt closed chill wings on his heart. She looked toward the noise, then lowered her head again, until all he could see was her eyes.

"You must choose now."

52

Daughter of the Rising Sun

"It's an impossible choice!" Shard cried. "You said you had to know my heart—how can I know yours?"

"Ah, prince of the Silver Isles," Amaratsu said quietly. "King. A good question. You cannot. You can only trust."

Outside the cavern, her Winderost cousins battered and snarled at the narrow stone entry. Shard ruffed, looking toward the sounds.

The gentle touch of her talons directed him back. "If you make yourself a king, many will offer you friendship, and many will offer you power. You will make this decision many times over, Shard son-of-Baldr. Trust. Don't trust. Power for friendship. Some go mad with this decision before the end."

"I don't know to trust you," he said, though her eyes spoke of endless, peaceful snowing days in the Sunland, and wisdom beyond measure.

"Then choose power," she whispered. "And you will have nothing to fear. You will be as strong as the wingbrother you told me of, Kjorn, as strong as the Aesir, as strong as a dragon."

Shard shifted to move, but there was nowhere to go. He stood in her coils under her wing. She wove before him like a serpent.

"Your feathers could be as brightly silver as Kjorn's are gold. You could rule together across two lands with your brother, one like the sun, one like the moon, afraid of nothing, unstoppable, able to take anything you desire. The sons of kings, brothers as beautiful as the first sons of Tyr and Tor."

But isn't that what Sverin and Kajar did? Choose power over trust?

He knew this was the same question and trouble that had befallen his own father during the Conquering, and Per, and Sverin, even Shard himself and Kjorn. But Sverin slipped toward witless anger and fear. He made no new friends, distrusting Vanir, wolves and anything else outside of his own small circle of Aesir.

Shard drew a deep, bracing breath.

"If power was Kajar's choice, if power means trying to kill you, I won't choose that."

"Because you think you can't fight me?"

"No." Shard lifted his wings, horrified, looking down the beautiful length of her scales.

The light tapping from the pearl had quieted, and something about that sent dread through his veins. "Even if I knew I could, I wouldn't. You've helped me, fed me, spoken with me, given me your name. You've done nothing an enemy would do."

"That is how some enemies work."

Dragons screamed rage outside, and another tumble of broken rock showered in. They would be inside soon. They would attack.

Knowing that, Shard made his decision.

"I choose friendship." He met her eyes squarely, digging his talons against the floor. "Even if it means my death. I will die trusting."

"As Kajar's dragon friend did," Amaratsu murmured, lifting her wings. The crystal light glimmered on and through the feathers like sunlight on ice. "As your father did."

"As I will?" Shard whispered. With a flick of her talon, she could end his life.

For a moment she poised above him, a serpent of ice and blinding white wings.

A beautiful, terrible death.

Her soft, joyous purr rumbled the ground beneath him.

"Oh no," she breathed. "No, Shard of the Silver Isles. I was right to sing you here. You are the Summer King and we will be great friends, you and I. For a brief time."

"A brief time?"

"I called you here with the Song of Last Light," she reminded.

Shard realized that her soft voice wasn't like the wind, it was like winter, growing brittle and weary. She wasn't young and beautiful. She was old, white as bone. He saw in her eyes a time when her scales shone the color of spring buds. In summer, those scales had shed to a golden like buttercups, and then the rich brown of loamy soil in autumn, her mane the blazing red of a rowan berry.

"The song was for you," Shard breathed. "You're dying."

"I was born in the spring," she murmured, ears twitching to the violent sounds at the entrance to the cavern. "So I would die in the spring, except that I choose to give my life another way."

"Fighting them? No, we can fight them together! I will fly with you!"

"Oh, Shard." She touched his feathers, her talons gentle as a mother gryfon. The tapping sound, like a claw on rock, gently resumed. Relief swelled at the back of Shard's mind even though he didn't quite know why. He only knew that noise from the pearl was good, was hopeful.

"Dragons of the Sunland live only one cycle of seasons before returning to the elements. I will die in the spring, anyway. But if I sacrifice, I will have power to protect you, and my—"

"Only one cycle of seasons?" Shard stared at her as it dawned on him, impossibly. Her wisdom. Her naiveté. Her seeming age and her strange youth.

"You mean, you were born *last spring*? You're one year old? How is that…but you knew of Kajar, of all of it…"

"Of course. The tale is told to all, as a warning. That is why we are still shut away from the world."

"But…a year? One year, of life?"

She dipped her head. "We don't need as long to live this life. We suffer joy, love, sorrow, live as part of the earth and sky and return to it again. Gryfons and birds and other creatures lead such long lives, even our cousins, wrought again and again with trouble, challenge and sorrow. We bring with us all the songs of our previous life, we are born again and again from the spirit of the world." She tilted her head around. "Perhaps if you learned more quickly, you would die sooner, as well."

She didn't mean it to be funny, but Shard forced himself not to laugh in disbelief.

She was only one year old. It was absurd.

Yet, sometimes Shard felt he'd lived a lifetime in the last year. Perhaps that was all a Sunlander needed. There were mayflies on the Sun Isle that lived but a day, but it seemed a dragon like Amaratsu should be different. Born in spring, mated, loving, losing her mate, all of that would be all she had of life.

A roar shook the cavern, and a few glowing flakes of lichen fluttered down and went dim like dying embers.

"Shard," Amaratsu said quickly. "My friend. I was selfish to ask friendship of you but I need your help."

"Anything," Shard breathed, shaking off his amazement. She had given his name back to him, told him the truth about the Red Kings. Given him friendship.

"Soon my son will hatch. You must sing him all the songs of the world that you know." She shifted to reveal the smooth, iridescent pearl within her coils.

Not a pearl.

An egg.

"I—"

"He will grow like a bird, more swiftly than you can blink, my friend. The songs and wisdom of the Sunland will be in his blood, but no knowledge of the world. He will learn quickly, and I wish him to learn from you, not my Voiceless cousins. They wish to steal him. Or worse. My son needs you, now, a kindred spirit."

"I won't know what to do!"

Her laugh fell like tinkling crystals. "Keep him warm. Be yourself. Be his friend. Remember what I said to you. Dragons of the Sunland shape the world based on the first songs they hear, the first things that they know of it. I wish him to know you, to know that all creatures can be his brothers."

"Why did you bring him here, if you thought your mate was dead?"

For a moment she was silent, her coils gently shifting down, and down, so that the egg slid neatly between Shard's feet. He could've wrapped both forelegs around it.

"The Summer King song gave me hope for change. So long in the Sunland we have done the same things over and over. I believe if he learns of the world in a new way, he will face it in a new way. And so I brought him here when I sought my mate, and listened to the winds for sign of his first friend. It was you, Shard. Now my son will be winter-born, a difficult fate. He will need you."

"A son," Shard whispered, awash with amazement. "A brother…"

"A father," Amaratsu corrected, misunderstanding why Shard said the words. His belly felt cold, then warm, terrified.

At their voices, the tapping grew harder, more determined. *My mother and father wished me raised among the Aesir,* he thought, dazed, *so that we could find peace as a pride.* Amaratsu wished the same for her son, in a way.

Shard raised his head. "What will his name be?"

Relief flooded her gaze, and he saw within the wise depths of her eyes the plain, worried look of a mother. "Hikaru. If he ever journeys home to the Sunland, he must introduce himself as Amaratsu's son, Hikaru."

Amaratsu's son, Shard thought. *Dragons trace their blood through their mothers.*

"Hikaru," he whispered to the egg. "I'll teach him," he promised, back up to Amaratsu. "I'll do my best, I swear to you."

"And so I will for you. Promise me, Shard, whatever happens now, that you will not move."

"I can fight—"

"They will not see you at first. Only me. Promise me." She set her forepaws on the stone and arched her back, uncoiling her long body. "You will not move."

"I promise…"

"Tyr," she thrummed, her voice growing in power. "Father. Maker of the sky. Tor, mother of Midragur…grant me the gift that comes with sacrifice."

Shard lifted a forefoot, surprised. "Amaratsu—"

"Be well, my friend." She touched her nose to Shard's brow, then the egg. "My son." Then she lifted her head toward the entrance to the cavern, and raised her wings.

Shard made to follow but the egg began to roll. He caught it, shouting, "Wait! Amaratsu—" then he froze, remembering his promise.

The wyrms of the Winderost crashed through the broken tunnel.

Shard couldn't count them all in the confusion of muddy dark wings, screaming and breaking rock. The cavern shook and stones rattled down. He stood over the dragon egg, wings flared.

A dragon is shaped by the things he first hears.

As Amaratsu ramped up to strike, her great wings stretched wide, Shard forced himself from a fighting stance to mantle over the egg.

An insistent tapping resumed.

"Not yet," Shard said. "Not yet." He touched his beak to the egg, and the tapping stilled. "Listen. Hear your mother's power!"

He made things up, he didn't really know what he was saying. Something, anything to soothe the little life in the egg.

In the mountain cavern the Winderost dragons had enough room to fly, to circle warily. At first they looked small, so high above. Then they circled lower, swooping to examine. Amaratsu warned them back, hissing, with sharp, bobbing movements of her head. Their responding roars sounded almost like bitter, venomous laughter to Shard. He hunched low, wings draped around the egg. Amaratsu was twice as long as the largest of them but more delicately built. If they attacked, they would kill her.

They blocked the starry ceiling and Shard winced with each roar, each low swoop. Their stench filled the cavern. Rotting meat, sulfur, dirt. Old blood. Hatred.

Shard clutched the egg to his chest.

Amaratsu shrieked. At first Shard thought it a battle cry, then heard the sorrow in her voice.

"My brothers, my sisters, Please! This is not you! My blood will not save you. My son's blood will not give you what you want! You have names, strength, purpose—" rattling snarls and two dragons swooping down to threaten cut off her pleas.

Shard wanted to shout, to call her back, but he realized they had not attacked him because they hadn't realized exactly where he stood. Amaratsu blocked him. He blended with the stone floor, and his wings hid the egg.

For now, but we'll all die here! But he couldn't shout, couldn't disturb the egg so close to his heart, couldn't draw attention.

"Listen," he whispered instead, his bones shaking from the roars, flinching as stones fell around, rocked loose by the cacophony. "Listen to your mother."

The egg was quiet and still, but instead of feeling relief, Shard worried. Amaratsu cried out again, and again was met with the baleful snarls of witless beasts.

"Very well!" Amaratsu swore against the deafening roars. "Remain in the dark! But you will not have him."

Her voice shifted, and it was like no other creature in the world. The language of the wolves and boar, but deeper, colder, ancient. It was as if Amaratsu spoke with the very voice of the earth itself, the great shifting tremor of the First mountain and stone to rise out of Tor's sea.

"Great Spirits of earth, accept me back," she intoned, the words falling over each other in an avalanche.

The Horn of Midragur shuddered, tiny rocks skipping along the ground near Shard's talons. Amaratsu's voice swelled.

"Earth and stone," she breathed like a wind. "I am spring-born, I am your child and your sister and I will return to you. For my birthright, I give you my name and my voice. *Miyo's daughter, Amaratsu!*"

The Winderost wyrms dove as one.

Amaratsu reared up, stretching her wings wide. Jaws bared open toward her, talons reached, the deadly tails whipped as the wyrms shot down at her.

Shard cringed back, choking back an eagle scream, and prepared to make a last stand.

Wyrms clouded the air and all was black and screaming.

A strange creaking like massive, twisting ice tore the cavern.

Amaratsu whipped around, her scales catching all the light like crystal, and coiled sharply around Shard and the egg, forming a dome of her body, closing her wings to a protective mantle.

Shard ducked and closed his eyes, ears flat, fatally certain the wyrms would tear her apart, then Shard and the egg.

Roars battered the air, oddly muffled outside of the dome of Amaratsu's body.

Then all was still.

And silent.

Shard clutched the egg under his wings, too terrified to move. He had no idea what happened. He barely dared to breathe.

After a moment he heard dull, angry roars again, but now they sounded far away, as if they had flown outside of the cavern to the tunnels, or out of the mountain completely.

Another few breaths, and no louder sounds came. No talon touched him, no air around him stirred. Slowly, he lifted his head.

He loosed a soft cry of disbelief.

In her last moments, Amaratsu's strange plea had worked. It took a moment before Shard finally understood what she had asked of the earth and gods. She still coiled over Shard and the egg, enough room for Shard to stand and walk six paces in a circle. Enough room for the egg to hatch.

But the long body that seconds ago had been warm, sinuous and serpentine now glittered translucent, hard and cold, formed entirely of rough, shining crystal.

The earth had accepted her back.

"Thank you," Shard whispered, straining for sense before he lost his voice and his wit completely. In dying for them, she had given them safety and time.

The wyrms of the Winderost railed in fury outside, but the body of Amaratsu lay unbreakable, a solid, divinely-formed crystal.

Trembling, Shard peered out through the gleaming facets to see the dark wyrms circling, smashing their talons and horns against the crystal. Not even a flake drifted free.

"Well," he whispered calmly to the egg, while his guts rattled like leaves inside him. "I think it's…it's safer now."

After a pause, the light tapping resumed.

"Yes," Shard whispered. "It's all right now."

Not all right, his mind screamed. Amaratsu was dead, he was trapped, and the dragons waited outside. But he couldn't panic again. He couldn't fall Nameless again. This time, he could not fail.

He'd made a promise.

A dragon is shaped by the first things he hears. Amaratsu made sure he wouldn't hear violence his first moments in the world, had left him, trusting, to Shard's voice. He wondered if he should sing the Song of First Light as was their custom. Or Last Light, to honor Amaratsu, so that, born in a difficult time, the young dragon would understand death.

He will be winterborn, Amaratsu had said. *Already a difficult thing.* She'd brought her son there to bring peace. To help her violent cousins, and to end the nightmare of the Winderost. Through that, Shard would set all right in the Silver Isles.

Shard had thought it would all be connected, but he'd been more right than he ever could have guessed. Realizing that and growing calm, he knew what to do.

"My name is Shard," he whispered to the egg. "Son-of-Baldr. And Ragna," he added, thinking that the Sunland dragons traced their bloodline through their mothers. The tapping paused, then resumed eagerly, scraping, tapping. "Prince of the Silver Isles. I have a tale for you."

A tiny, translucent black talon pierced the egg.

A thrill unlike anything he had known swelled in Shard's heart.

"Well done," he whispered. "Well done, Hikaru."

The talon disappeared. An onyx snout replaced it, tipped with a sharp hatching beak like a bird. Shard fluffed with pleasure and lay down comfortably, unafraid of the dragons outside, trusting Amaratsu. He opened his wing to cup the egg and create a shield of warmth.

"This is the song that Tyr and Tor sang to the world when it was young as a fledging gryfon. As a gryfess sings to her kit of all the things to come, so they sang the world this song—of hope, of fear, of love."

The dragon kit stilled, then wriggled furiously to free his face. Shard couldn't help but purr as the dragon hatched, safe from the nightmare beyond Amaratsu's crystal walls.

All too soon they would have their enemies to face, their destinies to meet. Hikaru's life, Shard feared, would be very hard for the short time he was in the world. He would need friends, and strength.

Safe inside the crystal chamber, Shard sang the first song that Hikaru would hear.

The song that would shape him and what he thought of the world.

"One will rise higher," Shard's voice thrummed low.

Pearly eggshell dropped to the floor.

"One will see farther."

The sleek black scales shone so brightly that strange light pulsed out from the breaking shell.

"His wing beats will part the storm."

The small, blind dragon face sought his. Shard lowered his head. A tiny paw groped out to touch his beak as Shard's voice filled their crystal chamber.

> *"They will call him the Summer King*
> *And this will be his song."*

THE END

ACKNOWLEDGEMENTS

WOW, WE DID IT AGAIN! There's a lot of gratitude toward a lot of folks packed in this volume. Up front is Husband Man, Dax, who I gratefully acknowledge for his unending support in all areas. My mom and dad, for support both tangible and intangible. My fellow writer Tracy Davis, who got the first read, deserves kudos for taking it on in one large chunk, and for her thoughtful feedback.

Thanks to my ARC readers who helped me round up the last of the typos, and for their work on early reviews.

Big thanks to Kessie Carroll and Laura Nix, for the jokes that Halvden and Vald tell—I needed a little help on that one!

My Master Mind team—artist Jennifer Miller for another piece of stunning cover art that once again brings Shard and his world to life. Thanks to TERyvisions for turning a typo-laden word document into a beautiful Book, and a big, big thank you to my editor Joshua Essoe. I owe him this one. His feedback and critique truly helped me wrestle this story into the sequel that I wanted it to be.

Thanks to all the people who are currently giving shelf space to my book: Bookworks of Whitefish, Copperleaf Chocolate Company, Crystal Winters of Whitefish, Fact & Fiction of Missoula, Montana, and the Whitefish Community Library.

Finally, this printed first edition wouldn't be possible without the enthusiasm and support of my friends and Kickstarter backers! Thanks to all of you, truly, deeply.

I'd like to especially call out those who were willing and able to pledge $100 or more:

Andrea Tatjana
Sheryl R. Hayes
Lauren Head
Lauren Pitt
Sarah Brooks
Jessica Thorsell
Lorsey Clark
Anne Williams (Tyrrlin)
Chrissandra Porter
Rhonda Harms
Darryl Klippenstein
Cherice "Kota" McGhan
Tabitha Hazeltine
Cody R
Abigail Rice
Roberta Miller
Melissa A. Hartman
Sir Lynx
S.
Signe Stenmark

Kate Washington
Ella Lacey Bunsen
Thaner Cox
Christina McGinty-Carroll
Alexander Mays Bizzell
Sarah Hermann
Vicki Hsu
Edward Fan
Snowstorm
Maddy Gralak
Fride Holtgaard Digerud
Paul van Oven
Colin Trigger Whittle
Kristina Busby
Galit A.
Amanda "Moon Wolf" Kennedy
R. A. Meenan
Rhel ná DecVandé
Miriam "SunGryphon" Halbrooks
Linda van Rosmalen

The Stumptown Historical Society

And newlyweds Dwyn & Johnathan McIntyre, this being the honored first time where their married names appeared together.

You are all the wind under me. See you in the Silver Isles.

PHOTO BY JESSICA LOWRY WWW.JESSICALOWRY.COM

ABOUT THE AUTHOR

Jess E. Owen has been creating works of fantasy art and fiction for over a decade, and founded her own publishing company, Five Elements Press, to publish her own works and someday, that of others. She's a proud member of the Society of Children's Book Writers and Illustrators and the Authors of the Flathead. She lives with her husband in the mountains of northwest Montana, which offer daily inspiration for creating worlds of wise, wild creatures, magic, and adventure.

Jess can be contacted directly through her website, www.jessowen.com, or the SOTSK Facebook fan page, www.facebook.com/songofthesummerking .